"You and I got off to a rocky start the first time we met, *jah?*"

She nodded.

"Why? I didn't know you, and you didn't know me. So why did we immediately start arguing with each other?"

"I don't pretend to know."

"You're doing it again."

"Doing what?"

"Acting like you hate me so you don't have to face the truth."

"What truth? That I like you?"

"*Jah.*"

"That's the most absurd thing I have ever heard."

"Is it? Then why can Hannah see it?"

"Hannah is seeing what she wants to see."

But somehow he knew there was something more to it than that. "There's one way to find out for certain."

"How's that?" she asked.

He knew if he said the words there was no going back, but he couldn't stop himself. He was foolish and bold and possibly crazy. But he was certain this was one time when he needed to take a chance. "Kiss me . . ."

Books by Amy Lillard

The Wells Landing Series
CAROLINE'S SECRET
COURTING EMILY
LORIE'S HEART
JUST PLAIN SADIE
TITUS RETURNS
MARRYING JONAH
THE QUILTING CIRCLE

The Pontotoc Mississippi Series
A HOME FOR HANNAH
A LOVE FOR LEAH

Amish Mysteries
KAPPY KING AND THE PUPPY KAPER
KAPPY KING AND THE PICKLE KAPER

Published by Kensington Publishing Corporation

A Love For Leah

Amy Lillard

ZEBRA BOOKS
KENSINGTON PUBLISHING CORP.
http://www.kensingtonbooks.com

ZEBRA BOOKS are published by

Kensington Publishing Corp.
119 West 40th Street
New York, NY 10018

All Kensington titles, imprints, and distributed lines are available at special quantity discounts for bulk purchases for sales promotion, premiums, fund-raising, educational, or institutional use.

Special book excerpts or customized printings can also be created to fit specific needs. For details, write or phone the office of the Kensington Sales Manager: Attn.: Sales Department. Kensington Publishing Corp., 119 West 40th Street, New York, NY 10018. Phone: 1-800-221-2647.

Zebra and the Z logo Reg. U.S. Pat. & TM Off.
BOUQUET Reg. U.S. Pat. & TM Off.

First Printing: August 2018
ISBN-13: 978-1-4201-4568-7
ISBN-10: 1-4201-4568-1

eISBN-13: 978-1-4201-4569-4
eISBN-10: 1-4201-4569-X

10 9 8 7 6 5 4 3 2 1

Printed in the United States of America

*To my sister Susan and her beautiful daughter Olivia.
And to all the families created from tragedy and adoption.
God has a plan.*

ACKNOWLEDGMENTS

I can't speak for all authors of Amish fiction, but I am researching every chance I get. I love to travel to the places where my books are set. I love talking to the people, getting the "lay of the land," and otherwise living the experience so I can bring it to the reader. Inevitably I get home and start writing when questions arise.

As always I owe a big thank-you to my Amish friends in Lancaster who always answer my general questions and never remind me that I might have asked that one before. Thanks to the people of Pontotoc and the incredible Amish of Randolph. Your unique community is both amazing and beautiful in its simplicity.

Another big thank-you goes out to my reader Patti Gallagher who navigated this poor Baptist through the modern Mennonite church. Patti, you are a wonderful help and any mistakes on the workings of the Mennonite church are my own.

To my assistant, best friend, Girl Friday, and all around good-deed Carl, Stacey Barbalace, thanks always for being there to answer questions, proofread, and listen to me cry when things (aka, the plot) is not coming together as I had planned.

Thanks to my family for always standing behind me, even if among the encouraging words are not-so-subtle hints to catch up the laundry and cook something for supper. You are my heart and my life.

A super big thank-you goes out to the Seymour Agency and my wonderful editor at Kensington, John Scognamiglio. These books don't just write themselves you know! Thanks for all you do!

And thanks to you, the reader. Without you, this journey wouldn't be nearly as much fun. I'm glad we're on this ride together!

Chapter One

Leah's heart beat a little faster in her chest as she pulled her car down the lane leading to her parents' house. Coming home. It always felt the same, like riding a roller coaster with no restraints. Even after all this time.

"Who's that?" Brandon, her fifteen-year-old nephew, pointed to the buggy parked to one side. He may have only been in Amish country for a short while, but already he could tell the subtle differences in each individual buggy. The Amish might strive for community and sameness, but some things couldn't be completely contained.

"I don't know." And she really didn't care. Not to be rude, but she was too tired to give it much thought other than that her family seemed to have company a lot. She didn't need to know who it was as long as there was still a place for her at the table. She pulled her car next to the parked carriage and turned off the engine.

The evening sun had dipped behind the tree line. September was quickly approaching, and soon it would be dark. That was the thing about fall and winter. The days were shorter, and when she had so much to do. *Lord, please.*

That was her prayer of late. Only two words, but powerful. She had been praying the same prayer for weeks, ever since she decided to open Twice Blessed, a secondhand store on Main. She had prayed so often she figured God knew what she was about to say. No sense in wasting His time with too many words.

She rested her head against the steering wheel and released a heavy sigh. It felt good to just sit there for a moment and soak it all in: being home, the upcoming grand opening of her store, and life.

"Aunt Leah?"

She turned her head, opening her eyes to find Brandon looking in the passenger side window. A small frown of concern wrinkled his brow.

"Are you coming in?"

"Yeah." She sat up and grabbed her bag out of sheer habit. It wasn't like she needed her things at her childhood home.

She slung the strap over one shoulder and followed Brandon up the porch steps.

As usual, the Gingerich house was buzzing with activity. Brandon jumped right in, heading toward the back of the house where the kitchen was located. To get a snack or lend a hand, who knew? That was the thing about teenagers— they were hard to read.

"Hey, sis. How's the store coming?" Her twin sister, Hannah, swept in from the direction of the kitchen carrying a basket of bread. She deposited it on the table as Leah set her purse in a nearby chair.

"Good. Good." She moved in for a hug.

It felt more than good, more than wonderful, to feel her sister's arms around her. They had been so close growing up, but when Hannah decided to get a taste of the *Englisch* world, everything changed. It had taken fifteen years, but finally they were back on track.

"We have guests," Hannah whispered as she moved away.

"What kind of guests?"

"The male variety. One grown, one about six."

"Anyone we know?"

Hannah shook her head, her loosely tied prayer *kapp* strings swaying with the motion. It was still a little bit of a shock to see her sister in her Amish clothing. It had been so long since Hannah had worn Plain dresses. But Leah was starting to get used to it. "They're from Ethridge."

There were two Amish settlements in Tennessee. The one in Ethridge was the largest, while the one in Adamsville was small, like theirs in Pontotoc, Mississippi. Adamsville had sprung from nowhere when couples who lived in Pontotoc had too much family in Ethridge and grew homesick. The small town was a halfway point of sorts between the two communities.

"Where did Mamm find them?"

Eunice Gingerich seemed to always be on the lookout for lost souls. Maybe that was where Leah got it, that need to help her fellow man.

"You know Mamm."

That she did.

Hannah moved in close. "I think he's looking for a wife. Well, at least Mamm seems determined to find him one."

"Gracie?" Leah asked, speaking of their cousin.

Hannah shrugged. "If Gracie gets married, Mamm won't have any help."

"You're here."

"Just for a while." By this time next year, Hannah Gingerich McLean would marry Aaron Zook and become the mother of three new children she obviously adored.

Leah wasn't the least bit jealous. She had led an eventful life, one that she certainly couldn't have lived if she had remained in her small home community. She had traveled to faraway places, other countries, to build shelters for the poor, repair schools, and tell people about Jesus. Fulfilling.

"What are we whispering about?" Gracie glided into

the room, the platter of roast beef nearly hiding her face from them.

"Our supper guests."

Gracie's mouth formed a small O as she set the food on the table.

"Where's Tillie?" Leah asked. Their youngest sister was seriously dating her longtime friend Melvin Yoder. Well, as serious as dating could be before either one of them had joined the church. But once that decision was official, everyone expected they would marry as soon as possible.

"Picking the last of the tomatoes," Gracie said.

"He seems nice enough," Hannah said.

"Who? The man?" Leah asked.

Hannah nodded. "And Peter's a little cutie. But . . ."

"But what?" she asked.

"You'll see at supper. Now come help us set the table."

With all three women working, it didn't take long to get the food to the large dining table that sat in a room off the kitchen. In fact, it took longer to get all the people there. But once Leah's father came in from his workshop—she knew he was trying to squeeze every ounce of daylight from the sky—her younger brother, David, followed close behind. Jim, the eldest, had most likely headed to his own house across the way to eat with his own wife and children.

Introductions went all around. Leah did her best to hide her surprise when she was presented to Jamie Stoltzfus. To say he wasn't what she had expected would be a huge understatement. Not that she had known what to expect. Tall and broad, Jamie was younger than she had imagined, with reddish-blond hair and eyes the color of a spring sky. She could picture those eyes sparkling with laughter, but right now they were serious, with fine lines at the corners.

Worried. That was the word. His eyes were beautiful, but worried.

"How do you like Pontotoc so far?" Leah asked, looking from Jamie to Peter. He really was an adorable child. He favored his uncle quite a bit, enough that they could easily pass for father and son.

Peter ducked his head and stared down at his bare feet. Fall was coming, and soon he would be forced to wear shoes—a terrible time for most kids in the district.

Leah waited for Peter to glance back up, fighting his own shyness, but his gaze remained downcast. She looked to Jamie, who acted as if nothing was amiss. "Not much different from Tennessee. Just smaller."

Her mother bustled past with a pitcher of water and smiled. "You'll get used to it soon enough. There are days when I feel it's too big." She turned her attention to Peter. "What do you think?"

Peter's head dropped a little lower.

"He doesn't . . . talk." Jamie cleared his throat. "Not since the accident."

All conversation came to a halt. Normally Gingerich family time was busy and loud. Was it any wonder, with nearly ten people waiting to be fed?

"Oh." Mamm set the pitcher on the vinyl tablecloth and blinked. Her expression was one of shocked sympathy, but somehow Leah didn't think Jamie would appreciate the sentiment.

"It's all right though," Jamie said. His eyes held a bright light, as if he was doing everything possible to convince those around him, as well as himself.

Slowly the conversation around them had picked back up. Yet Peter kept his gaze trained firmly on the floor. Something about the boy touched Leah's heart. It could've been his mop of coppery brown hair that hung almost to his shoulders, or those blue eyes so like his uncle's. But it was more than that. It was the haunted look on his face, the shadows that deepened his eyes as if he had seen far too much in his short years.

"What happened to the back of your hand?" At Brandon's question, everyone's attention swung back to Peter. He seemed to withdraw into himself, making his presence even less than it had been before.

Gracie hurried over and linked her arm with Leah's. "My goodness," she chirped. "We forgot to put the butter on the table. Brandon, can you help me with the butter?" She said the words even as she steered Leah toward the doorway leading into the kitchen.

Brandon looked at her as if she had completely lost her mind. "Can't you—"

"I'll help too." Not one to be left out, Hannah eased past them all and into the next room.

They all bustled into the kitchen, where Brandon propped one hip on the smaller kitchen table and looked at his aunts and cousin. "Now, that wasn't obvious at all," he drawled. "I take it that it's some secret?"

Gracie shook her head. "Not a secret, but a painful memory."

They had only a moment to wait before Hannah picked up the rest of the story. "Did you hear about that fire in Ethridge?"

"About six months ago?" Gracie clarified.

Leah thought through all the news she remembered hearing in the last few months. "The house fire?"

"That's the one." Gracie nodded.

"But—" Leah looked back toward the dining room. She had spent enough time in both rooms to know that they couldn't be overheard, but she lowered her voice all the same. "His parents died."

"And his baby sister," Hannah filled in.

"Peter himself was in the hospital for a couple of months."

"Poor family." Leah made a mental note to add the Stoltzfuses to her prayer list. She might be exhausted and hanging on by a thread, but there were others out there still in need.

"So that mark," Brandon said, "it's a burn scar?"

"*Jah*," Gracie said. "But don't mention it. Peter is sensitive."

Brandon nodded. "I read this book once where these two kids run into a burning schoolhouse to save some other kids. One got really burned, but he died."

Leah's heart went out to what was left of the family—an uncle and a son. They had traveled so far for a chance to start over.

David poked his head into the kitchen and gave them all a small grin. "Dat said quit whatever it is you think you're doing and get back to the table. We have company and it's time to pray. Oh, and Mamm said bring the applesauce."

"*Jah*. Okay," Hannah murmured and moved to exit the kitchen. Leah grabbed the applesauce while Brandon and Gracie started toward the dining room once again.

The air around the table was thick with suppressed emotion. Leah could feel it like a weight pressing her down into her seat. The oppressive atmosphere did not change as everyone bowed their heads to pray. In no time, they were passing food around as everyone filled their plates. At least the conversation had started to flow again, though it was more stilted than smooth.

"What do you do, Jamie?" David asked as he scooped out a helping of mashed potatoes.

"For a living?" he asked.

"Of course."

Jamie cleared his throat. "I was hoping to get into a bit of handiwork."

"Like repairs and things?" David asked.

Jamie nodded. "I don't have enough land to farm. Farming's hard, going it alone."

Nods went all around the men at the table.

"Leah opened a store," Tillie blurted.

"Not yet," Leah murmured.

"Well, this week."

Jamie turned those incredibly blue eyes to her. "Is that so? What kind of store?"

"It's a resale shop. You know, clothes and house goods."

He nodded. "Where is it?" he asked. "In front of your house?"

Most all Amish in Pontotoc had a small store in front of their house in which to sell their family's products. Jams, jellies, pickles, and sauerkraut were peddled on a regular basis.

"It's on Main. Next to the Chinese restaurant."

"You're Mennonite," he said, as if for the first time noticing that she was dressed modestly, but not Plain. His face was passive as he spoke, but Leah saw the flash of censure in his eyes. A lot of people felt Mennonites were Amish who couldn't cut it. But that was far from the truth.

She lifted her chin. "That's right."

Around them, the conversation fell silent.

Jamie cleared his throat and dropped his gaze to his plate, but something in Leah couldn't let it go. How dare he pass judgment on her!

"Is there something wrong with being Mennonite?"

He seemed reluctant to answer. "They are more liberal, to be certain, *jah*?"

"And liberal is bad?"

"Leah, can you pass the potatoes, please?" Hannah's voice was unnaturally high-pitched, and she still had a mound of food on her plate, potatoes included.

"I want to hear what he has to say," Leah replied. She had been fighting these stereotypes ever since she had decided to join the Mennonite church. It was the closest she could be to the Amish without returning, but it was more than that. The message they preached, the love they shared, and the gospel of Jesus all spoke to her in a way Amish teachings never had. She turned her attention back to Jamie and raised one brow in challenge.

Jamie shrugged. "If it works between you and God . . ." he said, but didn't finish the statement. He didn't have to.

"Wow, Mamm, this roast is delicious," Tillie said. "That's one of the best things about fall. Cooking in the oven again. I mean, you can cook in the oven in the summertime, but it heats up the house so bad. This is the earliest I've ever seen you cook a roast. I don't think I ever remember you cooking a roast in the summer the entire time I was growing up. What about you, Leah?"

She turned to her sister. "No, I can't say as I remember a single one."

And just like that, the conversation shifted. The atmosphere at the table seemed to relax, but every time Leah caught Jamie looking at her, she could see the remains of the censure in his eyes. What was so wrong with being Mennonite? She prayed to the same God, dressed modestly, and didn't have to rely on a driver if she needed to go someplace. So she didn't wear a prayer *kapp*. Her hair was still covered when she prayed. And just because she didn't make her own clothes didn't mean she was less godly than her sisters, or anyone else for that matter. Having a car didn't change what was in a person's heart. Maybe that was what was wrong with Jamie Stoltzfus. Maybe he was struggling with his own faith and taking it out on her choices. It was a good thing she wouldn't have to see him again after tonight.

Come tomorrow, she would be far too busy with her shop to worry about the likes of him.

Jamie forked up another bite of the delicious roast and said a silent prayer of thanks. He had been eating his own cooking for days. Not that it was bad, but it wasn't *good*. Not like this.

The invitation from Eunice to come to supper tonight was a gift from heaven. He and Peter had been holed up in their tiny cabin at the edge of the Gingerich property doing everything they could to adjust to the move. But staying at his own house and eating his own food was not integrating him into this new community.

All he had wanted when he moved to Pontotoc was a fresh start. It was inevitable. No one there knew them. Oh, they knew his family or knew someone who did. None of the Southern communities were big enough to escape that. Everyone in Pontotoc knew someone in Ethridge. Everyone in Ethridge knew someone in Adamsville. Everyone in Adamsville knew someone in Pontotoc, and so on. If they didn't know one of his kin, then they had surely heard of the terrible fire that had claimed the lives of his brother, his sister-in-law, and their baby, Ellie.

"Handiwork, *jah?*" David asked again.

Jamie nodded. "I figure I can take Peter with me when I go to a job." He didn't want to leave the boy at home alone. Peter was having enough struggles adjusting to what had happened to his family.

"He's not in school?" This from Leah.

He had done his best not to look at her the entire time they had been seated at the table. It was a near impossible feat, as she was seated directly across from him. But even more than that, his gaze seemed to have developed a mind

of its own and liked to look at her despite his best efforts
not to.

"He doesn't talk." Was there a part of that he hadn't
made clear? He had hoped like everything that Peter would
come out of this chosen-mute state he had fallen into. The
boy could hear and see, he could think and respond, but he
wouldn't utter a word. It was beyond Jamie as to why, but
the doctors in Nashville had cited trauma and told Jamie
that he would come out of it when he came out of it. As
long as he was eating, sleeping, drinking, and otherwise
going about his normal day, not to worry about it. But
Jamie worried. Oh, how he worried.

"He could still be in school. You don't need to talk to get
an education."

"I suppose not," he reluctantly agreed, "but the teacher
in our last district had trouble keeping him occupied while
all the other students were doing their regular lessons."

"Maybe she just isn't a good teacher."

"She's my sister."

"Did anyone save room for pie?" Tillie jumped to her
feet as she asked, her chair scraping hard against the floor
as she stood so quickly. "I'll go get it."

"I'll help." Gracie followed her out of sight.

Leah let out a small cough. "I meant no harm."

"No," he said. She might not have meant any harm, but
she was by far the most opinionated person he had ever
met—Amish, Mennonite, or otherwise. Was she always
this contrary?

"Maybe that worked against him," Hannah mused. "You
know, since she's part of the family. You should consider
sending him to our school. Aaron has three kids there. I
could talk to them about Peter. They could look after him."

And this was the other thing: talking about him like he
wasn't there. How hard was that for Peter? Jamie could
only imagine.

"I wouldn't want to impose," Jamie murmured. He still wasn't certain how smart of an idea it was to send the boy to school this year. He had been working with him at home, hoping that he could give him a few lessons so he wouldn't be so far behind come next year, but it was beginning to be more than he could handle. He had worried that Peter would be swallowed up in the constant motion at the boy's grandparents' house, but it might be better than what Jamie could give him.

He pushed that thought away and centered it on Hannah once again. He had heard somewhere that she and Leah were twins, but they could hardly look more different. And it had nothing to do with the way they were dressed. Hannah had lighter hair and hazel eyes, while Leah's hair was dark like a raven and her eyes mossy green.

"It's not an imposition. In fact, the school is just across the road from Aaron's house. I'll go over there tomorrow and talk with the teacher." She gave him a pretty smile.

"*Danki*." What else could he say? He was grateful, even if the thought left a stone of dread in his stomach.

Just then, Tillie and Gracie came back into the room carrying pie and dessert plates. Thankfully, the subject of school was dropped.

Blackberry pie was Peter's favorite, and the boy dug in like a starving man. Jamie hid his smile. Peter might not talk these days, and he might be hard to handle in school, but he still had enthusiasm for a few things, and that had to be good. *Jah?*

"I thought you had gone home."

Leah turned as Hannah pushed open the screen door and stepped outside. She stopped the porch swing with her heels so her sister could join her. "Nah. I thought I would stay so Brandon would have more time with you."

Hannah laughed. "And he headed straight over to see Joshua."

Brandon had made fast friends with his cousin over the summer—a relationship that had the entire family's approval. Life had been difficult for Brandon in the past year, and he had shown it by growing out his hair, piercing his lip, and carrying around a generally bad attitude. After the death of his father, he moved to Pontotoc only to discover that the man he had called *father* his entire life wasn't.

His true father was his mother's first love, Aaron Zook. Theirs was a complicated story, but it was playing out in the time of God's will. Hannah had moved back, fallen in love with Aaron again—as if she had ever *not* been in love with him—and was preparing to join the Amish church. Aaron, who was a widower, had never known that he had a son. The two were making steps toward building as normal a relationship as they could, given the circumstances. Brandon had moved in with Leah, who promised to care for him while his mother stayed in her family's Amish home and worked toward her baptism the following year.

"Joshua's a good influence," Leah said, restarting the swing.

"Pontotoc is a good influence," Hannah countered. "Living with you has been a good influence. By the way, have I told you thanks?"

Leah smiled. "About a million times."

"Well, thank you. There. That's a million and one."

They sat in silence for a moment, the only sounds the creak of the swing's chains, the call of night birds, and the muffled voices drifting out of the windows.

"Any luck getting him to cut his hair?" Hannah asked. Since moving to Mississippi, Brandon had given up most of his snarly attitude and his lip ring, but he still held fast to his shoulder-length hair.

"He always keeps it clean and out of his face." Leah shrugged as if to say, *What's a surrogate* mamm *to do?*

Hannah sighed, then flashed her sister a quick smile. "I kinda like it."

Leah shook her head. "Then why ask him to cut it?"

"Dat. Have you seen the way he looks at Brandon?"

"I think you have it all wrong. When Dat looks at Brandon, he sees what the rest of us see: fifteen missing years. You denied him that. But he loves Brandon. It's written all over his face. Besides," she continued, "his hair isn't much longer than Peter's."

"I suppose," Hannah murmured. "What about that, huh?"

"What about what?" Okay, so she was playing dumb, but maybe if she acted unaware, Hannah would give up, thinking she was wrong.

"Uh, the sparks between you and Jamie."

Leah scoffed. "There were no sparks." At least none other than anger.

"I must be mistaken." Her sister's tone implied she was anything but.

They rocked back and forth for a few more moments, each one lost in the sounds of the night.

"He's just so opinionated," Leah said with a growl. She hopped to her feet and went to stand at the porch railing. "I mean, all that about Mennonites. Like we're the devil's minions because we have cars. Well, if it wasn't for people like me having a car, he wouldn't be in Mississippi, now would he?"

Hannah opened her mouth to reply, but Leah plowed on.

"And all that about being liberal. My skirt covers more than your dress. It's longer, you know. I don't go around showing my ankles. And my hair is covered when I pray." She shook her head.

"You said your fair share too," Hannah said.

Leah whirled to face her sister. "I was nothing if not nice to him."

"You questioned why Peter wasn't in school, called his sister a bad teacher, and asked about Peter's burn scar."

"That was Brandon."

Hannah gave a small nod. "I suppose it was."

"How were we supposed to know?"

They fell silent for a moment, then Hannah spoke. "You've been working so hard these last few weeks."

Leah nodded.

"Too hard?" There was concern in her sister's voice.

"Brandon has been the answer to my prayers, but he can't be there every minute with me. He has school and Shelly."

Brandon had met a girl his age at the library. Like him, Shelly took online classes there so she could use their computers to connect to the Internet. Shelly was smart and from a good family—a family that was also very conservative. They might not be Amish, but they lived a simple life "off the grid."

"Are you worried about tomorrow?" Hannah asked.

Leah sighed. "I'm excited. I've gotten all that I can get done completed, but there's still so much I want to do." She had racks of clothing, all separated by gender, but she wanted to eventually separate it all according to size. That way she could keep up with her inventory better and make sure she had what her customers were shopping for. She wanted to expand the kitchen selection to include small appliances. She wanted to build shelves to carry used books. And that was just the beginning. She had many more plans. More plans than she had room for.

"It's good to see you so excited about this."

She smiled. "Well, we can't all move home, reconnect with the love of our lives, and live happily ever after."

"Have you been to see Benuel?"

Leah waved away a hand and looked out over the dark yard. Not much moved this time of the evening, so she pretended interest in nothing at all. "Why would I go see him? He's moved on. He's getting married this fall."

Hannah nodded. "To Abby." She waited just long enough before continuing that Leah turned back to face her. "Our cousin."

"I know."

"Are you sure this isn't bothering you just a little?"

Leah sighed. "I'm positive." Whatever had existed between her and Benuel had passed a long time ago. Next month he was getting married to Abby Glick, and Leah was happy for them both. Leah might be a tad envious that Hannah was getting married, but she had decided a long time ago that marriage wasn't for her. She didn't quite belong in any world, not the *Englisch* or the Amish. The Mennonites were the closest she had come to a place where she could be comfortable, but she couldn't say one hundred percent it was where she was supposed to be. If she didn't know her own place in the world, how could she join her life with another's? Yet with each passing year she began to wonder if her decision had been a bit hasty. Now she had the shop to think about. It might not take the place of children or the loving arms of a faithful husband, but at least it filled her days. Right?

"Good." Hannah rose to her feet. "Abby came by this afternoon. She wanted to make sure that we got the invitation to the wedding and that the two of us will be there."

Leah was grateful for the cover of shadows. It hid the shock she was certain shone from her face like a beacon. "She wants us there?"

"She would like for us to help serve and to clean up afterward. Are you up for that?"

"Of course." She swallowed back the lump in her throat.

She would help her cousin. They were family, and that was what family did. They helped one another.

"Good," Hannah said and started for the door to the house. "I'll let her know."

Leah gathered up Brandon, and they got into the car to drive home. All the way back to town, Brandon talked nonstop about Joshua, Peter, and Jamie. Brandon seemed to have settled into his new life quite well. They were something of kindred spirits, Leah and him. He had been raised *Englisch* by an ex-Amish mother and an *Englisch* father who really hadn't been his father at all. Now he lived with a Mennonite in an apartment above a secondhand store in small-town Mississippi. Talk about adjustments.

"Are you ready for tomorrow?" Brandon asked as she parked the car.

"As ready as I'll ever be," she quipped, then stopped, one hand on the door to the shop. It was the biggest drawback she had seen with her business setup. She got to stay in the loft apartment for practically nothing, but she had to walk through the store to get to it.

"Though I think I might stay down here for a couple of hours and work on a few more shelves." She had arranged them and rearranged them to the point where she was starting to move items back to their original places.

"Uh-uh." Brandon took ahold of her elbow and nearly dragged her to the back room and up the steps. "You'll have plenty of time to do that tomorrow. Tonight you need a good night's sleep without any distractions."

So why did Jamie Stoltzfus's face pop into her mind? It wasn't like she wanted anything to do with the man. But a distraction? Heaven help her, he was.

"But—" she protested.

Brandon pointed toward her room. "Go," he said with mock seriousness.

Leah smiled. He really was a good kid. "How did you get so smart?"

He grinned in return. "Just comes naturally, I guess."

The door to Jamie's bedroom creaked slowly open, so slowly that it might have been caused by the breeze blowing in through the screen-covered windows. Yet it wasn't the wind. This had happened before.

"Come on," he said, moving to one side of the bed, then patting the empty space he had created. The sound of the flurry of little bare feet met his ears, then the mattress dipped slightly as Peter climbed into bed next to him.

It took only a second for Peter to snuggle down into the covers and become still once more. It was almost as if he needed to be close to Jamie, but he didn't want to be a bother. Honestly, Jamie didn't know why he ever made up the cot for the boy to sleep on in the front room. Every night since coming to live with him—first in Tennessee and now here—Peter crept into Jamie's room sometime during the night.

Jamie supposed it was because he hadn't been in the house when the fire had started. Peter's dog, Goldie, had just had a litter of pups, and Peter wanted to spend every moment he could with the precious canines. The best Jamie could figure, his parents had put him to bed, and Peter had snuck out to the barn and the warm, wriggling puppies sleeping there and had fallen asleep. Once the fire started, Peter woke, ran into the flames, and tried to save his family. But he was too late. As far as Jamie knew, this was Peter's way of never allowing that to happen again. The thought was heartbreaking.

It was a matter of minutes before Peter's breathing became deep and slow.

Jamie turned his eyes to the darkened ceiling. How many times had he prayed for the boy to find peace? Every day since that fateful winter night. It gave a whole new meaning to *pray without ceasing*. Every day he gave thanks. Every day he asked for peace and joy for the child. Every day he waited. But his faith was strong. God's will was beyond their understanding, but he could accept it. What he was having trouble swallowing was that there was nothing he could do to help Peter. One look at the boy and anyone could see the hurt and fear in his eyes. Jamie longed to take that from him, to give him back some joy in this earthly realm. Joy that would see him through until he was with his family once again.

He should have never made that deal with Sally's parents. It added another layer onto his stress. Now if Peter didn't talk by the end of three months, then Sally's parents were to take back over Peter's care. It was a devil of a bargain, but it was done now.

Ever so softly, he leaned over and planted a small kiss on the top of Peter's head. He loved the boy as if he were his own. It was the last piece of Joseph that he had. "Good night," he whispered. "I'll make it right again. Somehow, someway. You will be whole again."

Chapter Two

Madness. That was the only thing Leah could say about the grand opening. She had expected a soft opening with a few people wandering in off Main just to see what was happening. But the waitresses at the Boondocks Grill had put up a flyer in the window, and their steady lunch crowd had become Leah's stream of lookers.

She sold plenty as well. There were a number of junk shops and antique stores down Main. Hers was the only one she had seen with clothing and everyday housewares. But her goal had been to open, let the community know what the shop was about, and let God handle the rest. Evidently God had a few plans of His own.

And then there was the accident. Not that it was as major as that sounded. The shelf holding all the baskets of socks and other accessories fell. It could have been a lot worse. The only casualty was one of the baskets. It was crushed when the shelf fell on it. They had cleaned up the mess and set the baskets on a low table near the clothing section, but she still needed to have the shelf repaired. Since it was part of the original construction in the building, she decided to have all the shelves checked out, and as soon as possible.

"I think it's going good, don't you?" Brandon propped his hands on his hips and looked around the shop.

"*Jah*," she said.

"Why do you do that? Use the Dutch word? You're not Amish any longer."

Leah smiled and shook her head. "A person can't just stop being Amish. You are either Amish or ex."

"That still didn't answer my question."

"Because there is no one answer." She gave a small shrug. "Habit. Being back here. Comfort."

"It's comfortable?" Brandon shook his head. "That's weird." He continued to wag his head from side to side as he moved toward the back of the store to help a young couple get a baby toy off the top shelf.

Of course it was weird to Brandon. He was fifteen. Everything was weird to him. But Leah hadn't even realized she had used the Pennsylvania Dutch word for *yes*. It had simply come out of her mouth without any prompting from her brain.

She nudged the thought from her mind and moved behind the counter to ring up the next customer in line.

The day continued in the same vein until Leah was certain she wouldn't be able to get out of bed come tomorrow. Her feet ached, her leg muscles burned, and her brain was tired. It seemed that the worst part of running a secondhand shop was that people had a tendency to treat it like a garage sale and want to negotiate the price . . . on everything. Still, all in all, it was a *gut* day.

Oh, great, now Dutch words were invading her thoughts. Unlike most Amish children in the area, she and her siblings had learned English at home simultaneously with Pennsylvania Dutch. When she was younger her thoughts were a tangle of Dutch and English, but since moving out and living with the Mennonites for the last ten years, English had dominated her thoughts.

"Hope you're hungry," Brandon called as he came through their apartment door. The scrumptious aroma of Chinese food wafted in behind him.

"Starved." She slid onto the floor from her place on the couch as Brandon set their supper on the large, square coffee table. She didn't have a dining table, but no matter; she didn't have a dining room.

Brandon sat down across from her, accustomed to eating while sitting on the floor. He began to unpack the to-go bag of goodies. "Are you sure you don't want me to teach you how to use chopsticks?"

"Maybe another time." When she wasn't this tired . . . and hungry.

Brandon shrugged as if to say *Suit yourself*, unwrapped his chopsticks, then rubbed them together to smooth them out.

Leah fished a plastic fork out of the sack and dug into her orange chicken.

"What's the deal with that guy?"

"What guy?"

Brandon shrugged again, a sure sign he was hiding something. "The one who was at Mammi's last night."

She stopped searching for the perfect piece of chicken and eyed her nephew. She had almost forgotten about Jamie Stoltzfus. Almost. "Why?"

He shrugged. That was the third time. Definitely up to something. "I dunno. Did you know him before? You know, before you left?"

"Of course not."

Brandon mumbled something into his container of beef and broccoli.

"What was that?"

"Then why did he make you so angry?"

Why indeed? "I guess some people just aren't destined to get along."

"But that's not what Pastor Joel said last Sunday."

Now he decided to remember a church sermon. Why couldn't it have been the lesson on respecting elders or keeping up your personal appearance? "I don't recall." She sniffed.

Brandon stopped. "You were taking notes."

It was Leah's turn to shrug.

"He said we are going to have personal differences in our lives. We're going to meet back up with people who have hurt us, but we need to learn to forgive."

So he had. "What does this have to do with Jamie Stoltzfus?"

"That's why I asked if you had known him before. I thought maybe he had broken your heart long ago."

"Hardly." There was no way she would have been friends with someone as stuffy as Jamie Stoltzfus. *That's not true.* Back during her *rumspringa*, she had been the conservative one, while Hannah had been more . . . adventuresome. It was her sister's feisty spirit that had made Hannah want to see what was out there beyond the limits of Pontotoc, Mississippi.

"Then why did he make you so angry?"

She didn't have the answer to that. At least not one she wanted to share with Brandon. How could she tell him something she didn't quite understand herself? She had worked hard to find her place outside the Amish faith, and to have someone criticize that was too much. "It's been a long week, a long *month*, trying to get ready for the shop to open. I guess I was just a little hypersensitive." Even to her own ears it sounded weak, but it would have to do.

"That's good to know, because Dawdi hired him to come fix the shelves tomorrow."

* * *

The first thing on her to-do list was to reorganize the boxes of donated Amish clothing in the back room of the shop. No, the first thing was to talk to her father about jumping in and making decisions that he had no business making, and the second was to reorganize the donation boxes. But since her father was at home today, she would have to put that conversation off for a bit.

Leah stood and stretched the kinks out of her back. She had been trying to devise a system that allowed the district members to look at the clothing without it taking up too much space in her storeroom. It was a decent size, and she didn't keep much in the back, but when she figured in two or three racks of clothing, the space disappeared quickly.

"I need to pay you for this." Mary Yoder reached into her purse and pulled out her wallet. "How much? There's no tag."

Leah shook her head. "There's no charge."

"How are you going to make a living?"

"I'm selling the stuff out front."

Tears filled Mary's eyes. Her husband had recently died, leaving her alone to raise twin daughters. She was struggling, making jams and pickles to help supplement her fledgling bakery business. But that sort of thing took time, leaving her fewer opportunities to sew clothes for her family. People like Mary were the very reason Leah had opted for a free Amish clothes exchange. There wasn't a great deal of money in their community. Most relied on farming to earn their wage. When that was taken out of the equation, money got even tighter.

"I can't thank you enough. I'll repay you."

Leah gave her a small smile. "Just bring in some of Susan and Elizabeth's clothes when they outgrow them. I'm sure someone in the district could use them."

Mary nodded. "I will, Leah. I will."

Leah packed the clothing into a recycled plastic sack and sent Mary out the back door.

It might be the most satisfying transaction of the day. This was what it was all about. This was what made all her hard work worthwhile.

"Leah?" Brandon called from the doorway of the stockroom. "Jamie's here."

And just like that, her good mood took a nosedive.

It was something else, what a man would do for money. Jamie grabbed his leveler and placed it on the shelf. Perfect. Only two more and he could be done with this job and away from the piercing gaze of Leah Gingerich.

She had been staring at him since he had arrived. Watching him as if she suspected he'd run off with the family fortune. Not that he thought there was one. The Gingeriches seemed to be like everyone else in Pontotoc: hardworking, loyal, and down-to-earth. But not Leah. Well, she was hardworking, and she seemed loyal enough, but down-to-earth? Just the fact that she had left the Amish to turn Mennonite had him wondering where her heart lay. What was so wrong with her family and her friends that she needed electricity and a car to make her life better? Or maybe it was the clothing. Had she wanted to wear different styles and be more modern like the *Englisch* girls? He might not ever know, but there was something about her that chafed him.

He handed the leveler to Peter, who set it to one side. Without being asked, he handed Jamie the tape measure.

Jamie measured the spot for the next shelf and marked it with a carpenter's pencil. He turned back for the screwdriver, but Peter was already holding it out for him. All the while, he was more than aware of Leah's gaze following his every move.

He had asked if she wanted him to come after hours, but she said the shelves needed to be repaired as soon as possible. So here he was on a Saturday morning trying to finish the shelves before her ten o'clock opening time. Shouldn't she be dusting things and straightening the merchandise and not merely leaning up against the counter and watching him like a hawk follows prey?

The set of brackets went up without a fuss, and Jamie reached for his leveler again. Peter had it at the ready.

"That's quite a helper you've got there."

The words sounded loaded, like an intro into something more. "*Jah*," was all he said. Any more and she might feel obligated to tell him what was on her mind. And if it was anything like the other night at her parents' house, then he didn't want to know. Leah Gingerich was nothing if not strong and opinionated—two qualities that didn't always go together in the Amish world.

Perhaps that was why she had left. She was too opinionated and had had to leave because she—

He shook his head at himself. He didn't care why she had left. He didn't care one bit.

"What is it?" she asked. "Yes or no?"

"*Jah*. Yes, he is a *gut* helper."

Peter didn't even crack a smile at the compliment. It just wasn't natural, this lack of emotion coming from him. And it worried Jamie more and more. *Jah*, it had been nearly six months, time enough for the burns on his neck and hands to heal. The ones on his legs had been more severe and had required surgeries and grafts to repair. But even those wounds were now faded to scars. The doctors had told him that the muscle tissue had been damaged and would never be the same. Peter would always limp, and quite possibly might have to have special shoes made to keep his gait even. Chances were greater that his left leg would grow at a normal rate, but the right leg, which had sustained most of his injury, might end up shorter as time went on. Jamie prayed about it every night. The Lord's will would be done, but it didn't hurt putting in a word or two, just in case.

Leah fell silent, and Jamie went back to hanging the next shelf. Wasn't it ten yet? He could use some reprieve from her glacial stare.

The third shelf was firmly in place when another voice sounded behind him.

"Looking good, don't you think?"

Brandon McLean. Jamie had met Brandon at supper the other night, but how he fit into the Gingerich life equation, he didn't know. Jamie hadn't asked anyone, but just being in small-town Pontotoc, people were talking. He knew that Brandon was Hannah's son. Her husband had died in an accident recently, and she had returned to Pontotoc. How her son had ended up *Englisch*, Jamie might not ever know. Now, Hannah was marrying her long-ago sweetheart, Aaron Zook. As far as Jamie could gather, the wedding was to take place the following year.

"Yeah." Leah's answer was reluctant.

Was it him? Or men in general? Had she turned into one of those feminists like the *Englisch* had, those women who were always marching for equal rights? He shuddered at the thought. A Mennonite feminist. That was a new one.

"Almost done," Jamie tossed over his shoulder as he began work on the next-to-last shelf. He couldn't be finished soon enough.

"Doors open in ten minutes," Leah said. "Think you can handle it?"

"Of course," Brandon replied. "Where are you going?"

"To the back," Jamie heard Leah say. "I won't be long."

Jamie let out a small sigh of relief. At least she hadn't told Brandon to stare at him as she had been doing. It was much easier to work without someone scrutinizing his every move.

Out of the corner of his eye he saw Brandon move toward the front of the store to ready it for opening. They had already had a few people stop and peek in the windows, pointing out certain items as they passed. Whatever it was, it seemed that Leah's shop was on its way to being a success.

The last two shelves went up much quicker than the first ones. Or maybe because Leah was no longer following his every move, it just seemed faster. Whatever it was, he had the shelves all hung and the mess cleaned up before the first customers came through the doors. All except for the tools. Peter was currently loading those into the handled toolbox.

"Here we go."

Jamie turned at the sound of her voice, fully expecting her to hand him a check or maybe an envelope containing the payment for today's work. Instead, she was carting a cardboard box filled with . . . clothes?

"What's that?" he asked, his voice dropping an octave. Was she trying to pay him in goods?

Leah glanced quickly at Peter, then trained her gaze on Jamie once again. The shift had been so quick that he might not have seen it at all if he hadn't been staring at her the whole time.

"Let's . . ." She nudged him toward the back of the store.

Against his better judgment, Jamie followed behind. "*Jah?*" He tried to keep the skepticism out of his voice, but it was hard. He was trying to make ends meet—they all were—and he might even accept clothing as payment if that were the original agreement. But he needed money for groceries. Not someone else's castoffs.

"Your check is in this envelope. I have an account at the bank just down on Main. If you take it in there, they'll cash it for you."

"And the rest?" He nodded toward the clothes.

"For Peter."

His hands started to tremble, and he wanted to drop the box like a hot rock. Instead, he thrust it back at her. Surprise flashed in her eyes before she caught it, fumbling a little as he let go. "We don't want your charity." He barely got the words pushed between his clenched teeth.

"It's not. I mean . . ."

She couldn't even come up with a lie about it.

"Peter and I are just fine. There's no need for—" He waved around a hand instead of finishing his sentence. Lord knew, it was easier that way. He had never been so angry, so insulted, in all his life. "Come on, Peter," he called to the boy.

Peter jumped to his feet and took ahold of the toolbox handle. The thing was almost as big as he was.

"Now hold on a minute. This isn't charity. This is a loan. Peter can wear these clothes until he outgrows them, and then you can bring them back and swap them for 'new' ones." She made a weird hand gesture as she said the word *new*.

He wasn't about to answer. He spun on his heel and started for the back door. That was the way he came in, and it would be the way he would go out.

Then a hand on his arm stopped him. "What do you think charity is? A handout? Helping one's neighbor? The entire Amish way of life is built on helping your fellow man, and you think a couple of pairs of pants and a few shirts is too much?"

When she put it that way, she had a point, but he wasn't about to tell her that. His pride got in the way. It stuck in his throat and refused to budge. No other words could get out.

Peter caught up just as Leah thrust the box toward Jamie once again. "You need these."

He shook his head. "*Take heed that ye do not your alms before men, to be seen of them: otherwise ye have no reward of your Father which is in heaven,*" he quoted before storming out the back door.

The nerve of that man!

Leah fretted over Jamie's words until she was able to close the shop and head upstairs. She wanted to look up his quote in the Bible. Why she needed the chapter and verse, she didn't know. She wanted it, that was all.

And it did give her an idea for the shop. She should find some used Bibles to have in the store, for sale and just to look at. It would add a better ambiance to the place. And she could look up any wayward verses grouchy customers threw her way.

Honestly, what was that man's problem? He acted downright insulted, and all she had done was offer him a few clothes to get them through. Jamie's clothes weren't bad. Just a little worn in all the regular places, elbows and knees. But Peter was a mess. The shirt he'd had on at her *mamm*'s had been a bit small. Today's was too big. Same thing with his pants, which, on top of their varying sizes, also had holes in the knees and frayed hems. The clothes were perfectly fine for being around the house and working, but she had the means to give Peter something better. After all that he had been through, shouldn't he have at least that much?

She found the verse as Brandon came out of his bedroom all changed and ready to go. Matthew 6:1. *Take heed that ye do not your alms before men, to be seen of them: otherwise ye have no reward of your Father which is in heaven.*

"Doing a little reading?" he asked.

She shut her Bible quickly, and it snapped with the force. "Just a little. Are you all ready to go on your big date?"

"It's not a date. Shelly and I are going to study for a chemistry exam we have next week."

"And that's why you shaved and put on cologne." She rubbed a hand down his baby-smooth cheek.

He pulled away. "Aunt Leah," he protested. "It's after-shave."

She waved a hand. "Same thing."

He rolled his eyes, but these days the gesture was more playful than it had ever been before.

"Be home by ten."

"Ten thirty?"

"Ten fifteen," she acquiesced. "And that means leave her house at ten till. I want you *here* at ten fifteen. Not leaving her house."

"Yes, ma'am." He palmed his keys and headed for the door.

In seconds, silence had descended. How long had it been since she'd had quiet? She used to love it, back when she first moved to town, but tonight it came down like a thick fog, blanketing everything in gray.

She leaned her head back against the couch and closed her eyes. It had been one long week. Now she needed the silence. She did. She needed time to recharge, to rest. Tomorrow was Sunday. She would rest tonight, then go to church tomorrow. That should cheer her up.

But all she could think about was Jamie Stoltzfus and the unwarranted betrayal in his eyes as he thrust the box full of clothes back into her arms.

"Wow!" Brandon leaned forward in his seat to get a better look at the throng in front of them. "There are a ton of people here."

"Church," she whispered. Her parents were hosting their worship service today. She had forgotten all about it when she and Brandon had left their Mennonite church in town. She should just turn around and go back to her apartment, maybe sort through some more of the estate sale boxes she had picked up in New Albany last weekend. She was hoping to find a Bible or two in those treasures.

But she had already been spotted. It wasn't like she could hide the sound of her engine or the cloud of red dust billowing out behind her.

"Are we going to stay?" Brandon asked as she pulled her car alongside the row of buggies.

"Might as well," she muttered.

She had left Pontotoc before she had joined the church, so technically she wasn't shunned. Still there were a few, more conservative, members who took a step back as she walked past.

It shouldn't have stung, but it did. She was comfortable with her decision, but to have people she had known her entire life treat her like a toxic stranger . . .

Maybe she was overly sensitive since her confrontations with Jamie Stoltzfus, but honestly, why did she care what the man thought of her?

"Leah," her mother greeted her, clasping Leah's hands in her own. "I didn't expect to see you today."

"We thought we would surprise you." Leah gave a small shrug. She felt a little guilty that she had Brandon living with her so that Hannah could take back up with the Amish life, so she tried to bring him out every chance she got. Her shop was closed on Sundays, making it the perfect day for a nice long visit. Well, when there wasn't church, and it wasn't at her *mamm*'s house.

"It is a surprise. Get a plate and help yourself. Everyone has already eaten, but there's plenty left."

"*Danki.*" Leah motioned for Brandon to follow her, and together they made their way to the food tables.

"When I heard that the Amish have a meal after church, I thought it was a big spread."

"Like fried chicken and green beans?"

"Baked beans would be better, but yeah, something like that."

Leah grabbed a couple of paper plates and passed him one. "It's about convenience and togetherness."

"And not about eating?" Brandon asked.

"Not really. Plus, it's Sunday, and it's required that we do as little work as possible."

"'We'?" he echoed.

"I mean *them*." Why was she blushing? Must be the heat. After all, it was August in the South. "Be sure to get some pretzels." She pointed to the large plastic container of seasoned pretzels. "Those are Katie Esh's, and she makes the best seasoned pretzels from here to Ohio."

Brandon scooped a spoonful onto his plate next to the cheese slices and pretzels he had already dished out. "How do you know they're hers?"

Leah smiled and pointed to the container. "She's been bringing pretzels in that same container since before I was born."

A strange look passed over Brandon's face. She wasn't sure if it was astonishment or disbelief. "If you say so."

"I do." She chuckled. "Change is slow around here."

"I'll say." He grabbed a Dixie cup full of red gelatin and another of lemonade. "Do we sit at one of the tables?"

That she wasn't sure about. "Probably, yeah, but . . . I'm not sure I'm comfortable doing that. Let's go under the tree."

"Good plan."

Leah led the way to the large oak that sat at the edge of the yard just between the driveway and the horse corral. No one was sitting there, which surprised her. Usually the kids were all gathered around, drawing shapes in the dirt, playing games, and enjoying the shade. Not that shade was a valuable weapon against the Mississippi heat and humidity, but it helped some.

Then Leah remembered: Jim's bird dog had had puppies, and the kids were probably in the barn with the pups.

She eased down between the tree roots, shifting a bit to get comfortable—like that was possible sitting on a hundred acorns. Funny, she had sat under this tree more times than she could count, and she didn't remember the pain of acorns then. Ah, the oblivion of youth.

"Whoa," Brandon said, rearing back a little as someone came around the tree. It was Peter Stoltzfus.

"Hi, Peter," Leah said. "Do you mind if we sit with you? We thought it would be good to eat in the shade."

He nodded, his long hair swinging from side to side, even under the band of his hat.

"Thanks." Leah smiled. "Do you remember coming into my shop with your uncle?"

He nodded. Jamie was right. There was nothing wrong with the boy. He just didn't speak. But he was answering her just fine. Perhaps the teacher in Ethridge had made him nervous or anxious. Or perhaps it had been too soon for him to go back to his routine. The Amish thrived off routines. It came with being a farmer. If there was no rhythm to the day, then things got overlooked, chores were skipped, and animals and crops suffered. But for people who had endured a tragedy like Peter had, sometimes a break from routine was needed before a new routine could begin.

"Do you remember Brandon?" Leah asked.

Again Peter nodded.

"Hi," Brandon said.

Peter gave a small wave, then started picking up acorns and tossing them toward the closest fence post.

"Brandon is my nephew, like you are Jamie's."

This time Peter didn't acknowledge her words, but that was all right. Not every statement required a response.

Leah settled back against the tree and began to eat. She hated regretting coming over today, but she did. There was too much territory between the people in the community who understood and the people who wished she had never returned.

Okay, maybe she was being harsh, but she had seen the looks on their faces. It would take a lot more than bowing before the church and a vote by the membership to get her back in the good graces of the community. Even if she wasn't shunned, a great many people wished that she and Hannah had simply stayed away. Coming back only served as a reminder that people left to begin with.

She sighed and set her plate to one side. A few of the churchgoers had already hitched up their buggies and started for home. Soon it would be clear enough that she could sit on the front porch and visit with her *mamm* or Hannah. Until then, she was staying right where she was.

A tiny hand landed on her shoulder, and before she could fully register the fact, a small body came around the tree and settled in her lap. Peter snuggled into position as if he had been sitting on her his entire life.

"Uh . . ." Leah looked to Brandon, who shrugged. She lifted an awkward hand and removed his hat, setting it to one side. Then she ran a hand down his silky hair.

Peter rested his head against her and released a sigh so heavy and long, Leah wondered if he'd been holding it in half his young life. Or maybe just since he lost his parents.

She relaxed and continued to stroke his hair, murmuring inconsequential words as he let out another shuddering sigh.

Why it felt so right, she wasn't sure. But she knew that she was supposed to be there, in that moment, with him. And whatever else happened, happened.

She rested her head against the tree and closed her eyes. The rest of the world fell away. She would probably never have children of her own. It was a privilege that she had given up a long time ago. But for now, in this moment, this would do.

"What are you doing?"

Chapter Three

Leah jerked out of her near-trancelike state. The sound of the booming voice had her nearly jumping out of her skin. She jerked, and Peter did the same.

Then, as if he had only now become aware of what he had been doing, he pushed himself to his feet and hurried toward Jamie, his limp even more pronounced as he tried to run.

"He was behind the tree when we sat down," Leah said by way of explanation. Though her words explained nothing. How could she adequately explain when she had no reasoning herself?

Jamie's jaw hardened, and he lifted his chin a fraction of an inch. The look was almost appreciative, and yet she glimpsed a flash of envy before he grabbed Peter's hand and whirled away.

"What was that all about?" Brandon pushed himself up a bit straighter and stared after Jamie and Peter.

"I'm not sure. He doesn't want me around him, I guess." Surely she had only imagined the gratitude and jealousy in his glare. She had a feeling Jamie wasn't grateful to anyone but God. And even that she wondered about.

"The whole thing," Brandon said, waving a hand in front of him. "He sat in your lap."

Leah shrugged. "He needed a connection."

"He wanted a mommy."

Leah blew out a derisive sound. "No way." But for a moment there, it had felt like a mother-son relationship. She could only imagine that was how her sister felt when she sat on the couch next to Brandon or across from him at a restaurant.

"Yes way." Brandon pushed to his feet and retrieved her plate as well as his own. "That kid is in the market for a mommy, and you're the number one candidate."

Leah ignored Brandon's words as she helped with the cleanup. One after another, the plates and bowls were gathered up and deposited in the trash. In fact, she pushed the thoughts completely from her mind until she was sitting on the porch swing, waiting for her twin to join her. But it wasn't just Hannah who came out onto the porch; she was followed close behind by Tillie and Gracie.

"Whew." Tillie fanned herself. "I'm glad that's over. I mean, I enjoy hosting church and all, but it is *a lot* of work."

"It's a blessing," Gracie reminded her.

Tillie nodded. "I know. I know."

"It is a lot of work though," Gracie agreed.

Hannah nodded. "I had forgotten how much."

It took months to ready for a church service. Everything was cleaned. Baseboards, cabinets, under everything, and over everything.

"The good news is when you're done, your house is really clean."

"Until the next time," Tillie said.

Everyone laughed.

"You should have come out for the service, Leah," Gracie said. "You would have enjoyed it."

"Actually, I forgot Mamm and Dat were hosting today."

"That's because you weren't on your hands and knees scrubbing baseboards," Tillie said.

"You're right about that." But she had been doing other things—getting her store ready, taking care of Brandon. So he was practically grown and a good kid despite everything he had been through. It wasn't like he needed a great deal of watching after.

As if reading her thoughts, Hannah spoke. "Thank you for bringing him out today. I know you've been really busy with the store."

"Oh, that's right," Tillie said. "How is the store?"

"Doing good," Leah said. "Where is Brandon?"

Hannah pointed to the barn. The first melodies of a song floated to them on the breeze. "At the singing."

"I hope that goes okay," Gracie said. "Not like last time."

Earlier in the year, just after Brandon and Hannah had arrived in Pontotoc, he had gone to a volleyball game with Joshua. A boy had gotten upset because he thought the *Englischer* was flirting with his sister. The boy was something of a hothead, and a fight nearly broke out.

"I think the kids have decided where Brandon fits into everything."

"That's a miracle," Tillie said. "I didn't even know Brandon had it figured out."

Hannah shook her head. "Just that he's *Englisch*, but his parents are Amish, and he'll be hanging around. That's about it."

"That's complicated enough for me," Tillie said.

"What about you, Leah? Where do you fit in?" Gracie asked.

Leah pulled her gaze away from the barn and settled it on her cousin. "I don't. I'm Mennonite now."

"I guess it would be hard to give up electricity and your store . . ." Gracie mused.

"I don't know. You think the bishop wouldn't let her have her store?" Tillie asked.

Hannah shrugged. "It is in town."

Leah jumped to her feet. "Why do you think I would want to be Amish again?" She hadn't meant for her voice to sound quite so angry or loud. But even the singing in the barn stopped. "I mean . . . I don't know what I mean." She collapsed back into the swing.

"Touchy subject?" Gracie asked.

"Yeah, it's just . . ." It was just what? That she felt a little guilty that her sister had come back, while she was still out of the Amish church? Or maybe she was angry with the fact that if it hadn't been for Hannah, Leah herself would have never left. By now she would be married to Benuel King and have a passel of kids. Or maybe she was simply overtired from a stressful and busy opening. "It's been a long week."

"I'm sure." Gracie grabbed one of her hands in true Gracie style and squeezed her fingers reassuringly.

Leah smiled in response, but the image still remained: her happily married; a bunch of children. It was something she had dreamed of her entire life. Then things had changed.

She mentally shook away the thoughts. She loved her life. She had a great shop that was showing even greater promise. She had a roof over her head and food in her fridge. Well, maybe not in her fridge, but she wasn't hungry, and that was a lot more than she could say for some people. She should be grateful. She *was* grateful, but she was adding her thanks to her prayers that night. She needed God's help keeping everything in perspective.

Gracie released her hand and headed for the porch steps. "Eunice wanted me to check on the kids."

Hannah gave Leah's knee a quick pat. "I've got to go read to Mammi for a while."

Leah smiled at her sister. Hannah rose and made her way back into the house, and just like that, Leah was left alone with Tillie.

Her sister came closer and waited for Leah to stop rocking with her heels before she sat. Across the yard, Gracie let herself into the barn.

"How did you know?" Tillie asked in the setting sun.

Leah frowned. "How did I know what?"

"That you wanted to leave."

"Wanted to le—you're not still thinking about—" She shook her head. "Tillie, no."

"I'm just asking." But she turned her attention to her lap and proceeded to twist her fingers in the fabric of her apron.

"But you wouldn't be asking if you weren't considering it."

"You and Hannah." She pushed to her feet and went to stand by the porch railing. She folded her arms across her middle and looked out over the dusty yard that separated her *mamm* and *dat*'s house from Jim and Anna's. "It's all well and good for you two to leave, but I can't even think about it."

"Come sit down." Leah stopped the swing once more.

Tillie dropped her arms and shuffled back over.

"It's so hard to leave," Leah said. "Harder than I can ever tell you. Harder than you will ever know."

"But it can be done."

"Of course it can. The question is, why would you want to?"

"I have my reasons." She lifted her chin and stared out over the yard once more.

"Which means they aren't your reasons at all."

"Please." Tillie's tone was more than melancholy. "Leave Melvin out of this."

"How can I when I know he's the one trying to get you to leave?"

Tillie sniffed. "He's not. We're just talking about it."

"Uh-huh, and you've been talking about it long enough that one of you doesn't want to and the other does."

"It's really not like that." But even in the day's fading light, Leah could tell that her sister wasn't even fooling herself.

"If you really wanted to leave, then you would have been gone by now."

Tillie leaned back in the swing, folding her arms across herself once again. "Maybe" was all she said.

Leah sighed. "I'm sorry. It's just been a long week."

"So you keep saying," Tillie said with a nod.

"No one can make the decision for you. Not me or Gracie or Hannah. Not even Melvin."

But you let Hannah make the decision for you.

She pushed that voice away.

"I suppose," Tillie said.

"And I believe that your still being here says something."

Tillie nodded again. "I suppose you're right," she said, then pushed herself up from the swing. "Thanks, Leah."

"Anytime." Though she doubted she had added any new advice to the argument. Each person had to decide for themselves. She might have left to be with Hannah, but she had made the decision in a heartbeat. One minute she was being left behind, and the next she was standing on the side of the road waiting for someone to pick them up.

Leah watched as Tillie let herself into the house. It really had been a long week.

Laughter and the sound of voices rose in the air as Gracie and Brandon made their way back to the house.

"Are you ready to go?" Leah asked him.

He grinned. "I was born ready."

"Did you get to talk to your dad?" Leah asked once they were in the car and on the way home. Brandon had just recently discovered that Aaron Zook, his mother's one-time boyfriend, was his father, not Mitch McLean, the man who had raised him. Mitch had died in a boating accident earlier in the year, leaving Hannah and Brandon practically desti-tute as unknown debts started drifting in. Hannah had had no place to go but home. And once she had returned to Pontotoc, there was no keeping Brandon from the truth.

But it had all worked out. Or at least, they were working things out. Such a tangled mess took time to unwind.

"A little bit. It's hard, you know? I don't know what to say to him."

"You could tell him about school. And about the shop. Maybe about Shelly."

He blew out a disbelieving breath. "Me and Shelly are just friends."

"Shelly and I. And you can still tell him about her if you're only friends."

Brandon shook his head. "He wants . . . I think he wants to teach me things. You know, be a father to me."

"But you don't think you need that."

"Learning how to train horses is not going to help me."

"You never know. You might grow up and be a horse trainer."

"I doubt it."

"But would it hurt you to learn?"

He let out another breath, this one closer to a groan.

"I thought you liked watching him with the horses." It was a sight to behold, the poetry that was Aaron Zook with a horse. There was a beauty in it that wasn't from this world. Awe inspiring.

"That was before."

"Before what?"

"Nothing."

Before he found out that Aaron was his father. It would be tough news at any age, but Brandon was especially vulnerable. He had just lost the man he had always thought was his dad, then had to move out of the house he had always known to live in the middle of one of the most conservative Amish districts in the country. Culture shock didn't quite cover it.

"Give him a chance," Leah said softly. "This has to be just as hard on him."

"I guess."

But Leah could tell Brandon wasn't convinced. One day . . . *one day*, she prayed the two would be able to have as normal a relationship as possible. Given the circumstances.

"What were you and Aunt Tillie talking about?"

"Nothing." The word slipped out so easily, even if it wasn't the truth.

"Is she still thinking about leaving the Amish?"

Leah took her gaze from the road long enough to give him a quick look. "How did you know about that?"

Brandon shrugged. "People talk, you know. The Amish are the worst. But what do you expect, since they don't have television?"

"Who's been talking?"

"Everybody. Joshua and Libby mostly. But Anna and Jim when they think I'm not listening."

"I see." She didn't have a better answer to that. What would Tillie say if she knew everyone was speculating? Or perhaps she did know, and it was all a cry for someone to stop her?

"Do a lot of people leave?"

"Wh-what?" Leah pulled herself out of her thoughts.

"Do a lot of people leave? I mean like you and Mom. Are there a lot of you?"

"Enough, I suppose." She had no idea. She had heard statistics on the matter, but who truly knew how accurate they were? Leaving wasn't easy, and most who did tried several times before they were successful.

"What about turning Amish?"

"Turning Amish?"

"Yeah." He sat up a little straighter in his seat. They were almost into town. But at this time on a Sunday evening, hardly anyone was stirring around. "Mom is coming back. So that's different. Does anyone who's never been Amish before just decide they want to be?"

"I've heard of it happening once or twice, but it's not very common."

"But it does happen?"

"Yes." She pulled her car to a stop behind the shop. "But it's a hard life, and not many people can start living it on a whim."

"If it's so hard, why does anyone come back? Why does anyone stay?"

Leah put the car into park and turned off the engine, but she made no move to get out. "People have all sorts of reasons for coming back."

"Like Mom?"

She smiled at him. "I think your mom's case is a little bit different from most. People get out into the world, and it isn't what they thought. Or maybe they realize the world can separate them from God, so they come back. Most of us look for God in the first place we heard about Him."

He seemed to think about that for a moment. "Is that what Mom's doing? Finding God?"

"That's part of it, I suppose."

"And Aunt Tillie? Will she lose God if she leaves?"

The thought was heartbreaking. "It's possible, yes."

He nodded, then reached for his door handle to let himself out of the car.

Leah followed suit, locking it for the night.

"What about you?" he asked as they climbed the stairs.

"I didn't lose God. That's why I joined the Mennonite church." She unlocked their apartment and flipped on the lamp nearest the door.

"Not God," Brandon said. "Do you ever think about coming back?"

More times than I can count. But she couldn't say that out loud. She couldn't admit it. Admitting it wouldn't change one thing. She had left, and she had never come back. She might have returned to Pontotoc, but that was as close as she had gotten. She was happy with the decisions she had made. "No," she lied, realizing she had told two whoppers in so many hours. Less than. "Now go get ready for bed. We have a big day ahead of us tomorrow."

He couldn't believe he was coming in here again. Jamie opened the door to Twice Blessed with a quick sigh. It was as if he couldn't stay away from the woman. Which was ridiculous. They seemed to argue about something every time they were together. And he wanted to stay away from her. Far away from her.

Lord help me get through this day with friendship and kindness. Amen.

She was standing behind the counter when he walked in. She looked up and met his gaze as his heart gave a hard thump. *Jah*, he dreaded seeing her so much that his heart was beating out of normal rhythm. It was sort of sad, really, that two of God's creatures couldn't get along any better than that.

"Jamie," she greeted, then cleared her throat, most probably just to stall for time. "What are you doing here?"

He held up his toolbox. "Jim said you needed a hand with a few things."

She nodded. "But I thought Jim would come." *Or at the very least, David* was left unsaid, and yet it hung in the air around them.

"He asked me to."

She tilted her head to one side and seemed to contemplate the notion. Then she gave a delicate shrug and motioned for him to follow her. "I was hoping to have this done before the opening, but the parts didn't come in, and I was stuck waiting until now." She pointed to the industrial-looking setup of iron pipes and sturdy chains.

"I want to turn these into hanging clothing racks. Can you do that?"

Jamie looked over the materials, then turned his gaze toward the ceiling. "You want them to hang down from there?"

She nodded. "And I need two of them, one on top of the other. Just a little clearance room for after the clothes are hung."

He took out his tape measure and started measuring the distance from the ceiling and how high off the ground the lower rod would be. "How do you want—"

The bell over the door rang out its gentle warning.

"Excuse me." She held up one finger and moved toward the front of the shop.

He could hear her talking to whoever had just come in while he stood there with his hands on his hips and did nothing. Nothing but wait for her to come back and show him more of what she wanted.

She returned a few minutes later, and he showed her what he had come up with.

"I think that's too much clearance room," she said. "People need to be able to reach the clothing on the top bar just as easily as they can the bottom one."

"That's all well and good, but what happens when someone really short comes in? What are you going to do then?" he asked.

"Are you always this contentious, or is it only with me?"

He felt exactly the same. "I'm merely saying that you can't cater to everyone. There will always be someone who doesn't fit the criteria."

She propped her hands on her hips and studied the situation.

"Plus, if you hang the bars like I just showed you, then you still have space to hang something over the window to protect the fabric and yet let the sunshine in."

She chewed on her lower lip, and he had the feeling that she liked his idea but was too proud to admit it. "I like it," she finally said.

Jamie felt as if a light breeze would have knocked him to the floor. There was a soft side to Leah Gingerich after all. Besides the one that wanted to force handouts on him.

"Make it so," she said with a quick nod, then turned and wound her way back to the front of the store.

She had to admit that Jamie did good work. He was fast and thorough.

"All done." He came from the back of the store and placed his toolbox on her counter.

"I appreciate it." She opened the cash register and pulled out a few bills to pay him.

He shook his head. "No need."

She frowned. "I paid you the last time you came out."

"That was different."

"I don't see how." She waved the cash at him, but he refused to take it. "Fine," she said. "Let me pay your sitter. Where is Peter today?"

"At your *mamm*'s house."

He had left his child with her mother in order to come and do a favor for her brother, which was a favor to her, and he wouldn't take any money for the job. She shook her head to smooth out the tangle, but the thought still remained a jumbled mess in her mind. So why did she feel like he had somehow taken advantage of her family? Or maybe she felt like he was setting them up to owe him.

Maybe she had been living out too long. But the distaste still burned in her stomach.

"Just take the money."

He grabbed his things and started for the door. "Let me know if you have any problems with the fix."

And just like that, he was gone, leaving Leah at the counter still holding the money.

Chapter Four

"I still don't understand what you're doing," Brandon said that evening. He didn't bother to take his eyes from his phone as he spoke.

"I'm packing a box of essentials for Jamie and Peter."

Brandon looked up. "But this guy, he like, hates you, doesn't he?"

"I wouldn't go that far." Maybe she would, but she didn't like it when the words came out of someone else's mouth.

"I would. Why do you want to hang around this guy if he makes you angry?"

Leah turned from the cabinet where she had been collecting canned goods to share. She had a tendency to buy when things were on sale and always had plenty of canned fruits, vegetables, soup, and beans at the ready. "It's just something I have to do." *And when God tells you to do something, you should do it.*

She had been fighting that voice inside her head all day. The one that told her she needed to get some things together and take them out to Jamie and Peter's. After the fiasco with the clothing, she knew Jamie wasn't going to take kindly to her intrusion, but she had to do what God compelled her to do. And Heaven knew, she wouldn't be doing this without God's direction. She would like nothing more than to stay two counties away from the man. Technically, that wasn't possible. Far away would have to suffice.

"You want to drive with me out there or not?"

Brandon had turned his eyes back to the screen, but he shook his head. "No way."

"I'll let you drive." She jangled the keys encouragingly.

"Nope." He didn't even bother to look up.

"You don't want to practice driving?"

He dropped the phone to his lap. "As tempting as it might sound, I'm going to have to pass. I have a test tomorrow, and I don't have time to get blood out of my clothes."

"If you have a test, why are you playing a game?"

He grinned, that charming grin she had seen on Aaron's face time and again when they were growing up. Brandon might take after his mother in coloring, but he had his father's smile. No doubt about it. "I'm taking a break."

"If you're resting, then you can do it in the car while I drive."

He retrieved his phone. "No way. Bloodshed, remember."

Leah hoisted the cardboard box off the counter and staggered a bit under the weight. She hadn't expected the box to be quite this heavy. "You've got it all wrong. He's Amish, remember? That makes him a pacifist."

Brandon chuckled as she made her way to the door. "That man is anything but peaceful when it comes to you."

She shook her head. "Can you get this door for me?" Normally she would have tried to juggle the box, but it was heavy enough to topple her over if she wasn't careful.

Brandon stood and did as she asked.

"And be sure to study. Your *mamm* will have my hide if you don't have a good semester."

"I know." Brandon stood, one hand on the doorjamb, the other at his side.

"I know you know, but you've got to know enough to actually pass it tomorrow."

He bent down and gave her a quick buss on the cheek. "I've got this. Now go play Good Samaritan."

"I won't be gone long," she promised. After all, how long would it take before he tossed her out on her ear?

Jamie was just gathering the supper dishes and putting them in the sink when a knock sounded at his door. It had been so long since anyone had come visiting that he wasn't sure what it was at first. Then it sounded again.

"Who could that be at this time of night?" Must be someone who wasn't from around these parts. Sure, it was easier to stay up in the summertime when the time change gave them another hour of daylight to add to their day. But folks around here went to bed before the chickens. Another half an hour, and he would have been on his way to bed as well.

He checked on Peter, who was sitting at the table copying his letters into a paper tablet. It might not be the best way to learn them, but it beat nothing. Jamie hadn't given up the hope that Peter would overcome the ghosts that haunted him and begin to speak again. But one thing he knew for certain: all good things in time. When the Lord was ready for Peter to talk, He would move Peter's heart, and that would be that. In the meantime, Jamie was going to teach him everything he could at home. Maybe when Peter actually got to attend school, he wouldn't be so far behind his peers.

"Leah," Jamie breathed as he opened the door. She was the last person he had expected to see. And that was why she stole his breath from his lungs. He just hadn't been expecting her, was all. It was that and nothing more. Not the raven color of her hair or the clear green of her eyes.

For the first time, he noticed that she had a tiny band of freckles across her nose. A light dusting of cinnamon that added more charm to her features than he cared to acknowledge. He didn't want her to be charming. He needed her to be tough as nails, take-no-prisoners. Leah who wasn't vulnerable to the sun.

"Can I come in?"

That was when he noticed the box she was carrying. He took it from her and backed up a step so she could enter the tiny cabin he called home. One day he hoped to build himself and Peter a proper house, but for now this would do. The Lord had provided.

She looked around. He hadn't done much since moving in, just basic cleaning and such. "I love what you've done with the place." She spied Peter across the room and gave him a small wave. "Hey there, Peter."

He waved, then bent back over his work.

"What's all this?" Jamie carried the box over to the table and set it in front of the boy.

"Just a few things I thought you could use. Some canned goods and a few sets of clothing for Peter."

Jamie stilled. His stomach cramped, and his heart sank. "This is charity."

"Of course it's charity. I came to help."

"Take it back."

She shook her head. "*But you shall freely open your hand to him, and shall generously lend him sufficient for his need in whatever he lacks.*"

He took a step back.

"You're not the only one who can quote the Bible." She smirked, but the action was gone almost immediately. She had planned this. But why?

"Peter, why don't you take your things into my room? Go ahead and get ready for bed. It's almost time."

The boy nodded and slipped from his chair, picking up his things before taking them out of the kitchen.

"Why your room?"

He propped his hands on his hips. "Surely you remember that this is a two-room cabin."

She nodded.

He pointed toward the floor, then the door that led to the only bedroom.

"One. Two."

"One bedroom," she mused.

"I was having Peter sleep in here on a cot, but every night he gets up, sneaks into my room, climbs into bed with me, then goes back to sleep." Why was he telling her all this? "I moved his cot in there so he could sleep close. Now he starts out on the cot, but by morning he's right next to me." He gave her a cautious smile.

"Is he afraid?"

Jamie shrugged. "I suppose so. Or maybe he feels out of sorts. He lost his family and all. I moved us down here to get away from all the meaningful people who just seemed to make everything worse instead of better."

"You thought a new environment would give him a new outlook."

"Something like that." Lord, she was smart. He had never met anyone quite as smart as Leah Gingerich. From years of living in the *Englisch* world, no doubt.

But when she looked at Peter with sweet understanding, he could forget that she was Mennonite. At least for a time.

"Well, I guess I should be going." She eased toward the door.

"Take your box." He moved to fetch it from the table. He and Peter were getting along just fine. He had made up his mind when he took Peter from his grandparents that he wouldn't turn to others for help. If he was going to do this—raise Peter by himself—then he was going to do it.

Besides, if everything worked out like he planned, he would find himself a wife and get special permission to get married out of season, and the three of them would live happily ever after. Oh, and somewhere in there, Peter would start to talk again and the world would be returned to normal. At least that was his prayer and had been every night since the accident.

She shook her head. "You are the most stubborn man I have ever met."

He shrugged. He had been called worse. And he didn't care what Leah Gingerich thought. This wasn't her life.

"I'm sure you want what's best for Peter. But allowing him to walk around in clothes that are obviously not his . . ."

"His clothes were burned in the fire." His throat grew tight.

She nodded. "And the ones he has now are ill-fitting. Have him try on what I brought. Let him have some ownership of his things once again."

Did she somehow know that Peter's clothes were castoffs from his young uncles? It was what they had, and Jamie was grateful. Peter was grateful. "Worldly possessions are of no importance."

"Says the man who lives in a shack."

"From the woman who lives over her work."

"Touché."

He frowned. He had no idea what that meant, and there was no way he was asking her to explain. She was too intelligent by far, and he wouldn't show his ignorance for her enjoyment.

"Have him try on the clothes. If they don't fit, you can give them to Mamm. I'll pick them up next time I visit. But if they do, then you keep them for him to wear."

He opened his mouth to protest, but she shook her head. "It's just clothes. Fabric and thread. Stop making such a big deal out of it." Then with a smile that contained tones he didn't quite understand, she turned on her heel and headed out the door.

Leah resisted the urge to lean back against the door of the cabin and suck in a deep breath. There was so much about this situation she didn't understand. Why was he being so stubborn about accepting help from her, and why was she so adamant about giving it?

He had made it perfectly clear that he didn't want anything to do with her or the things she offered. She was not calling it "charity." Somehow that had gotten a bad connotation.

With a sigh, she made her way down the porch steps and got into her car. Thankfully, Jamie didn't follow after her. He didn't toss the box of goods she had brought out into the yard. That had to be a good sign, right?

She cranked the car and headed farther down the lane, to her parents' house. The lights were still on, though she knew everyone would be in bed soon. Still, she couldn't come all the way out without at least stopping by for a minute.

Having heard her car, Hannah came out onto the front porch to greet her. "Where's Brandon?" she asked.

"Nice to see you too, sister dear."

Hannah laughed. "*Jah*, all that. Now where's my son?"

"Studying." Leah used air quotes around the word.

"That bad, is it?"

Leah shook her head. "He's a great kid." As she said the words, Peter Stoltzfus's sweet face came into view.

"When he sets his mind to it. Seriously, he hasn't been giving you any trouble, has he?"

Leah skipped up the porch steps and gave her sister a quick squeeze. "He's fine. And a big help." Brandon had gone through a rough patch after his father died. But once he saw the family he could have, he settled down a bit. "I couldn't ask for a better flatmate."

"Have you been watching the BBC again?"

Leah placed one finger over her lips. "That's our little secret."

"Come sit with me." Hannah looped her arm through Leah's and led her over to the porch swing.

"It's almost dark," Leah said unnecessarily. And when it got dark in Mississippi Amish country, it got dark. A person couldn't see their hand in front of their face.

"Mamm's got the lamp on in the window. And I've got a flashlight."

As if on cue, Eunice Gingerich opened the front door. "Leah, is that you?" she asked through the screen door.

"Yes, Mamm."

"Everything okay?"

"Of course. I was . . ." Did she really want to tell her mother that she was down visiting with Jamie Stoltzfus? No, she decided. She didn't. But there was no way out of it. "I found some clothes I thought Peter might be able to wear, so I brought them out for him."

Mamm shook her head. "He's a stubborn one."

"Peter?" Hannah asked.

"That Jamie," Mamm said. "We like to never got him to accept the house."

"What do you mean?" Something in her mother's words seemed contradictory.

"The cabin. The bishop came to your father and asked him if he could help Jamie and Peter. Jim offered to let them stay with his family. David too, but he wouldn't hear of it."

"How'd you get him to take the cabin?"

Mamm pressed her lips together and shook her head. "Your father. I don't know what he said to him. But he convinced Jamie to move in."

Which explained why Jamie came to fix her racks that morning. He was staying on her parents' property for free. Not that they were keeping tabs—but she would bet Jamie was.

"Wait," she said as her mother's words fully sank in. "He's staying with you for free?"

Hannah gave her a strange look. Then Leah realized how her words actually sounded. "I mean . . . Never mind." She wouldn't be able to explain it even if she had all night. And she didn't.

"Is something wrong?" Mamm asked. Concern tainted her normally cheerful tone.

"Everything's fine." She stood. "But I need to be getting back to town."

Hannah stood as well. "Why don't you come back out tomorrow after work." She shook her head. "No, not tomorrow. I'm going over to Aaron's. How about the next day? You can come out, and we can have a better chance to visit."

Leah nodded and hugged her sister. "I would like that." But she knew there was more to the invitation than met the eye. Twins had a special bond. People could call it whatever they wanted, but it remained the same. Hannah knew that Leah had something on her mind, and her nosy twin wanted to know what it was.

"*Danki* for the invitation," Jamie said, nudging Peter forward.

Aaron stepped to one side to allow Jamie and Peter to enter.

"We're glad you're here," Hannah Gingerich said.

When Aaron had invited Jamie and Peter to supper, Jamie had naturally thought that it would be the three of them. A boy's night, so to speak. He had briefly wondered if Aaron could cook, then decided his efforts couldn't be any worse than Jamie's own. He hadn't expected Leah's sister, Hannah, to be there.

He had heard through the grapevine that Hannah and Aaron had been a couple a while back during their runaround years. But instead of joining the church, dating, and then getting married as was the usual custom, Hannah had taken off for the *Englisch* world, leaving a broken-hearted Aaron behind, if Jamie was getting the story right. He had heard a lot of stories since moving here. So many that it was hard to keep all of them in order.

But considering that Hannah was here at Aaron's, acting like a wife for all intents and purposes, then he supposed there was some validity to the tale. Plus, it would explain how Hannah came to have an *Englisch* son who lived with Leah. Well, sort of.

"Everybody, come eat," Hannah called from the kitchen door.

Jamie, Peter, and Aaron met at the table with another boy and two young girls: Andy, Laura Kate, and Essie.

"I love fried chicken," Essie said after prayer.

"Take one piece," Aaron instructed.

Hannah smiled at Jamie. "She likes to take a lot in case she's hungry later."

Jamie smiled. Essie was as cute as she could be, lively and vivacious. He had a feeling she stayed in trouble more than she stayed out of it, and suddenly he was reminded of Leah—not that the child physically resembled her. But they both had that same spunky manner, sparkling eyes, and mischievous smile.

Essie accidentally stuck her fingers in her mashed potatoes, then licked them off.

"Use your napkin," Aaron instructed. He barely glanced

her way as he said the words. Jamie had the feeling this was a nightly occurrence at the Zook house.

He looked over to Peter, who was as stiff and serious as Andy Zook as he silently ate his meal. Andy seemed like a good kid, polite with manners to spare. He ate his meal, didn't pester his sisters, and generally kept his eyes on his plate. Just like Peter. Except Peter was six and should be acting more like Essie. Not like at-least-twelve-year-old Andy.

Jamie dipped his head over his plate, closed his eyes, and said a little prayer for Peter. The boy was missing out on some of the best years of his life. The thought was heartbreaking. Wasn't it enough that he had lost his parents and his only sibling?

"Can I have another piece of chicken now?" Essie asked.

"If you eat it all tonight, you won't have any to take to school tomorrow," Laura Kate explained. The eldest Zook daughter was almost as serious as her brother, but not quite.

Essie tilted her head to one side as if contemplating the very difficult puzzle of eating her favorite chicken now or later. "Tomorrow, I guess," she said with a small pout. "But when I'm bigger, Hannah's going to teach me how to make it all by myself and I'm gonna have fried chicken every day."

"You'll sure enough be bigger then," Andy mumbled.

"What does that mean?" Essie asked. "Dat, what does Andy mean?"

"He means that it's not healthy to eat fried chicken every day. You have to eat other things as well."

"Like meatloaf and pork chops."

Hannah nodded with a smile. "And green beans and cabbage and—"

"Carrots?" Essie asked. "I like those."

"And carrots," Hannah agreed. "Now finish up so you can have pie before you help Andy do the dishes."

Essie scraped her plate clean, then nodded. "I'm done. I want to save my chicken for tomorrow."

Jamie finished his own meal and glanced over to Peter, who had done the same. He had no complaints when it came to the boy eating. He supposed that was good. Peter might not be talking, but he was eating and sleeping—if he counted the hours after Peter crawled in bed with him—and Jamie had to consider those good signs. There were a lot worse things than not speaking. He just wished he could convince Sally's parents of that.

After the accident, Jamie had heard of children similarly traumatized who stopped eating and nearly starved to death before they got help. Thank the good Lord, he didn't have to worry about that. And he had faith. Faith that when Peter's insides healed as well as his outsides, then he would talk again. The doctors assured him that there was nothing wrong with Peter's vocal cords or anything else that controlled speech. It was just a matter of time.

"Let's take our pie and coffee into the living room, where we can talk," Hannah suggested.

"Good idea," Aaron agreed. "Essie, will you take Peter outside and show him how we feed the goats?"

"*Jah*, Dat."

"But she's supposed to help me with the dishes," Andy grumbled.

"Laura Kate can help you," Aaron said.

"*Da-at*," Laura Kate protested. "It's not my turn."

"It'll be your turn tonight, and the two of you can switch tomorrow."

Laura Kate didn't seem overly happy about the idea, but she nodded and followed her brother into the kitchen.

Hannah also rose. "I'll get the dessert and meet you two

in the living room." She followed the children into the kitchen.

"Come on, Peter," Essie said, climbing down from her chair. "Let's go feed the goats."

Jamie took a step toward them as Essie grabbed Peter's elbow and started for the back door. But Aaron stopped him with one hand on his arm.

"They'll be fine."

Jamie tried to expel the tension from his shoulders. "*Jah.*"

"Come on." Aaron led him from the dining area into the living room.

Jamie cast one look back at Essie and Peter, then allowed Aaron to lead him away. They would be fine. He knew it. Essie didn't seem to mind that Peter hadn't said one word since they arrived. She held his arm and chatted nonstop as she led him out the back door.

Peter seemed to enjoy being around Essie as well. Maybe Leah was right, and he should put Peter in school. If their teacher was a good one, then perhaps she could bring Peter out of his shell.

He couldn't believe he was even thinking it, but Leah Gingerich might be right. Huh.

"Here we go." Hannah breezed into the room carrying a tray with three cups of coffee. Behind her, Laura Kate, looking very pleased with herself, carried a tray with three saucers of chocolate pie.

Once everyone had their dessert, Laura Kate took both trays back into the kitchen.

"She's a cute one," Jamie said. Strange, but before he became a single dad, he had never really thought about children and whether or not they were cute, or sullen, or even spunky. Now he seemed to be looking at other people's children and wondering if he was on the right track or if he was so far off, Peter would never recover.

"She's something," Aaron said with a laugh.

Jamie took a bite of his pie, using his full mouth as an excuse not to reply. He seemed to remember that Aaron hadn't been a widower for more than a year, and his children seemed to have adjusted just fine. Andy might be a little sullen, and Laura Kate might be a little too serious, but they were talking. Was he doing something wrong? Maybe they all helped one another.

"Our buddy bunch is meeting on Saturday. Would you like to come?" Hannah asked. "It'll give you a chance to meet a few people."

"*Jah*. That would be good." Except that buddy bunch groups were formed when the members were in their teens. Jamie could meet a lot of new people, or merely be on the outside of a close-knit clique.

"Peter can stay here with the kids," Aaron offered.

Jamie shifted uneasily in his seat. "*Jah*." Or maybe he could find a sitter. Maybe Eunice would watch Peter again. He hated to leave the boy behind, but he needed to get out and meet people. Maybe even a woman.

Perhaps that was what Peter needed. A mother.

"Will Leah be there?" Now, why had he asked that? She wasn't even Amish any longer. Of course she wouldn't be there. Except they seemed to accept the fact that she wasn't Amish and still welcomed her into their homes and lives.

"No," Hannah said slowly, looking to Aaron as if he knew something she didn't. "But Gracie might be. She joined the youth group after we did, and sometimes she comes. It just depends if anyone needs her." Hannah settled a little in her seat and gave an affirming nod.

Of course. Gracie was quite a bit younger than Hannah and Leah. It only made sense that she had joined the group later, when she herself had turned sixteen. And with the groups in Pontotoc being so much smaller than the ones in Ethridge, it only stood to reason that older members— members who had already joined the church—didn't recognize the dividing lines of the buddy bunch groups.

"Yes, Gracie."

Jamie didn't like the gleam in her eyes; he had seen it before. It had *matchmaker* written all over it. But that was okay. If he was looking for a mother for Peter . . .

The more the idea knocked around in his head, the more comfortable he got with it.

"Gracie's a sweet girl, wouldn't you say?" Hannah asked.

"Of course he would say that," Aaron interrupted. "Everyone says that."

"Well, that's because it's true. She's always willing to help. And she's a fantastic cook."

And she was pretty enough, he supposed. He hadn't really thought about a woman since Deborah. Beautiful Deborah. But Gracie Glick was about as different from Deborah as black was from white. Gracie was blond-haired and fair-skinned, with big blue eyes. Deborah was darker, with hair the color of fine chocolate and eyes like violets. She was more like Leah.

Where had that come from? Deborah was nothing like Leah in looks. So they both had dark hair, that was where the similarities ended. But in personalities? That was where they held a sameness. Deborah was opinionated, strong, and willful. He should have seen right off that she wouldn't make him a good wife. She may not have been born fancy Amish, but she was fancy Amish at heart. Just like Leah. Leah who left the Amish to become a Mennonite, drive a car, and have electricity in her store. Deborah wanted more than sometimes their community allowed.

But Gracie . . . Gracie was demure, helpful, and obedient.

She would make someone a good Amish wife. And that someone might as well be him.

"Come on," Leah said Wednesday evening. She shook the toe of Brandon's sneaker. He was lounging in the big comfortable chair she had found at an estate sale. She had thought she would sell it in the shop, but she liked the chair. Red and overstuffed, with rounded arms that begged a person to curl up on a rainy day and read a book. So far Brandon had gotten the most use out of it. She had barely had time to wash her hair, much less read a book for pleasure. But soon, she promised herself.

"Where are we going?"

"To Mammi's."

"My *mammi*'s or your *mammi*'s?"

She laughed. "They live in the same house. With your mother, remember?"

He nodded, but made no move to get up.

"She asked about you yesterday, so I thought it would be good for us to go back out tonight."

He peeled his gaze from his phone and actually looked at her. "I thought you went out there to see Jamie and Peter."

"I couldn't not stop in and see Mamm."

"My *mamm* or your *mamm*?"

"Again, same house."

Brandon laughed. "What does this have to do with me?"

"You need to come with me. Your mother misses you."

A shadow moved across his features, but it was gone so fast she wondered if she had imagined it. "She's probably over at Aaron's."

"I bet not."

He blew out a breath. "Yeah, right."

She laid one hand on his ankle, hoping the gesture came across as supportive. She was new at this surrogate parenting thing. "Listen, I know this has been hard on you. And you've handled it like a champ. But it's just as hard on your mom."

For a moment she thought he might protest, but he simply nodded and pushed himself to his feet. "Okay," he said. "I'm ready when you are."

"See," Leah said as she pulled into the drive at her parents' house. "I told you she would be here."

Hannah walked across the yard toward them. She smiled as she approached, that smile reserved just for her son. "Hey, you two."

"Hey, yourself." Leah turned off her car and got out. "We thought we'd come out and see if Mamm's got any pie."

Hannah chuckled. "Mamm always has pie. She even baked one special this morning."

"Apple?" Brandon asked hopefully.

"Cherry."

"Where'd she get the cherries?"

"Walmart. But don't tell anyone. She's afraid it might ruin her reputation."

"Why cherry?" Brandon asked with a frown.

"Peter and Jamie came over for supper tonight," Hannah said as they moved toward the house. "Mamm wanted to give them a special treat."

"Oh, yeah?" It seemed as if Jamie and Peter were always coming over.

"You know Mamm."

They moved up the porch and into the house. Tillie came out of the kitchen and wrapped them both in tight hugs.

Leah breathed a sigh of relief that her sister was still there. Maybe she was just overreacting.

"I heard Mamm baked a cherry pie," Leah said.

"There's still a couple of pieces left. But you better hurry. Jamie's been threatening to eat the rest of it all evening long."

Leah stopped. "He's still here?"

Tillie nodded. "On the back porch. Peter's with the twins looking at the puppies. Not that there's much to see. I mean, they're cute and all, but they don't even have their eyes open. All they want to do is eat and sleep."

"Sounds like a plan to me," Brandon quipped.

Tillie laughed. "Come on. I'll get you that pie."

They walked into the kitchen with more of the same. Laughter, jokes about pie, and friendly greetings. Leah lived for these times. She had missed them so much.

Once they had their pie and milk, Leah and Brandon sat at the small kitchen table. Tillie and Hannah joined them, while Mamm bustled off to take care of Mammi.

Leah forked up a bite and savored the tart flavor of the cherries mixed with the flaky goodness of her mother's pie crust. "Where's Gracie?" She hoped no one had called for her to come help with something. It seemed she was always flitting off to one relative or another's to make everyone's life easier, while her own seemed perpetually on hold.

Hannah gave a sly smile. "On the porch with Jamie."

"Why?" Leah asked.

Hannah shifted in her seat and shared a knowing look with Tillie. "He's come here to see her."

"What?" She couldn't stop herself. Leah hopped to her feet. "Jamie and Gracie?"

Three sets of eyes stared at her as if she had declared herself president. She realized then that she might have overreacted, just a bit, and she eased back into her chair. She picked up her fork and pretended nothing was wrong.

But everything was wrong. Jamie couldn't "see" Gracie. The idea was ridiculous.

"I mean, Jamie and Gracie?" It took all her composure to push the words out in a normal tone. Well, more normal than the one she had used earlier.

"What's wrong with you?" Tillie asked.

Leah shook her head and pushed her plate away. Her appetite was gone. Her mouth tasted like ash, and her stomach cramped.

"Are you going to eat that?" Brandon asked around his last bite of pie.

"Don't talk with your mouth full, please," Hannah coached.

Leah shook her head.

Brandon pulled her plate across the table and started in on what was left.

"Nothing's wrong," she said. "Just . . . Jamie and Gracie?"

Hannah smiled. "I think it's romantic."

"Me too." Tillie propped her elbow on the table and cupped her chin in one hand.

"Romantic?" Leah scoffed. "He's so . . ." She searched for the word. Opinionated? Bossy? Handsome? She shook that last thought away. "Conservative," she finally managed.

"That's a good thing around here," Hannah said.

"I guess," Leah grumbled. "But Gracie . . ."

"Is glowing," Tillie said. "He showed up, and she just beamed."

Leah shook her head, trying to get it all in perspective.

"I'm outta here." Brandon pushed his chair back from the table and set the plates in the sink.

"Where are you going?" Hannah asked.

"Over to see what Joshua's up to." He turned to Leah. "Come get me when you're ready to go." Then he kissed his mother on the cheek and started for the door.

Conversation stopped as Hannah watched him walk away.

"It's going to be okay," Leah said.

"I know," Hannah whispered. "But that doesn't stop me from praying about it every night."

"We all do," Tillie added.

"Then we can't lose," Leah said.

Hannah smiled. "It's tough, you know. When you know you're doing the right thing, but it's the hardest thing you've ever done."

"Even harder than leaving?" Tillie asked.

"Much harder than leaving," Hannah answered.

Tillie sat back in her seat and seemed to mull that over.

Leah wanted to go back to talking about Gracie and Jamie, but it seemed that conversation time had passed. Still, the thoughts tumbled around inside her head as Tillie and Hannah started talking about the merits of using lard over butter in a pie crust.

She felt as removed from that conversation as if she were in another state. How long had it been since she had made a pie? How long since she had done anything like that? She hardly even made dinner these days. It was all part of her new life. Her busy life as a business owner. It was a small price to pay for the freedom she now had. Wasn't it? And the good she was doing for the community. And being close to her family once again. But she needed to change that. She needed to start cooking again. Wintertime was coming. She could load some good things into the Crock-Pot and not make it her personal goal to keep the local Chinese restaurant in business.

"Leah?"

She started at Tillie's voice. Leah had the feeling this wasn't the first time her name had been called. "Yes?"

"Let's go check on Gracie and Jamie."

"She means *spy*," Hannah added.

"They really should have a chaperone."

"And I'm certain you are the person for the job."

"I am today." Tillie grinned and pushed herself up from the table. "Are you two coming?" she asked.

Leah caught Hannah's gaze and hoped she looked as disinterested as she intended. "You in?"

"One of us has to go. She'll start making up stuff if we don't."

"Not true," Tillie tossed over her shoulder and flounced toward the back door.

Chapter Five

Jamie shifted in his seat and glanced toward Gracie Glick. They had been out here on the porch since after supper. An hour, maybe, and he felt every second of it. Every so often he could sense the eyes of her family on the two of them as her kin peeked through the windows. It was to be expected, but it made him nervous all the same.

"Are you comfortable?" Gracie asked.

Sixty minutes alone, and she had asked him that at least ten times.

"I'm fine." He nodded his thanks and resisted the urge to shift again. If he did, he was afraid she might hop up and fuss over him like a mother hen.

Of course, when they were married, he wouldn't mind a little fussing from time to time.

Married. The word knocked around inside his head, pinging off his doubts. How was it that he came up with the idea one day and the next he was out "visiting"? After Deborah, he had thought he would never get married. He hadn't wanted to. Some people just weren't meant for marriage. Old Sam Ebersol, for one. And Ruth Yoder. He had known them both back in Tennessee, and they had never been married. People used to joke that the two of them should marry each other, but no one had the courage to say it to their faces. Knowing the two of them, they would have just laughed. But until after Deborah had called off their engagement, he had never thought he would be among their ranks. He had just gotten used to the idea of never getting married, and here he was out searching for a wife.

He was rusty. He had been living by himself for too long. Or with Peter. He wasn't much of a conversationalist. Now Jamie had all but forgotten how to chitchat.

"I'm going over to the schoolhouse to talk to the teacher about Peter."

Gracie nodded enthusiastically. "That's a good idea. I can come with you if you like. The teacher, Amanda Swartzentruber, is a friend of mine."

"That's okay. But *danki*." He should have taken her up on the offer, but he felt that was moving a bit fast. He hadn't even had the chance to talk to Peter about it before he had jumped in and started looking for a wife. He at least needed to prepare the boy.

"Oh, no." She sighed.

"What?" Jamie looked around, trying to find the cause of her distress.

"My cousins." She nodded toward Leah, Hannah, and Tillie as they held up the edge of their dresses and picked their way through the tangle of plants just off the porch.

Tillie turned and waved. "Don't mind us," she instructed. "We're just going to check the blackberry bramble and see if there's any fruit." She held up a galvanized pail as if to back up her claim.

Gracie pressed her lips together and shook her head. "Those bushes stopped producing months ago."

Tillie smiled. "You never know. It's been pretty warm these last couple of weeks. Maybe there are some late bloomers."

"You don't want blooms. You want berries," she called in return. "And there are no berries."

Her cousins simply smiled and waved and ignored everything she was trying to tell them.

"I'm sorry," Gracie said, ducking her head as she said the words. He had a feeling she was hiding the hot color in her cheeks.

"It's all right," he returned. "It just shows your family loves you very much."

She stared out over the tangle of brush to where her cousins were poking around, making only a half-hearted attempt at looking like they were searching for blackberries.

"I suppose," she said, dragging her lower lip between her teeth. He had seen that movement somewhere before. But he couldn't place it—Leah. He had seen Leah do that exact same thing. "It's still embarrassing."

"I remember one time Deborah's family did about the same thing, but they all came out into the front yard and checked every bolt and rivet in the family carriage."

She laughed, then a small frown worked its way between her brows. "Deborah?"

He shifted once again and cleared his throat. Why had he brought her up? "Deborah is my ex-fiancée."

Her expression grew somber. "I see." This time she shifted.

Great. Now he had made them both uncomfortable. And all it took was one name. "She, uh . . . she decided that she didn't want to be married with a family right away."

"Peter?"

He nodded. He hadn't thought about that time in a great while. He'd had more important things to think about. But all too often lately her name had dominated his thoughts.

Theirs had been a classic courtship. They were in the same youth group, joined the church in the same year, and started dating right away. He was certain she was the one. She was sweet and beautiful, a kind and caring person, and he loved her. How could he have known that his responsibilities would stand between them? He'd been beyond shocked when she came by his house one Sunday afternoon and told him they were through. He had planned on forever.

"I'm sorry," she said, reaching out to squeeze his hand reassuringly.

"Hey, now. We'll have none of that." This from Tillie. Then she laughed as if she had made the funniest joke known to man.

"I'm really sorry," Gracie said again and pulled away. "I don't have a great many opportunities like this, and I guess they think it's funny."

He chuckled. Honestly, he couldn't help himself. "It is a little funny. I mean, we decided to come out here and talk, and they are acting like we need constant supervision."

"They're just being nosy. There are no berries out there."

"We could go inside."

"And they'll be right behind us."

"Hey." He reached out and almost took her hand into his. Instead he placed his hand back in his own lap. This whole situation was stressing her out much more than it should have.

"It's just . . . just . . ." She stopped as if unable, or maybe it was unwilling, to go on. She shook her head. "Never mind."

Jamie sat back in his seat and tried not to sigh. This entire conversation was going nowhere. He should be asking her about her likes, dislikes, dreams for the future, and a thousand more questions that seemed to have deserted him. He needed to know what she thought about Peter and how she imagined the boy might handle their relationship. Would it upset him further, or would having a female around the house make it easier to cope?

The image of Peter curled up in Leah's lap Sunday after church had burned itself into his brain.

"It's getting dark," Gracie called to her cousins. "Perhaps you should give it up for the day."

Leah propped her hands on her hips and studied the sky as if she had never heard of the concept of a sunset before. "I suppose so."

"Shouldn't you be getting back home?" Gracie asked. If she had said that to anyone other than her cousin, she would have had to pray half the night begging for forgiveness.

"I've got an idea." Tillie turned to her cousins. "Let's have a sleepover."

Leah scoffed. "Aren't we a little old for that?"

"Allow me." Hannah took a step forward. "*Jah*, it's time for getting home. Be safe."

Tillie's expression was beyond gloomy.

"Perhaps we should pack it in for the night," Leah said.

"And a sleepover," Tillie bounced back quick.

"And a sleepover," she finally agreed.

Jamie stood. "I think this is where I leave." He grinned. He shouldn't have been so relieved, but he was. Maybe he could try again tomorrow. Nerves had a lot to do with both of their issues.

"Thanks, Gracie. I had a nice time." He almost choked on the lie. It wasn't that his time was terrible; he just wouldn't call it nice. "I'll see you tomorrow."

She nodded. He squeezed her fingers, then dropped her hands. Tomorrow. Surely everything would seem different then.

"You cannot be serious," Leah said some time later. The four women had settled themselves in the sewing room, crowded on the two beds, and whispered into the darkness. Just like they used to do. Except back then their age differences were more pronounced. And there had been a lot more room in the beds.

"Why shouldn't I?" Gracie asked.

Leah shook her head, even though she knew her cousin couldn't see her.

"He's cute," Tillie said.

"I'm sure Melvin would find that very interesting," Hannah said.

"Oh," Tillie protested. "That's not what I meant."

Hannah laughed. "I'm just playing."

"I love him," Tillie said, her voice taking on a hurt edge.

"Of course you do," Leah said.

"It's just hard, you know?" Tillie said.

Their chattering grew quiet.

"Nothing's easy," Hannah said. "Not leaving or staying."

"Amen," Leah whispered into the night.

"Staying is good," Gracie put in.

Somewhere in the room, someone drew in a deep breath to speak, but no words followed. Leah didn't know who it was; only that it wasn't her.

"Nothing's forever," Hannah finally said.

It was the truth. Except leaving. That was forever. Leah couldn't imagine how Hannah could return. Nothing would ever be the same. Or maybe she was okay with that. But Leah knew. She understood that nothing would ever be the same again. Some long-ago writer said you can never go home again. This must be what he was talking about. Being home was the best and the worst thing. Being here tonight with her sisters and cousin was more pain than pleasure. And yet she wouldn't have missed it for the world.

"It feels like forever," Tillie said.

"What's that supposed to mean?" Gracie said.

"I don't know," she muttered. "Let's talk about you and Jamie."

"There's nothing to talk about."

Leah could hear the wistfulness in her voice, and she was glad for the darkness that hid her wince. Jamie was no good for Gracie. Couldn't she see that?

"He seemed pretty chummy to me," Hannah said.

"He's just looking for a *mamm* for Peter." Leah hated the negative tone in her voice. But couldn't they see?

"I'm okay with that." Gracie's voice was barely above a whisper in the dark.

"Really?" Tillie asked.

"Well, *jah*. I . . . I have always wanted to be married."

"That's what every girl wants," Hannah agreed.

Just the thought broke Leah's heart. It was every girl's dream. They had all been raised to know their place in the community and their role in the family. They had all been raised to be married. Yet somehow, Leah had been cheated out of that. Or perhaps it simply wasn't in God's plan for her. Just as she had thought that it was not in God's plan for Gracie. Now her cousin was talking about getting married for marriage's sake. Gracie deserved better than that. Couldn't she see it?

"Eunice always says love will come," Gracie said. "I have to have faith that this is what God wants and love will come."

Leah shook her head. "I never heard her say that."

"Me neither," Hannah added.

"She does," Tillie agreed. "All the time."

"Maybe something she started after we left," Leah mused.

"But you and Melvin already love each other," Hannah pointed out.

"We're the lucky ones," Tillie said, but the sad note in her voice made Leah think about their conversation from the day before. Was Tillie really thinking about leaving the Amish? Because she was so in love with Melvin she would do anything to be with him.

You were in love with Benuel. Hannah was in love with Aaron.

It might be true that Hannah and Aaron were a couple once again and would be married by this time next year. That wasn't the issue. Hannah and Leah had both loved and both left. Tillie could too.

Love didn't always hold everything together.

Jamie looked around the one-room schoolhouse and tried to remain positive. This was the right plan. He hoped so, anyway.

"Do you have any questions?" Amanda Swartzentruber couldn't be a nicer person. She was kind and sweet, but he could tell that she had a handle on her classroom. Even if they *were* on their best behavior in front of their visitors, the entire class was attentive and joyous. And that was something Peter could use. Or so Jamie thought.

He looked around the room. Bright-colored posters about letters and manners, colors and presidents covered the walls. One bulletin board boasted pumpkins, apples, and scarecrows made from multicolored pieces of construction paper. It had been so warm lately that he hadn't given the time much thought. But it was already September, and soon fall would be upon them.

The room was inviting, warm, and cheerful. And yet he couldn't say the words that would authorize Peter to stay.

The boy squeezed his hand. Jamie looked down, but Peter was looking elsewhere. That gentle grasp had been for comfort and not about gaining his attention. How could he leave him here, with a stranger?

Then Leah's words came back to him. He needed to do this for Peter. He needed to give him a chance to start a normal life. And the boy couldn't do that if he was being shuffled around with Jamie everywhere he went and writing his letters at night after supper. He needed proper schooling. And maybe being around other kids now would help him find his voice again.

"Jamie?"

He stirred himself out of his thoughts and trained his gaze on the young teacher. If he had to guess, she was about Gracie's age—younger than Leah—and competent. Her blond hair was worn in their traditional style, which made her brown eyes stand out even more. "Sorry. What was that?"

"Would you like to stay through lunch, maybe play with the children during recess? That will give you both time to adjust."

He tried to shake his head, but he nodded instead. "*Jah*," he heard himself say. "That would be good."

He could find no fault in Amanda or any of her students. Most had more than one family member living in Ethridge, and they all tried to name someone they knew and waited patiently while Peter either nodded or shook his head if he didn't know the name.

Not even one of the students asked why he didn't speak or about the scars on the backs of his hands or the side of his neck. Perhaps the teacher had already had a talk with her class about the merits of being kind to those who are different.

When it came time for lunch, Essie Zook took Peter by the hand and led him to a space on the playground just to the school side of the swing set. "Come on," she urged. "I'll share my lunch with you. Don't tell Dat, but he always packs too much." Then vivacious mother hen Essie spread out her lunch and proceeded to divvy it up between the two of them.

"Sweet, huh?" Amanda sidled up beside him and took

a drink from her water cup. "Essie's a good girl. A little on the mischievous side, but she would be a good help bringing Peter out."

He had been thinking the same thing. "Good. Good."

The children started gathering up their lunch mess, washing their hands, and lining up to use the outhouse.

"*Danki* for your time," Jamie said. He let Essie work with Peter, showing him the order of things. He seemed to take to the girl, and Jamie was fine with that. She had shown him where to wash his hands and found him a place in the boys' line. Now Jamie was waiting for him to finish his business so they could leave. He had seen all he needed to. The school was more than adequate, the teacher kind and caring. Now all he had to do was convince himself that Peter would be all right here.

Oh, he knew it in his mind, but his heart was a different story. He had gone through so much to bring Peter here that he was terrified he was going to blow it for them both. And with his time to bring Peter out of his shell coming to an end . . . well, he needed to do something and he needed to do it quickly. "Once Peter's had his turn, we'll be out of your way."

"I have an idea," Amanda said as she stood at the door. "Why don't you leave Peter here. He can finish out the school day, and that way tomorrow won't be so difficult for him. Day one will be day two." She smiled. She really was trying to be helpful, so why did he feel like he'd been kicked in the gut by a stubborn mule? It was about the same feeling he got whenever he was around Leah Gingerich.

Amanda nodded encouragingly.

"*Jah*," he said, his voice rusty.

"Good, good. Then we'll see you at three."

"I should tell him." Jamie started toward Peter, still waiting in line.

Amanda stopped him with one hand on his arm. "Let me do it. It'll be less emotional that way."

Jamie swallowed hard. It might be the best way. Not make a big deal out of it. But he remembered all the times Peter had snuck into his room just to be close to another person. He didn't want to set back any progress he had made in healing. "He lost his family in a fire—"

"I know," she said gently. "He needs to learn to trust that you will come get him."

That sounded logical. So why did it feel wrong in his heart? "*Jah*," he heard himself saying. He made his way to his buggy, climbed in, and set his horse in motion. The children waved and called out farewells, but Peter must have been inside.

He's going to be okay. But Jamie just wished he could believe it was true.

This was perhaps the dumbest thing he had ever done. Peter was at school. So why had he driven into town to Twice Blessed?

He parked his carriage around back and tethered his mare to the steel post planted in the packed earth. He could be out looking for a job, maybe over at the mill seeing if they needed any help. Handiwork was sporadic, and he needed a little something more to make sure he and the boy had everything they needed.

Yet here he was, standing in back of Leah's store. Was he just trying to get mad today? But the last time he had seen Leah, she hadn't upset him. She had been pretending to pick blackberries off bushes that had long ago stopped producing fruit. It had been a thin ploy for Leah and her sisters to spy on him and Gracie. Like anything was going to happen. Not that any of that had happened the other evening. He had just made his intentions known—not in so many words, but they needed to take this slow. As much as he wanted to rush in and get married, whoever he did marry would want a few of the niceties that came along with courting and marriage. Even if that someone was as practical as Gracie Glick.

He let himself in the back way Leah had set up for her Amish patrons, with its horse-friendly parking and a section filled with Amish clothing for trade.

He stopped, trailing his fingers down one of the shirt-sleeves closest to him. Why had she done all this? Her store seemed to cater to *Englisch* and Mennonites more than Amish, and yet she made sure there was adequate and safe parking for horse and buggies and a free section in the back where any Amish who needed clothes could come and get something. And the most interesting part of all was that the Amish didn't even have to set foot in the main store.

He looked around. It was a good space, and it would be profitable if she filled it with actual goods for sale. Yet she hadn't. Why?

He shook his head and continued on into the store. He would never understand her, and he should stop trying.

"Jamie?" She blinked once when she caught sight of him, as if she were testing her vision.

"Hey." Not the most eloquent of greetings, but he was still trying to figure out why he was here. He didn't even like Leah. But she was the most plainspoken person he knew.

"Where's Peter?"

"That's why I'm here. I left him at school."

Her eyes grew wide. "You what?"

"I left him at school."

"I heard that. I mean *why*?"

He shrugged, but the motion felt like it was made with someone else's shoulders. "You said you thought the teacher was competent and could handle a child who didn't talk. So

I thought I would take the chance, and . . . I don't know." He blew out a heavy breath.

"When I came down here, from Tennessee," he began, "I said it was to give us a fresh start."

"Yes." She nodded, the light in her green eyes understanding.

"That wasn't exactly the truth."

"Okay."

"Sally's parents wanted to take him. Sally is—was his mother. She was the oldest, and she has younger siblings. But I was afraid that Peter would get lost in the shuffle of the ten kids they still have living at home and the six grandkids who are over there almost every day."

Leah whistled under her breath. "That's a big family."

Even bigger than most. "*Jah*. I told them that I could get him talking again and that I should have him."

"And you brought him here."

Jamie nodded. "I thought if he was away from all his familiar surroundings, that maybe he wouldn't be reminded at every turn and maybe he could start to heal."

She nodded. "I can see that. Or he might get so traumatized that he never speaks again."

"Don't say that." Jamie raised his voice, drawing the attention of the patrons shopping in the kitchen section. He shot them an apologetic smile and tipped his hat. "Don't say that," he repeated so only Leah could hear.

"It's entirely possible."

"I didn't know what else to do." He shook his head. "That boy is all I have left of my brother. You take care of Hannah's son. You should know what I'm talking about. I have to keep him safe. I have to make sure he heals."

Leah shook her head. "That's admirable and all, but whether or not he speaks again isn't entirely up to him and his healing. It's up to God."

"I know."

"But you're having a hard time accepting that."

He caught her gaze, stared into her eyes. "And you never questioned what God has planned for you?"

She looked away. "I didn't say that. Only that we accept it if it's what we want it to be."

He shook his head. "There's got to be more to it than that."

"Like what?"

"Do you think I would be here talking to you if I knew?"

"You suppose I have the answer?"

"You don't?" He raised his voice, once again drawing the attention of the shoppers. "Can we go somewhere and talk?"

A frown pulled at her forehead. "You want to talk to me? I thought you couldn't stand me."

"I never said that." But he felt the heat rising in his neck and up to his face.

"You didn't have to."

He cleared his throat. "I may not always agree with you, but you seem smart. Like maybe you would have a few answers the rest of us can't see."

"As flattered as I am, I have to wait until Brandon gets back from his lessons before I can go anywhere."

Was it part of God's plan that Brandon took the next moment to stroll through the front door of the shop?

"He's here." Jamie turned back to Leah. "Now you don't have an excuse."

She took off the tan apron she had been wearing over her clothes and hung it on a hook behind the cash register. There was a picture of a dove on the bib. He supposed it was sort of comforting, but he couldn't say for sure. Except that Leah looked all kinds of cute wearing it over her Mennonite clothes.

"Brandon, I'm going out," Leah said without preamble.

Brandon's gaze darted from Leah to Jamie and back again. "O-kay," he said. He took his own tan-colored apron off the peg next to hers. He slipped it over his head and tied it at the back. "Got anything that needs done around here?"

"You can sweep if you get bored, and if you are really desperate, you can restock the glass shelves. A lady came in today and took all that we had left out front."

"Got it, boss." He shot her a cheeky grin. "I'll keep things running while you go on your date."

"It's not a date." Leah and Jamie spoke at the same time.

"Yeah, okay." Brandon nodded. "Rendezvous, then."

Leah pressed a hand to her forehead. "That's even worse."

"Tête-à-tête?"

"You're not helping." Leah slung her purse over her shoulder and glanced back at her too-smart helper. "We're just going to the café at the end of the block, if you need anything."

Brandon grinned, a look that said he was entirely too pleased with himself. "I'm sure everything will be just fine."

Leah couldn't resist an eye roll as she stepped out into the warm, pre-fall sun.

"Down here, you say?" Jamie asked. He nodded toward the small café that took up the corner spot of the building. There were picnic tables on the far side where patrons could sit outside, but even on a day like today, when fall was approaching, the temperature was still too warm for sitting in the sun.

"You want to sit out here?" he asked.

Leah shook her head. "Do you mind if we go inside? I tend to sunburn easily, and I didn't bring a hat."

"*Jah*, sure." He held open the door for her to enter.

Like everything else in Pontotoc, the café was quaint, small, and unpretentious. Though Leah couldn't help but notice the looks that she and Jamie got as they ordered a couple of drinks and took them to the nearest table.

"What happens if it's part of God's will, and Peter

doesn't speak again? What then?" Leah asked once they were seated.

"I don't know." Jamie punched down his ice with the end of his straw, then took a cautious sip. "Their tea is good," he said. "My *mamm* used to make us tea when we were growing up. It tastes like hers."

Leah took a sip and nodded. "Really good. And how do your parents fit into all this?"

"They don't. They passed away when we were just out of school."

Which explained a lot, as far as Leah was concerned. "I'm sorry."

"God's will, right?"

"Wait. You can accept God's will when it happens to you, but not when it involves someone you love?"

He shook his head. "That's not what I meant."

"It's what you said." Well, practically.

"I guess it's easier for me to accept God's will for myself, but not when it affects others."

"It doesn't work like that."

"I know." He took another drink. "What about you?"

She drew back a bit. "What about me?"

"Is it God's will that you open this store? Or is it just something you wanted to do?"

She smiled. "I like to think God had a hand in it."

"Why?" he asked.

Did she really want to get into this with him? Some things were better left unsaid. "I felt it was time to come home." It was the truth. Just not all of it.

He tilted his head to one side and studied her. His blue eyes were intense, as if looking for secrets she didn't want to reveal. Or was she just being fearful? "Why now?"

"Why not now?" She let out a nervous laugh. This caring and concerned Jamie wasn't as comfortable to be around.

She was better when she knew they were adversaries. Or at the very least on opposite sides of the issue.

"You're not joining the church like your sister. So why now?"

"Well, you know." She shrugged.

"You don't want to tell me." He nodded. "I see."

She shook her head. "It's not like that." But it was exactly like that. "It's just hard for me to talk about."

"It's fine."

"No," she said. "It's not." She took a deep breath. "I've wanted to come back for a long time, but . . ."

"But?" he prompted.

"I never had the courage. I mean, I can't come back. You know."

"Sorry. I don't."

"I can't join the church and become Amish again." They were words she had never said to another.

"Why not? Your sister is."

"It's different for her."

"I don't see how." He frowned, concern and lack of understanding etching lines in his features.

"I found my place. My church." It was the best explanation she had. The safest.

"You can switch churches. And I know the bishop would welcome you back."

She shook her head. "I wish it were that simple."

He smiled, and once again she noticed how handsome he was. He should smile more often for sure. "Seems to me that you're the one making it complicated."

"About Peter."

"Subject change. I understand. Peter," he said. "He means everything to me."

"Then you should do everything you can to help him."

"I am. I will."

She twisted her glass from side to side, widening the

circle of condensation beneath it. "There's this man . . . in our church. He's a doctor."

"There's nothing wrong with Peter."

"Yes, Jamie, there is. Nothing that's his fault." She did her best to make her words understanding and kind. She adored Peter, and she only wanted the best for him.

His eyes narrowed. "What's that supposed to mean?"

All in. She had come this far. "This doctor works with suppressed memories and trauma cases like Peter's. I think he would be able to help him."

Jamie was so still for so long that Leah felt for a moment that they had somehow been suspended in time. "A head doctor?"

"A therapist, yes."

"Peter doesn't need that kind of help." His voice was low and menacing. "He needs God and prayers."

She reached toward him, but he had already pushed himself up from his seat. "*Danki*, Leah Gingerich. Thank you for distracting me with your cockamamy ideas about right and wrong. It kept me from constantly worrying about Peter. But now it's time I go."

"Jamie."

But he spun on one heel and stalked out the door.

Leah looked at his empty seat. So much for a "new Jamie." He was the same through and through. Too conservative. Too rigid. Too . . . Amish.

Chapter Six

The trip back to the school took entirely too long. Jamie was left with too much time to stew over what Leah had said. He wanted to hate her for it. But even if he hadn't been raised to hate no one, he wouldn't have been able to. Deep down, a part of him wanted her to be right. He needed an answer to the problems Peter faced, but was he so desperate for a solution that he was willing to sacrifice his beliefs to gain it?

No. He had to trust God. He had to pray harder, pray more, pray truly without ceasing.

Most of the children had already left the schoolhouse when Jamie pulled his buggy to a stop.

"See," Amanda said, pointing at him. "I told you he would be back."

The smile on Peter's face stretched clear across. One hand held his hat in place as he loped across the packed dirt drive and hoisted himself onto the side of the buggy. Little arms came through the window and hugged Jamie close.

"Did you miss me?" Jamie chuckled, his anger with Leah melting away.

If it was at all possible, Peter's grin grew even wider. He nodded enthusiastically, his hat falling from his head.

"You ready to go home?"

Peter jumped down, still nodding as he snatched up his hat and slapped it against one leg to knock the dust off.

"Tell Amanda goodbye," Jamie instructed.

Peter turned and waved, then came around the buggy and hopped in the other side.

"Everything go okay?" Jamie asked.

Amanda gave him a pretty smile. "As close to perfect as possible."

"Good. Good," Jamie said.

"We'll see you tomorrow, then?" she asked.

"Of course," Jamie said.

"Bye, Peter." Amanda gave them a small wave.

Jamie flicked the reins and started his mare into motion once more. He chanced a look at Peter as they rocked along. He seemed happy enough. Maybe even content. He had good times and bad times. Times when he seemed to miss his family more than others. He had nightmares and still wanted to sleep as close to Jamie as possible, but given the circumstances of his family's deaths, it was no wonder.

"We're all right, aren't we, boy?"

Peter nodded, flashing another of his all-encompassing smiles.

"*Jah*," Jamie said. Leah could make all the crazy assumptions she could think of, but he and Peter had an understanding. Peter would talk again. And soon. Jamie had to believe it was true. It couldn't be any other way.

A loud commotion outside had Jamie on his feet in a heartbeat. It was not quite seven o'clock on a Saturday morning. Who could be making all that noise? Their cabin was far enough away from the Gingerich houses that the sound of their morning chores had never been an issue. What was happening outside was loud . . . and close.

He checked the front window, but all he could see was a lumber truck. Maybe the driver had gotten turned around. It was easy to do out here, especially on the back roads, where there were few markers.

"Finish your breakfast," he told Peter.

The boy nodded and went back to work on his scrambled eggs, the one thing Jamie could make edible every time.

Jamie stepped out onto the porch and wished he had taken the time to have a more thorough look out the window. It would have given him an advantage to know what was happening before he was standing in front of everybody just staring in disbelief.

So many people stood in his front yard. There had to be at least ten men with hammers and determined expressions.

And in the middle of it all was Leah Gingerich.

"Just set the wood down over there," she told the driver.

No one was lost. No one had gotten turned around. But there had to be some mistake. He hadn't ordered any lumber, and he surely hadn't asked for ten men to come with it. He recognized the Gingeriches and Aaron Zook, but everyone else's face was a mystery. He must have seen them at church last Sunday, but he couldn't recall their names a week later.

"What's going on here?" he asked. He looked from one man to another. Finally Jim Gingerich stepped forward. "You know about barn raisings?"

Jamie nodded.

"Well, this is a room raising."

"What's that?"

"A room raising." Leah had finished bossing around the truck driver and had come to stand by her oldest brother. "We're here to build a second bedroom onto the cabin."

"But I didn't—"

Jim smiled. "That's okay, because Leah did."

"You?" He turned his attention to the beautiful woman

who had been a thorn in his side since the day he had met her. "You did all this?"

"Uh . . . yeah. I mean. It was nothing. Amish help one another."

"You're not Amish."

She shrugged. "I may have left the Amish, but that doesn't mean I'm not Amish at heart."

He frowned. "Is that what this is all about?" Around them the men started to get to work, staking out the spot where the new room would go. "Pretending to be Amish?"

"I'm not pretending to be anything."

"I see."

"I don't believe you do. I wanted to help you, so I put up a sign in the shop. You walked by it yesterday."

"And asked your brothers to help."

"Why is it that you have such trouble accepting any sort of help from me when I know that this cabin was given to you?"

"That's different." His tone had started to rise, and a few of the men had turned to see what was going on between them. He lowered his voice.

"It is certainly not any different at all." She tapped one foot on the ground, sending up little puffs of orange dust. "In fact, I'm beginning to think someone forgot to teach you manners. When a person helps you, you're supposed to say *danki*. I say you're welcome, then when somebody else needs help, you can lend a hand. That's how it works."

"*Danki*." He pushed the word through clenched teeth.

"You're welcome. See? That wasn't so hard. You'll thank me later."

"I already did." He turned on his heel and headed back to the house, her words still ringing in his ears. Why was it so hard for him to accept help from her? It just was.

* * *

It was the middle of the afternoon before Jamie could talk to Leah again. He had tried and tried, but he had no final answer to his question except that it was. Something about her set his teeth on edge. He supposed it was because she had turned her back on everything he held dear. She walked away from the Amish when things got tough. She might have only gone to the Mennonites, but as far as he was concerned, she had abandoned her heritage. Not everyone was lucky enough to be born Amish.

"I apologize for this morning," he said. He tried to sound polite, but his voice held a gruff edge. He caught her in the front yard. The rest of the men were in the back, taking a little break under the branches of the large pine there.

"I only wanted to help. I thought maybe if Peter had his own room . . . you know, a space to keep his clothes and his toys, that maybe . . ."

She had been thinking of Peter. Now he really felt like a heel. "Thank you," he said. This time he really meant it.

"I found a few things for him. A couple of shirts, a picture of a horse, and a wooden tractor."

And just like that, the easy feeling was gone. "Why would you get him a tractor?"

"So he can play with it." A frown settled itself between her brows.

"He can't play with a tractor. It's against the *Ordnung*."

She propped her hands on her hips. "Really? Don't you think the bishop has more important things to worry about than a six-year-old playing with a wooden toy? It doesn't have rubber tires. Like it matters. It's a toy."

"It's not part of our culture."

"UFOs are not part of the *Englisch* culture, and yet children play with spacecrafts."

He shook his head. "That doesn't make any sense at all."

"It does to me."

"Of course it does."

"What is wrong with you?" she asked. "Why are you so determined to follow every rule down to the last comma?"

"It's what we're supposed to do. It's what God wants from us."

"And not allowing a child to play with a wheeled toy is that important to God? I don't think so."

When she put it like that, he started to have his own doubts. He straightened his spine and cleared his throat. He wasn't going to let the questions ruin his faith. He had to have faith. It and Peter were all he had left. "No tractor," he said and stalked back toward the house.

"What is it with the two of you?"

Leah whirled around as Gracie came up from the main house. "Hey, cousin."

Gracie stopped next to her, waiting for an answer.

"Just two different people, I guess." And for some reason their "different" couldn't exist in the same space. Once they got near each other, it seemed they always found uncommon ground.

"Eunice wanted me to bring over some cookies," Gracie said. "She thought the men could use a break."

Leah nodded toward the back of the house. "They just took a rest, but you know men and food."

"*Danki.*" Gracie gave her another smile and headed around back.

Suddenly Leah had the feeling that her *mamm* had nothing to do with Gracie's decision to bring a snack to the workers. One worker in particular: Jamie Stoltzfus.

She eased around back, careful not to draw attention to herself. Gracie went around to all the men, offering them cookies from the plastic container. But every so often she would look up at Jamie as if she needed to know where he was at all times. Which was ridiculous. Unless she really was serious about courting him. And he really was serious about courting her.

Courting usually led to marriage, and Leah had just made it easier for him. She had arranged for Peter to have his own room. Now Jamie would have privacy, and when he got married . . .

She shook her head. That was a long time off. If ever. And surely not, if she could do something about it. Jamie was all wrong for Gracie. And Gracie was all wrong for him. Why couldn't they see that?

Maybe it was just an experiment.

Gracie moved away from the other men and approached Jamie. She cast her eyes down, then glanced up at him as if he were the center of the universe. She held the cookie container toward him, took a step closer, and smiled. Flirting with food.

It was sad, really. And someone had to do something about it.

Leah marched over to where they stood, all but wedging herself between them.

"Can I get one of those cookies?" she asked brightly. "I may not be wielding a hammer, but planning can sure take it out of a girl." She snatched a cookie from the bowl and shoved it into her mouth.

"You did plan all this, didn't you?" Gracie smiled, then turned her attention back to Jamie. "Hannah told me that she invited you to our get-together tonight. Please tell me you're coming."

Leah worked on chewing up the rest of the cookie as Jamie cast a quick glance her way. His attention flickered over her, then returned to Gracie. "I had thought I would. But I'll have to ask Eunice if she can watch Peter tonight."

"Oh, Leah will watch him. Won't you, Leah?"

And how could she say no? She had an entire cookie in her mouth.

"Of course," she mumbled around the rest of the cookie. She waited for Jamie to protest, to tell her that he didn't want her liberal influence to adversely affect Peter, but he didn't.

"Great." Gracie beamed another smile at Jamie. "I guess I should be going. Lots to do before tonight." She handed the container of cookies off to Leah, then waggled her fingers in an uncharacteristic wave. "See you then."

"*Jah*," Jamie said with a wave of his own.

Leah expelled a heavy sigh. "You have got to be kidding me," she grumbled. Was she the only one around here who hadn't lost her mind?

"What?" he asked.

"I'll be right back." She thrust the container of cookies at him, then hurried after her cousin.

She caught up with her at the bottom of the hill. Actually, she allowed Gracie to get far enough ahead that when Leah stopped her they would be midway between the two houses. No one needed to hear what Leah had to say.

"Gracie."

Her cousin whirled around with a hand pressed to her chest. "Leah! You scared me."

"Sorry. I just . . ." She just what? Wanted to talk to her for a minute? Wanted to tell her what a bad idea it was that she court Jamie? "Are you really going tonight?"

"*Jah*, of course. Tonight we're playing games at Aaron's house. That's always fun."

Leah frowned. "Going to Aaron's?"

"Playing games." Her eyes grew bright. "Maybe we'll break up into couples teams, and Jamie and I can be partners."

Leah winced. "About that . . ."

"What?"

"Do you really think it's a good idea for you to see Jamie? I mean, you hardly know him."

"That's why I'm seeing him, isn't it? To get to know each other better?"

"What happens if you get to know him, and you decide you don't like him?"

Gracie laughed. "What's not to like? He's handsome, and he cares about others. How many men would take their brother's child to raise?"

Leah thought of the conversation she and Jamie had had the day before. How he needed for Peter to start talking again, and why. "That's just it," she said. "Do really want to start off a marriage with a child?"

"You're getting ahead of yourself. We haven't even been on a real date yet."

Thank goodness for that. "But it would be a challenge. You wouldn't have any time at all to get used to being married."

"Lots of women get pregnant on their wedding night."

"Yes, and they have nine months at least to spend with their husbands before the baby arrives. I'm talking about from day one."

Gracie blinked as the truth sank in. Then she waved a hand as if dismissing Leah's words. "No matter. I'm going to be twenty-six next year. All my friends are married. All the members of our group are married. This may be my only chance. All my life—" She shook her head. "I've always been invisible," she finally said. "And I didn't mind it so much. Maybe that was just what God wanted for me. But now God is giving me a chance to change things. Don't get me wrong. I love helping everyone. I always have. But this is a chance at a family of my own. How can I pass that up?"

"For love."

"What?"

"For love," Leah said, louder this time. "Don't you think you should have love?"

Gracie frowned. "Love is a luxury I can't afford."

* * *

The room smelled of new paint and sawdust, a surprisingly fresh smell.

"What do you think?" Leah asked as she coaxed Peter into the room. "Now you have your very own space." She whirled around to look at it from all angles. "Of course, it still needs a little work, but in a day or two you should be able to move your things in here." She kept up her steady stream of ideas for the room. "My *mamm* has a wardrobe out in the barn that she said she would let you have. That way you'll have a place to keep your clothes. And I found a chest at a flea market that you can use as a toy box. I think it would look great at the end of the bed. Well, when you get your own bed. We'll have to see what we can do about getting that first, huh? How else are you going to sleep here?"

Peter looked around the room, his eyes wide in wonder. As far as rooms went, it was about as basic as it could be, just a floored box with new drywall and two windows to help draw in the breeze. But to Leah it represented so much more. It was a fresh start for Peter, a new space for him to begin again.

"You know you can talk to me, don't you?" she asked. "I know there are things that are hard to deal with, things that we might not want to think about. But sometimes if we talk them through, they don't seem quite as large as they did while they were in our heads. Do you know what I mean?"

He nodded slowly.

"Good. I want you to know that I'm here if you need me. And you can talk to me about anything, okay?"

Once again he nodded.

Leah smiled. Jamie was convinced that Peter could talk. What if he was right and Peter simply didn't want to speak?

He needed to know that someone was there for him when the time came that he wanted to share what had been going on in his head these last few months.

A noise sounded from the front of the house. "That might be Jamie. Do you want to go see?"

Peter slipped his hand into hers, and together they went into the front room.

Jamie took his hat off and hung it on the peg by the door. "Hi," he said. "Did you have a good evening?"

Leah swung their clasped hands and smiled down at the boy. "We did. We had supper with Eunice and Abner, then came back and played with some toys. Not the T-R-A-C-T-O-R, but some other things."

Jamie's expression softened. "Thank you. And about that . . . I think I may have overreacted a bit about the T-R-A-C-T-O-R."

You think? Somehow she kept those words confined in her own thoughts. "It happens," she said instead.

"And I want to apologize. You can give him the T-R-A-C-T— uh, tractor."

She smiled, though she did what she could to keep it from looking triumphant. "Thanks. It's in my car. I'll get it before I leave. So, how was the party?"

"It wasn't really a party," he said. "Just a group of friends getting together on Saturday night."

"News flash: that's a party."

He frowned.

"Sorry," she said. "What I mean is there's not much difference, is there?"

He shrugged. "Cake?"

She laughed. "Good point. Did you have a fun time?"

"*Jah*, I guess. It was a little awkward. I didn't know hardly anyone. Just Aaron and Hannah."

"And Gracie."

He shook his head. "Gracie wasn't there."

"She wasn't?" Leah tried to hide her surprise. Earlier, Gracie had seemed all excited about going. What had changed her mind? Maybe something Leah had said?

"And everyone was married. I was the odd man out."

"I bet." She tried to feel sympathy, but she just couldn't get it to replace the spark of joy. He had gone to the party and had an okay time. But he hadn't been able to spend more time with Gracie, and there were no single women in attendance. Leah shouldn't have been so happy about that, but she was.

Peter let go of her hand and made his way over to the couch. He climbed into the cushions and grabbed the book they had been reading earlier. He opened it and started flipping the pages, running one finger under the words as if he were actually reading it.

Leah cleared her throat. "I guess I should be going. Come with me out to the car and you can get the T-R-A-C-T-O-R."

Jamie chuckled.

"Good night, Peter," she called, trying not to be so aware of Jamie as he followed her out the door.

The night was warm with a cool wind that promised fall was on its way. Nighttime birds called to one another over the constant drone of insects. A billion stars twinkled in the dark sky. There were no stars like that in the city.

"Thanks again for watching Peter," Jamie said as they neared her car.

"No problem." She adjusted the strap on her purse, a strange thought occurring to her. She had watched Peter at the request of Gracie, who didn't even go to the event. Leah wasn't sure what to make of it, so she simply got the tractor from the back seat and handed it to Jamie. "I'll see you later." Leah gave him one last smile, then ducked into the driver seat. What else was there to say?

He pushed the door closed behind her and took a step

back. He gave a small wave, but made no move to go into the house.

A big part of her wanted to run down to her parents' and find out just why Gracie didn't go tonight, but another part of her just wanted to go home. She had been gone all day. Besides, she could find out what Gracie's problem was tomorrow when she and Brandon came over after church. Unlike the Amish, the Mennonites held church in a building and every Sunday. Frankly, Leah liked going to the shorter service, even if it meant she had to go more often. It reminded her weekly—every day, actually, with all the events her church offered—that she needed to keep open lines with God.

And that was always a fine plan.

She returned Jamie's wave. He gave a quick nod and turned for the cabin.

With a smile on her lips, she cranked her car and headed back to town.

The phone ringing in the middle of the night was never a good sign. It was one of the first things Leah had learned when she got out into the *Englisch* world. She fumbled with the bedside clock, then stopped to turn on the lamp so she could see it. Her cell phone's melodic chime persistently continued. It was just after midnight.

Who was calling at this hour?

She pushed herself up in the bed, finally awake enough to register that she should actually answer the phone. She thumbed it on and swiped to answer. "Hello?" She didn't bother to check the caller ID.

"Leah?" The frantic yet familiar voice came across the distance to her.

"Mamm?" She was instantly awake. "What's wrong?"

"Is Tillie there with you?" Her mother sounded like she

was about to cry. Leah could almost imagine her standing in their neighbor's kitchen pacing as she tried to put together the pieces of what was happening. "Please tell me she's there with you."

Leah shook her head. "No, she's not here." Unless she snuck in after Leah went to bed. Maybe Brandon had heard her but hadn't wanted to wake Leah so late.

"She's gone." Her mother sobbed. "I went into her room, and she isn't there. The bed's all made. Where could she be?"

A sinking feeling took up residence in Leah's stomach.

"Let me check the apartment." She pushed herself off the bed and made her way into the living room. Brandon was asleep on the couch with the TV still flickering, sending lights and shadows all around the room. If Brandon was out here, then maybe he had been the gentleman and given Tillie his bed. Possible.

"Where could she have gone?" Mamm asked. But Leah wasn't sure her *mamm* really wanted an answer. Or that she would like the only one that came to mind.

Leah eased past Brandon and opened the door to his bedroom, careful not to disturb anyone who might be sleeping on the other side. She shouldn't have bothered. His bed was empty, the covers thrown about just the way he had left them that morning. One day he would make his bed, she was certain of it. But today wasn't that day. Nor was it the day to bring it up.

"Leah?" Mamm asked.

"She's not here."

Her mother let out a ragged sigh. "What do we do? Where has she gone?"

"Mamm," Leah started. "Calm down. Who was Tillie out with?"

She sniffed. "Melvin."

"And he's the only one?"

"*Jah*. That I know of."

"When did you last see her?"

"Just after supper. They said they were going to the Rabers' to play cards. How can she just disappear like that?"

Leah didn't want to tell her mother what the woman should already know yet wasn't able to accept. Why else would she have panicked at midnight when her daughter hadn't come home? "Could it be that Tillie has left to experience the *Englisch* world?"

The thought was instantly sobering. Just having the words out and between them changed everything.

Her mother sniffed one last time. "Tillie would never do that."

Just like I wouldn't either.

"Maybe you should come with your car and help us find her," Mamm pleaded.

Leah bit back a sigh. She was more likely to help find the note Tillie had left explaining why she was leaving. But when Mamm called . . . "I'll be right there."

Leah debated for three and a half minutes on whether or not to wake Brandon. In the end, she left him a note explaining where she had gone and why, finishing with her doubts about being back in time for church. He had his own car and a driver's license. He could go or sleep in. Tomorrow was up to him.

The short drive to her parents' house seemed to take twice as long as normal. There wasn't any traffic on the road, so she could only blame the elongated perception on nerves. What was she going to find when she got to the house? How was she going to convince her *mamm* that Tillie was gone? Fine, but gone?

She said a small prayer of thanks that Hannah was there. She needed her sister to help. Leah had never wanted to leave the Amish. The possibility hadn't entered her thoughts until Hannah and her blasted *Englisch* magazines. Once Hannah got the idea in her head to leave, all Leah could do was try to keep up. She couldn't let her twin sister leave alone.

The whole house seemed awake when she got there. Lamps were lit in nearly every room, as if Mamm was afraid Tillie was lost and needed the light to find her way back. Or maybe in her anxious state, Mamm had lit them, then forgot to turn them off before going to the next room.

"Leah!" Mamm rushed out onto the porch as Leah pulled her car to a stop and got out. "Thank heavens you're okay. I was getting worried."

"Nothing to worry about, Mamm."

She shook her head. "There's plenty to worry about."

Hannah came out of the house and looked past Leah as if expecting someone else. Gracie was right behind her.

"I left him sleeping," Leah said. "Teenager and all."

Hannah smiled, but her face was still in shadows. Leah knew she missed Brandon; that alone was enough to dampen her expression. Add in the fact that Tillie was gone . . .

"Abner," Mamm called and headed toward the barn. She had a flashlight in one hand, the beam bobbing as she made her way.

"Is Dat in the barn?" Leah asked.

"You know how he is. Once the commotion started he headed for the workshop."

No one would ever accuse their father of handling situations straight on. He had to saw some wood, plane a surface, and paint whatever wasn't painted. The sheer work and concentration somehow got his thoughts back in order. But it shut his family out until he came to terms.

"Do you suppose he did that when we left?" Leah asked.

"No one's ever said, but I would imagine."

Leah nodded. "Has anyone looked for a note?"

Gracie shook her head. "Eunice doesn't want to believe that Tillie would actually leave."

"She finally got us all back in town, and then Tillie takes off." Hannah sighed.

No wonder Mamm was in denial.

Leah glanced back toward the workshop. She could hear her parents talking, but couldn't understand what was being said.

"She's been trying for over an hour to get him to take the buggy and go look for her."

"What about Melvin?"

"I think that's why Mamm wanted you to come out with your car. It would be easier for you to drive over there and see if he's home."

And safer. The buggies shared the roads with cars and trucks alike. It was dangerous enough in the daytime. At night? Far more dangerous than anyone should risk unless absolutely necessary. "Maybe we should look for a note first."

"Maybe," Hannah agreed.

"I checked down by the pond," Jim said, emerging from the darkness and nearly scaring her to death.

"What are you doing, Jim?" she gasped.

"Mamm wanted me to look down by the pond."

"She's not in the animal graveyard." This came from Jamie. Like Jim, he appeared out of the darkness, having turned off his flashlight—she supposed to save the batteries.

"What would she be doing at the pond or in the animal graveyard at this time of night?" It was late, and her mother was not allowing any thoughts other than that they would find Tillie because she had wandered off.

"What are you doing here?" Leah asked Jamie. Not that she was unhappy to see him. Even if they seemed to continually get on each other's last nerve, she wanted him to know how special it was that he was helping them.

"Your *mamm* came knocking on the door when she realized that Tillie wasn't home from her date." He shrugged. "I thought I should help."

Because that was what they did. They helped one another. She wanted to point that out to him, but refrained. No sense starting an argument with him. One would surely break out of its own accord soon enough.

"Thanks for helping," Leah said with a quick nod.

He pressed his lips together and dipped his chin in return.

"Leah, you want to help me check her room?" Hannah asked.

"Sure." They needed to find the note, and as quickly as possible. Mamm wasn't about to let any of this go until she knew for sure where Tillie was. And without that note, the next stop would be Melvin's parents' house to see if he was there. That was one of the main problems about not having phones in shanties close by, or even in the barn like she had heard some places in Lancaster County had. She knew the bishop would never go for the idea, but she could wish all the same.

Not that it mattered to her personally. She was, after all, Mennonite now. But it really would have helped her mother tonight.

"Where's David?" Leah looked around for her other brother.

Jim chuckled, but shook his head. "You know Dave. He could sleep through the house falling down around him."

Leah laughed, but the sound was too shrill in the serious darkness. "That's true." Too true.

"C'mon." Hannah looped one arm through Leah's and the other through Gracie's. "Let's go find that note."

* * *

It took another fifteen minutes to find the note. Leah wasn't sure if Tillie had been trying to make sure her mother found it, or if she had hid it to buy herself some time. At any rate, she had stuck it in the container of flour she kept in the pantry. Mamm always made biscuits on Sunday mornings. Maybe Tillie didn't want her to worry while she was cooking.

Mamm sat at the kitchen table dabbing her eyes with the end of her apron. "Read it again, please."

Leah dusted off her hands and shook the letter once again. Flour streaked her skirt and her long-sleeved shirt as if she had been hard at work cooking something. Like she cooked anything these days.

"*Dear Mamm, Dat, and family,*

It may come as a surprise to many of you, but this is something I have been thinking about for a long time now. I didn't make this decision hastily or without contemplation. Melvin and I have gone to the Englisch *world to see if there's anything there for us. We're not entirely sure what we will find, but only know that we need to see for ourselves. It's been Melvin's dream for a long while now to fix engines and work on cars.*"

Mamm sucked in a hiccupping sob.

"*We are safe, and we are together. I hope you find comfort in that. And we'll write as soon as we have any sort of news.*

Until then, we mean no disrespect. But this is something we have to do. I hope you understand.

Tillie."

"There's nothing else?" Mamm asked.

"No." Leah had answered the same question four times now, once after each time she had read the letter. She wasn't certain what her mother was looking for—maybe another note that said Tillie wasn't serious, and she was just over at a friend's spending the night? It was hard to say, but it was obvious that Mamm needed something more. "She says she's safe," Leah added.

Mamm shook her head, tears filling her eyes. "How can we know that to be true? She wrote that before she even left the house."

"I think she means that she and Melvin have a safe place to stay tonight," Hannah explained.

"And tomorrow?" Mamm asked.

"I'm sure she has someplace safe to stay tomorrow as well," Hannah clarified.

"Tillie's smart," Leah pointed out. "She knows how to take care of herself." At least she hoped she did.

They had all tried to warn Tillie against leaving. They had tried to explain that the grass wasn't always greener. But Leah had been through the same thing with Hannah. Tillie had to know for herself, firsthand.

Mamm wagged her head sadly from side to side.

Leah caught Hannah's gaze. In that instant they shared so much. Faith that Tillie would be safe. Hope that she would once again find her way home. And remorse over causing their mother so much pain all those years ago.

"I guess all we can do is wait." Mamm pushed to her feet and let out a heavy sigh.

"And pray," Gracie added.

Mamm nodded. "I pray. Let's just hope God is listening."

Chapter Seven

It was three a.m. before they convinced Mamm to lie down and get some rest. Pacing the floor wouldn't bring Tillie back to them. Only time and the good Lord's grace.

Hannah and Leah met Gracie out on the front porch. They were hoping for a measure of privacy, and they needed to be as quiet as possible to allow Mamm to rest.

"Do you really think she has someplace safe to stay?" Leah asked. If Tillie had wanted, she could have come to live with her and Brandon. It might have gotten a little crowded from time to time, but at least Tillie would be close. Or maybe that was the reason she didn't let Leah know; she wanted to do this on her own.

Gracie shook her head. "I don't know."

"I just never thought she would actually do it," Hannah lamented.

"None of us did," Leah said. Maybe they should have taken her questions and idle talk more seriously.

"It's that Melvin," Gracie said. "I don't mean to accuse him, but Tillie would never have left if it hadn't been for him."

"He did want to work on engines, but Tillie is a smart girl. She can make her own decisions," Hannah said.

"Yeah," Leah agreed. "Bad ones."

Gracie sighed. "So now we just wait?"

Hannah and Leah nodded.

"There's nothing more we can do until she decides to reach out to us," Hannah added.

But how many times had either one of them reached out after they left? Once, maybe twice. Reaching out meant tears and questions and facing how much the ones they left behind were hurting. Reaching out sounded like a fine idea, but in reality it was a painful process that was best avoided if at all possible.

But they could hope and pray that Tillie would call, tell them that she was safe, make them believe her, and then allow them to tell her all the reasons why she needed to come home immediately. Hopefully she would have a clear head. She would see the merit in their words and she would come back as soon as possible. Hopefully.

"Will you stay tonight?" Gracie asked.

"Please," Hannah added.

Leah made a vague gesture with one hand. "Brandon . . . and . . ."

"Brandon will be fine," Hannah said.

"You left him a note?" Gracie asked.

Leah nodded.

Hannah smiled, a little sadly. "Then he'll be out here in time for breakfast."

There was a full house for breakfast the next morning, but Tillie's presence still left a gaping hole. As predicted, Brandon drove in from town. Peter and Jamie walked down from their cabin, and David was there as well.

Sometime after the girls went to bed, they heard Dat come in. Hopefully whatever monsters that haunted him had moved on, and he had made his peace, but Leah had her doubts when first light came and he was back in his workshop once again. They might have lost a daughter, but they would gain a cabinet or chair out of the deal. Not exactly a good trade, but that was how it would be all the same.

"*Danki* for inviting us," Jamie said and rose from the table. "Should I—" He nodded in the general direction of the workshop, and Leah took it to mean did they want him to go talk to Abner.

Mamm shook her head. "Just sit for a while. Let your breakfast settle."

It was something Leah had been hearing her entire life.

Jamie nodded and eased back into his seat. He braced his elbows on the table in front of him and clasped his hands, as if praying.

Peter slid from his seat and tugged on Jamie's shirt-sleeve. Once he gained his uncle's attention, he pointed toward the barn.

"You want to go see the puppies?" Jamie asked.

Peter nodded.

"Go on ahead. But leave everything else alone," Jamie instructed. "Including Abner."

Peter nodded with a large grin, then all but skipped out the front door despite his constant limp.

"I've never seen him that happy," Gracie mused.

"He's coming around." Jamie wore a smile of his own.

Leah hoped he was right. Peter did look happy. And well-adjusted. Or maybe it was just that his clothes fit a little better than before. She made a mental note to keep an eye out for more items for him.

"Time for me to go." Brandon pushed his chair back from the table.

"Where are you going?" Leah and Hannah asked the question at the same time. They looked to each other, then back to Brandon.

He gave them a look only a teenager could deliver. "Really?"

"Really," they said, in unison once again.

"I thought I would go over to Shelly's." He glanced toward the battery-operated wall clock. "If I hurry I might be able to get there in time to go to church with them."

Hannah's eyebrows shot up so high, they almost blended with her hairline.

"And if you don't get there in time?" Leah asked. Her sister might be surprised about his interest in church and God, but Leah had seen it several times over the last few weeks. Of course, it didn't hurt that Shelly and her family were very devout churchgoers. Even if Brandon still claimed that he and Shelly were just friends.

Mamm grabbed a stack of dirty plates and bustled them into the kitchen.

"Go help her," Hannah mouthed to Leah.

Leah shook her head. At times like these, the kitchen was Mamm's domain. Leah wouldn't dare intrude. Plus, she wasn't sure what to say when Mamm started talking about Tillie. And one thing was certain: Mamm needed to talk about Tillie. Was it any wonder? If Leah's father would come out of the barn and talk to his wife about the issues they now faced, it would go a long way in everyone's healing, but she knew better than to mention it. There were some things just not discussed.

"Leah," Hannah admonished in an urgent whisper.

"You go," Leah returned.

"I'll go," Gracie pushed her chair back from the table and followed Mamm into the kitchen.

Jamie watched Gracie as she left the room. He had wanted a chance to talk to her this morning, another chance to get to know a little more about her. Maybe find out why she hadn't come to the gathering last night. For two people who were supposedly getting to know each other better, he didn't get to spend much time with her. Not that they were *officially* courting. That would come later, *after* they got to know each other better. But how was he supposed to get to know her if she was always off helping others?

He turned to find Leah staring at him.

"And that's the reason why you can't court her," she said.

"Leah," Hannah cautioned.

He blinked. Had he somehow missed part of the conversation? They were talking about dishes, and now Leah had switched to courting. He couldn't find the connection. "I beg your pardon?"

"That's the reason why you can't court Gracie."

"Le-ah."

"What's the reason?" Jamie shook his head. "Who said we were planning on courting?"

Leah scoffed. "Of course you are. What was all that on the back porch a couple of days ago? A prelude to courting." She answered her own question without giving him a chance to do so.

"And what is the reason again?"

"She's too sweet for you."

"Leah!"

"It's true," Leah said, swinging her attention from Jamie to Hannah. "She will do anything to please the people she cares about. And that means she's vulnerable to those who will take advantage of it."

"And you think I'll take advantage?"

Leah sniffed and hesitated as if not so sure of her earlier words. "It's only natural. Especially since it's more of a marriage of convenience."

He could feel the heat rising up in his neck. What kind

of person did she think he was? "I think that decision should be left up to Gracie. Don't you?"

She shook her head. Hannah stared at her, mouth hanging open in shock. "She's so in love with the idea of being married that she can't see how opinionated and stubborn you are."

"Now that's the pot calling the kettle."

"I call them like I see them."

"Thanks for that." Though without great effort his words sounded more sarcastic than he had wanted them to. But as usual Leah had more pressing matters to discuss.

"She can't court you because she is so in love with the idea of getting married that she will never be able to fall in love with you. All that's going to lead to is heartbreak."

The more she said, the angrier he became. "I don't believe this is any of your business."

"She's my cousin."

"What Leah is trying to say is, what exactly are your intentions where Gracie is concerned?" Hannah asked.

"And she's a grown woman," he shot back, ignoring Hannah's question. "I have heard of plenty of crazy reasons why one family doesn't want another courting their kin, but this is ridiculous."

"Hardly, when it's obvious that you aren't right for her."

"What gives you the right to decide that?" he returned.

"We just care about Gracie so much," Hannah continued.

Jamie turned his attention to Hannah. She was the logical one. She was the one he could talk to. "I think Gracie is a fine person. And I think she would be a good mother for Peter."

"See? That's all he wants. A mother for Peter," Leah said. "I knew it."

Jamie shook his head. "What's wrong with that? Many marriages have been based on less."

"That's true," Hannah said.

"That's crazy," Leah countered. "Marriage should have much more than that."

"Like what?" Jamie asked.

"Love," Leah said. "What about love?"

"What about it?" Love had ruined a lot in his life. Love was the reason he was here, in Mississippi, instead of home and married in Tennessee. He wouldn't trade his love for Peter for anything in the world, but romantic love? He could do without that for the rest of his life.

"Everyone deserves love," Leah said. "Especially someone like Gracie."

Love is a myth, he wanted to shout.

"Even you."

"My word," Mamm exclaimed as she bustled back into the room. "What is going on in here?"

"Nothing," Hannah quickly replied.

Jamie wasn't sure he could have answered in a normal tone. Leah Gingerich had a way of making his blood boil. True love. Who needed it?

"Nothing, Mamm," Leah agreed.

"Thanks again for breakfast." He pushed his chair back from the table and started gathering the rest of the dirty dishes and leftover food. Leah had no idea what she was talking about. Love was nothing but trouble.

"Leah, wait."

She stopped as Jamie strolled across the yard toward her. She had already said her goodbyes and was headed back to town. She needed a nap before figuring out what was for supper. Last night's long hours were beginning to catch up with her.

"What is it, Jamie?" She was too tired for any more of their verbal sparring. She had made her point. She had tried to make Gracie see reason, she had explained to Jamie all the reasons why he should leave Gracie be. Now she just had to have a little faith that it would all turn out the way it was supposed to.

He stopped short and rubbed his chin. After the night they had all had, rusty stubble covered his jaw. Once he married and grew his beard, the whiskers would be a coppery color. Interesting. "I just wanted to tell you that I would never set out to hurt anyone in this family."

She nodded. She believed him. He wasn't the enemy, just misinformed. Misguided.

"Especially Gracie. She's about the sweetest person I have ever met."

"And that's why you want to court her?" She jangled her keys in one hand, hoping the rattle would speed things up a bit. She needed him to say whatever it was he came out to say—then leave her to get on her way.

"Well, one of the reasons, I guess."

"You just want someone to cook and clean for you so you don't have to."

"You are mouthy and nosy," he said. "Perhaps a husband would keep you in line."

"Or not," she retorted. She was a slave to no man. "Why don't you admit it? A housekeeper would suit the same purpose for you. Cooking and cleaning."

"This from a woman who does neither."

"I happen to have a very busy shop right now. But I have cooked, and I have cleaned. And when I get married, that's not why I want the man to marry me, so I can push a broom and make biscuits."

His friendly manner disappeared in an instant, leaving his familiar disbelieving expression. "I doubt you even know how to make biscuits."

"I can make them in my sleep," she retorted and got into her car and headed for home.

* * *

Leah turned her car back out onto Topsy Road, then replayed her never-ending argument with Jamie in her mind. She had wanted to stay and talk to her mother and sister more, maybe explain to Gracie that she didn't have to settle for the first man who came along, but it seemed that Jamie was as determined to hang around as she was. He helped clear the table, spent some time out in the workshop with her *dat*, and looked at the puppies with Peter.

She knew they were neighbors and all, but this should have been a family matter. And he wasn't family.

Not yet, anyway.

Couldn't he see how wrong he and Gracie were for each other? Leah herself might be as nosy and mouthy as he accused her of being, but at least she spoke the truth. She didn't go hiding behind it or the *Ordnung* to justify her own needs.

Maybe it came from joining the Mennonites, or maybe it was all the time she spent in other, less fortunate countries. It didn't matter. She could see it clearly, and she couldn't let it happen right before her eyes and not do anything about it.

And she didn't care what he thought about her culinary skills or her unwillingness to be a "proper wife" and cook and clean for her husband. She might not be married, she might not even be marriage material, as they say, but she had a wonderful store that was serving the communities— both *Englisch* and Amish—quite well. Her life was great, fantastic even, and the last thing she needed was a husband dragging her down and telling her that she wasn't proper enough.

She ran a hand over her eyes and thought of her bed at home. She was proper enough. Once she had a nap she would be even better. And it didn't matter what Jamie Stoltzfus had to say.

"What is all this?" Brandon's eyes widened as he took in the pan of chicken sitting in the middle of the kitchen table.

"It's supper," Leah said with a reaffirming nod.

"It's burnt."

She frowned. "Just a little, on the edges. I had the stove turned up too high when I went to take a shower."

She had come home from her parents' house with Jamie's words ringing in her ears. But it wasn't like she was doing this to prove something to him. He wasn't even there. No, it just made her think that maybe she had let her life get in the way of her life lately. She had promised Hannah that she would take care of Brandon. And that didn't mean just ordering Chinese takeout every other night. He deserved a home-cooked meal every now and again. That was all.

He looked at the food, then back at her. "You made this?" Nothing in his tone was inspiring.

"I can cook, you know."

Brandon nodded. "Uh-huh."

She decided to ignore that. "Go wash your hands so we can eat before it gets cold."

With one last look at the slightly-too-done feast she had made, Brandon started toward the bathroom.

"See?" Leah asked halfway through their meal. "It's not so bad?"

Brandon rocked his head from side to side. "I guess not. Why all this sudden interest in cooking?"

"I thought it would be better if I cooked tonight."

"It would have been better if you hadn't burned it."

She shot him a look. "Are you always this cheeky?"

"What can I say? It's a talent of mine." He grinned. His

eyes sparkled just like his mother's, but the smile itself was all Aaron Zook.

Was it worth it? she wondered. Hannah had given up a great deal to become Amish once again. Not money, really, but living with her son, the comforts of the modern world, driving, freedom . . . Leah shook her head. It didn't matter. Those things were on the surface. Hannah and Aaron had loved each other for years, through marriages to other people, years apart, and distance. And a love like that couldn't be ignored.

Would it be the same for Tillie?

"What are you thinking about?" Brandon asked.

"Nothing," Leah lied. It seemed she had been doing a lot of that lately. "Why?"

"You were frowning something terrible."

Leah forced a laugh. "And you've been hanging out with your *mammi* too much."

"Hanging out with Mammi gets me pie." He gave a wink.

"And has you talking like an old-timer."

He placed one hand over his heart. "A small price to pay."

"I could make you a pie."

His eyes widened in what she suspected was horror. "That's . . . okay."

"You think I can't make pie."

"I'm sure you can do whatever you set your mind to," he said diplomatically.

"Uh-huh." She gathered her plate and took it to the sink.

"Thanks for supper," Brandon said.

"Even if it was burned."

"Even if." He kissed her cheek. "But, Aunt Leah, please don't burn the pie."

* * *

"It's just not the same without Tillie here." Gracie set down her knife and sighed.

"We planned this cousins' day weeks ago," Hannah reminded her.

"Before Tillie left," Leah added. But she had to agree with Gracie; it wasn't the same without Tillie. Her young sister had only been gone for three days, and this was the first cousins' day with all of them as adults, but it still wasn't the same. Just knowing that she was gone . . .

"It doesn't matter if Tillie's here or not—we have to get this soup canned before the festival."

"And we only have two weeks, I know." Gracie sighed. "It still doesn't feel right."

But they had to go on. This year, Leah had gotten a booth at the upcoming Bodock Festival. She planned to use it for small sales and to help get the word out about her shop, but even more importantly, she was selling canned goods for the Amish. The bishop had never been one for his district actually participating in the festivities. He found it unnecessary, since the increased traffic into town also brought about an increased traffic to the Amish houses and the ministores that most had set up in their front yards. But somehow they had convinced him to allow them this experiment. Leah would work the booth and sell the goods. The future of their being able to participate again might well be resting in her hands.

"I still think we should make apple butter or something."

"Next week," Hannah said. "This week is soup."

"Because anything we have left over, we can eat this winter." Leah nodded. "We know."

Hannah sniffed. "I thought it best to be practical. It's hard to make a meal out of apple butter in the winter."

Gracie grinned. "Maybe, but I'd like to try."

They all laughed, even Hannah. Gracie had the biggest

sweet tooth that Leah had ever seen. Even bigger than Brandon's, with his love of pie.

"I was thinking about making a pie tonight," Leah started. She chopped the ham to go in the soup while Gracie diced carrots and Hannah tackled the onions. The weather was still quite warm, and they had set up a table in the front yard, preferring to work outdoors instead of inside.

"A pie?" Hannah chuckled. "How long has it been since you made a pie?"

"Not so long ago that you should be laughing," Leah grumbled.

"Why all this interest in cooking?" Gracie asked. "*Jah*. You never liked to cook before."

Leah shrugged. "Liking it and needing to feed myself—and your son—are two different things."

"As are a pie and a casserole."

"I wanted to do something nice for Brandon. He got an A on his last test."

"That's fantastic." Hannah beamed like the proud mother she was. It was no wonder. Brandon had turned himself around these last couple of months. He had been struggling when they had moved back to Pontotoc. And now he was thriving. Leah couldn't be prouder herself. And that was the truth.

"What class?" Gracie asked,

"Uh," Leah faltered. "History . . . I think."

"I thought he had a chemistry test last time."

Leah snapped her fingers "That's right."

Hannah's eyes narrowed. She moved closer to Leah so only she could hear. "Why do I get the feeling you're not telling the truth?"

Leah started, surprised by her sister's observation. "I don't know."

"Maybe because you're not?" Hannah asked.

"Why would I lie about something like that?"

"I don't know. Maybe Jamie Stoltzfus?"

Leah forced a laugh, not so loud that it drew Gracie's attention. Just loud enough for Hannah to hear. "What does he have to do with it?"

"You tell me," Hannah shot back. She straightened and turned to Gracie. "Gracie, could you go into the house and get us another couple of onions? I don't think these will be enough." Hannah gestured to the box of onions they still had to chop. Gracie, being Gracie, nodded without question and bustled into the house as requested.

"Spill it," Hannah instructed.

"Spill what? There's nothing to spill."

"I don't believe you," Hannah said. "And here's why. Last night all that talk about him and Gracie not being right for each other. Now you want to make a pie?"

"I told you. The pie's for Brandon."

"And you're not trying to prove something to our good neighbor?"

"Why would I want to prove anything to him?" Leah scoffed.

"Because I think you like him."

Leah nearly choked. "That's," she sputtered, "that's the most ridiculous thing I have ever heard. I don't like Jamie; I despise him."

"The lady doth protest too much, methinks," Hannah quoted.

"Hush, it's not becoming for an Amish woman to quote Shakespeare."

"It's equally unbecoming for one to tell stories to themselves and everyone around them." Hannah smiled.

Leah didn't have time to respond, as just then Gracie came out of the house toting a small bag of onions. "Eunice said this will have to do. These are all the onions she has."

Hannah smiled. "That'll do just fine."

* * *

The last thing Leah wanted to think about was Jamie Stoltzfus, but he was on her mind all the time. Twenty-four-seven, as they say. Jamie, and Hannah's words.

Leah didn't like him. She absolutely didn't like him. The first time she saw him, she thought about how good-looking he was, and then he opened his mouth and cut down her way of living. What was to like about that? Looks weren't everything, and they surely couldn't make up for the differences in their personalities. And their goals. And dreams. And lifestyles.

It was simply ridiculous.

She was avoiding going out to her parents' house in fear that she would run into him. She wasn't sure she could look him in the face knowing what Hannah thought about the two of them. What if Hannah had told him the same thing? What if he was going around thinking that she liked him? Or at the very least knowing that Hannah thought she liked him? The very idea was mortifying. How would she ever be able to look at him the same again?

"Aren't we going out to Mammi's today?" Brandon asked as she settled in for the afternoon. She had a lot of paperwork to catch up on, and she had devised a new way to track the shop's inventory. "We usually go there after church."

Leah nodded. "I thought we might do something different today. Since I'm going out there again Tuesday for another cousins' day."

"But I'm not going then," Brandon reminded her. "Someone's got to stay here and mind the store."

"It's a church Sunday."

"That never stopped us before."

Leah sighed. She wanted to give him a good reason why they couldn't go to her mother's house today, but the truth was, she didn't have one. And the real reason she didn't want to go lived just up the lane.

"Fine," she said. "But we have to wait until this afternoon when they're home from church."

"Of course."

Until then, she had work to do. Too much work to give Jamie Stoltzfus another thought.

Chapter Eight

Brandon chatted all the way to Mamm's house. He talked about Shelly, the sermon at church, working on Tuesday so Leah could have a day off. And all Leah could think about was Jamie. Maybe he would be off visiting this afternoon. Maybe he wouldn't even be around.

It was a nice thought, but she knew it wasn't going to happen that way. He had made up his mind to court Gracie, and there was no reason for him to go back on it. Why would he? Gracie was smart, sweet, and funny. She was helpful and kind, and she could cook. A lot better than Leah, who seemed to have forgotten every kitchen lesson she had learned while growing up. She had cooked every night this week. Well, she had *tried* to cook something every night. Mostly she had made a mess of things. And Brandon, bless his heart, had paid the price for it. Maybe that was why he had wanted to come out to Mamm's so badly today. The poor kid needed something decent to eat.

"I hope Jamie and Peter are here," Brandon continued.

Of course he was wishing for the very thing she was trying to avoid. How could her life be any other way?

"Oh, yeah?" she asked.

"I like Peter," Brandon said with a nod.

That was something Leah could relate to. She liked Peter as well. But she knew Brandon and Peter had the connection of loss binding them together. Though she couldn't imagine how Peter felt, losing his entire family in one terrible accident. Was it any wonder the boy refused to talk?

Leah parked her car to one side of the barn and got out, Brandon close behind. Neither Jamie nor Peter was anywhere around, but she wasn't counting her chickens just yet. The way her luck was going lately . . .

"We thought you weren't coming," Mamm called from the doorway.

Leah waved. "You know I wouldn't miss Sunday afternoon at home."

Mamm beamed a smile that shone even through the rusty screen door. "Well, come on in. We're just about to have some sandwiches. Are you hungry?"

"Yes," Brandon exclaimed.

Mamm laughed. "Come on in, hungry boy." She opened the door and stepped back for Brandon to enter.

"Hey, sis," Hannah greeted Leah as she came into the house.

Leah did her best to look around for signs that Jamie might be there, all the while trying not to *look* like she was looking. No hat hung by the door, which meant her father was out in the barn. Dave was most likely with him. Was Jamie out there as well?

"Is he here?" The question finally got away from her. She tried not to ask, but there it was all the same.

"Did you come to see us or Jamie?" Hannah asked where no one else could hear.

"Hush, that," Leah admonished. "Is he here or not?"

Hannah grinned. "So you do care."

"How can I avoid him if I don't know where he is?" Leah asked.

"Why do you want to avoid him?" Hannah's tone was pure innocence, but she wasn't fooling Leah one bit.

"He's seeing our cousin. Or have you forgotten?"

"You said yourself that they aren't suited for each other." Leah rolled her eyes. "When did you start listening to me?"

Hannah glanced back over her shoulder, then looped her arm through Leah's. "Walk with me," she urged and started toward the front door, Leah in tow.

"It's been a busy week," Leah fussed. "What if I don't want to walk?"

Hannah simply smiled.

"Kidnapping is illegal," Leah reminded her.

Hannah dropped her arm, as if she knew that Leah would follow.

Heaven help her, she did.

"Are you going to tell me what it is, or are we going to walk until we can't take another step?" They were just over the rise from the pond behind Jim and Anna's house. Leah had heard Mamm say that the family had gone visiting and wouldn't be back until later in the week. They'd gone to Ethridge to see Anna's family there. Which meant no one was down there fishing. No one was throwing a ball around in this end of the pasture. She and Hannah could talk freely.

"There's something between you and Jamie," Hannah said.

Leah shook her head. There couldn't be anything between her and Jamie, for a variety of reasons, starting with the fact that he was seeing her cousin, even if they were ill-suited. And he didn't like Leah. She didn't like him, no matter how handsome he was, or how good with Peter. He was too conservative. And Amish. She was Mennonite. They might as well be oil and water. "There can't be anything between us."

"Sometimes love has other ideas."

"Love?" Leah scoffed. "This is about as far from love as

two people can get." So why did her heart beat a little faster in her chest when she thought of him?

"I know love when I see it."

"Sure you do."

"Don't be sarcastic. Who was it that said Benuel King liked you?"

"He liked me so much he's getting married in a few weeks. To someone else."

"That's only because you left."

"And this is his second marriage."

"He'd be married if we hadn't left."

"Are we still on for Tuesday? You know, apple butter?"

"Yes, and stop trying to change the subject."

"It's a dumb topic."

"I happen to take your happiness very seriously," Hannah said.

"My happiness? I'm happy. What makes you think I'm not happy? I am happy, you know."

"I know you *think* you're happy, but why else would you look at Jamie the way you do?"

"*Pbftft.*" Leah let out a derisive noise and flicked one hand. "I don't look at Jamie any differently than I look at Aaron or . . . or the bishop."

Hannah just smiled.

"I don't." She didn't. How could she? Jamie was all wrong for her, and she for him. And he was trying to get to know her cousin better. Never mind that they would make a terrible couple. Both were of age and had joined the church. If they wanted to ask for the bishop's permission to wed, who was she to say otherwise?

"Just don't close your mind to the idea, okay?"

Leah made a movement with her head, half-nod and half-shake. "Whatever."

"No. Not 'whatever.' How can you accept God's plans for you if you close your mind off to the possibilities?"

"You think this is God's plan for me?"

Hannah smiled and looped her arm through Leah's once more. "I know it is."

He could feel someone watching him. It was a creepy sensation.

Jamie looked around and could see no one, but this was a large Amish household. There was always someone around.

Still the hairs on the back of his neck stood on end. He raised one hand to smooth them down.

He had come down to Eunice and Abner's to visit, on the insistence of Hannah. Yet he had been surprised when he arrived. He'd figured it was a good time to get to know Gracie better. He needed a wife and a mother for Peter, but he wanted to at least like the woman he married. And he couldn't like her if he didn't get to know her. And he couldn't get to know her if she wasn't there.

Now he was sitting on the porch swing, rocking back and forth, just enjoying the afternoon. Everyone else was inside playing some sort of homemade Bible trivia game while Brandon had taken Peter down to the pond to fish. Maybe he should have gone with them. He could have tossed a line into the water and lain back against the fallen tree and taken a quick nap. If it weren't for Peter, he'd have headed home a long time ago.

"Can I talk to you for a second?"

Jamie turned as Leah Gingerich approached.

She was another surprise. Well, she shouldn't have been. He should have realized that she would be at her parents' house on a Sunday afternoon.

"*Jah*. Sure." He stopped the swing so she could sit next to him. She hesitated. "I don't bite, you know."

She let out an uncomfortable laugh and eased down

beside him. So much for trying to take the awkwardness out of the situation. She was sitting as far away from him as she possibly could and still be on the swing with him.

"Brandon and Peter still down at the pond?"

"*Jah*." He gave her a sideways look. "But I don't think that's why you came out here."

She shook her head and twisted her fingers in her lap.

He waited patiently as she chewed on her lip and gathered her thoughts.

"Have you talked to Hannah?" She stilled her hands and met his gaze straight on.

"Uh . . . *jah*," he faltered. "I guess. About what?"

She sucked in a deep breath. He wasn't aware anyone needed that much air. "About us."

"Us?" he frowned.

"Me and you." She gave a small nod.

"Why would I talk to Hannah about us?"

She shook her head and popped to her feet. "Never mind."

He caught her arm as she tried to escape. "What are you talking about?"

"Nothing." She tried to tug from his grasp, but he only tightened his hold. He wasn't ready to let her go yet. Nor was he ready to let this matter drop.

"Sit down."

To his surprise, she actually did as he asked.

"Now tell me why I would talk to Hannah about me and you?"

She looked toward the door. The main door was open, leaving only the screen door to separate them from the folks in the house. From inside, he could hear them laughing at their game, just one big family enjoying a Sunday afternoon.

"Let's walk." She started toward the porch steps, leaving

him no choice but to follow her if he wanted to know why she was acting so strange.

She started toward Jim and Anna's house, then stopped. "Can't go to the pond. Brandon and Peter are there." She turned and started up the lane toward his cabin.

Jamie followed behind. "Where are we going?"

She shook her head. "Just . . . up here." She didn't stop until she reached his porch. He wasn't sure if she was running from her thoughts or trying to make sure that the two of them were out in the open, but still alone. She stood facing the house. Just standing.

He stopped next to her, wondering how long he was going to have to wait before she told him whatever was on her mind.

She whirled toward him. "Hannah thinks I like you."

He blinked. "I would hope—"

"Not that kind of like." She shook her head impatiently. "Like-like."

He wasn't a hundred percent sure he understood. "You mean, romantically?" He almost hated to say the word out loud. It hung in the air between them, just hovering there waiting to be noticed.

She nodded.

"What did you say to her?"

"I told her that she was being ridiculous. But she kept on. I felt I should warn you. She'll probably start in on you next."

"Probably not. I mean, you two are sisters and everything."

Leah crossed her arms, her lower lip protruding just a little. "Did you ever talk to your sister about something like this?"

"Of course not."

"Your brother, then."

He shook his head.

"Sorry. I didn't mean to dig up painful memories."

"It's all right." But he knew the look on his face wasn't from her mention of Joseph, but something more. Hannah thought Leah liked him? She seemed to hate him. She never let him get a word in; every time they were together she picked a fight with him. She disagreed with how he was raising Peter and his Amish way of life.

Yet all he could bring to mind was how green her eyes were.

"I just thought you should know."

"Is that all?" he asked.

"I'm sorry."

"Is that the only reason why you told me these things? Because I should know?"

"Of course," she said. "Why else?"

Why else indeed? "Maybe because you want to know if I like you back." He hadn't meant to say the words out loud, but now that they were out, he silently challenged her to deny it.

"What?" She scoffed, but she didn't meet his gaze. "Why would I want you to like me back?"

"This conversation feels a lot like one I had in the third grade."

She propped her hands on her hips and cocked her head at a sassy angle. "Are you saying I'm immature?"

"I'm saying this conversation is." He shook his head. "Listen, Leah . . . I . . . I think Hannah may be right."

She blinked at him as if she had lost all power of speech. "Wh-what?"

"I think Han—"

"I heard what you said. Why did you say it?"

"You and I got off to a rocky start the first time we met, *jah?*"

She nodded.

"Why? I didn't know you, and you didn't know me. So why did we immediately start arguing with each other?"

"I don't pretend to know."

"You're doing it again."

"Doing what?"

"Acting like you hate me so you don't have to face the truth."

"What truth? That I like you?"

"*Jah*."

"That's the most absurd thing I have ever heard."

"Is it? Then why can Hannah see it?"

"Hannah is seeing what she wants to see."

But somehow he knew there was something more to it than that. "There's one way to find out for certain."

"How's that?" she asked.

He knew if he said the words there was no going back, but he couldn't stop himself. He was foolish and bold and possibly crazy. But he was certain this was one time when he needed to take a chance. "Kiss me."

"What?" Leah shook her head. "No no no no no." He had taken complete leave of his senses. Why would she ever kiss him? They didn't like each other—hadn't they already covered this?

"Are you afraid?"

She scoffed. "Of course not."

"Then what's the problem?"

"That's awfully forward."

He shrugged. "I'm finding my life has taken on an unusual urgency."

"Why should I change for your emergency?"

"Kissing me would prove there's nothing between us. You'd like that, right?"

She eyed him narrowly. "What's in it for you?"

"You're stalling." His blue eyes twinkled in challenge as a small smile pulled at the corners of his lips. He thought this was funny?

She couldn't let him get away with this. And she certainly couldn't let him get the upper hand. She took a step toward him. Then another. She could do this. She raised up on her toes and kissed him to the left of his mouth.

"Almost," he murmured.

She took a step back. "What?" Why was she shaking? It was only a kiss.

"Almost," he repeated, then he grasped her elbows and held her close.

His lips on hers was like nothing she had ever experienced before. Well, not that she had kissed very many men, or boys. She had spent her time in more noble pursuits. But this . . . this was better than she could have ever dreamed.

Electricity shot through her, similar to the time she unplugged the toaster when she was washing dishes. Tingling, shocking, and somehow pleasant.

Okay, better than pleasant. *Way* better than pleasant.

All too soon, he set her away from him, his eyes dark, but still twinkling.

"Well?" he asked.

"Is that it?" She gently pulled herself from his hold before she dared ask him to kiss her again.

"Are you saying you didn't feel that?"

"What?" She blinked innocently at him.

"The spark."

"Oh, that." She waved a dismissive hand.

"And I suppose that happens every time you kiss someone?"

She shrugged, unwilling to tell yet another bold-faced lie. "It's not supposed to?"

"Not every time, no." He propped his hands on his

hips, his eyes losing some of their sparkle. "Admit it," he commanded.

"Admit what?" She smoothed a hand over her prayer covering to hide the trembling in her fingers.

"Admit that you liked our kiss, and that you wouldn't mind doing it again."

Our kiss? Why did those two little words make her heart jump in excitement? "Do *you* want to do it again?"

He shook his head. "Once again we're adults having a third-grade conversation."

Third grade was being generous. "You have taken steps toward courting my cousin." She shook her head. There were a dozen reasons why she should have never kissed him, and even more as to why she could never kiss him again. Yet that was the best she could come up with?

"This has nothing to do with Gracie. Now admit it."

Leah blew out a breath, stirring the tendrils of hair that had escaped her bob. "Fine. It has nothing to do with Gracie."

He started toward her once again.

"Okay." She took a step back and held out one hand as if to stay him off. "It was . . . nice." She took another step back for good measure. "It was more than nice. Now what do we do about it?" she asked.

"Court?"

Spending time together would give them opportunities to know each other better. "How? You're Amish, and I'm Mennonite." They might as well have been olives and ice cream. They just didn't go together.

"Let's talk about it." He reached a hand toward her, pulling her closer as he settled down on the edge of the porch.

"There's nothing to talk about."

"I disagree."

She shook her head. "There's nothing to talk about, because there's no solution. If there was a possible answer to our dilemma, then maybe we would have something to discuss."

He shook his head.

Leah took two more steps away from him, needing to put a little distance between them. She told herself it was because she wanted to be able to see his face better, and standing so close to him made looking at him uncomfortable, but that was only a fraction of the problem. She wanted to lean in close, lay her head on his shoulder, breathe in the essence that was all Jamie.

And then what? Tell him it was good knowing him, she was glad they had cleared up the little misunderstanding about who wanted to kiss who and how would it be, and have a nice life?

No thank you. She eased away from him, but it didn't ease the thudding of her heart.

How did this happen? One minute she had been happy with her shop and her life, happy for her cousin—even if she believed that Gracie and Jamie were all wrong for each other. When had everything changed?

Hannah.

"What are you thinking?"

"That none of this would have ever happened if it hadn't been for Hannah and her big mouth."

"You can't blame your sister. This would have happened anyway. She just moved things along a bit quicker."

"There's nothing to move along."

"There is. We just have to decide what we can do about it."

She shook her head. "I'm not willing to join the Amish church. I've been out—" She shook her head. How could she explain that to him? How could she make him understand that she had lived and seen too much? She had grown accustomed to the conveniences allowed by her church. But most importantly, she had seen that she could live a good and godly life outside of the church, and she was happy in that life.

So many times in her youth she had been told that a person couldn't go out into the world and still live a godly life. Hannah was the perfect example of that. Her sister had made more mistakes than either of them cared to count. She had strayed far from her upbringing. But Leah hadn't. She had found a place where she could worship God, help others, do everything she would have in the Amish church, but without all the restrictions. She understood the need for them. So many people needed to have those constant distractions eliminated from their lives in order to hear God. But she had found a balance of her own, and it suited her just fine.

"I can't go back into the church," she finally said.

"Can't or won't?" he asked gently.

"Can't. Both."

"I'm an Amish man, Leah. I don't know anything else."

She understood that. Oh, how she understood.

"And I have Peter to think about."

Peter was the most important thing. How could she ask Jamie to leave the church and bring Peter with him after all that he had lost?

"So there's no way?" It should have felt as if the world had slipped out from under her, but it didn't. She was next to Jamie, and that made everything a little brighter. Besides, she had been running from her feelings, hiding from them for so long, and now that they were at the surface, there was no denying them.

"I don't believe that. Why would God put this love in front of us only to take it away?"

"Is that what this is? Love?" She had been afraid to say the word, yet it slipped from Jamie's lips with an uncanny ease. As if he was already comfortable with the idea of the two of them.

"It has the potential."

Boy, did it have potential.

But once upon a time, she had thought she had loved Benuel King. Yet she had left him behind. He had married, been widowed, and now he was getting married again.

Life went on. That much she knew.

"What do we do about it?"

"Wait. Give ourselves some time. Maybe something will come to us."

It was a risk she was willing to take. "And Gracie?"

"I'll explain everything to her."

"Everything?"

He shook his head. "I'll tell her that Peter isn't ready for me to be away so much. Surely she will understand that."

"And what happens if we can't find a way to be together?"

He sighed. "I don't know," he said. "I honestly don't know."

In the end, they decided to take it slow. Not worry about courting or dating or any other relationship ritual. And no more kissing.

There was really nothing they could do until they came up with a plan that would allow them to be together. Or if their prayers were answered and God delivered one to them.

But Jamie wasn't holding his breath. God did more than work in mysterious ways, and though Jamie would like to believe that he and Leah were part of God's plan, he wouldn't know for sure until it came to pass. In the meantime, he vowed to spend as much time with her as possible, get to know her better, and see what happened after that.

It was different this time. He was different. Never before had he challenged a woman to kiss him. Or a girl. Or anyone, for that matter. So why now? Why Leah? Because it was different. He was different. *She* was different.

He waved as he approached the Gingeriches' house. It was Tuesday and their designated cousins' day. He had heard them talk about it on Sunday, and he had waited until her car drove past today before heading down to see what was happening.

He still had to talk to Gracie and explain things to her. Yesterday would have been the perfect time, but he had a job at the bishop's house repairing the porch on the back. Turned out the job was bigger than he had anticipated, and he had barely made it home in time to meet Peter as he walked from school with Jim's kids. Jamie was glad to have them close. He would have worried about Peter walking home alone, but there was power in numbers.

"Apple butter?" he asked as he drew closer.

"Do you like apple butter?" Gracie asked.

"It's not my favorite."

"And what's that?" Gracie finished peeling the apple in her hands and passed it to Hannah.

"Kudzu jelly," Leah said.

Jamie grinned. "How did you know that?"

"That's what you eat on your biscuits. I figured you wouldn't eat it if you didn't like it."

True. But that she noticed was something in itself. It just went to show that there was more between them than anyone had suspected, even them.

"Here, Gracie." Hannah passed her the basket of apples that had already been peeled and cored and were waiting to be diced. "Cut these. You're getting too far ahead of the rest of us."

"We need Tillie here," Gracie grumbled.

The other women nodded. He knew they missed her. "Has anyone talked to her?"

They shook their heads.

"I was hoping she would at least call the phone shanty outside the school, but she hasn't," Hannah said.

"She never was much good at writing letters either," Gracie added.

"She'll be in touch soon," Jamie promised.

"How do you know?" Leah asked. Her words came out sharper than she had intended. Was it any wonder they were always at each other?

"If she misses you half as much as you miss her . . ."

"Good point," Hannah said.

"Well, I for one don't want to talk about it anymore."

"Do you want a glass of lemonade, Jamie?" Gracie set down her knife and dried her hands on a nearby towel.

"That sounds good."

"Come on, then." Gracie motioned for him to follow her inside.

The interior of the Gingerich home was beginning to feel more and more like he belonged there, as if it were his home as well. He had been there so many times, eaten supper, read the Bible. He wouldn't know what he would do without their kindness and support.

He followed Gracie to the kitchen, half listening as she chatted away about apple butter, missing her sister, and sewing a new shirt for Peter.

"You didn't have to do that, you know." He took a sip of his lemonade as he waited for her to pour her cousins a drink.

"I wanted to. He's a sweet little boy who deserves better than what he's had lately."

He couldn't argue with that.

"Gracie, I need to talk to you about something."

She dropped her hands to her sides and stared at him. "You don't want to see me after all."

"It's not a matter of want—"

"It's Leah, isn't it?"

He drew back in surprise. "What makes you say that?"

She gave a one-shoulder shrug and started pouring lemonade once again. "I can see what's happening between the two of you."

"You can?"

She placed the now-full glasses on a wooden tray and stored the lemonade back in the icebox. "It's all wrapped up in arguing and disagreements, but it's still there."

Were he and Leah the last to know?

"I'm sorry. I don't know what to say."

"It's no matter. I wasn't expecting anything anyway."

The sheer tone of her words nearly broke his heart. Gracie was a pretty girl, with a sweet heart bigger than the delta. She deserved more than she had been handed lately as well. "You'll find someone one day who loves you just for you," he finally said. "And no other reason." Like needing a mother for his orphaned nephew. But he didn't say that last part. It was simply understood.

"So are the two of you going to start courting?"

He shook his head. "I don't know what's going to happen. We have a lot standing in our way." More than he cared to list at the moment.

"God will find a way," Gracie said with a confidence he wished he felt. "He always does." She picked up the tray and headed for the front of the house.

"Just one more thing," he said, following behind her. "Please don't mention this to anyone. We're not sure how this will turn out, and we don't want it to get back to Peter."

Gracie nodded. "Your secret's safe with me," she said before breezing out into the September sunshine.

"I feel like we're teenagers sneaking around," Leah said as they strolled under the branches of the big oak. Peter was home from school and down visiting with his newfound friends who had just returned from Tennessee. But that didn't mean there weren't any eyes on them.

Gracie hadn't said a word about what she and Jamie had talked about when they went into the house together, but from her cousin's overbright smile and slightly too loud tone, she figured he had told her he couldn't court her. Whether or not he told her why, Leah had no idea.

Still, a large chunk of her heart went out to her cousin. That was Gracie, always an attendant, never a bride. Leah had to wonder if the young men there in Pontotoc were blind or merely stupid. Something was wrong with them if they couldn't see what a catch Gracie Glick really was.

"I think it's best if we keep this between ourselves until we figure out what we're going to do."

She shook her head. "I don't think there's anything we can do." How were a Mennonite woman and an Amish man supposed to make things work? The only way would be for one of them to change churches, and she couldn't see either of them giving up their church for anything.

"We can let God direct us," Jamie said simply.

Oh, how she wished she had his faith in the matter.

He grabbed her hand and squeezed her fingers. "Didn't we promise just two days ago to take this slow? To give it a chance and see where it took us?"

"*Jah*—I mean, yes."

"Then that's what we shall do."

He dropped her hand as Peter came galloping up the hill, one hand on his hat as he hurried along. He caught sight of Jamie, and his little legs pumped even faster. He ran at top speed straight for them, launching himself at Jamie and nearly knocking him back with the force of his embrace.

Jamie chuckled. "It's good to see you too, buddy." He hugged Peter tight. "Go on and get washed up for supper." He set Peter back on his feet and watched as he made his way to the water pump.

"He still hasn't said anything?" she quietly asked.

Jamie shook his head. "I keep praying that it's only a matter of time."

"There's that doctor—" she started, but Jamie cut her off before she could explain further.

"No thanks. There's nothing wrong with Peter that a lot of love and a little time won't cure."

Leah watched Peter disappear around the side of the cabin.

She hoped Jamie was right.

The rest of the week was taken up with work and preparing her booth for the Bodock Festival. Jamie said he wanted to take things slow, and that was the only way, considering how busy she was at the moment. But after this . . . well, she said a prayer every night that after the festival she and Jamie would have more time to spend together.

"Is this authentic Amish apple butter?"

Leah turned her attention to the couple who had just come up to her booth. "Yes, it is."

The woman's cool gaze raked over her. "You don't look Amish."

"That's because I'm not. But I used to be," she added as the woman went to set the jar back on her table. "I was raised Amish and then left to join the Mennonites." Why was she telling this woman, this *stranger*, half her life story? The woman didn't need to know all that. But it seemed as if Leah couldn't help herself.

"My sister and my cousin made it," she said, leaving out her part in the process, lest her hands cutting the apples made it less than authentic.

"And they're still Amish?" the woman asked.

Leah nodded.

"Okay, I'll take it, then."

Leah waited for the woman to deliver the rest of her ultimatum, but she stopped there and dug in her purse for the five dollars to pay for the apple butter. Leah placed the jar in the sack, along with the flyer she had made for the shop. "Thank you."

The woman gave a stern nod, then moved away to the next booth.

"Whew." She collapsed back in her seat.

"Tough crowd."

She jerked her attention to the man who approached. "Jamie! What are you doing here?"

"I thought I would bring Peter out and show him the festival."

"Have you ever been before?" she asked.

A flush of red stole into his cheeks. "Actually, no."

She didn't think many Amish attended the festival as either booth operators or visitors. In fact, Peter and Jamie were the first Amish people she had seen all day.

"Be sure to check out the cotton candy vendor. I've heard he has green apple this year. Do you like green apple?" she asked Peter.

He nodded in a gesture big enough to knock his hat off his head. Thankfully, he held it in place with one hand, even as he continued to nod.

"Not many Amish come out for the festival," Leah said. One year she had heard that they gave away cane fishing poles at the fishing competition and that brought out a lot of horse and buggies, but for the most part, as they usually did, the Amish of Pontotoc kept to themselves.

"I noticed." Jamie looked around as if to prove his point. Leah wasn't sure if he was talking about the lack of other Amish or the fact that everyone within twenty feet of them was staring.

"Does it bother you?" she asked. "The people who stare?"

He gave a rippling shrug. "It's not like I can do anything

about it. Did it bother you when you were still with the church?"

She supposed it had, but she had been too caught up in Sunday singings and other activities to give curious *Englischers* much mind. And now that she was with the Mennonite church, she didn't dress much differently than anyone else. Just her head covering gave her away. "A little, I guess. But that's not why you came by today," Leah said. It was more of a statement than a question.

"I knew you wouldn't be out to the house until Sunday. And I haven't seen you all week."

A warmth filled her. "Did you miss me?"

He nodded and swallowed hard.

How could two people go from practically hating each other to falling in love? It was as bizarre a thought as there ever was. But that was just the way love was. Or so she had heard. She might have been smitten with Benuel King back in the day, but her heart had never pounded like this. His kiss hadn't made her knees go weak or made her forget that she disagreed with him on a lot of points.

"I thought maybe tonight you could come out to the house and have supper with us. I figure you'll be tired and won't want to cook."

He got that right. As if cooking had ever been high on her list of priorities. If it had, she surely would have learned the art by now.

"What will we eat?"

"Cold chicken sandwiches and potato salad, courtesy of your *mamm*, of course. Maybe afterward we can sit and talk. You know, get to know each other better."

Suddenly a cold chicken sandwich sounded like the best supper a woman could ever have. "I'd like that," she said. "I'd like that a lot."

Peter tugged on Jamie's hand and pointed toward a game

where a person could win prizes by picking up a rubber duck from a kiddie pool.

"You want to go play that?" Jamie asked.

Peter nodded.

"I see no harm," Jamie said. He turned back to Leah. "I guess we'll see you—"

"Jamie Stoltzfus! I didn't think I was ever going to find you in this crowd."

Chapter Nine

Jamie turned at the sound of his name.

"Deborah?" he whispered. He almost rubbed his eyes to see if it would clear his vision. Deborah shouldn't be here. She was in Tennessee, most likely preparing to marry some unlucky fellow who didn't have the baggage of an orphaned nephew.

She smiled at him, and the crowd parted, the way good things just seemed to happen for Deborah. She looked the same as she always did. Same chocolate-brown hair and sparkling smile. Her dress was a deep green with a crisp black apron, and he was certain the color was meant to bring out the violet in her eyes. She was beautiful, and she knew it—a strange combination for a girl who lived in a world where physical beauty held no place of honor.

Peter took a step behind Jamie as she continued toward them. At least he had stopped tugging on Jamie's hand.

"Surprise," she said, her grin widening.

Surprise indeed.

"Aren't you happy to see me?"

Jamie stirred himself from his disbelieving stupor. "Of course." He had been concerned there for a moment that she was no more than a figment of his imagination. But now he knew she was real.

Behind him, he heard Leah suck in a breath. He wasn't sure if it was anger or hurt, but it wasn't a good sound.

"Why are you here?" He hoped the question didn't sound as accusatory to her ears as it did to his. Wait. Why did he care? She broke off their engagement. Why should he have to bend and fetch for her if she could throw him away like yesterday's scraps? Who was she to come here like nothing had happened?

"You aren't happy to see me?" She gave a pout that she could have only learned from her fancy *Englisch* friends. Friends he was certain her *vatter* didn't know she had.

No was on the tip of his tongue, but then Jesus's words from the Sermon on the Mount came to him. *All things whatsoever ye would that men should do to you, do ye even so to them.* Do unto others as you would have them do unto you. And not the other way around. Just because she had treated him poorly didn't give him the right to return the same attitude.

He gave a quick glance back at Leah. He could almost touch her confusion. The air was thick around them. *This changes everything,* her eyes seemed to say. He shook his head, then turned back to the woman he once thought he'd marry.

"It's not that," he finally replied. "You just caught me unprepared."

Peter took another step over, so that he was completely hidden by Jamie's legs.

Deborah clasped Jamie's hands in her own and swung their arms like she was playing a casual game of ring-around-the-rosy. Then she caught sight of Leah.

"Who is this?" she asked. Her beautiful eyes widened in curiosity.

Jamie cleared his throat. "Deborah King, Leah Gingerich."

"Nice to meet you." Deborah didn't release his hands. "Can we go somewhere and . . . talk?"

He didn't miss her slight hesitation in front of the last word. *Make up* would have been a better term, he had the feeling. *Can we go somewhere so I can convince you that I didn't mean a word of what I said?*

Why? Why was this happening now?

"We can go back to my house." He cleared his throat again. The words kept getting stuck there.

"Perfect." She leaned around him to look at Leah directly. "Nice you meet you, LeeAnn."

"Leah," she corrected, but Deborah was no longer listening.

"My buggy is behind the secondhand store."

She looped her arm through his, not even bothering to acknowledge that Peter was attached to one end of him. "Good," she said. "I dismissed the driver. I told him I'd find my own way from here."

And that was Deborah: confident to a fault. And only mindful of what she wanted to see. How had he ever imagined that he would marry her? And how was he going to get rid of her now?

"What do you mean you don't know who Deborah is?" Leah paced around her mother's front room in frustration. She'd had to drive past Jamie's cabin knowing that he and Deborah were in there talking. About what? She could only guess. But after the familiar way Deborah had treated Jamie at the Bodock Festival, it had to be something more. Or important.

"Is there one word in particular that you don't understand, or is it the whole concept of 'I don't know'?" Hannah shook her head. "Why do you even care?" Then her sister stopped, and it was as if the light had dawned in her thoughts. "You do like him. I knew it."

"It's not like that." And yet it was exactly like that.

"Oh, *jah?* Then what's it like?"

"We talked the other day—"

"Talked or argued?"

"We can have a conversation without arguing, you know."

Hannah chuckled. "Funny, I have yet to see one of those."

Leah crossed her arms. "It happens. From time to time. You know, occasionally." She wasn't making this any easier on herself.

"I see," Hannah said.

"Would you stop being that way. We just talked."

"About what?"

"Your questions aren't helping me figure out who Deborah is."

"My questions are trying to find out why you care who Deborah is."

Gracie came into the room with a dust rag and a broom. "I know who Deborah is," she said.

Leah's attention snapped to Gracie. "You do?" She and Hannah said the words at the same time.

Gracie nodded. "She's his fiancée. Or rather, she was. Until he got custody of Peter. After that, they broke up." She set about sweeping the floor. In the Mississippi heat without central air to cool things off, windows had to be left open all the time. Everything got a complimentary coating of orange dust, courtesy of Mother Nature.

"I didn't know he had a fiancée," Hannah said. She turned to look at Leah. "Did you?"

Leah shook her head. It seemed there were a lot of things about Jamie Stoltzfus that she didn't know. That was all part of the getting-to-know-you phase they had just headed into. But now it seemed . . .

"Why wouldn't he tell us that he had a fiancée?" Leah asked.

"Why would he?" Hannah retorted.

"Because he's going to court her," Gracie said matter-of-factly.

Hannah hopped to her feet and snapped her fingers. "I knew it. I knew it, I knew it, I knew it."

"No, that's not it at all." Leah tried to get ahold of the situation.

"He's not?" A slight frown puckered Gracie's brow. "But the other day he said—"

"You got this from Jamie?" Hannah crowed.

Leah rolled her eyes. This is just what she didn't need. There was a reason she and Jamie were taking it slow—or maybe that was *her* reasoning, and *his* was the fact that he had a fiancée waiting for him in Tennessee.

"*Jah*," Gracie said. "He told me that he couldn't court me because he thought he had feelings for Leah." She turned slowly to look at her cousin.

"What a skunk!" Hannah laughed.

"You think?" Leah's heart dropped. She had thought for just a minute that she might have the chance at happiness that the others around her had been afforded. Hannah, Anna and Jim, even Benuel had all found someone to love and who loved them in return. She supposed she had to accept that it just wasn't in God's plan for her.

"I thought he was different," Gracie and Leah muttered at the same time.

They looked at each other and laughed. What else was there to do?

"So you're not going to court Jamie Stoltzfus?" Brandon asked that evening over take-out Chinese.

"We never really talked about courting—just about talking."

"You were talking about talking?" He shook his head. "I don't think I will ever understand anyone over thirty."

"Just wait till you're one of us." Leah flashed him a smile.

"Does this mean you aren't going to cook anymore?"

"Why does your tone sound hopeful?"

He stopped to chew and swallow his bite of sweet and sour chicken before continuing. "No, just curious."

"It's a sin to lie, you know." She tossed her napkin at him.

Brandon moved to the side to dodge it. "You shouldn't have to work so hard," he said diplomatically. That was one thing he had picked up from Shelly. He knew more how to finesse the people round him.

"Why don't you learn to cook, then?"

He shook his head. "I shouldn't have to work that hard either. Though I wouldn't mind having some spaghetti every once in a while."

"Now, that I can make," Leah replied.

"Can you teach me? I want to make it for Shelly. It's her favorite."

"Are we dating now?"

"I told you; we're just friends. Can't friends treat each other to supper from time to time?"

"I suppose."

He nodded. "And you'll teach me?"

"Starting tomorrow."

"Thanks, Aunt Leah." He beamed her a smile, but this one she had trouble returning. Her throat had gotten clogged with stupid emotions, like remorse and regret and love for a nephew so strong.

She swallowed them back and managed a smile of her own. "You're welcome."

She was not going to let this define her. Sure, she had thought Jamie was special; that the two of them could have something. But this just proved how wrong she was. They had been looking for a sign, a way for God to tell them they had made the correct choice. And here it was in the form of a fiancée returned.

Deborah and Jamie might have broken up once before, but they were better suited than he and Leah could ever be. How were they supposed to work out all their differences concerning faith and church? There was too much at stake to take this lightly. There were Peter and God and both of their families. Any decision they made would affect them all. She couldn't say that he would be better off with Deborah, but we would definitely be better off without her.

This wasn't exactly how he thought the day would end. Actually, it was nowhere near where he wanted it to be.

"Well, it certainly is cozy." Deborah glanced around the cabin, her expression a careful mask of indifference.

For the first time since they had built the room onto the cabin, Jamie was glad Peter had his own space. When they arrived at the cabin, he had sent Peter to his room to play.

"Why are you here, Deborah?" Jamie settled down on the worn sofa he had gotten from Twice Blessed. As a matter of fact, Leah had helped him with most of the furnishings in the now-three-room cabin.

"I think maybe I acted a bit . . . hasty."

"Concerning?"

"The wedding." She beamed at him, that smile that used to melt his insides. Now it left him bewildered.

"There is no wedding."

"And that's why I'm here."

He shook his head. "I must be missing something."

"It's simple, really. I should have never told you that I wouldn't marry you. I didn't think things through. I mean, you surprised me with Peter. I just needed some time to adjust."

"And you're adjusted now?"

"Very." There went that smile again. It was starting to become unnerving.

"Peter isn't a shock. He's a little boy who's lost almost everything in his life."

"I just didn't understand why you felt the need to take him. Not when Sally's parents were willing to raise him."

He was not getting into this with her again. They had been over it too many times to count.

He stood. "I think it's time you should go."

She blinked at him, then shook her head. "Go? I don't want to go."

"But I want you to. In fact, I'm insisting."

"No." She settled a little deeper into the couch cushions. "I came to convince you to marry me, and I'm not leaving here until I do."

Jamie sighed. "Where are you staying?"

"With Sarah Hostetler."

Jamie had met her. She was a young widow who had opened a candy shop to make ends meet for herself and her three young children. "I'll take you over there."

"But I don't want to go."

"Deborah, this is getting us nowhere."

She seemed to think about it for a moment. Finally, she stood. "All right, then. *Jah.* You can take me to Sarah's, but I'm not leaving Pontotoc until you say you're going with me."

"We did okay at the festival, huh?" Hannah asked the following Sunday.

Leah nodded. "I would say that one hundred and fifty dollars apiece is pretty good."

Gracie fanned out her cash. "I don't think I've ever seen this much money in one place. I mean, a number in the bank account book, but not in my hands. Can we do it again?"

"There's only one festival," Leah reminded them.

"But we could sell the goods in your shop."

"You already have the shop out front," Leah pointed out.

Like most families in the area, the Gingeriches had a small shed at the front of their property where they sold canned goods, bright plastic beaded jewelry and key chains, and Mamm's goat milk products.

"*Jah*, but if we had a couple of shelves of product in Twice Blessed, then we would be able to reach people who don't come all the way out here."

"She's got a point, you know. And it might help spread the word for other farms."

Leah turned the idea over in her head. Most of the farms made various jellies and jams, but the Gingeriches were the only family in the area who sold apple butter. The Danny Yoders and the John Bylers were the only families who sold sauerkraut. And Sarah Hostetler had made a name for her marvelous candies. If anyone came in the store and asked for something Leah didn't have, she would be able to direct them to the correct house for the items. It would help her store and her family as well as the entire community.

"I guess I could move some things around and we can put the jars up front."

"Where the kitchen goods are now?" Hannah asked. "That's a great place. People walking by will be able to see them."

"You'll need more shelves too," Gracie mused.

Hannah smiled. "I know just the person to do it. In fact, I'm going to ask him right now." She turned and started toward Jamie's cabin.

Leah grabbed her arm. "He has . . . company."

"Company?" Gracie and Hannah asked at the same time.

"His ex-fiancée."

"She's still here?" Hannah asked.

"Last I heard."

"Have you talked to him?" Gracie asked.

Leah shook her head. The last thing she wanted was to compete with the beautiful Deborah King. Like she *could* compete. Deborah was one thing Leah could never be again: Amish. "I don't think it's going to work out between us." That was an understatement. She had been waiting around for God to give them a sign or an answer. And He had. One look at Deborah, and Leah knew she and Jamie didn't have a hope. Too much separated them. Too much that could never be bridged.

"What happened?" they asked.

"Nothing." She gave a quick shrug that felt stiff and unnatural. "We're too different." She looked to Gracie. "I'm sorry. He was interested in you, and I ruined it. And for what?"

Gracie waved away her concern. "I'm not sure we would have been good as a couple either. We never seemed to be able to talk about anything."

"And now this?" Leah smiled.

"I think maybe you saved me from a lot a heartache."

"Gracie, he doesn't deserve you," Leah said.

"You too," Gracie said. The words were meant to make her feel better, but they only made her stomach hurt.

"I'm sorry I didn't get by to see you yesterday," Jamie said.

Yesterday had been Sunday. An off-Sunday. Leah and Brandon had made their usual trip to visit with family and had stayed as long as they could. She'd had to drive by Jamie's cabin arriving and leaving. But she hadn't seen him at all. Which meant one thing: He had better things to do besides spend time with her. Specifically spending time with Deborah. She knew this would happen, but it didn't make it hurt any less.

"It's no problem," she said with an offhand wave. Her mother or Hannah must have asked him to come work on her shelves, for he'd been at the shop first thing. Leah supposed it was only logical that she hire him to do the work, but it didn't make it any easier.

"I need to explain."

"There's nothing to explain."

He raised one brow. "Deborah."

"You don't owe me an explanation." She started tossing clothes into a laundry basket so she could easily move them to the back.

"I can't see how you figure that."

She shook her head. "Really, Jamie. You don't need to do this." More clothes in the basket.

"Leah, would you stop that and listen to me for just a minute?"

She rested her hands against the edge of the basket, but they itched to reach for more clothing. She needed to keep moving, keep busy until she accepted the inevitable. "Explain," she ordered.

"I didn't ask Deborah to come here."

She nodded. That much was evident when Deborah had called out, "Surprise."

"She came down here all on her own," he continued.

"Why?"

"What?"

"Why did she come down here?"

"To get back together." He turned red as he spoke the words.

"There you go." She moved to take the basket to the back.

"Leah, wait." He lunged toward her, stopping her with one hand on her arm. "You didn't ask if I wanted to get back with her."

She glanced down at his fingers where they lay against her thin, long-sleeved T-shirt. Then back to his eyes. "It doesn't matter."

"What?" He pulled away as if he had been burned.

"She came down here to find you. She obviously cares about you. And you two belong together."

He propped his hands on his hips. "What makes you say that?"

"You're Amish. She's Amish."

"Maybe I don't want an Amish girl. Maybe I've decided that I'd rather have a Mennonite lady."

She stopped and, unable to help herself, burst out laughing. "That is without a doubt the dumbest thing I've ever heard."

"I didn't mean for it to be funny, but if it helps you understand."

She set the basket on the table in the back. She would have Shelly fold the items for storage. Cooler weather was on the way, and short-sleeved shirts would be a memory until next year. "It's not about understanding."

"Then tell me what it is." His tone was so urgent, so caring that she almost told him that everything would be okay. But she couldn't. She owed them both that much.

"When we talked, I thought everything would turn out okay. We just had to believe."

"What changed?"

"I prayed for a sign. For direction so we would know that

we were doing the right thing. I prayed for an answer to our differences."

"And?"

"Deborah showed up."

"You think Deborah is a sign from God?"

Leah shook her head. "But her arrival is."

"Would you listen to yourself?"

"I can hear me just fine," she returned.

"Then you know how ridiculous you sound."

"I know that regardless of how hard it is to face the truth, you and I are too different to make any sort of relationship deeper than friendship possible."

He couldn't believe his ears. Was she really saying that? Her mouth moved and sounds came out, but he hoped he was hearing something someone else was saying. "I don't get a say in this?"

"What good would that do?"

"I don't know. But this is my life too. And if I want to keep looking for a solution, then I will."

Leah shook her head. "It's useless," she said. "The sooner we face that, the better."

"There's an answer," he insisted. "We just have to have faith. We have to believe, and it will be."

"Faith isn't going to get us through this. Don't you see? Faith isn't always the answer."

"I'm not giving up on you, and I'm never giving up on us."

Having said his piece, he went back to the front of the store. He had faith, and it was the answer. He knew that with enough time, the Lord would move Leah's heart, she would join the church, and they could get married.

Okay, so he was jumping ahead of himself. But there

it was. One day he hoped to marry Leah Gingerich. It was strange. He had never felt so sure of anything in all his life. And if that wasn't a sign from above, he didn't know what was.

Jamie finished the shelves, packed up his tools, and headed for home. He didn't say another word about Deborah or getting married the rest of his time there at Twice Blessed. He had planted the seeds. Now all he had to do was show her that there was a way.

"I was about ready to leave." Deborah rose to her feet from her place sitting on the edge of his porch.

"What are you doing here, Deborah?"

"I came to visit. I thought maybe you would want to go with me over to Sarah Hostetler's candy shop to see what we can find."

"I'm sure we'll find candy." He started to unhitch his horse. He didn't have another job today, so he was walking down and helping Abner, Jim, and David finish a gazebo the city commissioned to place in the park in town.

She smiled. "Okay. You got me. I just wanted to spend some time with you, and I remembered how much of a sweet tooth you have. I thought it might be fun."

Sarah's candy was some of the best he had ever eaten, and he liked supporting her shop, but that didn't mean he needed candy right then or that he wanted to go with Deborah to get it.

"I've got work to do," he said. "Maybe another time." Like never.

"If you have to work, why are you unhitching your horse?"

He sighed. "If you must know, I'm going down to work with the Abner Gingeriches."

"Don't they make sheds and things? I heard my brothers talking about it."

"They make all sorts of things." He turned his mare loose in the pasture with a silent promise for a good brushing later.

"And you help them a lot?"

"When I don't have another job to do." Abner had almost too much business for the three of them to keep up with. But Jamie wanted to work for himself and not at a job that had been handed to him. Abner had told him it wasn't like that, but it felt too much like charity for Jamie's comfort.

He and Peter were making it just fine. If things changed for them, then he would consider working with Abner more, but until that time, he was happy doing exactly what he was doing.

"You're not going to make this easy for me, are you?"

Jamie shook his head. "There's nothing to be easy or hard," he said. He needed to get down to Abner's and help, but he had to take care of this first.

He led Deborah over to the porch and sat on its edge. She settled down next to him.

"There was a time when I thought the two of us would get married," he started.

"Me too."

"But things have changed."

"Because you moved here? Everyone knows it's just a matter of time before you come back home. Once the time has passed and Peter hasn't spoken, well, I figured you'll move back to be close to him."

Her words settled around him like a cold fog. "You think I'm going to lose him."

"Has he talked any since you've been down here?"

"That's beside the point. You think I won't have Peter, so now you want me back?"

"Noooo. I told you. I realized that I was too quick in calling off the wedding. I didn't think things through."

Because she realized after the fact that he might not have Peter forever. But he wasn't letting Sally's parents take the boy from him. Peter needed to know that he was loved and safe, not just another mouth to feed.

Jamie wasn't doing this again. He stood. "I've got to go to work, Deborah. I'll see you later." He stalked off toward Abner's with her last words ringing in his ears: "Of course you will."

"I can't believe she's still here," Gracie said at their following cousins' day.

Gracie might be confused, but Leah knew exactly why she was hanging around. She wanted Jamie for her own once again. It was a realization that Leah could understand. But that didn't mean she had to like it. She knew it was only a matter of time before Jamie came to his senses and married Deborah. She would give him the stable Amish home that Peter so desperately needed.

"I heard that she told Jamie she wasn't leaving until he promised to move back to Tennessee."

"So he doesn't want to marry her?" Gracie frowned. "I don't understand."

"It's simple, really," Hannah said. "Jamie and Deborah broke up, and he moved down here to get away. He decided he needed a mother for Peter, so he was going to court you. Then he fell for Leah and had to tell you that he wanted to court her. Then Deborah showed up, and now Leah doesn't want anything to do with him. But he doesn't want anything to do with Deborah. It's like a bad romcom."

"Who's romcom?"

Hannah laughed. "Don't worry about it."

Gracie shook her head and began mixing up the ingredients for the lavender-scented goat milk lotion they were making. It would be one of the first products that she would sell in her store.

The girls fell quiet as they worked, each one lost in her own thoughts.

"He thinks faith will solve everything," Leah said, her words sounding overloud.

"What do you mean?" Hannah asked.

"Can't faith overcome everything?" Gracie added.

"It's not about faith. This is about reality."

"Sweetie, you are going to have to be a little more specific if you want our help."

"I don't need help," Leah said. "It's not like anyone can change anything."

"Faith?" Gracie asked.

Leah shook her head. "Jamie thinks he can just believe that there will be an answer, so there will be."

"An answer to what?" Hannah asked.

"How we can be together."

"And there's not one?"

She shook her head. "Too many differences stand in our way."

"And you're both stubborn as mules."

She shot Hannah a look. "Thanks, sister dear. You are too kind."

"Tell me it's not true."

She couldn't—not without telling a lie.

Chapter Ten

Could faith overcome anything? Honestly, Leah wasn't
sure. She had been told her entire life that faith was all a
person needed. If you had faith, then God would take care
of the rest.

But she had never seen it at work. She'd had faith as a
young woman going into her runaround years, and she had
left to protect her sister. No amount of faith could keep
Hannah in Amish country. She'd had faith when Hannah
told her she was marrying Mitch McLean. And that hadn't
turned out at all, unless she counted Brandon on the plus
side. He was definitely a plus as far as she was concerned.

She supposed faith had played a big part in her decision
to go to Central and South America and work as a mission-
ary. The living conditions in the places she had been were
abysmal. Faith played a part in every sip of water and every
bite of food, every minute of sleep and every beautiful
sunrise.

But this was something entirely different. It was one
thing to pray and believe that God would help work it out,
and another to go blindly into whatever life handed out.
Jamie was a smart man; smart enough to understand. Smart
enough to figure it out. Smart enough to do more than just

trust in God when it came to Peter. She wanted to shake Jamie—something, *anything* to get him to see clearly.

And the two of them? That was another matter entirely.

"Are you going to sit there all evening and stare at Jim's house, or are you coming to help me at Jamie's?"

Leah stirred herself from her thoughts and turned to find Gracie standing just outside the front door of the house, a large Dutch oven in her hands.

"What are you doing at Jamie's?"

"We talked about this yesterday." Gracie tsked. "Eunice wants me to go up there and make sure they have something to eat for the next few days. You said you would help."

She didn't recall. But she supposed she had. As much as she disliked cooking, it sounded like something she would do, offer to cook for someone in need, but lately her brain seemed too full and things kept slipping out. Like promises to help. Good thing she drove out here after work. Brandon had gone to supper with Shelly and her family, and Leah couldn't stand being in the apartment all alone.

It was ridiculous. When she had moved in that had been her intention: to live alone. But now that she had Brandon, or maybe it was all the time she was spending out on the farm with her family—whatever it was, the place seemed too empty with only herself for company.

"Are you coming?" Gracie asked. A small frown of worry stretched itself across her forehead.

"Of course." Leah pushed to her feet. She didn't want Gracie to have to go to Jamie's by herself. Who knew what she might find? Leah herself had hardly seen Jamie since the beautiful Deborah had arrived in Pontotoc. That in itself was telling. He had his love back at his side, and Leah was certain they were busy making plans for their future together. Just the three of them: Jamie, Deborah, and Peter.

So busy that Deborah couldn't be bothered to cook for them. Mamm probably just wanted Gracie and Leah to spy on the couple and make sure nothing untoward was going on.

"What are we cooking?" Leah asked as they trudged up the slight hill toward Jamie's cabin.

"Eunice thought a pot of beans would be good, and a couple of pans of cornbread." Gracie gave a small shrug. "Now that the weather is starting to turn, warmer meals will be more welcome."

Leah nodded.

"And I thought I would make them some fried chicken for tonight."

Ugh. Leah loved fried chicken, but it was messy and involved. "What's tonight?"

Gracie shrugged and switched the Dutch oven from one arm to the other. "I don't know. Eunice just said she wanted him to have something special for tonight."

Because he was having Deborah over? Had Jamie requested something special for a special evening? She shook her head at herself. She was looking for things that weren't there. Jamie didn't want charity from anyone. Wouldn't this be a form of charity? What about the other meals? She shifted the bags in her arms and rubbed the bridge of her nose.

"Headache?" Gracie asked.

"Trying to be," Leah replied. And she had no one to blame but herself.

They made their way across the small strip of grass that served as Jamie's yard and up onto the porch. Gracie knocked once on the door, then let herself in.

"Is he here?" Leah asked. She really didn't want to run into him, but she wanted to find out everything she could about the mysterious Deborah. How had she not known that he was previously engaged? They were talking about courting and seeing if they could make their lives compatible.

Why had he not mentioned that little detail? Was he, like the *Englisch* said, a player?

His kind face came to mind, with his sparkling eyes and charming freckles. He was the most wholesome player she had ever seen, if there was such a thing.

"I think he's outside. I mean, his buggy is here. And Peter should be home from school."

He might be outside or Deborah could have swung by in Sarah's buggy to pick him up. Him and Peter.

Gracie set the Dutch oven on the worktable and motioned for Leah to do the same with the sacks. She did, then started unloading the food she had brought: beans, cornmeal, chicken, spices. She supposed Jamie didn't have these things in the cabin. Not surprisingly, but it seemed as if Gracie had thought of everything.

Just then the back door flung open, and Peter plowed through. His limp seemed more pronounced today. Leah wondered if it had to do with his increased speed or whatever had put that frown on his face.

"What's wrong?" she asked.

Peter pointed out the window.

"Go check," Gracie said, then started opening cabinets to find the things she needed. First out was the chopping board.

Leah couldn't see anything unusual out the window, and she turned back to Peter.

He pointed to the front room. Maybe she needed to look out that window.

"I'll be right back," she said and made her way to the front of the house and the window that overlooked the yard.

A buggy was pulling up the drive with Deborah King holding the reins.

Leah stepped back out of the window and out of Deborah's line of sight.

"What is it?" Gracie called from the kitchen.

Leah held one finger over her lips, thinking she would ease back into the kitchen without Deborah being any the wiser. Then she heard Jamie's voice from outside and her footsteps stilled.

"What are you doing here?" He didn't even bother to say hello to Deborah. That meant something, but Leah was hesitant to be too hopeful. It was possible that she hadn't heard their first words to each other.

"Of course I thought I would come by and see you."

Leah rolled her eyes and somehow managed to keep quiet.

"You should go home." Jamie's words were gentle but firm. He didn't want Deborah there? Why not?

"I told you," Deborah said, *Don't be silly* clearly coloring her tone. "I'm not leaving until you agree to come back with me."

"I'm not coming back."

"You aren't serious."

He sounded serious enough to Leah, but what did she know? She had just met him a couple of weeks before. Leah had no idea how long Jamie and Deborah had known each other, but she'd bet it was a sight longer than that.

"I am."

"You say that now—"

"And I'll be saying it tomorrow."

"Jamie, I know you want what's best for Peter. We all want that. But if he doesn't speak . . . well, you can't force that."

"I'm not trying to force it." Once again his tone was patient. Just one of the things that made him such a good father to Peter.

"You're putting a time limit on it."

"Sally's parents did that. Not me."

"See?" Deborah's voice sounded falsely bright. "That's exactly why you should return to Ethridge."

"Deborah."

"Just think about it."

"There's nothing to think about."

"Promise me," she demanded. "Promise me you'll think about it."

"I promise."

What else could he say? He was tired and hungry and ready to go in the house and eat whatever it was that smelled so good. Eunice had told him that she was sending Gracie up to cook for him tonight. He tried to talk her out of it, but once Eunice got her mind wrapped around an idea, there was no pulling her off it. Never mind that it might be a little awkward for him, and possibly even Gracie, Eunice sent her niece to his house to cook.

Now he was a little bit glad that she hadn't listened to him. Something was smelling wonderful inside. All he had to do was send Deborah home, uh, back to Sarah's, and he could rest and enjoy what was left of his evening with Peter.

"I'm glad you stopped by," he said, standing and hoping she would do the same. Thankfully she did.

"I meant what I said," she reminded him as they stepped off the porch and started toward her buggy.

"About?"

"I'm not leaving here until you agree to go back with me."

"To Ethridge?"

"Ethridge, wedding." She smiled. Once upon a time he had thought that smile was the most beautiful sight he had ever seen. Now he saw through the tool she had used to make him forget anything and everything other than her.

"Deborah," he started, not really wanting to get into it with her again, but not able to let it go.

"I know, I know." She shook her head. "I know what your mouth is saying, but I also know what's in your heart. I hurt you. I understand that. And you need time. But I'm not giving up on us."

Before he could take in his next breath of air, she climbed into her buggy. She flashed him another of those shy-but-dazzling smiles as she pulled her buggy from in front of his house.

Jamie stood in the front yard and watched her drive away. He felt a little like he had when he had hit his head on one of the rafters in the barn when he was a teenager. Dazed, a little sick to his stomach, and filled with a dread he couldn't name. He just knew nothing was ever going to be the same again.

"Will you get back in here?" Gracie called from the kitchen.

Leah watched Jamie watch Deborah drive away and tried to figure out what was going on inside his head. Was he missing her already? Was he wishing he had called her back? One thing was certain—for all his talk about not going back to Ethridge, the pair seemed pretty intimate just before she left.

They were a couple, and anyone could see that. They might have had their disagreements, but they were from the same place. They had a history. She couldn't compete with that. And Deborah was the one thing that she could never be again: Amish.

"Leah," Gracie called again. "Give that man some privacy and get in here and help me."

Reluctantly, she moved away from the window and returned to the kitchen area.

"Sorry," she mumbled and took up the masher to cream the potatoes. "It's just that . . ." She stopped, shook her head, and started to work again. A moment passed. "I mean . . ." She stopped mashing. "They're a couple, you know?"

"What are you talking about?" Gracie asked.

Leah was reminded that her cousin hadn't been by her side, witnessing the familiarity between Deborah and Jamie. "They're a couple." She made sure her voice was low and didn't draw Peter's attention. He was sitting on the floor close behind them. She had to get this out of her system, but she didn't want to taint Peter's idea of the situation.

Gracie turned from stirring the gravy, a small frown wrinkling her brow. "Jamie and Deborah?"

"If you could have seen what I just saw."

"And what was that?"

Leah sighed. "The two of them. Together. All . . . cozy."

"Cozy?"

"Exactly. And after he started seeing you, then saying he wants to court me. And all along, he's been waiting for her to come back."

"Deborah?"

"Of course, Deborah."

"I don't like Deborah."

Leah whirled around to look at Peter. He was still sitting on the floor, playing with plastic horses and a fence that looked to be made out of Popsicle sticks.

"Did he just . . . ?" Gracie dropped the spoon she had used to stir the gravy and approached the boy. He was galloping his horses all around his makeshift corral. Not once had he looked up after speaking.

Maybe she was hearing things. Maybe he hadn't said anything at all.

Then they were both hearing things, because Gracie had witnessed it too.

"What was that?" Leah asked. "What did you say?"

Peter didn't bother to look up from his play. "I don't like Deborah."

She drew back and cast a quick glance at Gracie.

Her cousin shrugged.

"Why is that?" she asked Peter.

He refused to answer, preferring instead to line up his horses in the improvised pasture.

"Peter," she coaxed. "It's okay to talk to me, to tell me and Gracie what's on your mind. Would you like that?"

If he would or wouldn't, she never knew. He continued to line up his horses. Unable to get him to speak again, Gracie and Leah went back to their cooking.

A little bit later, Jamie came in through the back door.

"Something smells good." He took a deep breath. "We're eating fine tonight, Peter."

The boy nodded, but didn't say a word.

"Jamie." Leah wiped her hands on a dish towel and turned to face him. "Can I talk to you outside for a moment?"

"Leah." Gracie frowned.

Jamie's attention switched from one of them to the other and back again.

"Alone," Leah continued.

"*Jah*. Sure."

Thankfully Gracie just shook her head and turned back toward the stove.

Leah stepped out onto the back porch, which was little more than a handful of two-by-fours nailed to the back of the cabin. Being on it would offer them a little privacy while Gracie and Peter were inside, but not enough for peace of mind. Leah stepped out into the grass and walked a few more feet into the yard.

"Are you going to tell me why you wanted to come out here?" Jamie asked. "If this is about Deborah, I can explain."

Leah raised her gaze to his. "It's not about Deborah. Well, it is, but it's not." She shook her head.

"You're not quite making sense," he said in a gentlemanly tone.

Suddenly, what had seemed like a good idea thirty seconds ago didn't seem quite so brilliant. But she had to tell him. He had to know.

"Peter talked."

He looked as if all the air had been sucked out of his lungs. "What?" A smile toyed with the corners of his lips, but didn't quite come to fruition. It was as if he wanted to be happy, but was scared to allow himself to be until he heard her say those words again.

"Peter talked. Inside. When we were cooking."

Jamie's face split into a wide grin. "That's good! That's wonderful!" He looked ready to dance a jig right there on his tiny porch. It was what he had been waiting for, and it would mean he got to keep Peter with him in Pontotoc. That was what they both needed.

He grabbed her hands, his joy infectious. "Do you know what this means?"

Leah couldn't help but smile. "I do."

"What did he say?"

"He said . . ."

Jamie patiently waited.

How could she tell him that Peter didn't like Deborah? It would look as if perhaps she had put those words in his mouth, or at the very least, Jamie would know they had been talking about her in front of the boy. She took a deep breath. He could be mad all he wanted. Peter had spoken for the first time in months, and that was what they had to keep in mind. "He said he didn't like Deborah."

If Jamie found the news surprising, it didn't show in his expression "That's what he said?"

Leah nodded. "Listen, Jamie, I know that's strange, but well, that's what he said."

Jamie's joy seemed to leak out of him like air from a pinpricked balloon.

"No. It's okay. The important thing is he spoke, right?"

Leah gave him an encouraging smile. "That's right. Now we know he can speak, but something is making him not to want to." Unless it was important enough to say. And for some reason he had chosen his dislike of Jamie's ex-fiancée on which to break his silence. Did it mean that much to him?

And what did that do to their relationship?

It wasn't any of her concern, except that she and Jamie might have had something special if things could have been different. But things weren't different, and she had seen the intimate goodbye between Jamie and Deborah. Now Peter was talking, sort of. Would Jamie take him back to Ethridge now?

"Is that all?" Jamie asked.

"He said it twice." That didn't come out exactly the way she thought. She meant for it to be encouraging.

"And nothing else?"

"I'd tried to get him to talk, but he wouldn't." Now she sounded like a jealous liar.

"It's a start, *jah?*"

Leah smiled. "That's right. It's a start." So why did her heart feel like it was breaking in two?

"Will you and Gracie stay and eat?" Jamie asked as they headed back into the house.

Leah stopped, just long enough for him to wonder why

the question needed such contemplation. "I probably should be getting back home."

"Brandon?"

"Yeah. He'll be home soon. He went to the library to study for a test with Shelly."

Gracie turned as they came into the kitchen.

"You don't have to go, you know."

"Go where?" Gracie asked.

"Home."

"I thought you would come back to the house," Gracie said.

"I thought the two of you would stay here and eat."

Leah shook her head. "Why would we do that?"

He made a gesture with his arm, encompassing all the bubbling pots and waiting food. "You cooked enough for an army."

"Mamm just wanted you to have food for the week," she explained.

"An army could never eat this much," Gracie said with a laugh. "But seriously, we wanted you to have it for later."

Jamie gave a quick nod. "I would bet that we can sit down and eat until we're so full we think we'll pop, and there would still be enough left for the rest of the week. What do you say, Peter? You want the girls to stay and eat with us?" He leaned a little closer to the boy. "And remember what I told you. Never give up a chance to eat dinner with a beautiful girl."

Peter nodded enthusiastically, then scooped up his horses and Popsicle stick fences and deposited them in the basket by the couch. He dusted his hands, then stood there, waiting for the grown-ups' decision.

"You wouldn't want to disappoint a little boy, would you?" Jamie looked at Gracie and Leah in turn. They didn't come better than these two. Gracie always helpful. Leah smart as a whip and able to tell it like it is. No matter what happened between him and Leah, he felt blessed to call both of them friend. "Come on," he coaxed. "Don't make us eat all by ourselves."

"As long as you're okay with that," Gracie said.

"I'm okay with it," Jamie said. "Are you okay with it?"

So one or two times they had discussed courting. But he hadn't even held her hand. It wasn't like him and Deborah. Not at all. And Leah—he would do almost anything to spend more time with her. How else was he going to convince her to quit being stubborn and continue on the way God had intended her to be: Amish?

"Sure." Gracie flashed him a quick smile.

Jamie turned to Leah. What could she say but yes?

"Fine." She crossed her arms and shook her head. "But right after supper, I have to go home."

Peter sat quietly throughout the entire meal. Jamie wanted to talk to him about speaking to Leah and Gracie, but he felt that was a conversation better had when they were alone. For now, Jamie pretended he knew nothing as he ate, talked, and otherwise carried on as he normally would. He asked Peter the same questions he would have regardless, and Peter answered them in his silent way.

What would make a child not speak? Or speak once, only negative words, and not speak again? It was baffling. Unless Peter talked again, Jamie had no proof that he was speaking at all. Jamie couldn't go back to Sally's parents and tell them that Peter had said something. Until Peter was ready to talk to everyone, it was as if he hadn't spoken and all.

"Don't you think, Jamie?" Gracie asked.

Jamie pulled himself from his own thoughts and switched

his attention to his blond dinner companion. "What was that?"

"The weddings are fixing to start," Gracie said. "I think it would be more fun if they were held throughout the year, don't you?"

"I don't know. I never really thought about it, I guess."

"Well, I for one think it's better to have them year-round," Gracie said. "Like the *Englisch* do." She turned her attention to her cousin. "Leah?"

Leah looked up and shook her head. "Don't get me involved in this."

"I'm just saying," Gracie said. "Sometimes you have two weddings to go to in one day, and you have to choose one over the other. If we had them year-round and maybe on days other than Tuesdays and Thursdays, maybe people would be able to attend all the weddings they wanted."

"Or maybe not, because they have work to do in June," Leah said.

"Maybe." Gracie tilted her head to one side as if seriously contemplating the matter.

Jamie envied her in that moment. He wished he had nothing more pressing to worry about than on what days Amish weddings were held, and in what month. He chanced a look back over to Peter, who sat eating his food, quiet as usual. Why had he picked today to speak? And why about Deborah? Was Peter just getting more comfortable around Leah and Gracie? Maybe. But it didn't make sense. He had been with Jamie longer and hadn't spoken in front of him. But tonight, after supper was eaten and the mess cleaned up, he was going to have a long talk with Peter. And he could only hope that Peter would talk back.

"I think we should use flowers too," Gracie said. "I mean, you spend all that time growing and nurturing them and watering them in this heat. It only makes sense to benefit from your efforts."

"I don't know anyone who has flowers like that," Leah pointed out. They were absent for the very reasons Gracie stated. It was too hot and too much work for something that couldn't be eaten.

"What's wrong with flowers?" Gracie continued as if Leah hadn't spoken. "They're not vain or prideful. Are they?" She looked from Leah to Jamie and back again

"Are you thinking of getting married, Gracie?" Jamie asked. He thought he'd made himself clear when he went back on his intentions to court. But maybe she hadn't understood.

Gracie shook her head. "Gracious, no." She folded her napkin into her lap with a little too much attention to detail. "I'm just talking. But our cousin is getting married. In a couple of weeks."

"*Jah?*" He swiveled his attention between the cousins. Gracie seemed a little too bright, a little too talkative and chipper, while Leah seemed almost sullen in her silence. Neither one was acting like herself. What did it mean? That he shouldn't've invited them to supper? Or perhaps he should figure out a way to change the subject.

"Abby. That's our cousin. She's marrying Leah's old flame." Gracie leaned closer to Jamie as she talked, then let out a giggle.

"That was a long time ago," Leah said. But a telling flush of pink rose into her cheeks.

"Really? Your cousin's marrying your old boyfriend?"

Leah sighed. "That was fifteen years ago and another marriage for him."

So whatever had been between them was long gone? Then why did she look so wistful? Did she still harbor feelings for him?

Hannah had returned after fifteen years and gotten back with her lost love. Maybe Leah'd been hoping for the same. They might look different on the outside and have different likes and dislikes. They were even members of different churches. But they were sisters—*twin* sisters.

"I'm going to be an attendant," Gracie said. "Always an attendant." Then her attitude shifted from solemn back into high gear. "You are coming, aren't you, Leah?"

Leah shook her head. "I don't think that's a good idea."

"Of course it's a good idea. She's our cousin."

"It might be awkward."

"Only if you let it," Gracie returned.

"Not if you go with someone. Like a date."

Gracie and Leah swung their attention to him. It was a little unnerving having their stares on him so intense. He was beginning to wonder if they'd forgotten he was at the table.

"Gracious me," Gracie said. "That's a great idea."

But Leah was already shaking her head. "It's not a great idea. It's a bad idea."

"It's growing on me," Gracie said.

"Then go take a bath," Leah said through clenched teeth.

He understood her reluctance, and yet he didn't. Being with her was like being on one of those rides at the fair, the ones shaped like a ball cut in half. They went around in a circle until a body couldn't stand up once the ride stopped. They had argued, then disagreed, they had helped each other, then decided to court, she called it off, and now he was offering to be her date at her ex-boyfriend's wedding. *Jah*, dizzying was right.

"It doesn't have to be that kind of date," he amended. The main thing was to get her to go with him. How could he convince her that they were meant for each other if he didn't get to spend any time with her?

"I said I wasn't even going," Leah said.

"This way you can't *not* go."

Leah seemed to think about it an eternity. She looked as if she was about to decline. He had to do something.

"Listen, I came down here, and I didn't know anyone. Well, except for your parents, and I barely knew them. Peter didn't know anyone at all. This community has embraced us the entire time we've been here. But more than that, I feel very fortunate to call the two of you friend. And if friends can't help one another . . . well, then, what good is there?"

He could tell the moment her resolve weakened. He didn't know what caused the shift. It could be that she missed the Amish ways. Or perhaps she just missed being with her family and doing all the things they had done once before. It had to be hard going away Amish and coming back Mennonite. But he had to show her just how easy it would be, how *great* it would be when she joined the Amish church.

"As friends?" Leah pinned him with a quick stare.

"Of course." But he crossed his fingers under the table, as he had done as a child.

"Then I would be happy to." She smiled, and when she smiled like that, Jamie knew he could promise her the world and not think twice about it.

All in all, it was an enjoyable evening as far as Jamie was concerned. Peter seemed to have a good time as well, though he didn't speak again. Jamie didn't have any doubts that he had talked to Leah; she wouldn't lie to him about something so important, or about anything, really. But he was beginning to wonder if she had heard something else and not his nephew's voice.

"And the little rabbit and all her rabbit friends lived in

the hollowed-out log for the rest of their days. The end."
Jamie closed the book and brushed the hair back from
Peter's face.

"Good night," he said, kissing the boy's forehead. He
wanted to scoop him up and hold him so close he would
have to speak to protest being held so tight, but Jamie refrained. He loved the boy with all his heart, but he knew
Peter needed love and space. It was a tough combination.

Jamie pulled the covers up under Peter's chin, knowing
that before he sat down in the front room, the boy would
have already kicked the covers to the bottom of the bed.
Jamie didn't know why he bothered, other than he felt he
had to tuck Peter in. Wasn't that what a good parent did?
One of his parents tucked him in every night until he was
ten years old and he asked them to stop. He'd had good
parents. And he in turn wanted to be one as well.

"Sleep tight," he murmured and headed for the door.
Something stopped him there, and he turned around. Jamie
sucked in a breath and made his way back over to the bed.
"I hope you know you can talk to me," he said into the
darkness. "I love you, and I want you to be able to tell me
everything."

Only silence met his words.

"I know these last few months have been hard on you.
Harder than any of us know. But I want you to believe
that I have your best interests in mind. Everything I do, I
do for you."

There was a shift in the bed, then a little hand reached
out to him, little fingers curving around his own.

Jamie nearly wept. Peter was there; he was still in there
somewhere. He just had no idea how to pull him out of it.

He squeezed Peter's fingers, then released his hand to
leave the room. Maybe prayer. More prayer. The Bible said
prayer was the answer to everything, and he had to believe
it was true.

Chapter Eleven

If Jamie had to guess, he would've said that sometime around midnight Peter crept into his room. It was the same as always. Jamie had become a light sleeper since taking on the care of Peter. He had always heard mothers talk about "*mamm* hearing," when the smallest sound in the house or one of their children stirring would wake them in the middle of the night. He wondered how women with ten or twelve kids did it, but he supposed the women got used to it. He was getting used to the other things. Like Peter sneaking into his room, crawling in bed beside him, and sleeping the rest of the night curled up next to him. He didn't mind it; in fact it was sort of a comfort to have Peter there close. He could hear his even breathing, the small shuddering sighs, and he could feel the silk of the boy's hair. He had promised to protect Peter, to care for him now and always, and it seemed like a much easier task if Peter was next to him.

"Come on," he urged. The only sound to meet his ears was the pat of Peter's bare feet as he loped across the plank floor. A dip in the mattress, the squeak of the springs, and then Peter was beside him, snuggling down in the crook of his arm like he was born to do just that, like this was his place and no one else's.

Jamie would always have room for Peter right there beside him, until the time when Peter didn't need it anymore. If he needed it for the rest of his life, so be it. Peter came first, and any woman he decided to marry would have to accept that. One day he hoped to have a relationship. They could work around this crazy sleeping arrangement Peter had developed. But for now, Jamie was just happy to have the boy at his side. Never mind that they had just built a room onto the house so Peter would have his own space. It didn't matter that he had his toys in there, his writing tablet, the wooden tractor Leah had given him, and all the other treasures he managed to save. No, this was what was important to Peter. And it always would be. Jamie knew one thing was certain. Until he found someone who loved the boy the way he did, this was the way it would remain.

"Jamie, where's the dog?" Leah asked the following day. She hadn't added anything else—no sweet greeting, or those niceties that people toss around like cheap confetti. Something that Jamie had said about the night of the accident had tickled her brain until she couldn't stand it anymore. This morning she had realized what it was. She scooted out of the shop as soon as she could, saying a little prayer along the way that she would get to Jamie's before Peter came home from school. This was a conversation best held between the two of them alone.

"What dog?"

"When you told me about the accident that killed Peter's parents, you told me that Peter had a dog. He was in the barn with her the night of the fire. What happened to his dog?"

His mouth turned grim. "Goldie ran into the house after Peter." He shook his head.

Leah's heart fell to her toes. The boy had lost everything. His family, his sense of security, and his faithful dog.

"Why do you ask?"

"I thought maybe if you brought Peter's dog down here that he might come around a little faster. You know, start to heal."

"That isn't possible."

"You could get him a new dog." The idea rushed from her like clear water from a mountain spring. Of course! The answer was so simple, and it had been just out of sight this entire time.

"I can't get a dog."

"Of course you can." The more she thought about it, the more perfect the idea became. "I read this article the other day about therapy dogs."

"Therapy dogs?" Jamie did not look convinced. But she had known going into this that he was a stubborn man. He would hold on to his conservative ideals with both hands if need be. But she could convince him. After all, he wanted what was best for Peter.

"Yes." She nodded enthusiastically, unable to contain her excitement. "They use dogs for all kinds of things. They have dogs that can tell if a person is about to have a seizure and ones to help the blind."

"I don't understand how this will help Peter. He can see, and he doesn't have seizures. The dog surely can't speak for him."

"But he can care for the dog, and he'll have his sense of place back. Don't you see?"

"I'm trying."

"It's like this." Leah pulled him over to the house and sat on the edge of the porch. "Peter lost everything, even his dog. Now you are trying to be the family he lost."

"And you think he needs a replacement dog."

"Something like that." But when he said it that way, it seemed crazy at best.

"I don't know." He shook his head and kicked at a clod of dirt to the left of his foot. He had on shoes, which meant he had been out running errands, or maybe even working. Had he been to see Deborah?

"Promise me you'll think about it."

He nodded, though she could see the reluctance. The idea was brilliant, and with a little help, she was sure she could get Jamie to see it her way.

She pushed herself up from the porch and started back to her car. "I've got to go," she said. "I left Brandon at the shop all alone."

"I thought he only worked alone on Tuesdays."

"He works with Shelly on Tuesdays."

"I see."

Leah opened the car door and slid behind the wheel, ideas spinning in her head. A dog was just what Peter needed. Maybe not a new golden retriever, but another faithful, loyal dog he could help care for. It would give his life more purpose, new direction, and a whole lot of doggy kisses. The way she did the math, it was a perfect equation all around. "I'll see you."

He gave a small wave as she started the car.

"And Leah? Thanks for not bringing a dog out here today."

She smiled. "Next time you might not be so lucky."

Jamie watched as Leah pulled her car out of the drive and headed back for town. Was she right? Did Peter need another dog as a companion and friend? Would it make a difference? More than anything, he needed a difference for Peter, but with everything happening, and his deadline to have Peter speaking quickly approaching, he was afraid what he needed bordered on a miracle. And though dogs were great, he had never seen one bring forth a miracle.

"Everybody is going to be there." Gracie looked to Hannah for confirmation. That in itself didn't bother Leah, but the look her sister sent back did. Why did she get the feeling they were trying to set her up?

"Everybody?" she asked, looking from one to the other.

Hannah and Gracie nodded.

"Including Sarah Hostetler?"

Clearly that was not the name Gracie had been expecting. "Why Sarah?"

"Because if Sarah is there, then I'm sure her guest will be in tow."

"Guest?" Hannah's expression was all too innocent.

"One Deborah King from Ethridge."

"I wouldn't know why," Gracie mused. "It's not like she's in our group or anything. She wouldn't be invited."

"I'm not in the group," Leah pointed out.

"That's different." With a quick flick of one hand, Hannah whisked her words away.

"Did you invite Jamie?"

"No," Hannah said, while at the same time, Gracie said, "Of course."

"Which is it?"

"He'll be there," Hannah said.

If he was going to be there, so would Deborah. And the whole thing was just too confusing. Leah saw what she saw, and yet Jamie continued to act like one day he hoped there could be something between the two of them. And yet she could see no way that they could overcome their differences.

"I'll pass." As much as she hated it, he would be better off with someone like Deborah. Even better, someone like Gracie, but that might just be weird now.

"Are you afraid?" Hannah asked, a mischievous light shining in her hazel eyes.

"No," she scoffed.

"I think you are. What do you think, Gracie?"

Gracie nodded. "Looks that way to me."

Leah knew Gracie was just going along with Hannah, but still . . .

"Quit," she said. "I'm not afraid. I'd just rather not go and have to watch the two of them all night."

"We don't even know if either one of them is going to be there," her sister said.

"Who says anything is going to be between the two of them?" Gracie asked.

"Chicken," Hannah added.

"Fine," Leah said. "I'll go, but—"

"No buts," Hannah said. "Just relax and have fun."

"An ice-cream party?" Leah asked. "Isn't it a little late in the year for that?"

"It's never too late in the year for ice cream," Gracie explained.

"Quit complaining," Hannah said as she pulled the buggy to a stop next to the line of carriages waiting for their owners. "It's supposed to be fun."

It might be if it wasn't going to end up heartbreaking. Jamie had told her that it was over between him and Deborah. But she had seen their goodbye last Sunday. It had been nearly a week, and the image was as etched in her mind as if it had been there since time began. One thing was certain: Jamie and Deborah might have a few problems, but it would be no time at all before they got those worked out.

And poor Peter, who didn't like Deborah, would end up with her as a mother. Leah made a note to say a prayer for

Peter to gain peace where Deborah was concerned. He had been through too much to let this stop him.

"Get that sack," Hannah ordered as Leah crawled from the back of the buggy.

She handed the bag out to her sister, then swung down from the carriage. "What's in it?"

"We were all supposed to bring our favorite ice-cream toppings. I suppose we'll set them all out and make our own sundaes."

Oh, joy. The ice cream would be good, and Leah had no problem with most toppings, but how was she supposed to watch everyone eating their ice cream and enjoying themselves when she would rather be at home?

Sulking.

She was not sulking. She was merely being aware. Some things didn't work out the way a person wanted them to. Her and Jamie? They were definitely one of those things.

"How did I let you talk me into this?" Leah asked as they headed across the yard. Until that moment, Leah hadn't realized where they were: Sarah Hostetler's house. Any hope that Deborah wouldn't be at the party was gone in an instant. Deborah was staying with Sarah; of course she would be invited. With the way Leah's luck was going, Deborah was probably the guest of honor.

"You know you wanted to come," Hannah said.

"Why didn't you ride with Aaron?" Why hadn't she thought of this before? The setup stench was beginning to reek.

"He was coming with Jamie."

Of course.

Leah sighed. She wished she had insisted she bring her car. That way she could make an early escape. As it was now, she was going to need more ice cream than she had ever needed in her life.

* * *

"Okay, everybody, listen up." Sarah Hostetler raised her hands above her head and clapped them to get everyone's attention. The whole of the group stood in Sarah's large kitchen-dining room area, awaiting party instructions. "Now I know that many of you have been to ice-cream parties before, but this one is different. This is an ice cream *exchange*. First, you'll draw a name out of the jar. If you get your own name, you have to draw again. Yes, I'm talking to you, Daniel Hostetler." Laughter rose all around.

Leah shifted from one foot to the other and wondered yet again how she had managed to get into this mess. She was getting her bowl of ice cream, wolfing it down at the risk of brain freeze, then demanding that Hannah take her home.

"Once you get your name, do not tell anybody who you have. Draw five pieces of paper out of the next jar, and those will be the toppings that go on the sundae."

"You don't think we can pick out our own ice-cream toppings?" one of the males asked. Leah thought it was Sam Yoder, Sarah's brother.

"I surely don't, brother. You'll pick five pieces of paper from the second jar, and that's how you'll prepare your sundae."

"You already said that," someone grumbled. Most likely Sam again.

Sarah frowned, but didn't return the volley. "Once your sundae is complete, you find the person whose name you got and present them with their sundae. Are you ready? Go!"

There was a flurry of fabric as participants moved toward the jars to draw out their name and toppings. Leah hung back. She wasn't a part of the group, not really, so she wanted everyone else to have their turn first.

She hadn't seen Jamie since she arrived. Nor had she seen Aaron. Hannah disappeared first thing to find him, leaving Leah and Gracie to fend for themselves.

"I don't think he's here." Disappointment colored Gracie's voice.

"Who?"

She shot Leah a sideways smile. "Never mind. Here he comes."

Leah looked behind her. Jamie was making his way toward them, his destination clear.

Heavens, he was handsome. Add in his generous heart, and she could almost overlook that he was a conservative Amish. Almost. There was that little matter of the church.

"I guess this is the happening place to be, *jah?*" he asked, glancing around at the crowd of people.

Gracie followed his gaze with her own. "Oh, it's always like this when we get together."

Leah remembered all those singings and trips. The community was close and supportive. They spent a lot of time together, and as they grew so did the group, adding husbands and wives into the mix.

"It wasn't that night at Aaron's. There were only about five people there."

Gracie turned a bright shade of pink. "That's because it really wasn't a group function."

Leah could almost see when her words hit home with Jamie. "Oh," he said slowly. "I get it. And that's why you didn't come."

"I didn't want it to be so obvious that they were trying to set us up. It's—" She shook her head.

"What?" Leah asked.

"It's embarrassing."

"You don't want to tell us?" Jamie guessed.

"No, that everybody tries to set me up and it never seems to take."

"Did you three get your names?" Sarah Hostetler breezed up, stopping when she saw nothing in their hands.

"Not yet," Leah said.

"No time like now." Sarah grabbed the women by one arm each and urged them toward the jars. "You too, Jamie," she tossed over one shoulder.

Leah caught the tiniest of smiles playing around his lips, then she turned back front. It was going to be one interesting evening.

"There you are."

Jamie cringed at the words, or rather at the sound of her voice. "Deborah." He spun round to face her, pasting on a smile he hoped looked sincere. He wanted to break it off with her, not destroy her self-worth. But he was beginning to wonder if the two were one and the same.

"I've got your ice-cream sundae." She held the bowl up as if to entice him with her efforts. Her smile was dazzling. Everyone was milling around finding the person they had made the sundae for and accepting their own. The pairings were odd. Aaron had drawn Sam Yoder's name, and Hannah was handing off her concoction to their hostess herself.

He cleared his throat. "You, uh, drew my name?" It was almost a question.

"Very lucky, I'd say." Her smile widened, if that was even possible.

"Very lucky," he murmured in return.

Deborah leaned in a bit closer. "I drew the papers for the toppings, but didn't use them. I know what you like on ice cream, so I got those toppings instead."

Not exactly the purpose of the activity. At least as far as he could tell. Wasn't this about talking to other people? Trying new things? Getting out of the box?

"That's uh . . . great," he finally said.

"Here's your ice cream," Leah said, stopping short when she saw the two of them standing together.

Deborah's hand fluttered to her chest. "My ice cream?" she gushed.

"Actually it's . . . Jamie's." Her words trailed off as she noticed the ice cream he already held. "Is that for someone else?"

He let out a small cough. One of them hadn't drawn his name out of the jar, and he had a feeling it wasn't Leah. "It's mine."

A frown puckered her brow. "Oh."

"Isn't that something?" Deborah said. "Sarah must have put Jamie's name in twice. Or maybe it was Sam. I think he was in charge of the names."

"That's something, all right," Leah muttered.

Not that he could blame her. It was a little awkward being presented with two sundaes and knowing full well that Deborah hadn't pulled his name from the jar.

Deborah peered into the bowl Leah still held. "You drew toppings, didn't you?" She wrinkled her nose. "I only say that because of the pineapple. Jamie hates pineapple."

He wouldn't go that far. He would say that it wasn't his favorite, but it had been a while since he had eaten any; maybe it was time to try it again.

Leah's expression was unreadable. He wasn't sure if she wanted to dump the ice cream on his head or over Deborah's. He was leaning toward Deborah.

"Did you not get an ice cream, Leah?" he asked. Maybe if he changed the subject . . .

"It's okay," Leah said. "You don't have to eat it." She spun on one heel and marched away.

"Nice going," Gracie said. He had been so busy trying to smooth over ruffled feathers that he hadn't even seen her arrive. "Here." She thrust one of the sundaes she held toward Deborah.

She accepted it, albeit reluctantly. "This is mine?" By the tone of her voice, anyone walking by would think it was laced with poison.

"I drew your name," Gracie explained. "Now take this so I can go see about my cousin."

Jamie thrust his ice cream at her instead. "I'll check on her."

"But—" Deborah said, but he was already walking away.

It took a very long five minutes to find her. Everyone was milling around, and with the constant shift of bodies he had no means of navigation. Finally, he caught her by the front door. She looked ready to bolt.

"Leah," he called.

She shook her head. "Don't. Just don't."

"I'm sorry. I wanted to come here and spend a little time with you." They couldn't exactly date, or even call it dating, but he had to have a way to see her, talk to her, get to know her better. He had to have a way to show her everything she was missing and all she could gain by joining the Amish church.

"It's okay. Go see Deborah. I'm leaving." She escaped out the door before he could utter another word.

She shut the door behind her, leaving him to rattle the doorknob before he finally got the thing open. "Leah," he called, but she was already striding across the yard. He took off after her.

He caught her with ease, touching her arm to stop her. She didn't turn around, so he walked in front of her so he could see her face. The sun was starting to set, painting the sky pink and orange as it descended. It wouldn't be much longer before everyone would start leaving so they could get home before it went down completely.

"I'm sorry," he said. "I didn't know she was going to be here. Nor did I realize this would hurt you so."

"It's not that, Jamie. Not at all."

"Then what is it?"

She gestured toward the house, a wild, flailing motion with one arm. "That's where you belong. Not with me. But there with the Amish. Deborah's little ice-cream stunt only brought home what I already knew. I don't belong here, and you do. You belong with Deborah."

He blinked. That was about as far from what he had expected her to say as possible. "I belong with Deborah?"

She shook her head. "That's not what I mean. You should court someone you will be able to ask to marry you. Not a Mennonite like me."

He wanted to tell her how easy it would be to change that, but he kept his mouth shut. She knew. Her sister was following that path now, and Leah could too, but he wanted it to be her idea, her plan. "Peter doesn't like her," he said. Not the best argument for his case, but it was out there, and he had to go with it.

"I should have never told you he said that."

He took a step closer, clasping his hands on her arms just above the bend of her elbows. "Do you always wear long sleeves?" he asked, unsure of where the question had come from.

"Most times."

"Even in the summer heat?"

She shrugged. "I did when I was Amish."

That was true, but when she was Amish, her sleeves were full and didn't hang so close to her skin. These T-shirts were snug, but still very modest. She thought she was liberal for a Plain woman, but he knew that deep down she was as conservative as he was. Well, almost.

"I'm sorry I told you Peter said that about Deborah," she finally said.

"I'm glad you told me. Though Peter has made his feelings known without words."

She frowned and took a step back, forcing him to follow or release her. He opted for the latter. It was safer by far.

"Why would you marry someone Peter hates?" she asked.

"Why would you tell me to?" he returned. "And *hate* is such a strong word."

One dark brow raised in disbelief.

"I'm not marrying Deborah, though I can't seem to convince her of that."

She laughed. That had to be a good sign.

"I'm not marrying anybody right now," he continued. "This whole mess with Gracie just showed me that I don't want a marriage like that. I want to marry for love. Peter deserves that. I deserve that." It was mostly the truth. He wanted to marry Leah for love. He just had to convince her to return to her roots and love him back.

"You do," she said, her voice thick. "We all do."

Leah swallowed back her tears and watched Jamie's expression for any sort of change. She wasn't sure what she was expecting, just . . . something.

"Thanks for the explanation," she said. "If you see my sister, tell her I walked home."

"You can't walk home."

"I know the way."

"It'll be dark before you get halfway there."

She looked back at the house. "I'm not going back in there." She didn't belong there. She had felt every difference. She hadn't thought it would be like that. But at her parents' house, things weren't like that. She didn't notice the differences in their clothing, her hair, her head covering. But here? She noticed it all. She was the odd man out, and it didn't sit well.

"I'll drive you home." He took her elbow again and

started toward the row of buggies. She hated it when he grabbed her like that. Hated it and loved it, all in the same moment. His fingers left little tingling trails of joy, and at the same time her reaction was for nothing. There could never be anything between them.

Why, Lord? Why torture me this way? What lesson do You want me to learn?

"How will Aaron get home?" She tried digging in her feet, but she didn't want to resist—not that badly anyway. She stumbled along behind him, waiting for his answer.

"He's a smart man. He'll figure it out."

"You're going to take his buggy?"

"It's my buggy."

She couldn't argue with that. And chances were Aaron would come out with Hannah, see that his ride was gone, realize what had happened, and catch a ride with his intended.

"Don't you think we should tell someone that we're leaving?" Sarah maybe.

He stopped. "Do you honestly want to go back in there?"

Leah nodded. "Let's go."

They were halfway home before her words sank in. "You really don't think you belong with the Amish?" That could be a problem for his plans.

"I left, remember?"

"That doesn't mean you don't belong. This is where you grew up." How could she not belong to that?

"It doesn't mean anything. Not after you leave."

He wanted to ask her to explain, but he was afraid that if he did, she would stop answering altogether. "What about Hannah?"

"Hannah's different."

He wasn't sure how, but he wanted to understand. "How is it different for her?"

"She wanted to come back not long after we left, but she heard that Aaron was already courting someone else. She figured that if he could find somebody else so quickly, that maybe he never really loved her to begin with."

"But he did."

"That's right. And she's never stopped loving him. Now Hannah sees all the wasted time, all the years they could have been together but weren't. She would walk through fire to be with him."

Jamie wanted a love like that. He had never really thought about it before. Not until he met Leah Gingerich. "What about you?"

"I like Aaron. I always have. But I'm not walking through anything other than grass for him."

He swayed and bumped their shoulders together as they rode along. "That's not what I mean."

"I know."

"So why didn't you come back?" Had her love also been seeing someone else?

"When Hannah decided not to go back home, well, I couldn't *leave* her. I never wanted to jump the fence to begin with. I only did it to help her. And I couldn't do that if we lived in two different places."

"I have a feeling that's not the end of the story."

She gave a half shrug. "We got into a terrible argument. She disappeared, and that was that."

"And that's when you joined the Mennonites."

"I traveled a bit, went on a few mission trips overseas. *That's* when I found the Mennonites."

"You met them and knew you were home?"

"Sort of." She stared off at nothing. The sun was about down, and he couldn't see her face in the fading light. But her tone was wistful, full of wonder and awe. "The Mennonites are special. They are like the Amish, but not. I'm not making any sense, am I?"

"Not much." He turned the buggy onto the lane that led to her parents' house. In a few short minutes, they would be there. He would take his buggy to his cabin, and she would get into her car and head back to town.

"You just have to spend some time with them to understand," she said. Still not much by way of an explanation. And he wanted one. He needed it.

"So invite me." The words slipped so easily from his lips.

"What?" She seemed almost as surprised by his words as he was.

"Invite me to an event and let me see how they are." He wanted to know what was so special about them it could keep her away from her born heritage. Maybe if he saw it, he would start to understand for himself.

"There's a rock painting event Monday night."

He stopped, looked in her direction for a moment. She seemed serious enough, but it was starting to get dark. "Rock painting?"

She nodded. "I wasn't going to go, but we can take Peter with us. That might be good for him."

"Hold on a minute. What's a rock painting event?"

"The church is painting Bible verses on rocks to put out for people to find."

"And people are just going to find them?" He couldn't wrap his mind around the concept. The road they were traveling was composed of rocks. Rocks and rocks and rocks. How would anyone find a special one with a Bible verse painted on it in all the rocks?

"Well, yeah. I mean, there are groups and individuals who do this all over. They even have sites online to help people find them. Pastor Joel thought that since *Englischers* are already looking for the rocks, we could use it as part of our ministry."

"The verses are a message?"

"Right."

"And that's all you paint on them?"

"As far as I know, you can paint them however you like, as long as there's a verse on it."

"Sounds like fun." And strangely enough, it did. "Okay," he said, with more confidence than he felt. "Monday night, we paint rocks."

Chapter Twelve

How did that backfire on her? She hadn't had any intentions of inviting Jamie anywhere, and here they were setting a date for their next not-date. She couldn't date him. She wasn't a member of the church, but she didn't know what else to call it other than a date.

She stiffened her resolve. She would just have to keep it all in perspective. She was doing this to show him what her church was all about. This was for Peter, who needed to see that life was still good, fun, and worthy. Plus, it would be beneficial for them all to participate in such a satisfying and uplifting endeavor. It was that and nothing more. A not-date between almost-friends and a little boy who needed hope.

Jamie pulled his buggy close to the house. The sun was almost down, and the shadows had already started creeping across the land.

"Thank you for bringing me home." She had started to climb down when Jamie stopped her.

"Don't," he said. "Just sit with me for a minute more."

"It's about dark. You're not going to have any light to get up to your house."

"Let me worry about that."

Why did he want to sit with her? She felt that she was in dangerous territory. Too much could happen on an Indian summer evening as the sun disappeared. "I need to go in." Her voice was near breathless, as if she had been running a great distance.

"I want to kiss you," he admitted.

Her heart soared, then immediately fell. "That's not a good idea."

"It sounds like a great idea to me."

"Jamie—" But she had no way to finish that sentence. She wanted to kiss him, but she knew how useless it was. How damaging. It would only make things harder for them in the future. "We've already talked about this."

"You don't want to kiss me?"

She shook her head. How were they even having this conversation? "Wanting to has nothing to do with this."

"So you do want to kiss me."

"Jamie, please." But she couldn't continue. "You're making this harder than it has to be."

"You know, I could say the same thing about you."

"Me?"

"Why are you fighting this so hard?"

"Why am I . . . Jamie, anything we could have between us will not be able to last."

"Only if you keep looking at it like it's impossible."

"It *is* impossible." She was beginning to regret inviting him to the rock painting event next week. He was reading more into it than could ever be.

"See? There you go again."

"Mennonite. Amish." She pointed toward herself, then him.

"I think we both already know that."

"Amish and Mennonite don't date." Shouldn't fall in love; couldn't get married.

"Says who?"

"Says the *Ordn*—" This was getting them nowhere. "Forget it." She pulled away and climbed down from the carriage. "I will not kiss you. Not now. Not in the future."

She stalked toward her car, not turning around as he spoke one last time.

"So it's a maybe, then?"

Jamie watched as Leah flounced toward her car as if her walk alone would prove her point.

He bit back a chuckle as she scrambled with the door, finally managing to get it open. She hopped inside as if it offered protection from all worries and concerns.

Maybe this hadn't been the best way to woo her, but he was running out of ideas where she was concerned. She was smart and savvy, different from any other woman he had met.

He flicked the reins and started his horse in motion once again. He still had to get home, brush down the horse, and thank Libby Gingerich for sitting with Peter tonight. Peter had taken best to Leah, but right after her was Jim and Anna's oldest, and the last couple of weeks she had become his go-to sitter when he needed to go out. He hated leaving the boy, but since he was out doing his best to find the child a mother, he pushed his guilt aside and went about his business.

Except Leah was proving to be harder to crack than he had ever imagined. Still, she had invited him out on Tuesday. That had to mean something.

Rock painting didn't sound particularly exciting, but spending time with her and Peter . . . well, he couldn't find anything wrong with that plan.

* * *

Peter snuggled a little closer into Jamie's side and laid his head on his shoulder. Jamie gently nudged him, doing his best to stir him awake without letting anyone around them know that Peter was about to fall asleep sitting there.

Like he would be the only one to fall asleep in church. Les Byler usually fell asleep sometime after the first prayer and softly snored until the last one was given. Of course, Les was older than dirt and had served the church his entire ninety-plus years. Jamie might be new to Pontotoc, but he knew people in Ethridge who knew Les, and everyone said the same thing. The man might fall asleep sitting up on his bench, but he knew more about the Bible than the minister, the bishop, and both preachers rolled into one.

Peter's head softly collided with his shoulder once again. Jamie gently roused the boy. He understood. He remembered nodding off from time to time in church himself. But he'd had Joseph there to nudge him in the ribs, sometimes not-so-gently, to keep him awake. Jamie missed his brother so much. Not that Jamie had had enough time to grieve. He'd barely gotten the news before he had to make the arrangements for the funeral. After that, he'd been involved in trying to do what was best for his nephew. Then moving. And . . .

Jamie closed his eyes as the truth washed over him. He hadn't had time at all to grieve for his brother. He hadn't had time to make his peace. Maybe that was something he needed to correct, and soon. Maybe it was time for him and Peter to travel back to Ethridge and visit the graves of Joseph, Sally, and Ellie Stoltzfus. He and Peter both could use a little more closure before starting this second new phase in their lives.

Jamie opened his eyes and did his best to focus on what the minister was saying. Strawberry Dan Swartzentruber was about the driest man he had ever heard speak. But

Jamie tried to be fair. Strawberry Dan took his time when speaking, drawing out each word and making it hard to follow along at times.

He was a lot like Johnny Zook, back in his home district. Jamie knew that Johnny had been terrified to take his appointment as preacher. He wasn't big on getting up in front of a crowd. But since the church elders were chosen by God, they had to trust that the Lord knew what He was doing. Though Jamie supposed there was one in every district— one preacher who bored everyone to tears.

And his sleepiness had nothing to do with Leah Gingerich. He hadn't lain awake half the night wondering how he was going to convince her that they should be together. Or so he kept telling himself.

He roused himself out of his own thoughts and centered his attention back on Strawberry Dan. It wasn't the message. That was engaging. But there was something about the drone of his voice that had Jamie biting back a yawn.

He squinted and blinked, doing his best to shake off the tired feeling. He couldn't make Peter stay awake if he himself was nodding off.

Jamie allowed his gaze to roam over the room, thinking the change of focus might help. Instead, his look collided with Deborah's.

She smiled at him. Had she been sitting there all morning just waiting for him to look at her? Surely not. And he should never be so arrogant to think that she had been. But it wasn't a far jump from her hanging around Pontotoc and refusing to go back to Tennessee until he agreed that they were meant to be together. He had one woman he couldn't convince to give him a chance and another who wouldn't leave him alone.

He peeled his gaze away from Deborah, but he could feel her stare on him. Eyes back front, he feigned fascination in the sermon.

How many times had he looked across a congregation to seek out Deborah? So many he couldn't count. But that was before she had shown him her true spirit, before his brother's death, and before Peter had become the most important thing to him.

What he wouldn't give to have Leah be on the other side of the congregation, smiling, waiting for him to meet her after church. Leah. Not Deborah. But according to Leah, that would never happen.

A few rows in front of Deborah, Jamie could make out Eunice, Gracie, and Hannah. The ladies sat close together, shoulders almost brushing as they listened to the words Strawberry Dan was saying. In such a short time, that family had come to mean so much to him. They had befriended him, helped him, and they continued to do so each and every day. He knew that God had sent him to them to help guide him, and he made sure he said his prayers of thanks every day.

He managed to keep his mind on the message for the rest of the sermon. In no time at all he was standing in the yard in the sweet October sunshine.

"Glad to see you today." Deborah sidled up alongside him, smiling as she did so.

"Where else would I be?"

She shrugged, a delicate motion that looked as if she changed her mind about it midway through. "I don't know. I'm just glad you're here."

"Why are you still here?" he asked. He looked over her head toward the field where the children had started to play. They hadn't even eaten yet, and already a ball game had begun. Peter sat off to one side, under the shade of a large tree, plucking grass and tossing it aside. He was with the other children, in the same vicinity, but not a part of them. That was what Jamie had worried about when he sent Peter to school. The boy might be able to sit at a desk and do the work, but he wasn't a part of the group. And he might not ever be. The thought made Jamie's stomach hurt. He wanted so much more for him.

"Jamie." Deborah snapped her fingers just under his nose, snapping him out of his thoughts. "Are you okay?"

He cleared his throat and nodded. "Fine," he managed, yet he felt anything but. This time last year his life had been completely in order. Now . . . it seemed to be in total chaos. Too much was happening too quickly.

"You're stressed," Deborah said.

He made a noise somewhere between agreement and denial.

"You should come back to Ethridge. Where you belong."

He shook his head. "There's nothing for me there."

"What are you talking about? Your entire life is there."

"It was." Once upon a time, her words had been true. His life had been in Ethridge. His brother, his brother's family, his sister, all his friends, Deborah. But with Joseph's death, all that changed, and the longer he stayed in Pontotoc, the more it became home. Eunice, Gracie, Hannah, and the rest of the Gingeriches had been more than kind to him. They had been like family. "But I belong here now."

She made a disbelieving noise. "You don't mean that."

"I do."

Just then there was the call to prayer. Jamie bowed his head and thanked God for all the many blessings he had received, as well as the ones he didn't deserve that he knew would come regardless. God was good.

"Where did you get this?" Mamm's hand shook as she held the envelope as if it might contain something that would explode.

"It was in the mailbox," Brandon explained.

Mamm turned it this way and that, examining it from every angle. "But it's Sunday."

"I figure someone found it in their stack of mail and stuck it in the mailbox as they drove by on their way to church." It made perfect sense to Leah.

"Are you going to open it?" Gracie asked.

They were all seated around the table in the dining area. Even Dat had come in from the barn to hear what Tillie had written. It was the first time anyone had heard from her since she left, and the prospect of what it might contain made Leah's mouth dry.

She could only hope and pray that everything was fine with Tillie and Melvin. Hope and pray and pray and hope.

"Eunice." Dat's voice was low.

"*Jah.*" Mamm sucked in a deep breath. "Right." Hands still trembling, she tore open the envelope.

"*Dear family,*" she read. "*I know it's been a long time since we left, but it's been really busy trying to get everything set up. Melvin got a job at a garage (where they work on all sorts of cars). He was thrilled. He thought it would be harder to find a job. He was so excited when he came home his first day.*

Anyway, I didn't want you to worry. We are fine and safe. We're working, and we have a place to stay.

I love you always,

Tillie."

Mamm sighed. She held the letter up and read it again, this time to herself.

"Mamm," Leah said. "Mamm."

Her mother dropped the letter from in front of her face. The sheen of tears in her eyes almost did Leah in.

"She's fine. She said as much," Hannah reminded her.

"They're working. That's good," Gracie added.

The chair legs scraped loudly against the wooden floor

as Dat abruptly stood. The chair wobbled, then fell backward
as he stomped from the house.

"Abner," Mamm called, but her voice was weak, as if
reading Tillie's letter had taken all that she had.

The front door slammed, and Mamm wilted in her chair.

"I'll go . . ." Jim stood, followed by David and soon the
Gingerich women were the only ones around the table.

"He doesn't understand how she can leave everything
behind." Mamm shook her head. "It about killed him when
the two of you left, but at least you had each other. Tillie
has no one."

"Melvin is with her," Gracie reminded.

"He doesn't count. He's the reason she left in the first
place. If he hadn't wanted to work on engines and whatnot,
then she would still be here today."

You don't know that, Leah wanted to say, but she refrained. Mamm wasn't in the mood to listen to reason. Her
heart was breaking. She was grateful that she had heard
from her daughter, but sad that the news was not about her
return.

Leah reached across the table and caught her *mamm's*
hands in her own. "Tillie made her choice, and hopefully
she'll realize how wrong it is and return. But until then, you
can't make yourself sick thinking this was something you
could have prevented."

"She's right, Mamm," Hannah said.

Gracie merely nodded.

"But we had all of you here for a time. All three together." Mamm sniffed, but the tears stayed hidden.

"And you will again," Gracie said. "I just know it."

Leah couldn't protest against her prediction. She needed
her mother to gain back her faith and trust. But the truth
of the matter was that Leah would never be a whole part of
the community again.

A knock sounded on the front door. Mamm started as

if she'd been goosed, then she looked to the wall clock hanging over the sideboard. "That must be Jamie." She used the tail of her apron to wipe her eyes. "I invited him and Peter to come to supper, but that was before . . ."

She stood, turned around as if she was uncertain where to go, then started for the kitchen. "Somebody get that. I've got to see about supper."

Jamie raised his hand to knock once again, but the door was opened before he could finish his intent.

Leah stood on the other side, looking even better than she had in his church daydream.

"Hi," he said with a happy little grin. He had known that she would be here when Eunice invited him, but it was an added bonus that she opened the door for him.

She smiled in return, but he noticed that it didn't quite make it past her lips.

"What's wrong?" he asked.

She stepped to one side to allow him and Peter to enter. "We got a letter from Tillie. Mamm's a little upset."

"There wasn't bad news, I hope."

"Not if you don't count that she's not coming home anytime soon."

He nodded a bit grimly. "Maybe we should go home." He started to herd Peter back to the door.

But Leah shook her head. "Y'all being here will be good for her."

He hesitated. "Are you sure?" He didn't want to go home. He wanted to spend as much time as possible with Leah. All of it and more.

"Positive." She smiled, and this one was more like he was used to. "Come on in the dining room. We were just talking."

Jamie followed behind Leah, with Peter trailing after.

"Peter? Would you like to write your letters?" she asked.

He shrugged.

"Read a book?"

He nodded.

"Go on in the living room, and I'll bring you something to read."

"You have books for him?" Jamie couldn't stop the question.

"Of course. I found them for the shop, then brought them home, thinking Peter might need something to do here."

His heart became a little more hers. "Thank you," he said. "That means a lot."

Leah shrugged, as if she took such care with everyone she encountered in a day. "Just trying to help."

There was that smile again, and he wanted to swoop in and kiss her, taste that curve of her lips. But he didn't. He followed her into the dining room, then sat as she took books in for Peter.

"How's she doing?" Jamie asked after he greeted Hannah and Gracie. He sat opposite them at the table, a small spark of hope flaring inside him that when Leah returned to the dining room she would take the chair next to him.

"Tillie?" Gracie asked. "She's fine, I guess. It's hard to tell from her letter."

"Speaking from experience," Hannah started, "it's hard to write home. She doesn't want to worry us, but she wants us to know that she's safe."

"How can we not be worried? She's out among the *Englisch*."

Jamie hadn't realized how close Tillie and Gracie were until that moment. The age difference between them was greater when compared to the one between Gracie and Leah and Hannah, but Leah and Hannah had been gone most of Tillie's life. And as far as he knew, Gracie had been living with the Gingeriches almost that long. They were more like sisters than cousins.

Leah floated in from the kitchen. Jamie supposed that she had gone from giving Peter books to checking on Eunice. That was just the kind of person she was.

"Is she okay in there?" Hannah asked.

"She will be," Leah replied.

Gracie pushed her chair back from the table and stood. "I should go help." And just like that, she was gone.

Hannah looked from one of them to the other. "This is fun." She rose from her seat. "I'm not going to make excuses. I'm leaving so the two of you can be alone."

And she was gone before Leah could utter even one protest.

Leah looked at her hands, then up to meet his gaze.

Jamie drummed his fingers on the tabletop. "*Danki* for getting the books for Peter."

She nodded. "You already said that."

"I did?" Why had everything turned so awkward? He shook his head again and started to stand. "Maybe we should go."

"No," Leah said. "Please stay. I think Mamm needs this right now."

"What? More people to feed?"

"Normalcy."

Jamie eased back into his chair. "She misses Tillie a lot, *jah?*"

"*Jah*." Leah gave him a small smile. "Dat does too. He just shows it differently."

Jamie glanced around. "Where is Abner?"

"In the barn working on something or another."

"On Sunday?" He frowned.

"I'm not sure whatever he's working on can be called

actual work. Think of it more as therapy. That swing on the back porch?"

"*Jah?*"

"He made that when Hannah and I left. Mamm told me about it years later. It took him months to craft it. He worked on it between projects and every chance he got. She said it was as if he couldn't bear to be still. That if he was, too many memories and thoughts haunted him, so he chased them away by building."

"And what the bishop doesn't know won't hurt him?" Jamie supplied.

"Exactly." Leah smiled. "And Mamm needs to cook. Well, she cooks all the time anyway. When she's happy, when someone is hurting. Special holidays. She shows her love and her sadness through food."

"Which means she's in there cooking enough for half the district to eat."

"You'll stay?" Leah asked.

How could he refuse? The Gingeriches had been like family; more than family. Of course, it didn't hurt that there was food involved. Food that he didn't have to cook himself. "It's the least I can do."

The supper dishes were drying in the drainer and the sun was dropping in the sky as Leah and Jamie settled down on the porch swing out front.

Brandon had taken Peter into the barn to check the puppies again before they headed back to town. Brandon had become such a help to Leah, she wasn't sure what she would have done without him. Oh, everyone says a person makes it with what they have, but she knew how valuable Brandon truly was to her. And he was good with Peter too. Brandon had come such a long way since the beginning of the summer. Leah couldn't have been prouder, and she knew Hannah felt the same. Aaron too. They may not have been able to raise their son together, but they were still getting a second chance—just as he was.

"You haven't changed your mind about rock painting tomorrow, have you?" she asked.

Jamie eased into the swing next to her. "Are you taking back your invitation?"

"No. Of course not. It's just . . . well, I want you to be sure about what you're getting into."

"We're painting rocks. How hard can that be?"

"It's not the painting that's the problem. You and Peter will be the only Amish there."

"Is that going to be a problem?"

She shook her head. "Everyone is welcome in our church. I just wanted to make sure you understood."

His blue eyes narrowed. "Why do I feel like you're trying to talk me out of coming altogether?"

"I'm not. I just—"

He held one finger to his lips. "You are." His normally unclouded disposition evaporated like a puddle in the sun. "Will it embarrass you if Peter and I go? I've already told him about it, but I'm sure he'll understand if I explain it to him. Even though I'm not sure exactly what *it* is."

"No." Leah had to raise her voice to be heard over Jamie's musings. "I'm not embarrassed. I just didn't want you to feel like you've been put on the spot."

"I won't feel that way at all," he assured her.

"And if they start asking you questions?"

"Is that what this is about?"

She felt the heat rise into her cheeks. She hadn't meant it to come out like that. "I just know how people can be. They're going to want to know all about you and Peter and how you know me and my family."

"Then I'll tell them."

"And why we're there together."

"Now I understand."

She shook her head. "That isn't what I meant. I don't know what to tell people." And even more importantly, she wasn't sure what she could say that would keep Jamie from reading too much into the evening. They were friends, and that was all they could ever be. And she wanted that friendship. For as long as she could possibly have it.

"Tell them the truth," he said simply.

"What is the truth?"

"That I'm crazy about you, and I want you to join the Amish church."

She shouldn't have asked. It was one thing to know it, and quite another to hear him say it out loud. Part of her rejoiced that he cared about her, but that joy quickly faded as reality set in. "That's never going to happen, Jamie. I'm never going to join the church." Too much time had passed. Too much stood in her way. Couldn't he see that?

It had been so difficult since she had been back. She had been flooded with memories, bombarded with nostalgia, and filled with regret. But it didn't change a thing.

He shrugged as if her words hadn't affected him at all. "Tell them whatever you want, Leah. I don't care."

"What happened between you and Jamie tonight?" Brandon asked on the way home.

She shot him a quick look, then turned her attention back to the road ahead. Darkness had fallen, and it wouldn't do to run into a dog or, even worse, a deer because she wasn't watching where she was going.

"Did your mother put you up to asking that?"

"Of course not." But the words were so animated that she knew he was not telling her the truth.

"Uh-huh."

"Seriously."

"Whatever you say."

"You don't believe me? You don't think I care about you and your love life?"

She almost choked, coughed a couple of times, then pulled herself together. "My what?"

"Your lo—"

"I heard you. There is no love life."

"Only because you won't accept what's right there in front of you."

She narrowed her gaze and shot him another look. "Did you learn that from your mother too?"

"Why do you think Mom put me up to this?"

"You forget we're twins."

He nodded slowly. "I think she's right, you know."

"About what?"

"Jamie. He seems so . . . perfect for you."

Leah gave an unladylike snort. "Jamie? Me and Jamie? That's the craziest thing I've ever heard."

"What's so insane about it? You two are made for each other."

"Now, I *know* your mother put you up to that."

He sat back in his seat and crossed his arms. "Maybe. But I believe it too."

At least this time she was prepared for his absurd claims. She merely shook her head. "Then you are both wrong. Jamie and I couldn't be worse for each other. We have nothing in common. We don't like the same things. We don't even go to the same church."

"Neither do me and Shelly."

"I thought the two of you weren't dating."

He shrugged, but the darkness hid his expression. "We're not. I just said that to make a point."

"You have a point?" Leah asked.

"That you two are different but could be together if you were a couple, which you aren't because you keep telling yourself that you have nothing to offer him."

"Huh?" Leah stuttered.

"That you two—"

Leah held up a hand to stop his words. "Don't repeat it. The first time gave me a headache."

"Because you know it's true."

She wasn't about to argue with a fifteen-year-old. Or maybe a part of her knew she wasn't going to win this one. "It's not always that easy," she finally said. "You can like someone who's all wrong for you."

"Jamie's not all wrong though."

"I know you think that, but you were raised *Englisch.* Church beliefs are a big deal among the Plain people. Even more so around here."

"I guess so." His tone turned petulant. "But I know one thing—if I found someone I loved, I wouldn't let them go. Not for anything in the world."

"Are you ready for this?" Leah asked the following evening when she stopped by to pick up Jamie and Peter.

Peter hopped into the back seat as if he had been doing it his entire life.

Jamie eased into the front seat and eyed her suspiciously. "Why do I feel like you're trying to talk me out of going?"

She shook her head and waited for everyone to buckle their seat belts before putting the car into gear. Peter didn't have a problem with his belt, and she assumed because it hadn't been that long since he had traveled from Ethridge and he remembered how to fasten it.

It might not have been long since he had ridden in a fast-moving vehicle, but the fascination of traveling fast hadn't worn off. He twisted in his seat and peered out the window, his nose pressed against the glass as the world zoomed past.

"Are you?" Jamie asked again.

She wanted to play dumb and ask what he was talking about, but she didn't. He wanted to know if she was trying to talk him out of going to this rock painting frolic at the church. She was and she wasn't. She wanted him to go, but it worried her. It had seemed like a good enough idea when she had invited him. She would show him what her church was all about. She had attended an Amish church most of her life, right up until the time that she had left with Hannah. Jamie, on the other hand, had always attended Amish services and had never been to another sort of church. He didn't understand the draw the Mennonites held for her. The peace, love, and understanding, without the hard constraints of the Amish church.

Not that she thought the Amish church was bad, or even detrimental. It simply was what it was. She moved out and moved on. She could see the benefits that he couldn't in the more liberal ways. Just because they allowed electricity and cars didn't mean that they were not doing God's work. Because they had electricity and cars, they were better able to do His work in different places and on different levels. But how could she explain this to Jamie?

By showing him her church: the love, the peace, and the understanding.

And then what?

He would renounce his Amish ways and jump the fence with her?

If Peter's grandparents wanted him back now, imagine what they would do if Jamie decided to join the Mennonite church. They would swoop in and snatch the boy away before Jamie even had time to kneel before the congregation. It was just that simple and just that complicated.

And she was making it worse by inviting him here. She should have left well enough alone. She shouldn't have made this plan. It was a stupid plan and would do more harm than good.

If Jamie deciding that he loved her church and wanted to become Mennonite was something that was never going to happen, then she had to leave him alone. She had to separate herself from him and Peter both. Neither she nor Jamie was willing to change churches. Neither one of them was willing to give up the life that they had made. And if they weren't careful, Peter would pay the price.

She made up her mind then and there: after tonight, there would be no more almost-but-not-quite-a-date dates with Jamie Stoltzfus. There were too many hearts at stake.

Chapter Thirteen

She parked the car in the church parking lot and sat for a moment. She closed her eyes in quick prayer and hoped that the good Lord was listening. The prayer was short and to the point. *Help me get through this night, and I promise never to bother Jamie or Peter again. Amen.*

It had nothing to do with Deborah and her plans of marriage.

That was another thing she needed to talk to Jamie about. He might not have fathered Peter in the traditional sense, but he was as good a father to the boy as any man could be. Jamie didn't need a wife to help him care for Peter. He simply needed to pour all the love and attention onto him, and God would handle the rest. Peter had already spoken—granted, negative words concerning his feelings for Deborah, but it was just a matter of time before he spoke again. Once he was speaking, his grandparents had no cause to demand they get to care for him. All Jamie had to do was love the child and wait. He could do that with both arms tied behind his back.

"Leah?" Jamie asked beside her. His voice was filled

with light concern. "Are you okay? I mean, we don't have to go in—"

She shook her head and adjusted the rearview mirror so she could see Peter. "Are you ready to go paint some rocks?" she asked him.

He nodded enthusiastically, nearly slinging his hat into the seat next to him.

"All right, then. Let's go." She looked back to Jamie. "Are you ready?"

"Of course. You?" he asked in return.

Leah forced a smile. "As ready as I'll ever be."

Jamie wasn't sure what to expect when he walked into the church, but it wasn't anything like he imagined. Not that he'd had any experience with church buildings, *Englisch* or Mennonite.

They walked into what appeared to be a side building set at the end of the main church. Leah called it the *rec hall*, though he didn't quite understand what that meant. The place was equipped with several classrooms off a main room and even included a kitchen. The large area was separated from the stove and fridge with a low counter that stretched the entire length of the room. The rest was lined with long tables and chairs where people had already begun to gather, greeting one another as they found their seats.

At both ends of each table, someone had placed two plastic tubs, one filled with rocks and the other with paints in every color imaginable. Beside each set of paints was a plastic cup filled with brushes.

"Let's sit over here." Leah directed them to the end of one of the tables.

Jamie noticed that she spoke to several people as she entered and even more as she settled into the seats she had chosen. She smiled politely and introduced him and Peter to the people who stopped and asked. If they thought it was peculiar that he and Peter were Amish, they didn't say. They, like Leah, smiled and nodded, then went about their business. The men looked like regular *Englischers*, with blue jeans and patterned shirts. The women were dressed like Leah, with long skirts and modest sleeves. Some had small black prayer coverings on their bobs. The children were a mixture of the two, most dressing in the same manner as their parents.

Not long after Leah, Peter, and Jamie found their chairs, a young man stepped before the crowd. If Jamie had to guess he would say that he was in his midthirties. He had sandy blond hair and dark brown eyes. His smile was engaging as he clapped his hands together to get everyone's attention.

"Most of you know who I am, but I see a few unfamiliar faces in the crowd. For you, I'll introduce myself. I'm Pastor Joel. Tonight's project is about fun and fellowship," he started.

"And the word of God," some helpful artist added.

The man laughed. "Yes, that too. In the center of each table is a basket containing slips of paper with Bible verses written on them. You can choose one from the basket, quote one from memory, or find your own. However you feel moved. Paint the rock, the verse, and any decoration on your rock that you're compelled to. After they dry, we're going to take them around and hide them through our town for other rock hunters to find. Any questions?"

A young boy raised his hand.

"Yes, William?"

"Can I paint more than one?"

The pastor chuckled. "You may paint as many as you want. But remember, the more you paint, the more you will be responsible for hiding around town. Are you up for that?"

"Yes, sir." William gave an enthusiastic nod.

"Perfect. Any more questions?" When no one had any, Pastor Joel bowed his head. "Let us pray. Father in Heaven, thank you for the blessings You have given us this day. Lord, allow tonight to be fun and productive. Keep our hands, minds, and hearts on target and help us all to fulfill Your word. In Jesus' name. Amen." He looked around the room. "Let's paint. Everyone take turns getting your supplies. Don't forget to get a cup of clean water for cleaning your paintbrush, and have fun."

The room became a flurry of excited yet controlled activity. They waited a bit before getting their supplies. Peter sat patiently watching as the others ran for paint and brushes and then started picking out verses.

"Are you ready?" Leah asked Peter.

He nodded and slid from his chair.

"Sit tight," Leah told Jamie. "We'll bring you back supplies, okay?"

"Sounds good to me."

"Any special color?" she asked.

"Whatever you like," he said with a small smile.

Jamie watched as they went to the end of the table and started gathering brushes and paints. Leah kept up a steady stream of conversation, even though Peter only answered her with one gesture or another. She never seemed to get frustrated that he wouldn't talk. It was as if his lack of speech was just a part of who he was and not a traumatic choice he had made.

In no time at all they had gathered rocks, paints, and brushes along with a cup of water for cleaning up, then they returned to their seats.

"We got black, blue, and red," Leah said. "I wanted to get yellow so you could make green, but there wasn't one."

He smiled. "This is fine." But how did she know that green was his favorite color? He didn't recall saying anything about it to her. He had a couple of green shirts, but like most of the men in Pontotoc, he usually wore blue, for nothing other than tradition.

"We can make purple though, right, Peter?"

He nodded.

"Why don't you get us verses we can put on our rocks?"

He scrambled down and made his way to the center of the table, where the promised verses waited.

"Get us a few if you want to make more than one rock." And he had a feeling Peter would want to. Jamie himself was a little excited by the prospect. It was refreshing. Who had ever heard of a ministry to reach the people involving rocks?

Peter returned to his chair with a handful of the slips of paper and a huge smile on his face. Jamie would have never thought it possible, but tonight was going to be therapeutic—for them all.

"Are you going to paint? Or are you going to just sit there and stare?"

Leah started as Jamie leaned in close. Had she been staring? It was obvious she wasn't painting; she didn't even have a paintbrush in her hands. But she hadn't meant to stare.

The joy on Peter's face was near rapturous, and she wondered if she was getting a look at how he had been before the accident.

She took up her brush and dipped it in the green paint Peter had scuttled to get after painting his first rock. "I'm painting, of course." She swabbed the color over the top of the rock and shot Jamie a smile.

So far they had a purple rock with John 1:12 and a cross

for decoration. They didn't have enough room on it to paint all the verse so they'd merely left it off, hoping instead that whoever found the rock would look up the verse to uncover the full message. *Yet to all who did receive him, to those who believed in his name, he gave the right to become children of God.*

Brandon and Shelly were sitting a couple of tables over and up toward the front a little more. He had wanted to drive them himself, even though he swore it wasn't a date. Not that Leah thought Shelly's parents would allow her to officially date a boy. Maybe saying there was nothing between them was Brandon and Shelly's way of making sure they could spend time together.

Leah made a mental note to talk to him about that. It was right up there with sneaking around, and a relationship shouldn't be based on a togetherness that had to be hidden. Even if it was only just beginning—or maybe especially because it was only just beginning.

Leah looked around and noticed that several people were writing on their rocks with a black magic marker. "Peter, can you get us a marker like that?" She nodded toward the nearest woman wielding a Sharpie.

Peter nodded in that accommodating way of his and slid from his chair to get the item for her.

"I do believe that boy would do anything for you," Jamie mused.

"He's a good boy," Leah returned. A good boy who had been handed a raw deal, then a wonderful man to help him through it. But Leah knew that Jamie was still concerned that Peter wouldn't talk in time for his cutoff with the grandparents.

"Have you given any more thought to talking to Pastor Joel about the problem?"

"What can he offer that no one else already has?"

"A new perspective?" She gave a small shrug.

"Perspective is not what I need." He sighed.

"Still . . ."

Jamie shook his head. He picked up a rock painted with a large red heart and Mark 11:24. *Therefore I tell you, whatever you ask for in prayer, believe that you have received it, and it will be yours.*

It was a scripture he seemed to live by, but as the days passed, Leah could see his faith begin to wane. Just the thought of that saddened her. There had to be something more they could do.

He set the rock back on the table and forced a smile.

"Hi, Leah. I see you brought some friends tonight."

Jamie turned in his seat to find the pastor standing behind his chair.

The man reached out a hand to shake. His grip was firm, his eyes warm, and his demeanor welcoming.

"Pastor Joel, this is Jamie Stoltzfus and his son, Peter. They're neighbors to my parents."

"Good. Good." Pastor Joel nodded as if having them there was the finest thing he could have asked for. But Leah knew he was always like that: polite, welcoming, open. "Hi there, Peter." He reached his hand out to the boy, who had just returned with the requested marker.

Peter shook his hand and climbed back into his seat without a word.

"He, uh . . . doesn't talk." Jamie lowered his voice in what Leah assumed was an attempt to keep him from hearing, but Peter was too close. It wasn't possible that he hadn't heard the words unless he was extremely hard of hearing. And he wasn't.

She wanted to say something to Jamie, kick him under the table, anything to make him realize that he was potentially damaging Peter's self-confidence by saying things like that in front of him. But it was really none of her business, and Peter had already gone back to painting *Jesus loves you* on a blue rock.

"Puts a whole new spin on unwholesome talk, now doesn't it?"

Leah couldn't remember the exact verse he was referencing, but she did remember it was in Ephesians and dealt with only speaking goodness. She nodded, and Jamie did the same.

"Pastor Joel!"—from across the room, someone called his name.

"I think I'm being paged." He nodded toward Peter and Jamie. "Thank you for coming out tonight. It's good to finally meet you."

Pastor Joel moved away to address the people who had called him, and Leah turned her attention back to her rock.

She had managed to procure one of a decent size, along with some white paint to go with her red. She mixed the two to make a sweetheart pink. On one side she painted I Corinthians 13:2. *If I have the gift of prophecy and can fathom all mysteries and all knowledge, and if I have a faith that can move mountains, but do not have love, I am nothing.*

She had seen her sister find love, as well as her brother; even Brandon found a bit of puppy love, though he had a hard time admitting that there was anything more than friendship between him and Shelly. Was it so bad for Leah to pray for a little of that love herself? But what happened when the one person she thought she could love if given half the chance didn't have the same beliefs as her? Maybe she should paint a rock about being unequally yoked, though she knew Amish and Mennonite didn't count in that aspect. They both believed in God. They both believed in church and family, in love and caring for one another. Why did it have to be more difficult than that?

Inwardly she sighed while she pasted on a smile for Peter's sake. It just did. And as terrible of an answer as that was, it was the truth all the same.

"What did he mean tonight?" Jamie asked. It had taken him until the trip home to gather enough courage to ask. Well, *courage* was not the right word. But he had tried to convince himself all evening that he had heard wrong. That Pastor Joel hadn't said what he'd thought he heard.

"What did who mean?"

"The pastor. He said, 'It's good to finally meet you.' Why would he say finally?"

She gave a loose-shouldered shrug, but kept her hands on the steering wheel. "I may have mentioned you and Peter once or twice."

"In a private conversation with the pastor?"

"A request for prayer."

White-hot something shot through him. Anger? Regret? That feeling as if he'd stepped off a cliff and there was no turning back. "Why would you do that?"

She switched her gaze from the road to him, then back again. "Are you saying that you can't use prayers?"

"That's not the point, and you know it."

"There is power in numbers, and the more people praying, the better chance that prayer has."

He wasn't sure if he believed all that. Didn't God hear the smallest prayer? But he hated that Leah had felt sorry for him. So sorry that she begged her church to remember him when they talked to God.

"It's arrogant," he finally said. His voice was choked as if someone had tied something too tightly around his neck.

"Arrogant? To ask for prayers?" She scoffed. "Maybe if you asked for yourself, but not when someone else asks for you—scratch that." She took one hand from the wheel and waved it around as if erasing words from a blackboard. "Asking for prayers and praying . . . there's nothing arrogant about it. It's humbling. Maybe that's your problem," she said as she turned the car into the flattened area that served as a driveway for Jamie's cabin. "You think you're arrogant if you talk to God, but it only means you have a relationship with Him. And how can that be a bad thing?"

Leah's words continued to knock around inside his head even after he and Peter had come into the house and she had driven away. He got Peter ready for bed and read him a story, then he said his prayers and Jamie tucked him in for the night. Well, at least until he gave up and headed into Jamie's room.

He had no way of knowing what Peter prayed for. Had he been asking for a relief for his silence? Maybe not, if he could talk the way Leah seemed to think he could. With all the burns on his neck and surgeries to that area, it had even been speculated that there had been some undetected damage that caused his muteness.

Yet Leah had said he'd told her that he didn't like Deborah. Had he really said those words? Before the accident Peter had been a smart, funny, and vivacious little boy.

But Jamie had no way of knowing what Peter had asked for in his prayers. Suddenly he wanted to know more than anything. A mantle of urgency settled around his shoulders. There was so much at stake. So much still unresolved.

He sat back down on the edge of Peter's bed and pushed the boy's hair back from his face. "Peter, I haven't mentioned this before, but maybe it's time."

Peter watched with those large blue eyes as Jamie heaved a great sigh and continued.

"If you don't speak soon, your *mammi* and *dawdi* Yoder

are going to come get you and take you back to Ethridge with them. I don't know how you feel about this, but I would miss you so much, I don't think I could stand it. That's why I need you to talk. Soon. *Jah?*" He leaned down and planted a quick kiss on Peter's forehead.

The boy nodded and snuggled down into the covers.

That was all Jamie could do for now. That, pray, and trust in God. But the last two hadn't worked so far. Maybe it was time for more drastic measures.

He made his way back into the living area of the house and stared at the basket of painted rocks sitting on the table. He had promised Leah that they would go with the rest of the congregation and place those around Pontotoc on Saturday. Now they sat in their little basket, just a colorful reminder of one of the best nights of his life.

He had brought all the rocks home until Saturday so Peter could look at them. The boy hadn't wanted to part with the treasures, so Leah agreed that he could hold on to them until the next event.

Jamie plucked one of the rocks from the basket, this one larger than some of the rest. A cheery yellow and orange sun stared back at him. Hebrews 11:1 was printed across the bright body, and it must have been one of the rocks they had done later in the night, for this one had the entire verse written there. *Now faith is confidence in what we hope for and assurance about what we do not see.*

Faith. It all came down to faith. Faith that Peter would talk again. Faith that Jamie was doing right by the boy. Faith that one day Leah would see the two of them the way he did and not as an impossibility. Faith that it would all turn out in the end.

But after a while faith could wane, falter, fall. Then where did that leave him?

Maybe he was looking at this all wrong. Maybe it wasn't about faith, but about hanging on to the sure deal. Was he damaging Peter further by not forcing him to speak? Should he have taken him to a head doctor, as Leah had suggested? Or was he making paths where there were none?

He never should have agreed to the Yoders' terms, but what was done was done. But that didn't mean he had to give up without a fight. And fight he would. For Leah and for Peter. For them all.

"I heard you had a date last night," Gracie said as they sat around the kitchen table adding fragrances to the four-ounce bottles of goat milk lotion.

Gracie was in charge of lavender, while Leah wielded the orange and Hannah the peppermint. They had decided to give each fragrance a small run to see how they would sell. Already these three fragrances had been the most popular, selling out in the first week. Lemon peppermint, rosemary mint, and lavender eucalyptus were still hanging in there, but not selling as quickly as the pure fragrances. They had decided to take today and build up that stock before moving on and experimenting with the soaps.

For Leah, this endeavor was almost as thrilling as opening the store. She had wanted to make a place that could afford her a living, but also serve the community. Adding the goat milk products to the shop only added to that. It helped her store, brought in traffic, helped her mother, and gave her time with her sister and cousin—time she had missed when she had been away. She might not feel like she could join the church and step back into her Amish life, but she was grateful for any time she could spend with family.

"I did not have a date," she said emphatically. Almost too emphatically. She winced as Hannah and Gracie noticed her slip.

"I see. It wasn't a date." Hannah winked at Gracie, who took it up as she turned to Leah. "*Jah*, not a date at all. I see."

Leah shook her head. "I just wanted Jamie to see what my church is like, and I thought Peter would enjoy painting the rocks. That's all."

"Sure." Hannah nodded. "We understand." She winked at Gracie, who offered an exaggerated copy right back.

"Why don't y'all believe me?" She shot them both an exasperated look.

"Maybe because we've seen the two of you together," Hannah explained.

Gracie nodded in agreement.

"What? Arguing?"

"You may argue, but that's only because you both have strong beliefs and even stronger personalities."

"And he's Amish, and I'm Mennonite. He's more conservative and thinks I'm too liberal."

Hannah shook her head. "Amish and Mennonite. It matters, but it doesn't. You know what I mean?"

She did and she didn't. And one thing she understood above all others: it shouldn't matter, but it did. "Jamie and I are friends."

Gracie and Hannah nodded politely.

"Of course," Gracie said. "How can it be any other way? After all, I heard he was heading back to Ethridge soon."

Leah's heart fell. He hadn't said anything to her about it last night, but she wouldn't be surprised. He had picked up and left his life there. He had a fiancée—ex-fiancée—a sister, and aunts and uncles, she was sure. Peter probably had even more, if she took into account his mother's family. What was keeping Jamie in Pontotoc? "He is?"

Gracie shrugged. "I don't know for a fact, but that's what everyone is saying."

"Everyone being . . . ?" Hannah asked.

"Sarah Hostetler for one. And I figure she knows, since Deborah King is staying with her."

And once upon a time, Deborah had meant something to Jamie.

"Peter doesn't like Deborah," Leah said.

"Yes, I know. I was there." Gracie shot her a look.

"I'm not sure Peter has much of a say in this," Hannah added.

And he wouldn't, but Leah worried that Peter would regress if Jamie was getting back with Deborah. Yet there was nothing she could do about it. "Do you really think he's moving back?"

Gracie gave another quick shrug and looked to Hannah. "I wouldn't know. Maybe the question you should ask is, what's keeping him here?"

Chapter Fourteen

Jamie pulled his carriage to a stop and hopped to the ground. He looked back to Peter, who slouched in the back seat as if trying to disappear into the bench itself.

He motioned for the boy to get down. "Come on."

Peter flinched, but otherwise didn't move.

"I know you're not asleep. Come on. Get down." He did everything he could to keep the exasperation out of his voice. He was still so new at this parenting stuff, and he had no idea how to handle this one. But as soon as he got the mare put away and Peter settled in with some chores, he was marching down to see Eunice. Surely she would have some advice for him. She had raised five children, and barring the fact that three of them left the Amish at some point in their lives, they hadn't turned out too bad.

Head bowed, Peter climbed down from the carriage and dragged his feet as he trudged toward the house.

"Get out the broom first thing," Jamie said. "I want to be able to eat off that floor when I come back."

Peter didn't acknowledge his words, but Jamie knew he heard him. They had already talked about this on the way home. First sweeping, then mopping, then Jamie would have to come up with something else. There wasn't a lot to do in their two-room cabin, and Peter was going to be responsible for all of it for a long time after today's meeting with the teacher.

Jamie watched him disappear into the house, then sighed and unhitched the mare. Twenty-five minutes later, after the horse was watered and fed and he had checked on Peter, Jamie was on his way down to Eunice's.

He was almost to the bottom of the hill before he noticed Leah's car parked off to one side. He was just about to turn around and head back the way he came when Eunice called out to him from the backyard.

He'd been spotted. No turning back now. "Hi, Eunice," he called in return. Plus, going back home was a chicken move. How could he help Peter if he was avoiding Leah?

"What brings you down today?" She snapped the sheet to release the wrinkles, then hung it on the line. Tuesday must be linens day. Eunice had the line swaying with towels and bedding.

"Peter." He heaved a great sigh. "He's having trouble in school."

Eunice stopped gathering up the dry laundry she had taken off the line and eyed him. "I thought he was doing good."

"Me too. But I went to get him today and Amanda said he had been running around and acting up all day."

"And yesterday he was fine?"

"I wouldn't say that. She mentioned that he had been struggling a bit. She thinks the kids have been teasing him. She hasn't heard it herself, but she said that he seemed fine, then everything changed."

"When did this change happen?"

Jamie shrugged. "Middle of September, maybe."

"Did something happen then?" Eunice asked. She picked

up her basket of clean clothes and started for the house. Jamie took it from her and walked beside her the whole way.

"I don't think so. I mean, not that I can remember."

"All I know to do is pray," she said, opening the back door and urging him inside. He didn't want to go. What if Leah was inside? Of course she was. He would see her, say hello, and act like last night wasn't the best night of his life. Well, was the best night of his life until he found out that she had shared his business with her church. Then things had taken a turn. But up until then . . .

And after he had made a problem where there should have been none. Why? His own stupid pride. Leah thought he needed prayers, which he took to mean he was less of a man, he wasn't together, he didn't have his life all figured out. He was weak.

He was stupid, that's what he was. He had been trying to show her all that they could have together, and he'd all but picked an argument with her over a generous gesture on her part.

"I've tried that."

Eunice shot him a quick smile. "Prayer isn't something you try and move on to the next thing. *Pray without ceasing. In every thing give thanks: for this is the will of God in Christ Jesus concerning you,*" she quoted.

Thessalonians, if he remembered correctly, though he couldn't recall the exact chapter or verse. It had been one of his mother's favorites. Whenever he had a problem, even at his age, she told him to take it to the Lord in prayer. So why did this problem seem like it was too much to be solved by prayer alone? Because it was important. It wasn't just his life at stake. It was Peter's. Parenting was an awesome responsibility, and he doubted every day if he'd really be able to see this through. He had the desire in his heart; he just didn't know if he had the ability in him as well.

"Hey, Jamie," Hannah greeted as he carried the basket

into the house and set it on the kitchen table. This table wasn't as large as the one in the dining room, and as far as Jamie could tell, was used more for cooking preparations and quick snacks. Today it made a great place to set clean laundry.

"Hi," he returned.

"Where's Peter?" she asked.

He sighed, then straightened, his disposition immediately improving. "You have Brandon," he said.

"Yeeesss," she said slowly, her smile stiff.

"No, I mean . . ." He shook his head. "Peter's having some trouble in school, and I'm pretty new at the whole parenting thing. I have no idea what I should do."

"What kind of trouble?" Hannah asked.

Before he could answer, Eunice bustled them to the door that led into the dining room. "You two sit down. I'll bring in some coffee. Go on, now."

And his worst fear was realized as he stepped into the dining room.

Leah sat at the table with Gracie, each intent on the bottles they had lined up on either side of themselves. Leah was adding what appeared to be drops of essential oils while Gracie wiped down the bottles and added a label with the name and contents.

"Look who's here," Gracie said as she continued to wipe bottles.

"Hi."

"Jamie just told me that Peter's having trouble in school."

He started to protest at Hannah's familiarity, but none of them seemed surprised. It occurred to him then: that was what this family was all about. It might have taken years to get them all here and together now—minus Tillie, of course—but they were a family unit that pulled together and helped one another. Perhaps that was why Hannah and Leah were able to return to a life that had once been theirs.

But if that was the case, then why did Leah feel that she couldn't join the church? Granted, the Mennonite church she attended seemed like a great place for worship and fellowship. He had walked in and immediately felt welcome. He couldn't always say that about his Amish church home. Things had been a little different since he had come to Pontotoc, but that was simply because he was on the fringes. One of them, but not one of them. Not yet anyway.

"Sit down," Gracie commanded. "Tell us what's going on."

He sat and explained the situation to them. Halfway to the end of his tale, Eunice bustled in with coffee and cookies. Everyone grabbed a snack as he continued on to the end.

"Middle of September, huh?" Gracie mused. "That was the Bodock Festival, *jah?*"

Jamie had almost forgotten about the festival. "*Jah*, I suppose."

"Did something happen during that time?" Hannah asked.

As they talked, the women continued their work. It was something he had learned from the other women in his life. Amish women didn't have much time to sit still, even if it was to help a friend. His *mamm* and *mammi* had always been up to something: canning, chopping, cooking, preserving. "Busy hands," his *mammi* used to always say.

"Not that I recall." But honestly, the days had started to blend one into the other.

Leah snapped her fingers. "That was when Deborah came down."

"Oh, *jah*." Gracie nodded. "I remember now."

It had only been a couple of weeks before. So why did those few events seem like a lifetime ago? Because he had been living a lifetime in each day, loving Leah when he knew there would never be more than right now between them? Sounded logical enough.

"Deborah came down, and Peter got into trouble?" Leah asked. "That doesn't sound like him."

"He hasn't been in any trouble since then. At least none that I know about. This is the first time that I've had to have a conference with the teacher. And just between us, I don't think she wants him back in her classroom."

"Oh, Jamie." This from Leah.

Jamie held up one hand to stop her words. "It's okay. Lesson learned."

"It's not okay. He's a special little boy, and he's obviously hurting very badly to misbehave on purpose," Leah continued.

On purpose? "I don't think . . ." He let the words trail away. Had Peter acted out on purpose? Because of Deborah?

"Where's Peter now?" Leah asked.

Jamie jerked a thumb over one shoulder. "At the house doing chores."

"Do you want me to talk to him?" Leah asked.

"I'm not sure what good it will do."

Leah pushed herself to her feet, grabbed a couple of the cookies, and folded them into a paper napkin. "Stay here. Let me see what I can do."

The stricken look on Jamie's face stayed with her on the short walk up the hill to his cabin. Leah knocked twice, then let herself inside.

"Peter," she called as she stepped over the threshold. He was nowhere in the front of the house, so she made her way to his newly built room. In the couple of weeks that he had been there, he had made the space his own. He had even tacked a picture of a dog onto his wall. It was a golden retriever, just like he had lost in the fire.

Peter himself was sprawled across the bed on his stomach, face hidden in his folded arms.

"Peter?" she quietly asked. Was he asleep? Should she wake him? "Peter, sit up so I can talk to you."

He must not have been asleep. He pushed himself into a sitting position, wiping the back of one scarred hand against his eyes. Whether he was swiping away sleep or tears, she didn't know.

"I hear you had a bad time at school today."

He nodded, but kept his gaze trained on his lap.

Leah eased farther into the room and sat on the end of the bed next to him.

"Can you tell me about it?"

He shook his head.

"Peter." She used her tone as a warning. "You and I both know that you can talk, but that you won't. How are you supposed to tell folks around you what you need if you don't use your words?"

He gave a rippling shrug.

"I have a feeling you needed something from the teacher yesterday, and you were disruptive instead of talking. Am I right?"

He started shaking his head, then switched and nodded instead.

Tears pricked the backs of Leah's eyes. The boy could speak. She had heard him. So why did he tell her that he didn't like Deborah, but when he truly needed something, he kept the words to himself?

"There has to be another way, Peter." Except the boy couldn't write his words. He could make letters and numbers, but his thoughts were trapped inside his own head. Well, for the most part. He could tell her that he didn't like

Deborah, something that held no bearing, but he couldn't express other needs.

"The words fail you," Leah whispered. "You can't bring the important words out, can you? They're stuck in your brain, buried in the memories of the accident."

He dropped his chin to his chest. It was more than enough answer for her.

"Look at me, Peter."

He tilted his chin back up and his gaze met hers.

"We will get through this. I'll talk to Jamie. We'll come up with a plan to help you." Lord knew, he had suffered long enough.

"What are you saying?" Jamie asked half an hour or so later.

Leah had kissed Peter on the forehead, given him the cookies she had brought, then hurried back down the hill to talk to Jamie. "We both know Peter can talk."

He nodded, but the puckered frown remained on his forehead.

"But his words are all jumbled up with his memories of that night."

"So he can't speak because of the memorics?"

"Sort of. He just can't wade through all of that when he really needs to. Those memories shut down his speech when he really needs them."

"So why doesn't he speak when he can?"

"My guess is he doesn't even try. It's too frustrating for him."

Jamie sighed and sat back into the swing.

Leah could only imagine how he felt; how over-whelming it would be to have a child with problems like Peter's and not know how to help him. "There is that doctor who goes to my church."

"A doctor?"

"I told you about him once."

But Jamie shook his head. "I can't take him to that kind of doctor." He said the words as if the man were a witch doctor instead of medically trained. She knew that it was just Jamie's conservative nature. Her father would have behaved the same way. But it was frustrating nonetheless.

"Promise me you'll think about it," she asked quietly. "Peter deserves better than to be locked in his own head."

For a moment she thought he might protest, then he slowly nodded. "*Jah*," he finally said. "I'll think about it, but nothing more."

He hadn't meant to fib to Leah. He did one more thing to help Peter, and that was pray about it. But these days it almost seemed as if God wasn't listening. Or perhaps Jamie wasn't getting his answer quickly enough. Patience was a virtue, or so they said, but he was so worried about Peter that Jamie was finding it impossible to be anything other than exasperated. He needed to know the way, and he needed it right now.

The next day was Wednesday, and Jamie was loath to send him to school. The teacher hadn't said that Peter was not able to come back, but Jamie could tell that the young woman was reluctant. She had tried to help Peter, but once he became a hindrance to the other students, everything changed.

"I guess you're hanging out with me today, buddy," Jamie said over breakfast.

Peter nodded and took an overlarge bite of his cereal. Jamie hated giving the boy food out of a box, but they were both tired of eating scrambled eggs. It might be the only thing Jamie could cook without ruining, but prepared correctly or not, eggs every day grew tiresome.

Peter didn't look overly upset about not going to school. Then again, what kid would miss it? No one liked school except the really smart kids who knew all the answers and the teacher's pets, who were usually one and the same.

"I promised Abner I'd help him with a new shed today. You can take your tablet down and write out your letters and numbers while you sit on the front porch. You can take your reader out there as well. No going into the house and eating all the cookies today either. You do that too many times and you'll ruin your supper but good."

Peter nodded, then they said their after-meal prayer, and he took his bowl to the sink. A few minutes later he was equipped with his markers and notepad for writing.

Jamie grabbed his hat, and together the two of them headed for the Gingeriches'. Having Peter out of school for whatever reason didn't sit well with him. He felt like he was short-changing the boy. His education might just be starting, but it was starting. It was Jamie's job as his guardian to see it through.

The idea of online school flitted through his head. He shook it away. He was Amish. He couldn't enroll Peter in a computer school. They didn't have electricity or all that other fancy stuff people needed for that sort of thing.

Brandon and Leah do. Well, they had a way to make it work. Was that what he needed? A plan to make it work?

He couldn't fathom. He was Amish. He'd been born that way, raised that way, and he would die that way. It was hard to shake such hard-learned lessons. Even if he wanted to. And who said he did? He merely wanted Peter to have a decent life, a chance despite everything that stood in his way.

And so much was in his way.

He looked down at the boy who strode along beside him,

his short legs and pronounced limp leaving him struggling to keep up.

Jamie slowed a bit to help, but didn't say a word about it.

Leah's offer to talk to one of the people, a head doctor, in her church once again came to the front of his mind. Was it possible? Was it godly? He wasn't sure such a study would be. People were born with problems all the time. It was part of God's will. As Amish they accepted it and moved on. How could he call this anything other than God's will as well? How could he justify tampering with Peter's mind in such a way? Did he have the right? Was it even holy?

Those were answers he didn't have. The one thing he did have? Faith. And that was going to have to see them through. He was going to pray; pray without ceasing until he had his answer. Then and only then would be know what to do.

"Excuse me? Do you have this in grapefruit?"

Leah looked from the lady to the bottle of lotion she held. "I'm sorry, I don't currently, but I can get you a bottle in a day or so."

Ever since she had put the bottles of her mother's goat milk lotion on the front wall just inside the window of the shop, people had been asking about it nonstop. Yesterday she, Hannah, and Gracie had made more bottles of lotion, and today they were flying off the shelves.

"Would you?" the woman gushed. "My friend has the lavender. I love how it feels on my skin, but lavender smells like my grandmother." She wrinkled her nose. "Don't get me wrong. I love my grandmother. I just don't want to smell like her."

Leah smiled sympathetically. Her *mammi* smelled like

liniment and cinnamon. She didn't want to smell like that either. "Do you want pure grapefruit or a combination? Like vanilla grapefruit or eucalyptus grapefruit?"

The woman paused. "Are you making this just for me?"

Leah gave a quick shrug. "It's no problem. I can mix it up in the next day or so. If you like. You just need to tell me what you want the smell to be like, and I'll have it for you by Friday for sure."

The woman's smile was so bright it would have dimmed Independence Day fireworks. "I've never had my own fragrance before."

"I guess not many people have," Leah said.

"Can you make grapefruit, orange, and vanilla?"

"Of course."

"And the cost?" the woman asked.

"It's the same."

"I'll take it. Marjorie Hale." She reached out a hand to shake.

Leah took it and introduced herself.

"And you own this place?"

"Yes."

"I'll be sure to tell all my friends. That is, if you're willing to make them each a signature fragrance."

Signature fragrance? "I don't see why not."

Marjorie smiled. "Good. Good. But just between you and me, you could charge twice that, and everyone will still clamor to buy it."

"Are you serious?" Gracie asked later that afternoon. Once Brandon had finished his schoolwork, Leah had asked him and Shelly to mind the store so she could come out and talk to her new business partners.

"I'm ashamed that I didn't think of it," Hannah said. "It's brilliant."

"Being back with the Amish has made you soft," Leah said. They all laughed.

"I mean really, it's the perfect opportunity there in town. And if women can come in and design a fragrance all their own, how amazing is that?" Hannah asked.

Gracie's brow puckered. "Very?" she asked hesitantly.

Leah smiled. "Right answer." Unlike Leah and Hannah, Gracie hadn't spent any time in the I-am-different-and-special *Englisch* world. The Amish strove for togetherness, community, and sameness. Standing out wasn't encouraged. In fact, it was frowned upon. She had heard many an *Englischer* comment that by being the same, the Amish stood apart. That was irony at its finest. But if she were going to be in town and running the shop, what better way to promote the fragrances than with a custom fragrance bar to appeal to the women who wanted to stand apart from their peers?

"What about sales?" Hannah asked. "I mean, the single fragrances seem to be selling better than anything else."

"Right." Leah nodded. "We keep those, even the ones mixed two to a bottle, like lavender vanilla. Those will always be good sellers. This is something different."

"And we're just going to make lotions?" Gracie asked.

"We don't have to. We can offer whatever product we have in the fragrance. Goat milk soap. Or even sulfate-free shampoos and conditioners."

Gracie gasped. "I don't know how to make those. Just soap and lotion."

"We can learn how. Or not. We don't have to do it at all. We can make this as large or small as we want. It's up to us, and since we're already using the shop space, there's no overhead."

Gracie looked up at the ceiling.

"She means no hidden expenses," Hannah explained.

"Oh." Gracie nodded. "Of course."

"What do you say?" Leah asked, looking from one of them to the other.

"I say we do it." Hannah's eyes lit with excitement.

"I'm in," Gracie said, still frowning. "But what's a sulfate?"

"Are these the only Amish clothes you have?" a strangely familiar voice asked the following day.

Leah turned from her chore of checking tags and hangers to look at the woman. Deborah King. Jamie's ex-fiancée. If Deborah recalled meeting her, the recognition didn't show on her face. But Leah definitely remembered meeting Deborah.

"There are more items in the far back section. But they are trade items. If at all possible." Why was Deborah King in her shop looking to buy Amish clothing?

"I don't have anything to trade. That's why I'm here. Can I buy some of the items?"

It was on the tip of Leah's tongue to tell her yes, then charge her double, but that wasn't fair. She needn't be so mean-spirited. "The items aren't inventoried for sale, but you can take whatever you need, on one condition."

Deborah eyed her skeptically. They must be distrustful up in Tennessee. "What's that?"

"That once you're finished with the items, you donate them to someone in need."

Immediately Deborah's demeanor shifted. "Oh. *Jah*. Of course."

"Then take what you need." Leah turned and made her way back to the front of the store, but she could feel the violet stare of Deborah King nearly burning a hole in her back.

She might think Leah was all kinds a fool for giving

things away, but it was what the Lord had called her to do. And so it was exactly how she was going to go about it. Her heart felt light at the prospect as she went to the front of the store to rearrange the lotion shelves. She needed to add a sign advertising their new offering of custom-made fragrances. Marjorie Hale would be in tomorrow to pick up her fragrance, and if she wanted it all to herself, she could pay an extra fee to have it exclusively. Well, Marjorie wouldn't—since she had virtually developed the idea, Leah decided she would give the woman a discount. And with any luck this would be the start of a new business adventure for her, Hannah, and Gracie.

"I can't keep washing my clothes every other day," a woman said on the other side of the partition. Deborah King again.

"You should wear one at home like the rest of us and save your best dress for when you go out. Toting water is too much of a chore to be so frivolous." That was Sarah Hostetler.

"I'm not trying to be frivolous, but I can't be going around in a dirty housedress and apron."

So her solution was washing her clothes every day? In a community with no indoor running water, Leah had to agree with Sarah: frivolous.

"What if Jamie comes over?" Deborah continued.

Sarah sighed. Even though they were separated by a large slab of drywall, Leah could still hear it. "That's just the thing. Do you really think he's coming over? He hasn't been over since that first day."

"He's just hurt. I need to give him some time." Deborah's tone turned defensive.

"He's had almost three weeks."

"Not nearly enough. A man like that has his pride. He

may keep it hidden from the church, but trust me, it's there."

Leah could attest to that.

"It's just a matter of time," Deborah said, "before he realizes what he's missing and we go back to Ethridge. Together."

Sarah didn't comment. Leah wished that she did. She would like to know what others around Deborah thought about her and Jamie as a couple.

If Leah was being perfectly honest with herself, she would acknowledge that she was a little jealous of the relationship Deborah thought she had with Jamie. If Leah believed it to be real, she might be a lot jealous. But according to him, there was nothing more between him and Deborah King. And she hoped it was true. For Peter's sake.

"You know what Mammi always told us," Sarah said.

Leah hadn't realized that she and Deborah were kin.

"No, but I'm sure you're going to tell me."

"You can lead a horse to water, but you can't make him drink."

"Is that what you think I'm doing?" Deborah laughed. "Not at all. I'm just reminding him that he's thirsty."

Deborah's words and her throaty laugh followed Leah for the rest of the day. She heard them as she straightened all the racks and restocked the shelves with kitchen glasses and flatware. As she swept the floor, dusted out the windowsills, and turned the sign to closed.

Those words and that sultry laugh shouldn't have bothered her. She shouldn't have given either one a second thought, but here she was with them replaying in her head like a stuck recording.

"What up, Aunt Leah?" Brandon asked as she let herself into their apartment.

"Huh?" She focused her gaze on him, only then realizing that she had been walking in something of a daze.

"You okay?" A concerned frown lined his forehead.

"Yeah, sure. Fine. I'm fine."

"Uh-huh. You just keep telling yourself that."

She set her bag on one counter and pulled out a chair from the kitchen table. She plopped down into it and propped her chin in one hand. "What do you think about the Amish?" she asked.

"Huh?"

"What do you—"

He nodded. "I heard what you said. I just don't know why you're asking me."

Leah shrugged. "You never had any experience with the Amish before you came here. What do you think about them?"

He eyed her for a moment, and she was certain he was trying to figure out if she was pranking him or not. Satisfied, he pulled out the chair across from her and sat. "They're strict."

"And?"

"Loving." He smiled. "They make the best pie and—"

"And what?" she asked when his words cut off.

"They seem to really love God. I mean, I went to school with kids and had friends who said they loved God, but not like the Amish do."

"God's will," she supplied.

"I'm sorry?" he asked.

"The Amish believe in God's will. If their dog gets sick, it's God's will."

He frowned. "God cares about my dog? I mean, if I had one."

"Not a single sparrow can fall from the sky without the Father knowing about it," Leah paraphrased.

Brandon seemed to let that sink in. "Pastor Joel spoke on that a few sermons ago."

"That's right."

"What does this have to do with you and Jamie?" he asked.

Leah drew back. "What?"

"You and Jamie," he said, slower this time. "Isn't he why you came in all moony-eyed?"

"Whatever." She waved a hand as if the motion alone would dispel his question.

"Come on, Aunt Leah. I see how you look at him when you don't think anyone's watching."

"I don't look at him like anything."

Brandon grinned. "He looks at you like that too."

"He does?" She straightened. "I mean, whatever."

"Uh-huh." His grin deepened.

"There is nothing between me and Jamie. And there never will be." Saying the words out loud should have been therapeutic, but it only made her stomach hurt.

"Why not?"

"Long story short? He's Amish, and I'm Mennonite."

"It's really that big of a deal?" he asked.

"Mountainous."

He gave a loose-shouldered shrug. "Then change it."

"What?"

"Change. It."

She shook her head. "It's not that easy."

"Seems like it to me."

He was right, but only if the person was willing to change it. She couldn't become Amish again. It just wasn't possible. How could she take such steps back? Simply feeling like it was retreating was enough to tell her that joining the Amish church wasn't an option for her. And Jamie wasn't joining the Mennonite church. What happened when two people who cared about each other were too stubborn to give? They lived alone for the rest of their lives.

Pride or not, Leah wasn't sure spinsterhood was a goal she wanted for herself. But could she change it? There was only one way to find out.

Saturday morning dawned an imperfect day. Unless a person liked cloudy, overcast, and growing-chilly sorts of days. It was only mid-October, but the air held a bite that promised winter was on the way. However, this was northern Mississippi. Today could be forty degrees and tomorrow nearly eighty. There was no telling what the weather would bring.

The rock painters met in the church parking lot and devised a plan for dropping off their offerings all over town. Leah and Jamie drew Main Street, while Brandon and Shelly drew the other side of town.

"Can Peter go with us?" Brandon asked.

"Is that what you want, Peter?" Leah asked.

He nodded in that enthusiastic way of his. He hadn't been back to school. Not since the problem earlier in the week. Leah couldn't blame Jamie for not wanting to send him back to a school where it appeared he was failing, but she knew that he couldn't stay out forever. Sooner or later he would have to go back. And she wasn't convinced that he could thrive in such an environment.

"Jamie?" Leah asked, turning toward him.

"It's all right with me. You know where we'll be if you need us," he added.

"We'll be fine." Brandon smiled down at Peter. "Won't we?"

He nodded again, and the three of them headed off to Brandon's car. The teen had really taken to Jamie's son. As far as Leah was concerned, it was just another check mark in the "win column."

Jamie was stiff as he watched Shelly and Brandon drive off with Peter. Was he regretting letting Peter leave with the teens?

"Brandon won't let anything happen to him." She did her best to reassure Jamie.

He merely nodded. "I know." He turned away, but the car was long gone.

"Come on," she said. "I'll drive us over to Main."

She parked her car in her usual place behind the shop, and together she and Jamie started walking down Main. They left one rock in the window at Twice Blessed and another under the picnic tables at the end of the building. But they still had several to leave.

They walked and talked about nothing and generally had a good time in each other's company.

"Are you worried about Peter?" she asked.

"Because he's with Brandon?"

She shook her head. "About school."

"A little." Which meant a lot. But that was Jamie, allowing his faith to downplay his emotions.

"You won't be able to keep him out for long."

"I know. But I can't send him back there." They walked in silence for a couple of heartbeats. "I've been wondering about computer school."

Leah stumbled. "You what?"

"Is it so unbelievable?"

She shook her head and tried to get her bearings back. "No. Uh, yes. Yes, it is."

"I feel like I'm out of options."

"You have them. I know sometimes it feels like you don't, but they're there, just waiting to be discovered."

"That's my prayer."

Leah stopped. "Jamie, come to church with me and Brandon tomorrow."

It was his turn to falter. "What?"

"Come to church with us. We would love to have you, and you might learn something new."

Chapter Fifteen

Leah's request stopped Jamie in his tracks. "Church?" He said the word as if he'd never heard it before.

"Why not?" She shrugged. "It's an off-Sunday."

He shook his head, then nodded. "*Jah*. It's not a church Sunday for us."

"But?" she prompted.

"But it's not part of the *Ordnung*."

"There's nothing in the rules that says you can't come visit a church with me."

That was true, but he felt like he was manipulating the words until they suited his purpose. Yet he was curious about her church. He wasn't sure when it started. Maybe when they were painting rocks. Or maybe it was the first time he had seen Leah Gingerich with her conservative prayer covering and modern car.

"Jamie."

He turned his attention to her.

"Come with me. I want to show you our church."

"Why?"

"Does there have to be a reason?"

His stomach fell as he realized the motivation behind the

invitation. "Is this so you can get your doctor friend to look at Peter?"

The shock on her face couldn't have been feigned. "No. Of course not. I mean, I would love for the doctor to talk with Peter, but I would never arrange for something like that behind your back. Never."

He believed her. "I'm sorry," he said. "All this stuff with Peter and Sally's parents." He shook his head. "It's got me all jittery."

She smiled, and he felt as if he were in the direct presence of the sun. "It's okay. You love Peter, and you want what's best for him."

"And you do too," he said.

"Absolutely."

They walked down Main Street, looking for places where they could leave rocks for future hunters. The town's annual pumpkin-decorating contest was in full swing. Each store had some sort of pumpkin plopped out front. Some were carved, but more were painted with everything from the Mississippi State Bulldog to the Rams, the local high school mascot.

"Did you make a pumpkin?" he asked.

Leah shook her head. "The city wanted everyone to participate, but it didn't seem right. Not quite godly. You know, maybe even a little pagan."

"You could have painted one," he said.

"Like we did the rocks?"

"Exactly. That's not so pagan, is it?"

She shrugged. "Not sure. But it seems a little better than carving a scary face into one."

"Right. No jack-o'-lantern; just a painted pumpkin."

Leah grabbed his sleeve. "We could paint it with a Bible verse."

"Just like the rocks." His grin widened.

"Do you think Peter would like to help?"

"I know he would."

They walked a few steps in silence.

"We could paint it tomorrow after church," Leah offered.

"Is it really that important to you, that I see your church up close?"

"Yes," she said simply. "I think you might even like it."

"*Jah*. Okay then," he found himself saying.

"You'll do it?" Her face could barely contain her wide grin. "You and Peter will come to church with me?"

He nodded as she bounced on her toes like an excited schoolgirl. He had no idea why this was so important to her; only that it was.

They left two more rocks on their trip down Main, then turned to make their way back to the shop.

"Did you put that one out?" Leah pointed to a painted rock at the end of the building.

Jamie shook his head, then made his way over to fetch it. The rock didn't look familiar. It was about the size of his palm and almost perfectly round. Someone had painted it pale green, with a large multicolored cross and small red hearts. Around its edge they had written a verse. *Ephesians 2:8 For it is by grace you have been saved, through faith— and this is not from yourselves, it is the gift of God.*

"It has to be one of ours," Leah mused. "Unless another church is putting them out as well."

Jamie turned the rock over. There was nothing on the back. Leah's church had marked theirs on the back in case anyone wanted to contact the church about the message they had painted on the front. He flipped it back over and read the verse again.

By grace you have been saved.

"Or maybe a family," Leah mused. "I could see Shelly's family doing something like this too."

By grace you have been saved. It is the gift of God.
"Jamie?"

He jerked his gaze from the rock to Leah. "What?"

"Are you up for something to eat? I thought we might go get a burger. You know, the five of us."

By grace you have been saved.

"Five?"

"Me, you, Peter, Brandon, and Shelly."

"*Jah.*" He nodded. *It is the gift from God.* "That sounds fine."

They stopped for a burger at the café at the edge of the building. It was a beautiful fall day, and they opted to be outside at the picnic tables around the side.

Leah looked across the table to where Shelly, Brandon, and Peter sat. Jamie was next to her, and she couldn't help but wonder what the passersby thought of them. A Mennonite, two Amish, a conservative Christian, and an *Englischer*. She supposed they appeared like some sort of new-world blended family.

What would happen if she and Jamie could find a way to remain together? What would happen to Brandon? Nothing, if she stayed with her church. And that was how it would have to be. She had promised Hannah that she would take care of her son. Even if Leah wanted to join the Amish church, bend her knee, and ask for forgiveness, she couldn't. She had Brandon to think about.

"Did you know there's a rumor going round that you are returning to Ethridge?"

He wiped his mouth, his eyes wide over the napkin in his hand. "No." He swallowed, his voice thick.

"So you're not? Planning to return to Ethridge?"

"No. Not at all."

She tried not to look too relieved. "I'm glad. I thought you were settling in here nicely."

The kids had found one of those super bouncy balls they sell out of gumball machines. They had taken it to the end of the building, where they could throw it against the bricks and take turns catching it. Such a simple pastime, but it seemed to bring Peter great joy.

"I am. It's just—"

"Peter," she finished for him.

"*Jah*. Peter."

The name was simple, Biblical. Peter had been a devout follower of Christ, His rock. And yet there was nothing simple about it. Little Peter was hurting, suffering under his scars, and Jamie felt helpless against it. He didn't have to say the words. Leah knew. She could feel his despair. And she would do anything to help him ease those feelings. In both of them.

"What about Deborah?" Leah hadn't meant to ask the question. It had been knocking around in her head since yesterday, when Deborah had been in Twice Blessed.

Leah had wanted to tell Jamie about Deborah's plans to win him over, of her taking clothes so she would have more to wear while she was here. How she washed her clothes often so that her best would always be clean just in case. But how could she without sounding hopelessly jealous?

"What about her?" Jamie asked.

"She's been down here a long time."

He sighed. "She said she wasn't leaving until I agree to go back with her."

Leah wasn't sure how to respond. She made what she hoped was an understanding yet commiserating face, then tilted her head from side to side.

"Every night I pray that tomorrow will be the day she gives up."

When he should be praying for Peter.

"Aunt Leah! Jamie! Look!" Brandon called from the edge of the building.

Just over the last of the picnic tables, Leah could see Shelly bent at the waist and Peter crouched on the ground, his arms around the dirtiest dog she had ever seen.

Mud caked the beast's tan face, coloring its fur a rusty brown and clumping it together. Amid all the dirt and filth, Leah met sweet brown eyes that begged for love and attention. And maybe what was left of her hamburger.

She stood and took the scraps over to the dog. He gobbled down the burger, nearly choked, then started on the fries.

"What do we do with it?" Brandon asked.

"I think Peter wants to keep him," Shelly said.

Leah was reminded of the dog that Peter had lost in the fire. She had been thinking a dog would help his healing along, and she had said as much to Jamie, but she had no say further than that.

"I think he belongs to somebody." Leah pointed to the equally dirty collar almost hidden in the matted fur. Upon closer inspection, Leah could see that once upon a time, the collar had been a sweet baby blue.

After he was cleaned up, the dog would probably be cute. The kind of mid-sized dog with shaggy, tan fur that might answer to a name like Scrappy.

"There aren't any tags," Shelly pointed out.

"Maybe he belongs to someone around here." Leah glanced around to see if anyone appeared to be looking for a pooch.

"This dirty?" Brandon said. "He's been out here for a while."

"Doesn't hurt to ask," Leah said.

They almost had to pry Peter's arms from around the dog's neck. They used Brandon's belt as a leash and walked the dog down the street. He pranced on the end of the makeshift lead as he if he had been born to walk there. Leah knew he had to belong to someone. But who?

No one was missing a dog from any of the stores they visited.

"What do we do now?" Brandon asked.

"We can't take him home," Leah said. "We don't have enough room."

Shelly took a step back, holding her arms up as if surrendering. "Don't look at me. My parents would have a cow if I brought home a puppy."

"You think he's a puppy?" Jamie asked.

"He's not quite a year," Leah estimated. "But he probably won't get much bigger than this."

"I guess we could take him with us." Jamie's tone was reluctant. "If we leave him here, he'll probably get hit by a car."

Leah nodded.

"But we can't keep him," Jamie told Peter. "Do you understand that? He belongs to someone, and they are probably looking for him."

"Shelly and I can make some signs at the library." Brandon took out his cell phone and snapped a picture of the mutt.

Shelly nodded, her ponytail swinging from side to side. "I'll hand them out."

Jamie sighed. "I guess it's up to us to feed him and give him a bath."

Leah laughed. "I guess I could help with that too."

"Then let's do it," Jamie said, and together their odd little family, plus filthy stray dog, made their way down Main Street.

How did Jamie end up with a dog in a cabin with two— make that three—rooms? There was no fenced-in yard. Most folks around these parts let their dogs run free, but he didn't want to do that. Too many people drove too fast

down the winding gravel roads. What good would it do to
bring the dog home to keep him from getting run over in
town only to let him loose in the country? And he was reluctant to put the mutt on a chain. He'd had a friend who
had done that, and his dog had wound around a tree and
choked himself to death. The last thing, the *very last* thing
he needed was Peter coming outside to find a dead dog in
his yard. It was going to be hard enough when they found
the real owner.

But there Jamie sat on the couch that Leah had helped
him find. Peter sat at the coffee table, writing his letters.
The pooch lay curled up next to the boy, his chin propped
on one bent leg.

The dog was a loving creature. All he seemed to want
was a little bit of food and as much attention as anyone
could spare.

Someone had to be looking for the mutt. And it was only
a matter of time before they called Brandon's phone to in-
quire.

Jamie looked to boy and dog, who seemed so content to
be together. He supposed he would cross that bridge when
he got there, as they say. The dog needed to stay somewhere, and his cabin just happened to be the where. Everything else could be dealt with as it came.

Jamie pulled on the tail end of his vest the following
morning and surveyed himself in the small mirror that
hung next to his bed. Leah had told him that he could wear
whatever he wanted to the service, but he couldn't see past
wearing his church clothes.

The dog had slept with Peter the night before. Jamie
wasn't all for animals in the house, but he didn't have the
heart to tell the boy that the dog had to sleep elsewhere.
After all, they would have to keep him in the house for a

while. And if he was already inside, what harm was it if he stayed in Peter's room? From there it was a short hop— literally—to the foot of Peter's bed.

Jamie's secret hope was that the dog would provide Peter whatever it was he needed in order to fight back the terrible memories he faced and talk again. Time was running short. There were only a couple more weeks before Sally's parents would come to get him, whether they had room, love, and attention for another child or not.

Somehow Jamie had to get Peter talking. And somehow he had to do it in the next two weeks.

He heard the crunch of gravel from outside and knew that Leah and Brandon were there to get them.

"Peter? Are you ready?" He asked the question, but he knew Peter wouldn't answer. Couldn't blame a man for trying.

Jamie gave his vest another tug, then made his way into the main room. Peter was standing next to the couch, his own white shirt neat and crisp, thanks to Leah. The shirt had miraculously appeared in her donation box at the shop. It was a little too clean and free of stains to be anything but new. He figured Gracie had made it at Leah's request. He just couldn't imagine Leah sitting down at a treadle machine and piecing a garment together. The image just wouldn't come. And that wasn't bad. Leah was a little untraditional, but that was just Leah.

"Are you ready?" Jamie resisted the urge to tug on his vest once again. He felt like his clothes had shrunk. Or maybe he had gained a little weight. Most probably he was simply uncomfortable.

He had never been to another church. Not even once in his entire life. Why did he agree to go to Leah's church with her this morning?

Why did it matter so much?

Because he had faith in his God, in his religion, in his

faith. His faith was all that he had left. But lately . . . lately it had seemed like his faith was wearing thin. Lately he had been wondering if there was more out there than what he had been told his entire life. And it scared him. Straight down to his bones. He was terrified, quaking. What if he found something different only to discover that it really wasn't more? That it was an illusion. What would that do to his faith, his works? To everything he held so dear?

Peter nodded, the dog sitting at his feet as if he was trying to be the best dog he could be so they would have no choice but to keep him.

Yesterday, Brandon and Shelly had posted a bunch of flyers around town, and hopefully before the end of the week, the rightful owners would come get their dog. But when that happened, Jamie was going to have to get Peter another dog. Leah was right. Peter may not have said a word since the pup had come into their lives, but he was the happiest that Jamie had seen him in a long, long time.

He nodded toward the boy. "Let's go, then."

Walking into the actual church shouldn't have felt different than walking into an Amish home where the furniture had been moved aside and the benches had been set up for the service. But it did.

There seemed to be a reverent quiet about the place. The sort of hush that made him want to whisper, even though those around him were speaking in normal tones. He wanted to walk softly as well, even though the carpet beneath his feet cushioned his footfalls.

Aside from the air of expectancy, the church was . . . different than he had expected. Not that he'd had an idea in mind. All he had ever known were the homes of his friends and neighbors. But this was a building set aside especially for one thing. Church. Even the fancier houses that had a bonus room to hold church in used that space for storage and other things until their turn for service came around. This . . . this was a luxury beyond anything he had ever seen. Carpet, flowers, a big wooden cross draped with a stretch of deep purple cloth. The walls were painted a soft, inviting white, and the ceiling was lined with dark wooden beams. Aside from the place up front where he assumed the pastor would stand and deliver his word for the day, it was mostly like the church he was accustomed to. In a bare bones sort of way. Floor, walls, ceiling, benches to sit. But the atmosphere—that truly set the whole place apart. The atmosphere said, *This place is special, so special we only do one thing here: worship the Lord.*

Jamie cleared his throat as Peter moved a little closer to him. The boy was wide-eyed, taking in everything like a sponge absorbs water.

Leah led the way down the center aisle, just a few steps ahead of them. She tossed a small smile over her shoulder. "I usually sit here." She stopped about midway along the line of benches and pointed to a spot on the right. "Is that okay with the two of you?"

Jamie stopped. "You mean . . ." She had to mean that they were sitting together. He glanced around at the other couples who had already found their places. There were women and men on both sides of the center. At least now he wouldn't spend half of the service looking at her seated across the room. This way she would be right next to him. He cleared his throat again. "This is fine."

They sat together with Peter sandwiched between. He swung his legs and looked at the paper they were handed when they came in. It told of the songs they were going to sing, the verses they would read in the service, and what had happened within the church since they met last Sunday.

Jamie wasn't sure why Peter found it so mesmerizing,

but he stared at it as if he could read every word. He studied each page and held Leah's hand. Just like a family.

The sermon was enjoyable, interesting, and different than what he was accustomed to, aside from the fact that it was in English. The words of the pastor stayed with Jamie as the final announcements were read, the final prayer prayed, and the invitation offered to stay after and talk with others about God and His grace if someone needed special attention or prayer. These words mixed with the verse on the rock Jamie had found the day before.

Pastor Joel had preached from John 11:25. *Jesus said to her, "I am the resurrection and the life. The one who believes in me will live, even though they die."*

There was nothing there about how you were to live your life. It simply was. And yesterday the verse on the rock had talked about grace being a gift. Just a gift, and you were saved. Was it really that simple? He had wanted to walk up front, kneel down with the preacher, and ask about being saved by grace. God's grace. It had such a nice, firm ring to it. Trustworthy. But he had managed to keep his spot on the deep purple carpet. His legs had trembled with his effort to remain in place. He swayed even as if someone was pushing him from behind. This message went against everything he had ever been told in his life, and yet he wanted to know more. He didn't feel as if his church had lied to him, merely that it had told him only part of God's love. God's grace.

But he couldn't make himself go forward. It was uncertainty. He wanted to be sure of what he was finding out. Yet how could he know unless he asked? Wasn't that what the *Englisch* called a catch-22? But he had remained in place with Peter next to him and Leah on the other side of him. Brandon had found a place nearer the back, sitting with friends.

And then church was over. They met with a few of Leah's friends, then got back into her car and headed toward home. His home, the Gingeriches' home.

"Mamm's is always good for an after-church meal," Leah said as they headed down Topsy Road.

Jamie had traveled the road many times, but usually in a horse and carriage. Strangely enough, he was beginning to get used to traveling in a car. At least it wasn't as unnerving today as it had been the day before, or even the time before that.

"I could go for some of Mammi's pie," Brandon said from the back seat.

Peter nodded.

Why wouldn't he talk? Jamie so needed him to talk.

"Are you still going to the wedding with me and Gracie on Thursday?" Leah asked as she pulled her car to a stop at her parents' house.

"I said I would."

Leah breathed a sigh. "I was hoping you would say that."

Jamie got out of the car. The boys ran for the house to be the first one to the porch, thereby winning the biggest piece of pie. Brandon had Peter in both agility and ability, but Peter was pulling ahead. Brandon might have let him win, but Peter was thrilled all the same.

For Leah, the week went about as usual. Tuesday was cousins' day, and they continued their endeavor to stock, restock, and build up the goat milk products she carried in the shop. Twice Blessed's business was steady and true. She even had a few people come by with their cell phones and snap a quick picture of the rock she had "hidden" in her front window. Some ventured in, while others snapped and moved on along.

But Thursday? That was weighing on her. Why had she invited Jamie to go with her? Just so she wouldn't have to go alone? She and Hannah had promised to go together and help with the cleanup afterward, but Hannah's plans had changed when Aaron had a horse show in Oxford. Hannah was staying at his house while he was out of town to get the kids ready for school and put to bed in the evening. Hannah was going long enough to see the couple get married, and then she had to scoot back home. Which would leave Leah alone at her once-upon-a-time boyfriend's wedding. No, thank you.

So Leah had asked Jamie. Like a lovesick idiot. Not that she had delusions that anything could actually be between her and Jamie. But she did want to be his friend. She had grown fond of him. More than fond, if she was being truly honest with herself. He could make her madder than any person she had ever met, and quicker than everyone as well. But there was something about him that seemed to draw her to him, whether she wanted to be or not. It was as if something inside him called to something inside her. What? She had no idea. But it was there all the same.

She had prayed and prayed about it. She and Jamie were simply too different to be anything other than friends. Neither one was ready to give up their church; neither one was willing to ask the other to change their way of life. What could become of that? Nothing. Absolutely nothing. So why had God put these feelings inside her? Did Jamie feel the same? She thought He did, but she couldn't be certain. They had both been cautious not to cross any lines. At least none that couldn't be uncrossed.

"Are you ready?" Jamie asked as he pulled the buggy to a stop in front of her *mamm*'s house.

"As I'll ever be," she muttered under her breath, then flashed him a bright smile. "Of course."

She made her way down the porch steps as Peter was coming up them. The dog was padding along at his heels.

"Have a good time with Eunice," she said.

He smiled and nodded. If he was anything like Brandon, he would be just fine as long as there was pie.

"Hi, Peter. No, no, no," she heard her mother say as she got into the buggy next to Jamie. "The pooch has to stay outside. He'll be fine on the porch. Come on in and help me get him some water to drink. It's October, but still plenty warm out."

Leah had thought it was just her. It did seem warmer than usual, but she wasn't about to comment on it. Now she didn't have to.

"I'm still not sure about this." She waved a hand at her lap.

"What about it? You look fine to me."

It had nothing to do with looking fine. She knew she looked appropriate. Good, even. But she didn't look the same.

She was wearing her best: a long, dark purple dress with a shallow scooped neck and three-quarter sleeves. She liked what the color did for her hair and her eyes. They looked almost jade. She wanted to look her best for a lot of reasons, but she knew she would be the only one there who wasn't Amish. Her dress covered just as much as the Amish dresses; it just fit a little closer and didn't have an apron. The color was dark enough to pass muster, but she knew the truth. She would stick out like a sore thumb. She should have just stayed at home, but she had wanted to see Abby and Benuel find their happiness. She had to come, if only to prove to everyone that since she was back, she hadn't regretted her decisions. And she didn't. Mostly.

But sitting there with half of the district watching her as much as they were watching the actual ceremony . . .

"Are you okay?" he asked.

She wanted to shake her head no, but she nodded instead. "I'm fine." *As fine as frog hair.*

"Why do I feel like you're not telling me the entire truth?"

"Maybe because I'm not. But don't ask why. I can't explain."

"As long as you're okay," he said, casting her a quick glance.

"I am, truly. I promise."

They rode in silence for a few moments.

"You don't have to go," he said.

Suddenly she was aware that he had stopped the buggy, and she realized that they were at the turnoff to Abby's house. The home itself set back off the road just a bit, but not enough to conceal all the buggies that had already begun to gather there. Most everyone in the district would be here today. She would get out and face them all.

Or . . . they could just keep going. But what would that accomplish? It would just delay the inevitable face-off she would have with the community. She wasn't technically under the *Bann*, but that didn't mean she would be well received either.

Strangely enough, she hadn't seen Benuel since that fateful night fifteen years ago. She wasn't sure how she would feel when she saw him. If her heart would still flutter. Would his smile mean as much to her now as it had back then? But most importantly, would seeing him again make her regret the decisions she had made? Regrets were a waste of time, but most were beyond a person's control. And that was where Leah really had a problem with things. How could she be happy if she were living with tons of regrets? Would it be better to face them, or to leave and never know?

"Leah?" Jamie asked.

He had to be the bravest man she knew. He took in a boy
with troubles to keep him from getting lost in the shuffle of
another's home. He had moved over a hundred miles from
home to live in a cabin and help her father build sheds and
fix random problems in their community. That took more
than bravery; that took a fortitude that she found admirable.
And she was contemplating missing a wedding because it
might be uncomfortable? She should be ashamed.

"Let's go," she said with a quick nod at the turnoff. "Time
to face the music."

Fifteen years away, and Amish weddings hadn't changed
one bit.

They pulled up and were met by young male members
of Benuel's family. They were parking the buggies, unhitching the horses, and turning them out to pasture. As usual,
they had numbers to put on each horse's bridle and on each
buggy to match the numbers they gave each owner. With
that many buggies, horses, and owners, this was the only
way to make sure everything got back to the right person at
the end of the day.

Together Jamie and Leah walked to the milling crowd
of people, all waiting on the festivities to begin. Amish
weddings were a great deal like their church services. The
bishop and other elders were preparing for their sermons,
while the bride and her attendants were upstairs getting
ready. The groom was most likely hiding out in the barn
with his male kin, where they would be teasing one another
and acting like this wasn't the most important day of his life.

Since this was a second wedding, a great deal of the
traditions would be skipped, like the picking of partners for
the meal and the singing afterward, but the food, cake, and
joy would all be the same.

"Jamie Stoltzfus?"

He turned as Abby's father, Joe John Glick, came hurrying up. Joe John was dressed for the wedding in his Sunday best black vest and crisp smoky blue shirt that Leah suspected perfectly matched his daughter's wedding dress.

"I didn't think you would ever get here. Come quick," Joe John continued. "We need your help getting the tables up, and one has a broken leg. We've tried everything to fix it, to no avail. But I hear you're good with a hammer and saw."

Jamie gave a humble shrug. "I do all right."

"We need you," Joe John said.

"Of course." Jamie shot her an apologetic glance.

She waved it away. "Go do your thing," she said. It seemed she was destined to be alone at this wedding. Well, so be it.

"I'll find you when I'm finished," Jamie promised.

Leah merely nodded.

"*Danki, danki,*" Joe John said as he led Jamie away, leaving Leah standing all alone in the crowd.

Not knowing what else she should do, she walked like she had a purpose to the edge of the soybean field. Or rather what had been a soybean field before the last harvest. Now it was just a square of clumped earth and fragments of once-thriving plants.

Leah sighed. She should hold her head high and go back in there and pretend like whatever it was, she would have it no other way. But right that moment she just didn't have it in her. She needed a little time alone, just a few seconds when she knew no one but God was watching and she could give in to the unexplainable tears, if only for a second or two.

Remembering the creek that ran behind Joe John's shop, Leah headed for the crop of trees on the far side of the house. Just a few moments alone. That was all she needed.

She picked her way through the bramble, feeling somehow that the woods were thicker when she was younger, the trees taller, but that couldn't be the case. An ice storm a few years back cleared away a lot of timber, and the trees had to be taller now than back then. It only stood to reason. But it seemed as if nothing was making much sense today. And that was why she didn't even flinch when she cleared the line of trees, spotted the creek, and saw Benuel King sitting on the opposite bank.

"Don't you have a wedding to get to?" she asked without greeting.

He startled when she spoke, so lost in his thoughts or whatever, that he hadn't heard her come up. *Must be something heavy,* she thought. She hadn't expected anyone to be down here, and hadn't tried in the least to temper her footfalls as she walked through the woods.

"*Jah,*" he said. He stood and dusted off the seat of his pants. His wedding pants. He wore the same blue-gray shirt as her uncle Joe John and an expression that was almost as harried.

He picked his way across the creek, using half-submerged rocks and a fallen log to return to her side.

She stood there like the moss, just being, as he started past.

She should say something. But she didn't know what. *You look good?* And he did. *I handled things badly. I know it's been a long time, but I hope you forgive me?* Or maybe *You've moved on, why do I feel like I'm only treading water?*

He walked one step past her, then stopped. "You told me you were coming back."

She didn't have to ask what he was talking about. She knew. "I didn't mean to lie to you."

"I waited, you know. For a while, I waited and prayed that you would come back. And as much as I cared for you,

I'm glad you didn't. If you had, I wouldn't have married Mary Ann, and I wouldn't have Davey and Jonah."

"And you wouldn't be marrying Abby."

He smiled, and the motion lit his face with love and excitement.

"I just didn't want to break your heart."

"You didn't. Well, you did for a while, but I got over it. I moved on." He looked pointedly at her clothes. "You did too." He stopped, tilted his head to one side, and studied her from this new angle. "Tell me, Leah. Are you happy?"

Chapter Sixteen

Was she happy?

Leah stopped, let his words sink in. He was next to her, almost past her, but she couldn't see his expression, didn't know what he was thinking. She had to take it all at face value. Was she happy?

"Yes," she said simply, and she knew it was true. She was happy. She had made a good life. Maybe not the life she thought she would have when she was sixteen and making eyes at Benuel across the barn at a Sunday night singing. But it was a good life. Even though she couldn't go back and change how it came out, she loved it. She was happy. "What about you?" she asked. "Are you happy?"

He didn't take as long as she had to answer. "Yes. My life has been good so far."

And she prayed it would continue that same way. "Good. I'm glad."

Out of the corner of her eye, she saw him nod. "See you at the wedding, Leah." And then he was gone.

By the time Leah got back to the house, everyone was getting in place for the wedding to start. But this time her step was lighter. She hadn't realized what a burden leaving her Amish life behind had put on her. She wasn't completely at peace with every decision she had made, every regret that haunted her dreams, but this was a start. A very good one.

She stopped next to Jamie, who looked surprised to see her.

"Did you think I skipped town?" she whispered for only him to hear.

"I was beginning to wonder."

She tempered her smile lest it stretch across the room. "Just taking care of some unfinished business."

"Do I even want to know?" he asked.

She shot him a wink. "I'll tell you on the ride home." Then she moved away to take her place with the other women.

"Go on ahead without me," Leah said hours later. The wedding had gone off without a hitch, if a person didn't count the groom's youngest crying for his *Dat-dat-dat* the entire ceremony. In the end, Benuel's mother had started for the back door, her youngest grandson in her arms, but Benuel stopped her. He vowed his love and his life to Abby Glick while cradling Jonah in his arms and bouncing him to keep him happy.

It was proof positive that life was full of compromises. And those weren't always bad things.

"I hate leaving you here," Jamie said.

"It's okay. I've got plenty of kin hanging around. I can catch a ride with someone."

Jamie took another step closer. "Are you being serious, or do you want me to keep on? I can get you out of here, you know. If you're ready to go." He said the words where only she could hear.

Leah couldn't stop her smile. "I'm being serious. Everything's fine. I'm just trying to help."

He frowned and took a step back, his gaze steadily studying her as if he couldn't quite trust what she was saying.

"I promise," she said. She understood his reluctance. Only a few short hours ago she had been more than reluctant to even attend the wedding. Now she was even more willing to stay and help clean up as promised. She hadn't had an opportunity to explain it all to him. Of course he was confused. "I'll come by and explain once we're done here," she promised.

Finally, he nodded. "*Jah*. Okay. I'll see you in a bit then?"

She nodded, then watched as he turned on his heel and walked toward the row of parked buggies. He turned once when he was halfway there.

She waved and smiled to assure him that everything was indeed okay. He waved in return and started his footsteps once again.

It was well after dark when Leah finally returned to her parents' house, where she had left her car in order to ride with Jamie to the wedding.

A light was still on at Jamie's, and she warred with herself on whether or not to stop and talk to him. A big part of her wanted to keep on driving, as if stopping would somehow change everything beyond what they could handle.

But she stopped anyway. She had promised she would.

Sure, they had too many differences to have more than a friendship between them, but if that was all she could have, then she would take it. She couldn't imagine her life without Jamie and Peter in it. At least in some form.

Jamie wrenched open the door as soon as she knocked. "Hi." His smile was so bright she could even see it even though he was backlit from the light in the living room.

"I was afraid you had already gone to bed," she said.

He stepped to one side and allowed her to enter. "Peter has. He had a big day with Eunice."

Leah nodded. "He didn't happen to—"

Jamie's smile dimmed but remained in place. "No."

"Where's the dog?"

He motioned for her to follow him.

A small sliver of light fell across the foot of the bed as Jamie pushed open Peter's bedroom door. The pooch raised his head, saw there was no threat to the boy, and laid it back on his paws once again. He was at the foot of the bed, almost guarding Peter.

"Looks like he's settling in nicely," Leah whispered.

"*Jah*. Is it bad that I've prayed no one comes for the mutt?"

"I suppose that's only natural. He's been here almost a week." Leah smiled, then nodded for Jamie to close the door. She was suddenly overwhelmed with the need to tuck Peter in, pull his covers up, and kiss his sweet cheek. Maybe she would babysit again when Jamie found someone to court.

The thought sent her stomach plummeting to her shoes. One day Jamie would start to date someone, the person who would eventually serve as Peter's mother. A someone who would get all Jamie's tender looks and sweet smiles. They would probably have children together. Sweet babies to fill a whole house.

He wouldn't live in the cabin then. He would have a big, rambling, white house with extra rooms for such a large family.

But that would be with someone much younger than Leah. She had made her decisions, just as her sister had. She had chosen to serve God, not flirt and date. There were no babies in her future, just as there was no wedding.

Today she had watched as Benuel and Abby pledged their lives each to the other. And just like that, two families became one. And she was sure they would add to it, other babies to grow and grow.

"Leah? What's wrong?"

She glanced into Jamie's sweet and caring blue eyes. What was wrong? Everything. She should have never come home. There was nothing for her. Not really. But the decision had been made, people were depending on her, and there was no going back.

She shook her head. "Just tired. I think I need to go home and rest."

He frowned, and she could tell that he wasn't quite buying her excuse. "*Jah*. Okay."

She headed back to the door. "I just wanted to stop in on my way home."

"I thought you were going to tell me what happened at the wedding."

"Nothing." She faked a smile. "Nothing at all." It was mostly true. The real, life-altering revelations had been right here.

"Are you sure?"

Her smile wavered, then tightened as she made her resolve. "Positive."

He nodded, though he seemed reluctant to let her go. "Be careful driving."

She nodded as tears stung the back of her eyes. "I will," she said and closed the cabin door behind her.

Jamie was splitting firewood at the back of the cabin when the unfamiliar car pulled into his drive. Most likely an *Englischer* looking for Abner's shed company. Jamie buried the ax in the fat log he was using as a stand and wiped one sleeve across his forehead. It might be the middle of October, but it was plenty warm outside when a body was chopping wood.

The man shut off his car and got out, followed by a woman Jamie supposed was his wife. They were in their thirties, a nice-looking couple with a shiny car and smiling faces.

"Can I help you?" he asked.

"We're here about the dog." The man held up a piece of paper, and Jamie figured it was one of the flyers Brandon and Shelly had made, then hung down Main Street.

Inside the house, Jamie could hear the pooch barking, most likely with his paws up on the windowsill and his tail wagging like crazy.

"He had on a blue collar, but I found his tags in the yard," the woman said.

"He's been gone about five weeks." The man shook his head. "We thought he was gone for good."

"Then we saw your sign. I said, that's our Teddy."

The man nodded. "He's really our son's dog. But we all love him."

Just then the front door opened. Peter and the dog stepped out onto the porch.

The mutt took one look at the people and raced toward them, tail wagging but no barking. He braced his feet on the man's thigh, doing everything he could to lick the man's face. Unsuccessful, he raced toward the woman and gave her the same greeting.

Jamie swallowed hard. They had known all along that it would come to this. But after a week and no word, he'd begun to believe that maybe it wouldn't. Maybe the dog had been brought to this area and the owners were far enough away that they would never suspect the dog was still alive and well. In this fantasy of his, Peter got to keep the dog and the previous owners found one even better.

But this show of affection just proved that the pooch— Teddy—had belonged to them first.

"He looks wonderful," the woman said. "You've taken such good care of him. Thank you."

Jamie nodded his response, not sure he could trust his voice yet. These were the proper owners, and Peter would have to give the dog over. It was going to break his heart. Just thinking about it nearly broke Jamie's in two. But their ownership was obvious.

The man reached into his pants pocket and brought out his wallet. "Let me pay you for your trouble."

He couldn't take the man's money. He held up one hand. "No need." His voice sounded rusty and unused.

The man took out two twenties and forced them on Jamie. "Please," he said. "Let me do this much at least."

"*Jah*." He didn't have it in him to contest the man. "*Danki*." He cleared his throat. "Thank you."

"Thank *you*." The man took a couple of steps forward, the dog following each step like magic. He reached out a hand to shake, and Jamie took it. His afternoon of chores had come to an end, he was certain. He and Peter may have talked about someone coming to get the dog, but the theory and the reality were two different things.

"Come on, Teddy," the man called to the dog.

Teddy followed behind him, waiting patiently as he opened the car door. Then Teddy disappeared inside, popping up again once the door was closed behind him. He propped his feet up on the side and let out a bark Jamie could barely hear, tail wagging the entire time.

"No!"

Jamie whirled around, startled by the sound coming from behind him.

Peter was in motion. "Noooooooo," he cried, hobbling down the porch steps and across the yard.

By now the couple had gotten into their car and started to back away. Their intention was clear: they were leaving with the dog.

Peter kept coming, bellowing, "No! No! Nooooooo!"

The man stopped the car as Jamie snaked out one arm and caught Peter, pulling him close.

"It's okay," Jamie said, wrapping his arms around Peter as he continued to struggle. Each word he spoke was like a double-edged blade to his heart. Peter was speaking, something he had prayed over for months, but he was hurting, devastated even by the loss he was faced with once again. His anguish rolled off him, sending ripples through the air.

The man hesitated, his expression clearly stating that he had eyes and he could see and everything was far from okay. But he pressed his lips together and gave a quick nod.

"It's not fairrrrrrrrr!" Peter howled. "It's not rightttttttt!"

Jamie held him in his arms until the car had disappeared. Once released, Peter ran in his stumbling gait toward the road, even though the car was gone. Halfway there he tripped and fell. He landed hard on the ground and lay there, facedown, tiny shoulders shaking with his sobs.

One thing was certain. She couldn't carry on this way.

Leah had spent the morning straightening racks, restocking the lotions and soaps, and thinking about Jamie. She had thought that she could have him as a friend, but the more she knew about him, the more she cared about him. The more she wanted to know about him. The deeper her feelings ran. Until the obvious was staring her in the face: any relationship she could have with Jamie Stoltzfus would only leave her heartbroken. Was that something she could handle? She wasn't entirely sure. She wanted to spend time with him, she wanted to know him even better, be his friend in all ways. To triumph when he did and mourn alongside him. But one big obstacle stood in their way. Church. Not God, but religion. However, that was a big obstacle in their world.

After she had left the Amish she had heard tales, and

even gone to see a movie or two, about people of different religions who fell in love and, against all the odds standing in their way, managed to find a compromise to their beliefs. They managed to find a way to be together.

But, she reminded herself, that was only fiction. In the real world, the writers didn't have control over the endings; they couldn't manipulate the story to conclude the way they wanted. In the real world, it was up to God and to the people involved.

She pulled a green dress off the clothing rack and shook it out. It was an Amish dress, somehow mixed in with the *Englisch* ones. Even on a hanging bar it looked out of place. One among others. She trailed the fingers of one hand over the fabric. Could she do it? Could she go back to her Amish roots for love?

Was it worth it? Was it noble? Would God understand that she did it for love?

She couldn't wrap her mind around it. Joining the church in order to marry someone in that church seemed to cheapen both the religion and the relationship. How could she pray to God knowing that she had compromised both by bending her knee in front of the congregation?

It simply wasn't something she could do.

Nor could she remain friends with Jamie, see him day after day, and know that they would never have anything more than friendship. The idea broke her heart. And if not for her shop and Brandon, she would pick up and go somewhere, anywhere so she wouldn't have to face it all.

She walked the dress to the back and hung it amid the other Amish garments she stored for trade. Running away wasn't the answer. But it had become her habit. She had run away with her sister, then run away from her, left the country running away from God, then back again. This time she could not run. She would not.

"Now that's a face."

She turned as a woman approached. Deborah King, Jamie's one-time sweetheart. "Sorry," Leah murmured, chagrined that she hadn't even heard the woman come in. She had to get herself out of these thoughts and back into the world she actually inhabited.

"Can I help you today?" Leah asked.

Deborah smiled and held up a grocery sack. "I came to bring you some clothes to add to your donation stash."

"Thank you." Leah took the sack from her and glanced into it. There on the top was one of the very dresses that Deborah had taken when she had first come in. She looked back to the woman, questions in her eyes.

Deborah shrugged. "I'm going back home to Tennessee. I have plenty of things there."

"I see." But not quite. Hadn't she vowed to stay until Jamie decided to go back with her? Had something happened last night after the wedding? He hadn't said anything when she had dropped by to see him, but the whole visit had been beyond awkward. Perhaps she had been so lost in her own thoughts and emotions that she hadn't seen what was right in front of her face.

"You win."

Leah's attention jerked back to Deborah. "What? I win?"

"I saw how he looked at you. Even Sarah noticed it." She gave a tight smile.

"You're mistaken," Leah said. "We aren't a couple. We never could be." Why were those words so hard to say out loud? "He's Amish, and I'm Mennonite."

Deborah shook her head. "'There are none so blind,'" she paraphrased.

"I beg your pardon?"

"I wouldn't let a little something like that keep me from a man like Jamie Stoltzfus. *Danki* for the clothes." She turned on her heel and marched toward the door, leaving Leah staring after her.

* * *

"Thank you for coming up here," Jamie whispered to Gracie. She was such a help and never seemed put-upon when asked for a favor.

"You're welcome, of course," she whispered in return.

Jamie wasn't sure why they were being quiet. Peter had cried himself to sleep calling for Leah, howling that it wasn't fair, and otherwise screaming *no* over and over. Jamie had wanted Peter to speak, but not like this. Never like this.

"Go on into town," she said. "I'll be here if he wakes up, poor boy."

"I appreciate that, Gracie. I really do."

"My pleasure," she said in return. "Now, don't worry, and I'll see you when you get back."

He nodded, grabbed his hat, hitched up his mare, and headed for town.

He was torn between his two errands. Which one should he handle first? In the end, he headed for Twice Blessed, only to find that Leah had left Brandon and Shelly in charge of the store while she had gone on an errand. That could mean almost anything. Jamie thanked Brandon and headed for his second stop. The Second Street Mennonite Church.

There were several cars in the parking lot when he pulled up, but no horse and buggies. He parked next to a chain-link fence and tethered the horse to the top bar, praying nothing spooked her. She was a fine horse and never prone to skittishness, but he felt as if he were fighting uphill. Everything seemed hard, and his horse taking off, buggy in tow, through the town of Pontotoc would be the topper of the day.

He looked at the church building, trying to decide which way to go in. He had heard people talking on Sunday about the activities and had even seen a few in the church bulletin Peter had been thumbing through. The Second Street Mennonite Church was an "every day" church because there was something to do there every day. And it seemed as if today was no exception. The two times he had been there he had gone in different doors. Somewhere in the middle was the pastor's office. Jamie said a little prayer that Pastor Joel was in today and not out doing hospital rounds or home visits that he had heard about last sermon. He had missed Leah, and he needed advice. Badly.

With a sigh, he opened the side door to the rec hall and stepped inside. The interior was cool and quiet. He could hear muffled voices and children's laughter, but it seemed far away, removed by many walls. He remembered the way from Sunday and wound through the main room, past the Sunday School rooms, and into the carpeted section of the church. Sandwiched between the sanctuary and the rec hall was a line of offices he was told belonged to the pastor and the rest of the full-time church staff. Jamie walked the hallway, reading the names on each door. At the end, on the left, was a door marked *Joel Penner, Pastor*.

Please let him be here.

Otherwise, Jamie didn't have a clue how to proceed. He raised a hand and knocked on the door.

"Can I help you?"

He whirled around as the pastor made his way down the hall toward him.

"I—I was hoping I could talk to you about something." He took off his hat and twirled it in his hands, clutching the brim as he fidgeted.

"Of course." Pastor Joel shot him an understanding smile. It was comforting, even though Jamie knew he didn't understand. How could he understand something that Jamie himself didn't comprehend?

The man unlocked the door, flipped on the light, and motioned for Jamie to follow him.

He did, easing into the room as if it contained venomous snakes. *Relax. You're just asking. It doesn't mean anything else. In fact, you don't even have to ask about that. You can ask about the doctor and let the rest be.* Saved by grace. How could he believe in something so arrogant?

"What can I do you for?" Pastor Joel eased behind his desk and sat in the large leather chair. It was worn, well-used, and must have been there since the church was first built. Somehow, that was comforting. They weren't some fly-by-night religion. Not if they had a chair that old.

As silly as it even seemed to him, Jamie felt himself relax. Just a bit.

"I need to ask you about a member of the church. Leah—Leah told me about him. He's a head doctor. He helps children, I think."

Pastor Joel nodded. "I think I know who you're talking about." He waved toward the chair in front of his desk. "Go ahead. Have a seat."

Jamie looked to the chair and back to the pastor. He hesitated.

It looked safe enough. And so did he. He was fairly tall, of average build, with sandy blond hair in an *Englisch* cut and a finely trimmed mustache. He smiled when he talked, revealing lines at the corners of his brown eyes. Lines that said he smiled a lot. Or at least, that was what Jamie thought.

He eased down into the chair, but remained ready to pop back up again. He had to stay. He had to help Peter. But he couldn't stay long. He didn't want to leave the boy for any longer than necessary.

"I need him to help me with my nephew."

Pastor Joel nodded. "The boy who was with you on Sunday?"

He remembered them? Jamie shook his head at the

wonder of it all, then realized what he was doing and nodded instead. "I have custody of him for a time." He went on to explain about the fire, the death of Peter's family, and the promise he had made to Sally's parents. He finished his story with the morning's tragic tale of puppy love gone wrong.

The pastor nodded as Jamie spoke, listened intently, and otherwise kept an open expression. He didn't once ask why Jamie didn't take this to his bishop. He didn't turn him away since he wasn't a member of the church. He listened. In the end, he took out a piece of paper and wrote something on it, then pushed it across the desk to Jamie. "I'll call Bill and tell him that you think he might be able to help you and young Peter."

Jamie nearly wept with relief. He wasn't sure what he had expected in coming here, but it surely wasn't this open, caring, *loving* attitude. He cleared his throat and stood. "Thank you."

"Anytime." Pastor Joel smiled, his entire face creasing in those smile wrinkles.

Jamie turned for the door, half the weight that had been holding him down releasing. At least now he could breathe.

But at the door he stopped. There were two numbers written on the page.

"What's this second one?" he asked.

Pastor Joel smiled. "That's the number for Max Myron. He's a good friend of mine and a fine member of this church. He runs the Randolph Animal Shelter. He'll find you another dog, and a good one at that."

Jamie drove away from the church, the small piece of yellow paper nearly burning a hole in his pocket.

He was a chicken. Plain and simple. A coward of gigantic proportions. All he had to do was ask. That was all. Didn't

Jesus himself say *ask, and ye shall receive*? So why had he kept quiet?

Because he hadn't figured out how the God he had grown up with and the God he had heard about in the Mennonite church could be one and the same.

There had to be a way. How could he stop believing in one God and start believing in another? It just didn't make any sense, and frankly it was starting to make his head hurt.

But there was something about the message for Sunday's sermon that spoke to a different part of him. That part that struggled to pay attention in church, that part that wanted to question what he had been taught, or at the very least ask questions. But questioning the elders had always been frowned upon—at least by his family. He had never wanted to embarrass his *mudder* and *vatter*, so he'd kept quiet until keeping quiet was nothing more than a Sunday habit.

Chapter Seventeen

Leah pulled her car into the drive at her parents' house and stopped at the end of the lane. She wanted to talk to Jamie, but she wasn't going to allow herself that. Not until she had a few things straightened out in her own mind. No matter. His buggy wasn't in sight, so she could only suppose he had gone somewhere.

At least now she would have time to talk to Hannah. That was, if her sister was home.

Leah shut off the car, said a little prayer that her sister was there and got out of the car.

Thankfully, Hannah heard her and met her on the porch. "Driving a little fast today, aren't you, sis?"

"I need to talk to you," she said.

Hannah stopped. "Are you okay?"

"Yes. No, not sure." Leah shook her head. "How did you know?"

"What?" Hannah frowned. "Have you been in the sun too long?" she asked. "It's October, but this is Mississippi. Heatstroke is still possible this time of year."

Leah drew up short and pulled in a deep breath. "How did you know that you wanted to become Amish again?"

"It's not like I ever stopped being Amish," Hannah said.

Leah held up her hands to stay her sister's words. "Spare me all the philosophy. How did you know? Did you say, *I want to be Amish again because I love Aaron and I want to marry him; this is the only way it'll be possible*? Or did you say, *I love Aaron and the only way I can marry him is to be Amish again; guess I'll do that*?" She sucked in another breath, nearly winded from her ongoing tirade.

Hannah studied her for a few minutes, then wrapped her hand around Leah's arm, then marched her back down the porch steps.

Many a conversation had been had right there, sitting in the porch swing, but Hannah led her across the yard, past Jim and Anna's house, and all the way down to the pond.

"Why are you asking me these things?" she whispered.

"Why are you being so quiet?" Leah asked. "You dragged me down here so no one can overhear us."

Hannah shook her head. "I—I don't know. It just seems like something you don't want anyone overhearing."

She was right about that, but desperation had loosened her tongue and increased her impulsiveness. Another reason why she needed to think all this through.

"Well?" Hannah propped her hands on her hips and leveled her gaze to Leah's.

"I need to know." She couldn't say more. She couldn't risk it all. Not even with her sister.

"I wanted to be Amish again. But I suppose it was all part of the package. I had wanted to come back for so long. It took losing Mitch to free me. Once I came back . . ."

"Then you knew you wanted to stay."

Hannah nodded. "Is that how you feel?"

Did she? Leah shook her head. "I want to stay, but I'm happy in my church. I love my shop, the lotions, and the donations to help the needy families. I don't think I could do all that if I joined the church." But it was more than that. "I feel like this is where I belong."

"With the Mennonites?"

Leah nodded.

"Then there's your answer."

"But—"

"Jamie." Hannah gave a knowing nod.

Leah felt her heart crack, nearly break. How could love hurt so bad? Wasn't it supposed to be good, pure and true? Then why did it have the power to harm?

"Do you love him?"

"Yes." She nodded, but didn't say the rest: sometimes love wasn't enough.

"He loves you too, you know."

"You think so?" Tears welled in her eyes and threatened to spill down her cheeks. "Like it matters. There can never be anything between us."

"You can't believe that."

But she did. How else could it be?

"You should talk to him," Hannah said gently.

"Talking won't change anything. I can't ask him to leave the church. He can't ask me to join. There is no middle ground."

"What are you going to do now?" Hannah asked.

"I was hoping you could give me some answers."

"Sorry."

"Some big sister you are." Leah tried to laugh at her own attempt at humor, as bad as it was.

"Love," Hannah said. "Love is always the answer."

"Don't you mean God?" Leah asked.

"Well, sister, God is love."

Leah hugged her sister goodbye and got in her car about half an hour later. *I John 4:8. Whoever does not love does not know God, because God is love.*

It was a verse she solidly believed in. God gave them

love. Which meant it was part of God. So why was hers and
Jamie's destined for nowhere? There was more to it. There
had to be.

Or maybe she was simply overthinking it.

She waved at Hannah and started back up the lane, no
closer to an answer than she had been when she sped down
it over an hour ago. For now, maybe there was no answer.
Maybe there was just confusion, patience and confusion
until the answer was revealed.

But waiting felt a little like allowing life to happen to
her, which felt a little like being a victim. Is that what they
were?

She pushed that thought away. That was absolutely not
true. She might not know the answer to a lot of things, but
that was one she knew without question. God loved them.
They loved God. Somehow from there, everything would
work itself out.

Halfway between her *mamm*'s house and the cabin, she
spotted Gracie walking toward her.

Leah stopped and rolled down the window, greeting her
cousin's smile with one of her own.

"Hey, there," Leah said.

"Are you going up to see Jamie?" Gracie asked.

"I hadn't planned on it." It was better if they had some
space. Wasn't it? All this was complicated enough without
having to fight feelings that might not lead them anywhere.
It was just too hard, too confusing.

"Oh." Gracie's expression grew shadowed.

"What's wrong?"

She shook her head. "Peter."

Leah's heart almost stopped. "Something happened to
Peter."

"No. Not really. The people came to get the dog. Peter
got upset. It was bad." Gracie sighed. "I think Jamie could
use a friend."

"You could have stayed." Leah hated her own tone. It sounded accusatory, though she hadn't meant to say it.

"He said he wanted some time alone, but I don't know. When I left, he was sitting at the table staring at his Bible."

"Staring? Not reading."

She shook her head. "He couldn't have been reading it," Gracie explained. "It wasn't even open."

Jamie shifted in his chair, leaning back to see if he had heard a noise coming from Peter's room. It must have been something moving outside. He turned back to the book in front of him. His Bible.

He lightly trailed his fingers over the cover, almost testing its weight. He could open it. Look it up. Read what the Word said. Or he could . . . not.

He looked back to the piece of paper Pastor Joel had given him that very afternoon. There was something else written there. It had been printed there by the company that made the notepad. John 3:16. The book, chapter, and verse jumped out at him from the small bit of paper, but he had yet to gather enough courage to open his Bible and read what it said. Somehow he knew it would change everything. Was he ready for that?

A knock sounded on the door so loud that he nearly fell out of his chair. Or maybe it only seemed so loud because he had merely been too focused on what was waiting for him.

He stood, taking a deep breath to slow the erratic beating of his heart.

"Jamie?"

"Leah?" Her name was barely above a whisper.

He stumbled to the door and wrenched it open to find her standing there. "Hi." He wasn't sure what else to say. It felt like a lifetime since he had seen her.

"Peter?" she asked, nudging him aside so she could enter.

"He's still sleeping. Completely tired himself out."

She turned toward him, her shoulders tense. "What happened?"

"That might take a few minutes. You want something to drink?"

"Water," she said. "Water would be good."

He got her a glass of water, and got himself one too, then together they settled side by side on the couch.

He told her about the family who had come to get the dog, Peter's breakdown, and then going into town. He left out the part about getting the name of the doctor from her church and the tiny piece of paper with a Bible verse written on it. Something about it seemed familiar, but it wasn't one he knew by heart.

"I wish you had come to get me," Leah said.

"I got Gracie to come up and stay with him after I got him calmed down, but when I went into town you weren't at the shop."

"I'm sorry," she said. "So very sorry."

He nodded. "I know. Me too."

"What now?" she asked.

"I've got to get him to talk again. And . . ." He stopped, unable to outright say the words, as if saying them out loud would somehow make them bigger than real words. "I'm going to take Peter to that doctor. The head doctor from your church."

She reached out and clasped one of his hands in hers. Her touch was warm and welcome. He squeezed back.

"I think that's a fine idea," she said.

"I hope you're right."

She nodded and pulled her hand away. She seemed almost reluctant to let him go. Or was that simply wishful thinking on his part? "You have to try, right? Otherwise you'll never know."

And that was one thing he knew to be true.

"Will you go with me tomorrow?" he asked.

"To the appointment?"

He nodded. "It's at eleven o'clock."

"Do you want me to go?"

"I do. I . . . do," he said again. "You don't have to come in or anything. I would like to have some moral support."

"You got it," she said. "Pick you up at ten?"

"*Jah*," he said. "We'll be ready."

She shouldn't be nervous. It was an appointment where she would sit out in the waiting room and do just that— wait. Peter and Jamie would go in and talk to the doctor. Well, if Peter had started talking again.

Leah hadn't been completely shocked that Peter had melted down after the family came to get the dog. She *was* shocked that he had spoken for the first time in months— not counting his admission that he didn't like Deborah. Sometimes Leah felt like it was part of some dream and had never really happened at all. But yesterday had happened, and it had been major enough that the good doctor had come in on Saturday to talk to Peter and Jamie. Leah just hoped that he realized what it cost Jamie, internally, to come here and hand his problem to a doctor instead of putting all his faith in God.

She flipped through a year-old magazine and pretended to have interest in it during the five-minute intervals between checking the time. The hands on the clock seemed to be moving backward. She could almost see the second hand ticking in reverse, but somehow, miraculously, the hands moved forward ever so slowly.

Maybe she should have told Jamie that she would go into the counseling room with him. But she hadn't. She didn't have the right. She was a friend; nothing more. A friend that Peter had cried for after his heart was broken over losing another loved one. It didn't matter that it was a dog, or that he had only had the pooch for a short period of time. His world had come crashing in on him once again. Leah's own heart cracked at the thought. Tears stung her eyes, and she would give almost anything to be able to go back and be there for him. Hold him as he cried, rub his back, smooth his hair back from his face. She should have been there to help him.

She should have been there for Jamie as well. He loved the boy with all his heart. The thought of him having to deal with Peter, brokenhearted and sobbing, was almost enough to send her to tears right there as she waited. She managed to blink them back. Something had to change. She wasn't sure what or how, but something had to give.

The inner door opened, and the doctor stepped out into the waiting area. Leah had learned that they had gotten such an appointment as a favor to the pastor. Bill Stephens was a young doctor, though his certificates said he had been licensed for many years. Leah supposed he was either one of those prodigy babies or he had a young face. Young-looking or not, he had a calmness and peace about his demeanor that put her at ease the first time she had met him.

"Leah, can you come in here for a moment, please?"

"Of course." She stood and tossed her magazine into her vacated seat.

"Peter is going to stay out here and play, right, champ?"

Peter tilted his head back and nodded at the same time. It was an odd combination that almost had him spilling across the floor.

She was about to ask if Peter would be all right in the waiting area by himself when she noticed the doctor using some sort of eye signals to communicate with the receptionist.

The woman nodded in return, and Leah followed the doctor inside.

Jamie's expression was unreadable.

Leah met his gaze, but his clear blue eyes were murky and gave nothing away. Only the hard set of his mouth lent any indication of his true feelings, but even then it was hard to tell. He could be angry or upset, or maybe he just needed to use the restroom.

"Leah, thanks for coming out today. Jamie tells me that you drove him here?"

She nodded.

"That's very kind of you. You must be a good friend indeed."

She wouldn't say that. She tried, but she had failed Jamie and Peter both on so many occasions.

The doctor tapped the end of his ink pen on the notebook he held in his lap. "I sent Peter out to play so the three of us could talk."

Leah nodded understandingly, but Jamie remained still, almost slouched in his cream-colored leather chair, frown tacked firmly in place.

"I'm not sure how I fit into all this though," she said.

"Are you aware that when Peter started talking yesterday, you were the only person he asked for?"

She was.

"Not his mother or his father. Not even his uncle, who has been his caregiver all these months."

She had known that. But when he put it that way . . .

"I'm a friend," she said.

"I believe you're more than that."

Oh, how she wished that were true.

Jamie cleared his throat. "What do I do now?"

"This is going to take some time. Peter has lost so much. But you're right. He needs a dog. Or any kind of pet, for that matter. He's learned the hard way that life contains loss. Now he needs to know that there are rewards too."

"That's what this is? A reward for kicking and screaming in the yard?" Jamie's voice was more incredulous than gruff.

Bill shook his head. "It's reinforcement that the world is a good place. The dog will also teach him that life renews, it goes on. And it will teach him responsibility. But a dog is a big commitment. You have to be all in for this, or it won't work. Can you do that?"

Jamie nodded. "Pastor Joel gave me Max Myron's number. I'm supposed to call him about a dog."

Bill smiled and took a drink from his fountain cup, then placed the sweating paper back on the coaster. "That's a fine idea."

"What else?" Leah asked.

"He needs a stable home: mother, father, white picket fence, if necessary. He needs a routine, and everything that goes along with it."

"A routine?"

"Knowing what's going to happen and when will help ease his anxiety. If he knows that supper is going to be on the table every night at six on the dot, it's one less thing for him to have to be concerned about."

"I can help with that," Leah said.

"How? You can't even get supper on the table for you and Brandon. What are you going to do? Work all day in the shop, then cook and drive it to my house? That will get really old really fast."

"You have a better solution?" she asked.

"*Jah.*" His voice was stern, almost gruff. "You can marry me."

Chapter Eighteen

Leah stared at him blankly. It was perhaps the worst and the best thing he could have said to her. "I can't marry you." Her voice was barely above a whisper.

"Why not?"

"Perhaps you two could use some time alone." Bill started to rise from his seat.

"We're fine." Jamie waved away the man's protests as if he were flicking away an annoying bug.

"How many reasons do you need?" She really couldn't believe they were having this conversation, not after all the times these reasons had echoed in her head.

"I don't mind waiting outside." Bill started to stand once more, this time getting all the way to his feet.

"No need," Leah said.

"I don't need reasons. I don't want reasons. I want you."

How she wished that were true. But she knew the truth—the awful, ugly, painful truth.

"I'll just wait out front with P—"

"Sit down," they both roared together. Bill promptly plopped back into his seat. Leah barely registered his startled expression before she turned back to Jamie.

"There are so many reasons I'm not even going to tell you them all."

"Tell me one," he egged her on. "Just one."

"You're Amish, and I'm Mennonite."

"What if I told you that I don't want to be Amish any longer? Maybe I want to be Mennonite now."

Tears pricked at the back of Leah's eyes, and a lump filled her throat. "You can't do that," she said. "There's too much at stake here." She said the words even as Deborah's came back to her. *If I were you, I wouldn't let a little something like that keep me from a man like Jamie Stoltzfus.*

But she knew—Peter was the most important thing to him. He would do anything to protect him, help him, keep him. Anything, including renouncing his church for the sake of marriage. But what did that say about the marriage? It would always be second, always the thing that tore the faith away.

What they had, these feelings they shared, was too special to allow something, *anything* to make it less than God had intended.

"Did you not hear what I said?" he asked. "I don't want to be Amish any longer."

She blinked back the tears, swallowed the lump, and stood. "How I wish that were true."

Leah got halfway to the parking lot before she realized that she was their ride. They had all driven here together. The odd little family minus the two teenagers. But the truth was, they weren't an odd little family. They never had been. They never would be. It had only seemed so.

She sucked in a deep breath of the cool midmorning air. Before long, winter would be upon them. By then, she was certain, Jamie would have already found a wife. Maybe he would talk Deborah into coming back south and staying. Or maybe he and Gracie could work out some sort of agreement. That was most likely the better choice, but the thought of him married to her cousin left her cold, icy. The thought of him married to anyone else, actually, but she needed to get used to the idea. Soon it would be the reality.

She took another deep gulp of air, held it in her lungs, then released it slowly.

"You're still here."

Leah turned as Jamie and Peter came up behind her.

"I'm sort of your ride."

"You could have called Uber for us."

Leah drew back in surprise. "What do you know about Uber?"

"Plenty. See, I'm not uneducated or backward. I'm just an Amish man seeking the truth."

She thought it best to leave that one alone.

"Get in the car," she said.

He did as she bade, and before long they were on the road once more.

"What are we doing here?" Jamie asked. He looked at the sign hanging from the side of the beige-painted, cinder block building: *Randolph Animal Shelter*.

"You don't want to . . ." She cocked her head toward the building. "You know . . ."

"Get Peter a dog?"

"Yeah."

The entire ride over, Peter had been quiet. It was a state that Jamie was quite accustomed to, but now that he knew, for a fact, that there was nothing wrong with Peter's voice, he wanted him to use it.

But at the mention of the word *dog*, Peter slumped even farther down in the back seat. His chin hit his chest, his rusty hair swinging in front of his face. A week ago, the mention of a dog would have sent him over the top. He would have been so happy, clapping his hands and dancing around, even though dancing was so hard for him. He would have done it because a dog meant that much to him. Jamie hadn't realized it until Peter fell to the ground when Teddy and his rightful owners had backed out of their driveway.

He moved to get out of the car, but Peter and Leah stayed where they were. He leaned down and peered through the open window to where Leah sat. "Are you coming in?"

She gave a quick shrug. "I thought I would sit here."

"What about you?" he asked Peter.

His only answer was to kick the back of the seat in front of him with the toes of his scuffed black boots.

"You know," he started, switching his gaze from one of them to the other as he spoke, "the whole point of this was to pick out a dog and have a good time. Not sure what happened."

"Jamie . . ." Leah shot him a pained face. "I don't think . . . after our earlier conversation . . . that we should . . ."

"I see," he said. "You think that because I asked you to marry me and you said no, that now we can't be friends?"

"Something like that," she murmured.

"How wrong you are." He looked into the back seat, where Peter waited. "Okay, everybody out. It's time to look at dogs."

Leah could say that it was the most bizarre day she had ever had. It went from helping a friend to a marriage proposal to filling out forms to adopt a dog. The Randolph Animal Shelter had a screening process that even Pastor Joel's advance call couldn't get around. The man at the front desk wasn't Max Myron, but wore a khaki shirt with *Bobby* stitched across the left breast, just above where a pocket would be. He had a round, ruddy face, and the name suited him.

"Will the dog be in an enclosed yard?"

Uh-oh.

"*Jah*," Jamie said. He cleared his throat. "Yes."

The man asked a couple more questions about the purpose of the dog and whether Jamie had owned a pet before. She supposed he wanted to know if Jamie understood what he was getting into.

"All righty, then." The man turned away and grabbed a few more papers from one of the filing cabinets behind him.

While his back was turned, Leah leaned closer to Jamie. "What fenced-in backyard?"

"The one we're going to have. White picket fence, remember that?"

"Jamie." Her voice was both a warning and a plea. Didn't he understand? It had been the hardest thing she had ever done, turning him down. But it had to be. Normally after a crushing blow like that, she would have gone home and soaked in a tub of water laced with lavender oil. But here she was, running him all over town and helping him adopt a dog. "Will you stop doing that? It's bothersome."

"Marry me, and I'll quit."

"I can't." He was killing her slowly, just two words at a time. *Marry me.*

A rustle of papers brought her attention to the man behind the desk. "Is there a problem?" He eyed them over the top of his black-framed reading glasses.

"No." Leah cleared her throat.

Bobby smiled. "Okay, you three come with me, and I'll show you who's looking for a new home."

He stood and led them down a short corridor. At the end was a door. He pushed it open and stood to one side, holding it for them.

The smell of dog was almost overwhelming. It wasn't a bad smell, just a strong one, and Leah wondered how many animals they housed here.

The barking was almost deafening. The room they were in had the feel of a warehouse, only it was lined with cages and filled with canines of all shapes, sizes, and colors.

"Feel free to look around," Bobby hollered to them, using the clipboard he carried as a one-sided megaphone. "If you see one you like, we'll take him out into the yard and let you spend some time together."

Jamie nodded, then bent down and said something in Peter's ear. With all the barking, Leah couldn't hear what he said, but she supposed he was encouraging Peter to take a look around.

The entire time they had been in the shelter, he'd had his head down. Down so low it appeared someone had glued his chin to his chest.

Now, with Jamie's command, he moved forward, dragging his feet, chin still tucked.

"You want to look around?" Jamie hollered to her. "You need to like the dog too. After all, you'll probably be the one feeding him."

"Jamie."

"Once we're married." He smiled as if the plans had been in the works for months. He took a couple of steps into the room.

She held her ground.

"Come on," he coaxed. "Help us find a dog."

Walking down the aisles of cages was beyond heartbreaking. The dogs all barked, wagged their tails, and danced around as if auditioning for a part. Leah wanted to take all of them home. There were little dogs that looked to be part Chihuahua and medium-sized dogs that would be perfect for a boy like Peter. There were even a couple of dogs with legs almost as long as hers and deep, throaty barks. Great Dane mixes, most likely. There were puppies and middle-aged dogs and some with enough gray on their faces Leah wondered if they would live the rest of their lives in this shelter. The thought almost made her cry.

"Is that . . . ?" Jamie pointed to a cage where a shaggy golden-colored puppy braced her paws on the gate and tried to lick them through the chain link.

"Golden retriever puppy." Bobby nodded. "A mixed breed, probably. Just brought her in yesterday. She won't be here long."

She was about the cutest thing Leah had ever seen. Fuzzy paws, sweet brown eyes, and a wagging tail.

Jamie was staring at the dog as well. She didn't need to be a mind reader to know he thought the dog was perfect. A puppy to grow with Peter, a golden mix like the dog he had before. A dog to run and play with a little boy who needed a fresh start in life. In a word, perfect.

Bobby didn't even have to be asked. He grabbed a leash off the wall next to the door and unlocked the pen. The wriggling puppy danced sideways out of the cage, her back feet getting ahead of her front as she hurried to greet them. Leah wanted to snuggle her close and bury her nose in the soft golden fur.

"I'll get Peter," she volunteered.

Jamie nodded. "Meet you outside."

The room was more than two rows of pens, with an aisle down the middle. There were turns and switchbacks, each lined with more pens and more dogs. She was beginning to get worried when she finally found Peter. It was almost as if he had picked the dog farthest from the front. He was kneeling in the aisle in front of a gate, his hand palm up in an offering of trust.

"What'd you find?" Leah asked, slowing her footsteps as she came closer. From the other side of the large room, she heard a door shut. Once Bobby and Jamie were out of sight, the room got a fraction quieter as the dogs realized they were gone.

The pen in front of Peter contained a medium-sized dog with short hair and a skinny body. He was a mottled mixture of white, black, and tan and most probably had a great deal of blue heeler in there somewhere. His slim waist and pointed nose hinted at some greyhound. But it was his sad eyes and gray face that told most of his story. Even the wag of his tail was slow and hesitant, as if he were afraid to take the happiness of getting attention for granted.

"That's quite a dog," Leah said. Quite a dog and pretty much the exact opposite of the energetic puppy Jamie and Bobby had just taken outside.

"That dog's old."

Leah turned as Bobby came up behind them. She should have realized that he was back in the building by the increase in the barking volume, but she had been too busy watching Peter. She pressed a hand to her heart. "He seems to like him."

"That dog's got a story," Bobby said. "I suppose they all do, but he belonged to a vet. You know, Desert Storm or one of those." He shook his head as if that would help him remember. "The man who owned him suffered a lot of injuries. He came back, but everyone knew that eventually the wounds would get him. And they did."

"So his owner is deceased?"

"Yes, ma'am. And the poor pooch is old enough that no one wants to adopt him. Everyone wants puppies, or at the very least cute dogs. And that one is not cute."

She couldn't disagree with him on that, but it didn't make it any better. It didn't make it right. She felt a tug on her hand. She looked down into Peter's wounded eyes.

He pointed to the cage.

"Can you use your words?"

For a moment she thought he might refuse, then he sighed. "I want him."

* * *

When he had agreed to get Peter a dog, the canine in the back seat of Leah's car was the furthest thing from his mind. But Peter had chosen the dog. Leah said the dog chose them. He had been through almost as much as Peter. They both had loved and lost. And though Jamie was worried that the dog didn't have many more years left, Leah assured him that Peter wanted to spend them with the pooch.

Duke was his name, Jamie found out, called that by an owner who loved John Wayne films. Jamie had no idea who John Wayne was, but he figured if he was deserving enough to have a faithful companion named after him, he must have been something special.

He looked back over the seat to Peter and his new old dog. Bobby had given them a leash for the animal, but it didn't seem necessary. He knew what he was supposed to do, and he wasn't about to act up and ruin his adoption. How the dog knew all these things, Jamie wasn't sure, but he could look in his eyes and tell that somehow he did know. Smart dog.

Now he lay in the seat, his chin on Peter's leg. Peter looked out the window at the scenery going by and rubbed the dog's ear between his thumb and forefinger.

Duke let out a shuddering, utterly contented sigh.

"What are you going to do with him when you get him home?" Leah asked.

"I think he needs to be in the house. Bobby said he was housebroken. And it's not like he needs to have a yard to run in. He looks like he could take his last breath any minute." Just saying the words made him wonder if he should have tried to talk Peter into a younger dog.

"I know what you're thinking," Leah said. "And no."

"How do you know what I'm thinking?" Jamie asked.

She gave a quick shrug without even taking her hands from the wheel.

"When we're married, will you teach me to drive?" Jamie asked.

She rolled her eyes. "Would you stop that? You are not learning how to drive."

"So that's a no?"

"Jamie, seriously."

"I am being serious."

She turned the car into the drive at his cabin and cut the engine.

"Does that mean you're staying for a while?" he asked.

"I thought I would help you get all this in."

After their stop at the animal shelter, they had gone back into Pontotoc to Walmart and picked up what they would need for the dog. Jamie wasn't sure a dog needed *that* much stuff, but Leah assured him it was all necessary. Dog food, dog bed, dog bowl, toys, treats, and special shampoo.

"He's got more stuff than I do," he had grumbled, but Leah hadn't paid him any mind as she continued to load things into the basket.

Peter and Duke got out of the back seat and headed toward the house at a slow pace. Jamie noticed the dog walked with a slight limp. He thought he had read in the paperwork that just after the previous owner had been sent overseas, the dog had been hit by a car.

Jamie started to get out, but Leah stopped him with a hand on his arm. "Jamie." Her voice was quiet and hesitant. "Please stop asking me to marry you." She sucked in a shuddering breath. "I want to remain friends, but if you're going to do that, then I won't be able to come around."

"Because it makes you uncomfortable?"

"Because it breaks my heart."

Just what he wanted. Sort of. "Then marry me."

"Jamie." She groaned and laid her forehead against the steering wheel.

Jamie reached into his pocket and pulled out the yellow slip of paper Pastor Joel had given him. He wasn't sure how it pertained, but he knew on some level it did.

"What's John 3:16?"

She straightened, turned to face him. "What?"

"I mean, it's a Bible verse, that much I know. But what does it say? What does it mean?"

She looked at the paper he held in his hand. "Where did you get that?"

"Pastor Joel." He turned it where she could see.

She studied it. "It's a verse about God's love. That he sent Jesus here to die for us."

"And that is saved by grace?"

"Yeah," she said. "Mostly."

He let that wash over him, tried to fit it in with all the other things he had been taught in church. "Will you tell me more?"

She looked like she wanted to refuse. "You don't have to do this," she whispered.

"If you don't tell me, then I'll ask someone else. Pastor Joel, the head doctor. One of them will tell me."

She sighed. "Let's go in the house."

"And you'll tell me more then?" he asked.

"We'll talk about it."

Peter stayed out on the porch just sitting with Duke. Leah hoped the pooch would perk up in a day or two when it looked as if he was going to get to stay. Maybe once he got comfortable with the idea of having a new owner. Until then, Peter seemed content to rub his ears and simply sit by his side.

"Christians, Protestants," she said, "believe in saved by

grace. We are assured our place in Heaven because we believe in Jesus. Amish and Catholics believe that you have to do a little more." It was the best and fairest explanation she could come up with. She only knew what she believed, not exactly how to explain it to someone else.

"Works," he said.

"Exactly."

"How did you get to learn so much about religion?"

She really didn't know all that much. Not compared to others. "Once I left here, I knew I couldn't come back. Not and be a part of the church again. You know as well as I do that there's a reason we separate ourselves from the world."

"Hannah came back."

"I'm not Hannah."

He nodded in a *true* sort of way and waited for her to continue.

"So I started searching." She stood and wandered over to the window to check on Peter and Duke. They were in almost the same exact spot they had been in the last time she'd peeked out.

He seemed to let that all sink in. "Why the Mennonites?"

"I don't know. It just seemed right. I can wear a prayer covering. I can't imagine going without one."

"I saw a lot of women in the church without them."

"Personal preference," she explained.

"I don't think I can *not* wear a white shirt and a vest to church."

"You better not. Bishop Amos would have a fit." She laughed.

"I mean to Second Street."

Leah returned to her chair and took his hand into hers. "Jamie. You can't do that. You can't give up everything you have known."

"Why not? You did."

"That's different."

"How?"

She released his hand and stood. "I never wanted to leave. I only wanted to help Hannah. Keep her safe."

"You're a good sister."

"I'm not. I couldn't protect her. Not completely."

"She made her own choices."

"I did too."

"That's all I'm trying to do." His tone was simple, matter-of-fact.

"If you leave the Amish to marry me, what does that do to our relationship?"

"I would hope it would improve and grow."

"What if you regret your sacrifice?" He wasn't looking at this with open eyes. What kind of friend would she be if she let him jump into this rashly?

"Not going to happen."

"You can't know that."

"I wouldn't be leaving the Amish for you. I would be leaving for *us*. For Peter. To get him the help that he needs. To give him the family he deserves. If I were to find someone in the Amish church, it would be months before we could get married. Not taking into account how long it could take me to find them."

"The district's not that big. There's somebody."

"I don't want somebody," he quietly said. "I want you."

"Why?" The word fell from her lips before she even had time to think about it.

"Don't ask me questions I don't know the answer to. You challenge my every thought. You make me stand up for what I believe in, you question my every move, and somehow I'm a better person for it."

She wiped at her face, and he wondered if she was swiping away tears. "If I question you, then what's the answer?"

He looked back to the Bible laying open on the table. "I don't know."

She nodded. "Let me know if you ever find out." Then she turned and walked out the door.

How could things have gone this far when they knew there could never be more between them than what was already there?

For once in her life she wished Plain people wore makeup. She could use something to cover up the bruised-looking shadows beneath her eyes and add a little color to her lips and cheeks. She hadn't slept much at all the night before, Jamie's words ringing in her head like the bells of the cathedral in Mexico.

He made it sound so simple, so easy. Well, so had Hannah. As much as Leah wanted to believe, she couldn't. She had been down a similar road with her sister, and though everything turned out okay in the end, it had taken nearly fifteen years before that outcome.

Jamie thought he could just jump over to being Mennonite. She could understand such an attitude from *Englischers* who didn't always understand the subtle and complex differences between Amish and Mennonite, but he should know better.

Saved by grace took a lot of faith to accept, and still every day she did her best to keep up her works. That was why she had added the trade-in for the Amish. That was why she had taken on Brandon. That was why she did most of what she did for others. The religion of one's youth was so very hard to unlearn.

But Jamie was different. She had lived Amish for eighteen years; he had lived thirty or better. That was a long time to live one way, then suddenly change. Next to impossible. Especially if he was doing it for all the wrong reasons.

"You got a lot on your mind today," Brandon commented as she pulled her car into the church parking lot.

Out in the country, the Amish were already milling around getting ready for the three-plus hour sermon. Jamie would be among them in his white shirt and black vest. The clothes he said he never could break himself from wearing to church.

The religion of one's youth was so very hard to unlearn.

"Yeah," she muttered, not really wanting to talk about it. She was never up for rehashing her problems, but this one was especially hard. There were times when talking through a problem with a friend or relative could bring about a fresh solution. Not this time. There was nothing she could do or say to improve their relationship. He would always be Amish, and she would always be Mennonite.

A person can't just stop being Amish. You are either Amish or ex.

The words she had said to Brandon not so very long ago rattled around in her head. Jamie just thought he wanted to be ex-Amish. She wasn't under a *Bann*, since she hadn't joined before she left, but he was a member. He would be shunned by all his family.

He didn't have much family left. Just Peter and a sister in Tennessee. Leah knew her family would find a way around any shunning. Her heart gave a small leap of joy, but she squelched the feeling. She couldn't ask that of him. If she did and things went wrong, how would they ever forgive each other? Amish were taught to forgive, and as ex-Amish that value would still hold true, but the damage would still be done.

Leah got out of the car and slung her purse over one shoulder. She had to put a stop to those thoughts. She needed to give her mind a rest. It was time for church.

* * *

She did the best she could to follow along, marking all the blanks in the lesson sheet and making notes in the margins of her bulletin. But her mind kept drifting away to Jamie and Peter, sitting at someone's house on hard, backless benches listening to Amos Raber or Strawberry Dan or one of the others speak the message of the day.

Just before the final prayer, Pastor Joel came out from behind his podium and stood on the church floor. "If I could have everyone's attention for another moment, please."

Leah stopped gathering her things and trained her attention on the pastor.

"I had the pleasure of leading someone to Christ this morning." He grinned. "That's not exactly true. I helped someone to Christ on a different path. And I want to take a minute to introduce you to this person. Jamie, why don't you come on up here?"

Jamie?

Leah watched as the man she loved make his way down the aisle. She hadn't seen his buggy out back, or even in the side parking lot. How had he gotten here?

Better than that, *why* was he here?

Brandon elbowed her in the ribs. "That's Jamie," he whispered.

"I know who it is," she hissed back. The sight of him here, in her church on Sunday morning, a church Sunday for the Amish, made her heart sing with hope.

What was he doing here, and could she trust her wonderful suspicions? She couldn't allow herself to get her hopes up. Instead, she pushed those thoughts and her lifted spirits down until she could be sure.

"Folks, this is Jamie Stoltzfus. He visited our church last week with Sister Leah and Brother Brandon. Now you know we're always glad to have visitors of any sort, but I feel Jamie was called to be here. I won't tell you his entire story, I'm gonna leave that up to him, but I will tell you this. Up until this morning, Jamie was a member of the Amish church. But he came to me and asked me some pretty important questions. We talked about the Lord, His love, and His grace. I'm happy to report that Jamie has expressed an interest in baptism, joining our church, and helping us spread the word of Jesus."

A round of applause went up in the congregation. Beside her, Brandon clapped and clapped, but Leah felt as if her arms were glued to her sides. How could this be happening? Was it good or bad? How would she ever know?

"Don't you want to wait and talk to Jamie?" Brandon trailed behind her as she hurried to her car.

"No." She was more than afraid; she was terrified. How could he have done that? How could he have left his church, his life? Did he expect now that she would simply marry him because he had carried through with the one thing she told him not to do?

"I'm hungry," Leah said, unlocking the car and sliding behind the wheel. It might be nearing November, but the inside was still stiflingly warm. She turned on the air full blast to blow some of the hot out of the car.

"Okay." Brandon slid into the seat next to her. "Where are we eating?"

"You want to get pizza?" She backed the car out and waved at a few of the people who were also leaving. "Pizza sounds good."

Bradley Stone waved for her to stop. She would have loved to just keep driving, but he had made eye contact.

She stopped and rolled down the window.

"We're going to get pizza. You and Brandon want to go with us?"

She shook her head. "Thanks anyway. We were just talking about going to get a burger." She rolled up her window before he could say anything else. Then she waved and drove out of the parking lot as slow as she dared.

"Aunt Leah." Brandon had a white-knuckle grip on the dash. "What has gotten into you?"

"Nothing." She eased off the gas and shot him a quick smile.

"You're a terrible liar, you know."

She did. She couldn't even lie to herself. She didn't trust herself to be with Jamie right now. He had taken the first steps toward joining the church; the *Mennonite* church. Now she couldn't claim that religion was standing in their way. And despite her declaration that any relationship they could have after such a sacrifice would be tainted, she might not be able to tell him no if he asked to marry her now.

They ate lunch at a small café at the edge of town. She pretended that nothing was out of the ordinary, but she could feel Brandon's shrewd gaze on her the entire time.

"Can you take me back to the apartment?" he asked as she left a tip for the waitress and enough to pay their tab. "I want to go over to Shelly's."

"You're not going to Mammi's with me?"

"Not right away. I may get Shelly, and we can come over later. She said she wanted to see Peter's dog."

"Peter's dog is something else."

Brandon laughed. "That bad?"

She shook her head. "Duke's a great dog, but in dog years he's a *dawdi*."

"Peter's happy," he pointed out.

"Yes," she said. And that counted for a lot.

"Are you going to see Jamie?" he asked as they got into the car and headed back for Main.

"No." Her tone implied, *Why would I want to do something like that?*

"Chicken." The one word was quietly spoken.

"I am not," she protested.

"Then go see him."

"We're just friends," she reminded him. Though there had been a time . . .

"Like me and Shelly."

She started to say something, she didn't even know what, but was interrupted as Brandon laughed. "You have got it so bad. Just tell the man you'll marry him and get it over with."

"I can't marry Jamie."

"Why not?"

"A dozen reasons. A hundred dozen."

He frowned.

"Where would we live? He has a two-bedroom shack."

"Cabin," Brandon corrected.

"You and I live in a two-bedroom apartment, *over the shop*."

"You really are hopeless." He sighed. "No one gets married based on the idea of where they are going to live. You get married because you love someone. Maybe even you *need* someone. So you tie the knot, and then you find a place to live."

"It's not that simple."

He grinned. "Yeah, it is. You love him. He loves you. You now belong to the same church. Well, almost. The only thing standing in your way is you."

Leah refused to talk to Brandon the rest of the way back to the apartment. She didn't even wait for him to get his keys and get into the apartment before she left for her *mamm*'s house.

All the way there she had to push his words out of her head. The only thing standing in their way was her. That wasn't true. There was plenty standing in their way, like . . . like . . . well, there was plenty. She just couldn't think of anything on such short notice.

Oh, yeah, the biggest of all: changing religions for love was a dangerous sacrifice. One that could break a relationship.

She pulled into the lane leading to her parents' house. She would not stop at Jamie's. If Peter was outside, she would wave and keep driving as if she had never stopped there before. And soon, it wouldn't be so hard to drive past.

But no one was out front. She was both relieved and disappointed.

At the end of the lane, she pulled her car to a stop next to the barn and rolled up the windows to keep the red dirt dust out.

Orange pumpkins were stacked in a wagon parked to one side of the workshop. She supposed her brother David would be taking them to market come tomorrow morning. A beautiful crop they were.

And she remembered she still needed to get one to paint for her storefront. She walked over to the wagon and selected a nice one: not too big, not too little, round and plump. She put it in the back floorboard and shut the car once again.

That was when she saw it. A splash of red there in the remaining green grass that grew between the tree roots.

She turned to look at the color, knowing she had to be mistaken. What would a painted rock be doing out here on her parents' farm? She must have painted rocks on her mind, and it was causing her to see things. But there it was, in those few blades of grass.

She walked to it and picked it up. It was about as long as her palm, but only a couple of inches wide. The dark red paint had a fall tinge to it, but the yellow sun in one corner was all summer. *Colossians 3:14* was painted next to the sun.

Was she dreaming and none of this was actually happening? But the warmth of the real sun and the cool breeze were proof enough that it was real.

Colossians 3:14. She didn't know the verse. She would have to look it up when she got home. Or maybe later. Her Bible was still in the car.

She glanced toward the house. It looked empty. Who had left this rock? With a quick peek at her watch, she saw that her parents wouldn't be home for another forty minutes or so, and maybe even a little after that.

But Jamie's home.

She ignored that little voice. It didn't know what was good for it. Or maybe it did.

She decided to walk the short distance to Jamie's cabin. It was a perfect fall day, and she was enjoying the sun on her face and the rock painted with a sun in her hand. Her heart beat a little faster. Not because of the exercise, but because of the thought of the painted rock.

She couldn't allow herself to get too excited. It might not have even been meant for her. For all she knew, one of Jim and Anna's twins had found it in town yesterday and dropped it there on accident.

Or maybe Jamie hadn't given up on her after all.

There on the side of the road, Leah found another rock. This one was painted blue, with *John 15:12* on one side with a mosaic heart. This one she knew. *My command is this: Love each other as I have loved you.* On the other side someone had painted *Love me?* Coincidence? She was beginning to doubt.

She kept walking, and just to the right of the turn leading to Jamie's cabin was a green painted rock. This one said *I Peter 4:8*. And someone had taken the time to write the entire verse on the painted surface. *Above all, love each other deeply, because love covers over a multitude of sins.* On the back, the artist had written, *Sometimes love is the answer*.

Jamie was waiting for her when she got to his house. He stood on the porch watching her come toward him.

"That was some show in church this morning," she said by way of greeting.

"That was no show. That was the real thing."

She squinted against the afternoon sun. "You're really going to leave everything you know behind?"

"I have lots to learn ahead."

She wasn't sure how to respond. "I think you may have dropped something." She took a step closer and offered the rocks to him.

"Those were for you to find."

"Yeah?" Her heart beat a little faster. She had told Brandon that if Jamie asked her to marry him again, she might not be able to tell him no. But now, when the time was approaching, she found she didn't want to tell him no. Not about this. Not about anything.

"In fact, I have another one for you." He reached into his pocket and pulled out a rock. It was purple with a dove painted on it. Crude though it was, it still held a great deal of charm. In scrawling black, *Ecclesiastes 4:9–11* was written. She turned it over. *Marry me?* was written on the back.

"Do you know the verse?" he asked.

She shook her head, unable to speak. Or maybe she was merely afraid to break whatever wisps of connection were holding them together.

"*Two are better than one,*" he quoted. "*Because they have a good return for their labor: If either of them falls down, one can help the other up. But pity anyone who falls and has no one to help them up. Also, if two lie down together, they will keep warm. But how can one keep warm alone?*"

"How do we know?" she whispered. She wanted to ask if he had learned that for this moment, but she would rather believe it to be than ask him for sure.

He handed her two more rocks, simply painted in yellow and pink. Both had book, chapter, and verse written on them: *I Corinthians 16:13* and *Proverbs 31:10*. She would look them up later. "It's written all around us."

She looked at the rocks she held, painted by his hand with God's message of love and marriage. "I want to believe," she said. "I want to believe that we will never grow resentful or remorseful."

"There's only one way to find out," he said. "Let me prove it to you. Let me show you every day of our lives that I don't regret loving you, loving Jesus, or walking away."

He started down the steps toward her. Peter came out onto the porch, Duke right behind him. Once again Leah looked to the brightly painted rocks. God's word, Jamie's feelings.

"God led me here," he said when he was only an arm's length from her. "He led me and Peter to find you, find this church, find the truth, and find our happiness. It doesn't get any better than that."

Peter clapped as Jamie wrapped his arms around her. Jamie pulled her close and gently kissed her lips. "Marry me," he whispered.

It doesn't get any better than that.

That was one thing she knew to be true.

"Yes," she whispered in return. "Yes, I'll marry you."

Epilogue

On the first Saturday in December, Jamie and Leah were married. Such a quick engagement required a simple wedding, or at least that was what Leah kept telling him. But Jamie wanted as much finery and food as could be arranged.

The wedding party was a mixed lot, some Amish, some Mennonites, and a few *Englisch* thrown in for good measure, a variety that was a good reflection of the guests as well.

Leah had chosen a beautiful shade of green for the attendants to wear. She called it Christmas green, and no one saw any reason to say anything different. But since each of her attendants was from a different religion, they all had different dresses, all made from the same color fabric. Hannah wore a traditional Amish *frack*, complete with white church apron. Kayla, her friend from the Mennonite church, wore a dress similar to Leah's: almost to the floor with three-quarter sleeves, but in the green instead of Leah's bride-white. And Shelly wore yet another style, still green and still conservative, but with a more *Englisch* flair of billowing sleeves and an uneven hem. The men all looked handsomely the same, in their white shirts and black vests. Standing at the altar, Leah decided that Jamie had to be the most beautiful man she had ever seen. Her brother David and nephew Joshua stood next to him, and for once, Brandon didn't fuss about having to dress up.

There at the Second Street Mennonite Church, Leah and Jamie exchanged their vows and pledged to love God, each other, and Peter for as long as they lived. After their kiss, everyone went into the fellowship hall to have cake and give presents to the happy couple.

How ironic that Leah would marry first, before Hannah. But as far as church laws were concerned, Hannah and Aaron couldn't join their lives until she had finished her baptism classes and joined the church.

After a couple of hours of fun, food, and fellowship, the couple was ready to say their farewells to their guests and head to their rented beach house in Biloxi. A traditional honeymoon was out of the question, considering Peter's improving, but still fragile, state—though Leah told Jamie every day that Peter was stronger than he, Jamie, realized.

"It's a dumb tradition," Leah protested.

But Hannah shook her head. "It's fun and harmless. Now get up there on the steps and toss your bouquet." She ruffled the petals of the flowers: deep red roses and snow-white carnations.

Leah eyed her sister with a mixture of annoyance and indulgence. "The things I do for you, sister."

"And you still love me." Hannah smiled.

"You know I do."

"Are we going yet? Are we going yet? Are we going yet?" Peter rushed up and clasped her hand, pulling it as he jumped in place. They had told him they were taking him to the ocean, and he was beside himself with excitement. A new home, a new dog, and his first trip to the shore.

Well, it was the Gulf of Mexico, but Peter didn't know the difference and most likely wouldn't care a bit if he did.

"In just a minute." Leah smiled at him. Once he had started talking, he hadn't stopped. He talked from sunup to sundown, and all the hours in between. He talked about anything and everything. The color of the sky, a trick his dog had learned, the new kittens in the barn. He talked of love for Leah and Jamie and all of his new family members. He didn't talk about his other family. Leah supposed that some things were more painful than others. When he was ready, he would talk about the fateful night that took his family from him. Until then, she had promised to love him and look after him, and that was exactly what she was going to do.

Soon they would have the adoption papers all signed and legal. Peter would be theirs forever. Jamie had said it wasn't necessary, but Leah wanted the legal backup for Peter. Whenever he had any doubts, he could look at those documents and know that he was theirs and they were his. Just like Duke.

"What's the holdup?" Jamie sauntered up, looking from his wife to their waiting car. Someone, most likely Leah's brothers and nephews, had decorated the car with shoe polish, balloons, and a multitude of colored streamers. It looked a little like a carnival sitting there in front of the church. Leah could only imagine what it would look like going down the road all the way to the Gulf. *Honk, we just got married!* was painted on the back window.

"Hannah wants me to throw the wedding bouquet."

"Throw it? Like away?"

"Sort of."

"In the trash?" His frown clearly expressed his confusion. Leah's heart filled to near bursting. He still wore the white shirt and black vest, but Leah had a feeling she would get him in a blue shirt before long. Maybe even lavender. Even for church.

"Into the crowd," Leah replied.

"Into the crowd of unattached women," Hannah corrected. "Whoever catches it will be the next one to get married."

"Fine." He rolled his eyes as if to say, *Crazy traditions.* "Let's go."

Leah nodded and made her way up the steps as Hannah called for the crowd to gather round, with the unmarried women in the front. She saw her cousin Gracie there just before she turned to face the opposite direction the way Hannah had instructed.

Gracie was the sweetest and kindest person she knew.

Lord, if this tradition is really true . . . if whoever catches my bouquet will be the next one married . . . Lord, please let it be Gracie. She deserves a man to love. A man of her own who will love her and cherish her as she will him. Amen.

Leah closed her eyes and threw the bouquet over her shoulder.

From behind her she heard the rustle of fabric and the dull splat of feet as the women scrambled to be the one to come up with the flowers.

"You got it!"

Leah turned back at Hannah's exclamation. There was Gracie, still standing in the middle of all the women, clutching the bouquet in her hands. Her expression was one of mixed emotions. Should she dare hope? Who was she going to marry in this town? Was God giving her an opportunity that still had yet to show itself?

There was no way of knowing for sure.

Leah skipped down the porch steps and hugged her cousin. "You are the most worthy person I know. If anyone deserves to get married next, it's you."

Gracie looked down at the flowers trembling in her hands. Not many knew, but Leah did. Gracie wanted to get married more than she wanted anything else from life. But in a settlement the size of Pontotoc, there weren't many eligible bachelors. Would she have to travel to Adamsville or Ethridge, Tennessee, in order to find a husband? The thought broke Leah's heart. If her cousin did that, she would miss her terribly.

"If you believe, it will happen for you," Leah whispered next to Gracie's ear. She knew her cousin heard her. She shivered a bit, but continued to gaze down at the flowers she now held.

"Comeon-comeon-comeon-comeon," Peter chanted.

"Are you coming?" Jamie asked.

Leah glanced toward her husband. *Husband.* She liked the sound of that. "Yes," she called in return. How had she gotten so blessed? Blessed with more than she would ever believe she deserved. And she was going to live every day remembering and appreciating those blessings.

"Go on," Gracie said, with a small sniff.

"Believe," she said again. She squeezed Gracie's hand, then went to join her husband.

Believe. It was as simple as that. There had been a time when she hadn't thought she would ever get married. But had she believed? Only a little—yet love didn't need an entire field to grow. All it needed was a crack, a small spot to take root and never let go.

She should have seen that as it was coming, but she hadn't. Not until she was so deep into it that there was no going back, even if she wanted to.

Love was a hard lesson learned. Hannah had found love again. Leah had found it for the first time. She prayed that Gracie would be open to it when the time came. And it would. She just knew it.

Leah slid into the car next to Jamie. From the back seat,

Peter had already gotten out the map to track where they were as they drove south. She loved these two more than she had ever thought possible. Beside Peter, Duke was snoozing in the seat, no doubt let into the car by Brandon who took his best man duties very seriously.

They headed down the road, and Leah thought about the painted rocks Jamie had left for her. One had been marked with Colossians 3:14. At the time she'd had to look it up in her Bible, but now she knew the verse by heart: *And over all these virtues put on love, which binds them all together in perfect unity.*

Perfect unity. Her mismatched little family. They were all that and more.

Connect with Us

Visit us online at
KensingtonBooks.com
to read more from your favorite authors, see books
by series, view reading group guides, and more.

Join us on social media

for sneak peeks, chances to win books and prize packs,
and to share your thoughts with other readers.

facebook.com/kensingtonpublishing
twitter.com/kensingtonbooks

Tell us what you think!

To share your thoughts, submit a review,
or sign up for our eNewsletters, please visit:
KensingtonBooks.com/TellUs.